Leila

The Star Child

Darkness into Light

Author

Pat Basil Hayes.

 New Generation Publishing

Leila is gifted with very special powers, which were given to her by an Alien race of people. This Alien technology was infused into Leila's mind, while she was in her mother's womb, and before she was born. She will be the target for experimentation by some very unscrupulous other Aliens. They will try and abduct her, and remove her to their planet, so that this very advanced technology could be removed from Leila's mind/brain, could then be used to take over, and dominate other planets, and its people. However she is able to thwart their plans, even when she is a baby. Since then, she has remained anonymous, unidentified, clandestine, and secret on planet Earth. The time is fast approaching when she will inform the world and the universe of her powers.

Chapter 1

High above Planet Earth a UFO is in orbit, monitoring all discussions among all the Earth governments, trying to decide when and how they might help this unfortunate world. These Aliens are from a world called Pyseid. They are a very intelligent race of people able to decipher all known languages on this Planet Earth. The UFO is cloaked, which makes it invisible so that it will not be detected on radar or any other kind of monitoring on the Earth surface. This UFO has a contingent of six Aliens including Commander Xphat pronounced (X-Fa-at) and they are conversing in their own language, assembling all the information needed when they return to their own World Pyseid. They are not allowed to make contact or interfere in other planets problems. However, Planet Earth people are the same as the Aliens on the UFO. They are the same species (humanoid) as Earth people and they need all the information on how advanced those people are. Things are not looking good, this planet of people seem; to be at war in a very worrying way. They are placing all their ingenuity into destruction on the planet.

However, the visitors are going to try to find a way which might assist in saving the Planet from wilful damage perpetrated by its people. This particular race of Aliens are thousands of years ahead of Planet Earth, they would like to help.

They are having a discussion about all the spent rockets and satellites circulating in orbit above Earth. All this rubbish is going to cause all kinds of problems for future generations of Earth people, and if this rubbish is not removed accidents will ultimately happen. However, this is not part of their remit with regard to planet Earths survival. Any clean up will be the responsibility of Earth. The Aliens will just need to be very careful not to bump into any part of that rubbish, because it might cause damage to their spacecraft. So they will have to be very diligent, and keep an eye on all that debris, and wreckage flying about in orbit outside their craft.

Xphat walks to his second in command, captain Eyat and says, 'This planet is very primitive in comparison to our world. I would not like to live on that planet, would you captain? 'No sir, I would find it very difficult to blend in.' Eyat answers.

'Well, I certainly would not like to make my home down there, 'they are so primitive.' The Commander replies.

'I agree with you sir, it looks to be a very dangerous place to live, but that is never going to happen is it sir?

'I hope not, it's not a world I would choose to make my home in, Eyat. And I hope that I never have to make such a decision!'

'Anyway, that is none of our business our remit is to look at the situation, then report back to our world.'

How to make this work is going to be a very tricky subject matter. Discussions with the most senior people on their Planet Pyseid will not be easy. They will need to find a way to convince their government that Planet Earth is worth saving. There will be a lot of dissension but a plan to save Planet Earth must have consensus of the senior people of their home planet. They will not be easy to convince, as the Earth is very much a primitive planet in their eyes. They will not allow their technology on this primitive Earth planet, as it would have dire consequences on its indigenous people.

All this gathering of information is very important so that the personnel on the UFO can impress the higher echelons of power. Then they can make the necessary arrangements with the foremost science people on how to help Planet Earth and its people. The Commander knows that it will not be easy, however, he will not give any advice all he has to do is correlate all the pertinent information and deliver it back to his Planet. He walks around to all the Quantum computer stations where his people are engaged, making sure all the salient information needed has been correlated and placed on their computers, then he asks, 'Are we ready to leave?' All five Aliens nod their heads. 'Fine' he answers, 'set a course for our home planet Pyseid.'

Chapter 2

Back on Pyseid the UFO touches down. All the information gathered on Planet Earth has passed directly from the UFO's computers to a central administrative Quantum computer, an IPU (information processing unit) in the science building and the Commander makes a copy for the President. The Commander goes to the President's office where the President greets him and says, 'Welcome back Commander Xphat. Did you have a pleasant return home?'

The Commander places an IGD (information gathering device) on the President's desk with all the scientific information relevant to Planet Earth.

'Yes I did, sir!' he answers.

'What is your opinion of this Planet Earth?' the President asks.

The Commander replies. 'A very primitive planet, sir; it would appear that it is in need of assistance, its people would appear to be at war all the time. I think that they are heading for an impending disaster.'

'That is not good Commander it could affect this planet of ours in the long run, I'll not go into this for now, I'll wait to see what our scientists have to say when they examine all the information on this device. I'm sure it will be very interesting trying to come up with a plan to help this Planet and its people. I am very worried, Commander. I know that we should not be interfering in other planet's problems, but if we don't it could have dire consequences for our planet. I'll let the scientists decide then I'll place it in front of our most senior government people. That's all I can do for now Commander. Thank you Commander I'm sure that your hard work in collecting this information will be of great assistance to our scientists in their deliberations'.

Chapter 3

Two weeks pass. The scientists have not come up with a plan, although they have deciphered the information from their Quantum computers relating to the Earth planet and sent it electronically to the President's office. He receives it on his computer, digests it, he is not happy. He decides that his government should make the necessary recommendations for a plan, and then send them back to him as to what would be the best way to help planet Earth.

Another three weeks pass. His government are unable to form a consensus regarding the Earth planet. A plan is not forthcoming so this plan is electronically returned to the President for his perusal. The President is very unhappy with this situation so he calls his most experienced scientist to his office. The most experienced scientist on his Planet is Gia. She arrives at the receptionists office announces herself. 'My name is Gia, the President has sent for me.' She looks at the receptionist.

She points to the door and says, 'Please go in he is waiting for you!'

Gia knocks on the door a voice on the other side says, 'Come in please?' Inside she looks around sees the President seated at his desk and she says, 'You sent for me, sir!

The President's office is very palatial, beautifully laid out with lovely office furniture plus all the relevant stations of Quantum computers with global networking capabilities and self-editing software. All Quantum computers have voice communication to let relevant users know when a message is received so that they can attend to it as soon as possible after the message is finished.'

He points to a chair. 'Please sit down I need to talk to you about something very important concerning our Planet!

This unsettles Gia who looks worried, plus it takes the wind out of her sails. However the President has sent for her so it must be important and it would be wise to listen to him.

'I've been following your career in science and I need your assistance on a problem not of this planet but on another planet in a different Universe!'

Gia looks at him in astonishment and surprise asking, 'Are you sure that I'm the right person to find a solution to your problem sir?'

'Well, Gia, I've been reading your thesis on nanotechnology BIO/DNA and I know that you have made a very significant and viable scientific breakthrough. I would like to suggest' *he pauses for a few seconds* you and I will need to formulate some kind of plan to help the people of a world called Planet Earth.

'I don't want to give your technology to this world but I do need your help. The people that live on it look like us. They are humanoid and, as you know we have been monitoring them for some thousands of years. However, they are a war faring people and have been for two or three thousand years. They have now discovered atomic power and that is very worrying for us, because it could have a serious effect on our planet. They haven't worked out how to harness this power for peaceful means. They just make atomic bombs. As you probably know better than me, these bombs are extremely dangerous and I can't allow these stupid Earth people to put the whole Universe in a dangerous position, so I'm giving you the task of working out a plan to stop these idiots from blowing themselves up. If they lost control of this atomic power, it could prove disastrous. They could fragment their world then they could blow it up, which would be a detrimental and serious consequential problem for us and I will not let that happen. So, I would like you to go away and have a think about what I have told you!'

'What do you want me to do, sir?' Gia asks.

'I would like you to formulate a plan without giving our technology to an Alien race of people, to somehow putting a stop to their stupidity. You go away and return in a week's time with your plan. Thank you and goodbye Gia!'

'Yes, sir, I'll see what I can come up with,' Replies Gia. She looks very bemused by this discussion with the President and it has unsettles her.

'Good, off you go then, the President replied.

Chapter 4

Gia leaves the President's office perplexed and wondering what she is going to do to satisfy him. She says to herself. 'He is not in favour of educating the Earth people with my technology. Where do I start? I'll need help from someone. Who can be trusted?' This technology of mine is very sensitive, and in the wrong hands it could be disastrous. I shall need some time and luck if I'm to please the President.'

She returns to her office and sits down at her work station, trying to come up with something, anything, to give her a start. Unfortunately her brain will not function the way she wants, it seems to be frozen in time. But she needs to wake up to this situation, because the President is expecting her to come up with a plan of action. Who does she turn to?' She can't trust the other scientists because they are not privy to all the technology and nanotechnology and BIO/DNA that has been developed by her family over a very long period of time. She decides to go through the list of people in the science department and the only name that comes to mind is Oisin. (O-she-in) He is a very intelligent clever person and she has collaborated with him before. He works in the same department but in a different section. She decides to send him a message from her computer asking him to come to her office as soon as possible.

He replies back, 'I'm very busy but I can come tomorrow morning at ten if that is suitable?'

She sends him a reply, 'Yes that will be fine I'll see you in the morning!

Óisin has worked with Gia before on various kinds of scientific projects and he likes the way she works. She is a very fastidious person and her scientific knowledge is far above all the other scientists on his planet in a technological way.

He is looking forward to collaborating with her again. The next morning he goes straight to Gia's office and he knocks on her door.

She says, 'Please come in the door is open.'

Óisin walks in into the office walks over to Gia, gives her a big hug and a kiss saying, 'It's lovely to see you again, how can I help you.

'Well I need some help but this is only between you and me for the present. Nobody must know that you and I are working together again.

It's very important do you understand?''Yes I do,' Oisin replies.

I was called to the President's office yesterday where he informed me that our world is going to help this other planet in a different part of the Universe and I'm a little bit bewildered as to know what to do. He has given me a week to come up with some kind of a plan and he wants me to use my nanotechnology and my BIO/DNA but not to give that planet this technology. Does that make sense to you?'

'What do you mean?' Óisin asks.

'The planet, we call it Earth, the President is very worried because we sent one of our UFO's to monitor the day to day problems of that Planet. They returned about three weeks ago to give their considered opinion of that planet. He is worried that Earth will blow itself up which could have a detrimental effect on our planet!'

Óisin replies. 'What's that got to do with you?'

'The President needs a plan so he has trusted me to find one from somewhere, he wants a solution and he wants it as soon as possible. What do I do, Óisin? I can't just ignore him!' She waves her hands in despair, in walking around her office while looking at Óisin, then sits down in her chair at her desk. She is at her wits' end but she must find a way, a plan anything that will satisfy the President.

Óisin looks at her and says, 'Let's look at this in a logical way. He wants a plan, you have the technology. The only thing I can come up with is your technology. Perhaps we might be able to formulate something that would be satisfactory to the President!'

'Yes, but what?' Gia asks.

'Let us just talk about what he needs. It's not going to be easy but we must try. I'm sure we will come up with the right solution to please the President. We have six days so there is a little time to make some headway hopefully before the deadline given to you by the President!' Óisin answers.

Five days pass. Gia and Óisin have arrived at a solution to the request from the President.

Gia looks at Óisin and says, 'Well I think this might just please him?

'I agree!' replies Óisin.

'Good! Gia answers. 'Tomorrow morning we will go through it just in case we need to make any alterations before we present it to the President. Are you happy with that, Óisin?'

'Yes, I'm fine with that!' He replies.

She looks at Óisin and asks, 'Shall we go and have some lunch?

'I thought you would never ask!' he replies.

Chapter 5

Next morning Gia contacts the President by computer that she is available now to come to his office. She waits for a reply from the President. Óisin arrives in Gia's office to discuss other options in case the President might not sanction her plan, but they are confident that they will convince him that their plan is the only viable one.

Gia receives a message from the President on her computer, it reads; 'Please send me your plan now, I will read it, you make yourself available in one hour to be in my office to discuss this plan thank you.' She goes to her computer sends the plan to the President's office and waits a reply.

Gia bides her time then discusses her technology with Óisin with whom she has had a working partnership before. Her computer pings that a message is pending for her to read. She opens it up the reply from the President, and it reads, please come to my office as soon as you can I need to discuss your plan!' She looks at her timepiece then she says to Óisin, 'I think it is time to go to the President's office,' as she eases herself up from her chair. She tells the computer to close down she then walks to the door opens it and the two of them walk out into the corridor. They walk briskly to the President's office where the receptionist points to the President's door saying, 'He is waiting for you please go in!'

Gia knocks on the door.

'Please come in?' the President says.

Gia looks at Óisin and says, 'Right, this is our time to convince the President of our plan!'

She walks in with Óisin by her side and says, 'Good morning sir!

He looks up and is a bit startled. He knows Gia, and asks, 'Who is this other person by your side, Gia?'

'He is Óisin, sir, he has worked with me before on some other delicate technology, sir, and I will vouch for him!'

He is a bit worried as he looks at Gia. 'If you vouch for him that's good enough for me,' he sighs, as he gives a little smile and making a gesture with his hand. He says, 'Please sit down I would like to talk about your plan. I have read it and I like it. However there are a few little queries that I would like to talk about, so let us get down to business. Once we have clarified all of my worries I'll present this plan to our Senior Government Personnel then hopefully they will sanction it.'

I'll give it my wholehearted consent and I'm sure that they will give it the go ahead!' The President reads out the disturbing bits. When he has finished he says, 'I have to be very careful, as President that your plan doesn't return to haunt us. We have relatively good relations with all the people of our world. I as President must above all else consider all the adverse effects that might cause dissensions among our people. You are going to be ambassadors from our world, Pyseid, but you are under strict orders, on no account are you to make any contact with the indigenous people unless it becomes necessary that you have to trust someone of that World. You do understand; Gia this is a very big responsibility I'm placing on you but I trust your judgement and your scientific awareness. Now please don't let me down?'

'No, sir, I'll not let you down!' she replies.

Then she explains the significance of each part in detail. Three hours pass. When they finish going through the whole plan, the President looks up and says, 'Well I'm very happy with this plan. If it can be executed I'll be a very happy man.

'Thank you Gia and Óisin, you have been extremely helpful and I'm very grateful. I'll be in touch as soon as I receive confirmation back from the Senior Government people. Thank you and goodbye!'

Chapter 6

Gia and Óisin stand up, turn around, walk to the door open it. They walk through to the reception area and back to Gia's office. They do not exchange a word between the two of them until they are inside her office. Gia flops down into her chair.

Óisin on the other chair looks at Gia and says, 'This is a very big responsibility. Are you sure that we are the right people to carry this forward?'

'Yes, I think so I have the technology. I can't think of anyone else that could do it better than the two of us. You know that my technology is thousands of years ahead of all the other scientists in our world!'

'I agree with you but I'm a bit uneasy it could go wrong!' Óisin replies.

'I'm very excited. It's a challenge and I know that I will make it work!' she replies.

'Fine then, if you think it will work I'm happy to be at your side!' he answers.

'That's it then. All we have to do is wait to see what the government decides. It's going to be a very exciting time for us!'

Óisin looks at Gia and asks, 'Have you a realistic chance of convincing all the government departments to sanction your plan?'

'That's not my problem. All I had to do was convince the President, now it's up to him. I'm not a politician, all I have to do is wait for their decision and then you and I will put the plan into operation!'

'When do you think we might have an answer from the President?' Óisin enquires.

'My guess is about four weeks. You know how slow the government can be, they will go through every little detail until such time as all their colleagues have scrutinised every little word. Then and then only will they return the plan to the President. So we will wait to see what the outcome will be. Now you can return to your office. Thank you for all the help and backup you have given me. When I receive any correspondence from the President regarding the plan, I will let you know.'

Óisin leaves Gia's office and walks back to his office where he sits down.' His mind is running wild and he is trying to visualise, pre-empt something that might happen in the future, but he is totally lost. He knows that Gia is way ahead of him scientifically. He decides to leave this visualising to others and get on with his own work.

Five weeks pass before the President communicates a message to Gia's Quantum computer. 'Please come to my office immediately I need your advice.'

She leaves her office and hurries straight to the President's office. She enters the receptionist's office, she points to the President's door indicating to Gia to go in. Gia knocks, the President says, 'Please come in!'

She walks in and looks at the President. He points to a chair saying, 'Please sit down, I have some good news for you and I wanted you to be the first to hear it. Yesterday afternoon I received word from the deputy chairperson of the Senior Government Personnel that he would like to meet you as soon as possible with a view to clearing up some pertinent points about this plan of yours. Is that something you would be willing to do?'

'Yes, sir, that is fine with me!'

'Good, he replies, 'because he is on his way here to my office now. Nothing for you to be worried about, he has a few questions to ask you about the plan. He is a very pleasant man and I'm sure that you will be able to answer all of his queries.'

Then there is a knock on the door, 'Please come in,' the President says.

The door opens. A very tall and exceptionally attractive handsome person is standing in the President's office. He is immaculately dressed in a one piece suit which is a very dark grey. He goes and greets the President with a hug and a light kiss.

'Good morning, Matalik!' Then he points to Gia. 'This is Gia.' She stands up.

The two of them exchange greetings.'

The President says, 'Please sit down and let's iron out these queries. I need to clear all this business up this morning, so let us get down to it. Matalik, you have the queries about this plan so you ask Gia. I'm sure that she will give you the right answers, I'm also sure that she will impress you immensely.'

Gia is a little bit overwhelmed sitting with two of the highest government officials in her world and she is a bit nervous. She looks at Matalik then the President and asks, 'How can I help you? I'm presuming the questions are about my plan?'

Matalik looks at the President then at Gia and says, 'Firstly may I congratulate you on this marvellous scientific plan. It is really very impressive in fact it is amazing. The first question is, are you sure that this plan is viable? I'm not trying to place you under pressure but I need to be sure.'

'Yes I'm quite sure otherwise I would not have placed it in front of the President.'

Matalik replies, 'This plan is way above my head and I will not pretend to understand the technological make up. However let us clear all the salient points and as soon as that is done it will be up to the President to finalize your plan!' He sits down, looks at Gia and says, 'Please do not be afraid of me. All I need from you is that you will answer all my queries about your plan. He then goes through all the relevant questions with Gia, and marks them off on his note book computer as he goes along, it takes about two hours. He looks at Gia and says, 'you are a very interesting person and I'm sure that you will become very famous in the future, and, that can be only for the good of this world. I admire your work immensely as do all the government personnel and we wish you the very best in the future. Mr President, this plan is in your hands now and whatever decision you make, we, the government, will back you. Thank you and goodbye to both of you!' He stands up from his chair and leaves the room.

'That was very interesting I'm glad that you were able to answer all the queries and that you proved to his satisfaction and mine that your plan is worthy of recognition. I'm so glad my government has accepted your plan. I'll approve it and sign it off straight away now. The only thing left is for you to decide when you will be able to put this plan into operation. I'll need your decision by tomorrow morning. That's all. Gia, the only other thing I can say is good luck with this wonderful plan. Send me your answer in the morning.'

Gia rises up from her chair looks at the President and says, 'Thank you, Mr President you will not regret this decision. I'm very pleased to help and I hope you will be proud of me!'

'I'm sure I will be very proud of you!' the President replies.

Chapter 7

She walks out into the receptionist's office with a big smile on her face, which amuses the receptionist immensely. Gia can't wait to return to her office. She is so excited that she skips down the corridor sending a message to Óisin on her wrist computer which reads, 'Come to my office as soon as you can please. Thank you!'

He receives it (instantly), and replies, 'I'll be in your office in five minutes.'

Gia is back in her office and the excitement is building up inside her and before she knows it Óisin is knocking on her office door.

'Come in, Óisin!' she shouts.

Óisin walks into her office. She runs over to greet him, gives him a great big hug, saying, 'The President has given me the go ahead with the plan. I'm so excited I could cry. Now we can put this technology to use!' Gia is running around her office laughing and giggling like a little girl.

Óisin walks over to her, takes her by the hands, looks into her eyes and says, 'Slow down, take it easy I understand why you are excited. So am I. I'm very proud of you but you must steady yourself. There are very big issues and important decision to be made about your plan. It will not be easy, so let us get down to reality. Where do we go from here?'

'The first thing we will need is a Q.GSC (Quantum Galaxy Space Craft) a fast one. I'll contact the Space Authority you arrange anything else that we will need on our journey to this Planet Earth. You meet me at the Space Hub in twenty minutes. The President wants a reply by tomorrow morning so let's get on with the plan now!' replies Gia.

Chapter 8

Gia takes a hover car to the Space Hub, alights and walks to the main office. After showing the letter from the President to the receptionist, she is escorted to the Hub manager's office.

The Hub manager greets her saying, 'My name is Xbill,' as he looks at Gia, and then asks to see the letter from the President. He reads it. He looks up at Gia and says, 'According to this letter you need a Craft to take you to Earth. That's a long way, it's in another Galaxy. 'Please follow me.'

When they reach a different part of the building, he guides her inside where there is a sizeable amount of Space Crafts, big ones, small ones, with technicians working on them.

He turns to Gia and asks, 'Are you the only one going to this Earth planet?'

'No, I have another person called Óisin; he will be accompanying me on this trip!'

'I know Óisin very well, a great statistics person. I have been out with him many times. He is amazing, he makes flying look very easy. You are one very lucky person. He is the best flyer in our world.'

Óisin walks to the Space Hub, knows where he is going as he has been there many times before. As he walks inside the building he sees Gia and Xbill walks over to them. Xbill greets him saying, 'Welcome, Óisin, it's been a long time since I saw you last. Gia is telling me that you and she are going on a trip to this planet called Earth. May I ask why?'

Óisin looks at Gia she shakes her head and cuts in to the conversation. 'I'm sorry, Xbill, but we are not allowed to give you any information. It is top secret. Only the President can do that!'

'That's fine by me. I was only asking. Now, Óisin, what kind of craft would you like?'

'Well, I will need the fastest craft you have. What about Q.GSC?'

'Yes, that is available. We have just upgraded it, also the Antigravity is much easier to use and it's very quick. Please come with me.'

The three of them walk into another part of the building and there in front of them is Q.GSC, all big and bright. It is a stunning piece of technology.

'There you are, Óisin. Step aboard. You will need to synchronise your mind to the technology in this craft and you, Gia, you will need to do the same!'

The three of them enter the spacecraft. Óisin goes straight to the main deck and places his hands on the upgraded consol. He is now able to control the craft from his mind and he says, 'This is amazing. You have up graded the technology. I feel that I could do anything with it! I see that all the head up displays are upgraded as well a very sophisticated improved addition!'

'Yes, Óisin, I'm sure you will adapt your mind to this very sensitive upgrade. Here is the best bit; this craft is twice as fast as anything else in the fleet. The cloaking device is very best in the fleet, we have upgraded it and it is mind activated so that you will be invisible when you're in orbit above Planet Earth or any other planet you care to observe without them knowing you are there. How is that for science?'

Óisin looks at Xbill in amazement with a glint in his eyes and says, 'I can't wait to fly it. Please let me fly it now. Go on Xbill please let me fly it?'

'I'm not sure if I should let you have this very sophisticated craft, it's very fast very expensive and I could lose my job if anything were to go wrong.'

He looks at Óisin and has a fit of laughter. 'Of course you can take it for a spin. All three of us can go now to try it out. This will be the first time since the upgrade and I'm looking forward to flying with you again. It's in your hands now, Óisin!'

Óisin links his mind to the Quantum Computers in the craft, his mind relays to the computers; 'Open the hanger doors.' He sits down in front of the control consul then eases the craft up to about one metre above the floor and moves it forward until it is outside the hanger doors. He looks at Gia and Xbill and says, 'Are we ready? Then he sends a message to the computer *please take us two hundred miles above the planet.* No sooner has it left his mind and in thirty seconds the craft is at the required height above the planet. 'That is amazing. I like this craft now, the response is immediate, goodness it's very fast!' Óisin says.

'I told you it was going to be very fast!' replies Xbill.

Chapter 9

'Now, Gia, it's your turn. Please place your hands on the consol. It will not hurt you, all you will feel is a little tingling in your fingers.'

Gia looks at Óisin. He says, 'Go on place your hands on the consol. It's not going to bite you.'

She obliges, she places her hands on the consol; now her mind is one with the craft. She with draws her hands and says, 'That is amazing and now I'm able to fly this craft?'

'Yes, I can tell you now, you are a trained pilot and I'm sure that you will enjoy flying it. However, Óisin will be your captain and he will guide you in the advanced flying technicalities you will need on your journey to this----Earth planet. Shall we return to the hanger now, 'Please, take us down to the hanger, Óisin?'

Thirty seconds later the craft is outside the hangar doors, Óisin eases it inside the hangar and lets it settle down on its three legs and tells the computers telepathically from his mind to shut down and stop.

The three of them alight from the craft.

Gia looks at Óisin, then at Xbill and says. 'We will need this craft tomorrow morning, I will communicate with the President and tell him that we are leaving tomorrow morning.' She looks at Óisin and says, 'Will you please attend to all the needs we will have on our journey to Earth? I will see you both here in the morning at 9am.' She turns away and walks to her craft and drives back to her office.

Chapter 10

Gia arrives back in her office all excited. She is feeling so good now that her plan is going to help her planet and maybe this Planet Earth. She sits at her computer and sends a message to the President. 'I have been to see one of the Q.GSC's, it's an amazing craft. Óisin and I will be leaving in the morning for Planet Earth. I hope that you will wish us well, sir!'

The President replies, 'That is fantastic news Gia. I, plus all the Senior Government People wish you well on your long journey to Planet Earth and please be very careful.'

Gia sets about what she will need when she returns to the craft in the morning. She will need to transfer all the technology and technical information from her computer to the computers on the craft in the morning on a very high frequency radio link. That will not be a problem for her. Gia decides to send a message to Óisin. 'Please be in my office at 9am in the morning we are leaving for Planet Earth!'

He replies back, 'Fine I'll see you at 9am in the morning. I'm so excited. We are going on a very historic adventure and I'm happy to be of assistance. I think I'll meet you at the space hub. That will be much easier for me, hope you don't mind?'

'I'm fine with that.' She replies.

'This is a one off chance to do something very worthwhile for our World and I'm so glad you have chosen me!

Gia is now so excited now that she is finding it difficult to restrain herself from shouting out loud and waving her hands in the air. However she must restrain her excitement of carrying on with her work and stop dreaming. The rest of the day passes quickly. Before she finishes that evening she tidies up the office, tells her computers to close down. Placing a special code to keep it safe from prying eyes and then she retreats to the block of buildings where her living accommodation in the science complex is situated. There she makes 'an' evening meal of supplements which is the norm in her world.

Next morning she is awake early at around 6pm. She gets up, decides to have a dry shower. It is a biological cleaning device in the shower cubicle. When it has finished she does into her sitting room and turns on her computer to see if there are any messages which might need her attention. There are none, so she decides to have a small food supplement. She is now ready to get dressed and pack enough clothes for six long week's journey to this planet Earth. One last look around before she leaves. It's nearly time to go to the space hub. She walks out of her accommodation, locks her front door and walks to the space hub. When she arrives, Oisin is already there. She greets him saying, 'Did you have a good sleep last night?'

'Sort of,' he replies, 'I was twisting and turning all night. In the end I did fall asleep. And you, how did you spend your evening?'

'I fell asleep at my computer. However I did have a nice sleep in the end. Anyway are we ready to leave?'

Oisin answers, 'Xbill has not arrived yet. As soon as he signs off the craft into our care we will be away let's just go inside the craft to have a look and familiarise ourselves with the rest of the workings!'

After a few minutes Xbill enters the craft and says, 'Good morning Gia and Oisin, I'm sorry that I'm a little bit late. I see that you are excited and ready to leave for planet Earth. Well all I can say is happy voyage and safe return. I don't think that you need any more instructions from me, I will leave you to make your journey and see you when you return, Good-bye!' Then he vacates the craft.

Oisin looks at Gia and asks, 'Are you ready to help Earth and our Planet?'

'Yes I'm ready!' And she has a little smile to herself. 'How long will it take to travel to this Planet Earth?'

'I think it will be about one month according to our Q-computers before you arrive above Planet Earth, which gives us plenty of time to place your plan into operation. You have never been outside our planet before have you?'

'No, Gia replies, 'this is the first time that I'll have left our Planet in my life, but I'm looking forward to it!'

Oisin eases the craft up off the ground, sends a signal to the Q-computers to open the hangar doors. He moves the craft slowly out of the hanger. Then in thirty seconds they are in orbit and are on their way to Planet Earth. There isn't a lot to see in space so the two of them settle down just making sure that all the systems are working to capacity.

Chapter 11

In just over four weeks they have passed Jupiter. Oisin calculates the time on the Q-computer when they will arrive above Planet Earth. He then sends a message to the computers to cloak the craft from now, looks at Gia and says; 'Now we don't want anyone on Earth to know we are coming to observe them, with the intention of putting your plan into operation at a later date!'

Seven days later the craft is now in orbit above the Earth. Gia puts her plan into operation. The computers are scanning the planet for a suitable family into which her technology can be fused. It will take at least a week to search this whole planet, so Gia decides to split it into seven continents then into different sections so that she is able to find the best family from each section. Four days pass and the computers have chosen three families for consideration following Gia's criteria. One from a country called Canada, one from Australia and one from a country called England in the Europe confederation.

After two days pass the computers have correlated and simultaneously linked all the relevant and significant information of the three families and have arrived at a conclusion. The (chosen) family by the computers is the Carney family an English family.

Gia goes to the computers and asks, 'Is this the best family for my technology because I must be one hundred percent sure. Can you tell me why this family is your best choice?'

'Yes, the information plus the criteria you have given me on viewing all my systems tell me that this family is the best option.'

'Can you do another analysis with a breakdown of its constituent and element parts please?'

'The answer will be the same I have made all the relevant in depth analysis of all the criteria in my Quantum frame. The Earth family I have found to be the best suited to your BIO/DNA technology is the Carney family. Unless you change the criteria of the BIO/DNA you will receive the same answer. I am unable to make mistakes, I'm nonhuman, I have no likes or dislikes, I have reached a scientific analysis on your BIO/DNA and that is best suited to this Carney family!'

'Oisin, what do you think? Should I take this decision of our computers and implement my plan?'

He says, 'If you can come up with a better solution than the computers, good luck. I don't think you will better the computers.'

'Fine, 'What if I make the wrong decision? We could be in very big trouble with the President.'

'Look you have two options; option one accept the computer's analysis, and two, make your own decision. I know which option I would take.'

'What is that, Oisin?'

'I would take the computers' advice and analysis, it can't be wrong.'

Gia asks the Q-computers, 'When would you advise this plan be placed into operation?'

'In six months Earth time you will return to Planet Earth then start the process with the Carney family!'

Gia answers, 'Fine. If that is your recommendation, I'm fine with that. Maybe I should think about this on our way back to Pyseid!'

Oisin looks at Gia and asks, 'Shall we leave orbit and return to our own planet?'

'Yes I'm ready to leave.'

Oisin tells the computers, 'Take us back to our own planet, thank you,' and in seconds they are on their way home.

Chapter 12

On their return to their own planet Gia transfers all her nanotechnology back to her Q-computers, then sends a message to the President that the way is clear to place her plan into operation in about six months' time. If he needs any more information she is available at his convenience.

He sends one back: 'Please come to my office as soon as you can when you return.'

As the craft touches down Xbill is waiting for them. He has lots of questions for them as he needs to know how the craft performed.

As Oisin steps down onto the ground he says, 'Well how was the craft, Oisin. I mean how did it perform?'

'It is an amazing spacecraft; it's amazingly fast and very responsive. I love it. Everything went to plan regarding the craft, I'll make out a record of how the craft performed then I'll send it to you tomorrow if that is that alright with you?'

'Yes, that's fine with me. I'm so glad everything went ok, I was a little bit worried, Oisin!'

'I don't know why you were worried, 'the craft was in very good hands. We will need it again in about six month's time. Can I book the craft from today, will you book that date for me as soon as you can and let me know. I'll be in my office or you can contact me on my wrist phone. Thank you Xbill!'

'Come on, Oisin, we need to go to the President's office now. He will be waiting for us!'

Chapter 13

On arriving at the President's office the receptionist points to his office, Gia and Oisin walk to the door, Gia knocks. The President says, 'Please come in,' She walks inside with Oisin by her side, and the President greets them both with a hug and a kiss asking, 'How was your journey there and back?'

'Everything went like clockwork, sir,' Gia replies.

'Now tell me the whole story and I mean everything. I'm very excited, this is unique and the first time we will be making a positive intervention in another planet's culture and technology!' He points to the chairs, 'Please sit down, I'm so excited, and look my hands are trembling!' Gia and Oisin sit down and the two of them are smiling at each other, thinking the President is like a child with a new toy, but they do understand his excitement.

Gia goes through the whole plan as signed off by him. 'Mr President everything is now ready and in place for my technology to be given to an Earth family on planet Earth, but as relayed to us from the advice from the computers, we will need to return to this planet in about six months time to carry out the first part of the plan. We are hoping that you will give your permission to finish the work we have begun as we need to place this technology into the right person as explained in my plan'

'Well, I think you have done an excellent assignment so far, and I'm sure that your plan will prove to be exactly as you have predicted. I'm so proud of the two of you, I'm a very happy person now and I trust you implicitly. You get this right and you two will be heroes in this world, I can guarantee that. I expect that you will be doing some extra work on this technology while you are waiting to return to planet Earth?'

'Yes, sir, I have some updating to make to my technology which will enhance its capability even further.'

'You are amazing, Gia. Why don't you have this technology implanted into your mind?'

'Sir, my mind or that of anyone on this planet would not be able to use, absorb it, because it would scramble, mess up their minds, it is too powerful. The plan we have just discussed is the only way this can be implemented as far as planet Earth is concerned, and we are not in need of this plan ourselves, but you never know.' Gia has a little smile to herself.

'Good, I trust you to make the right decisions, That's it then, all we can do now is wait until the six months are up, then you and Oisin can go back to planet Earth and put the plan into operation. Thank you, Gia; we will meet again before your next appointment on planet Earth. Good bye and thank you again for all you have done for me up to now!'

'We are very grateful for your trust in Oisin and me, sir. We are sure that everything will work out fine in the future.'

She and Oisin rise up from their chairs and prepare to leave the President's office.

He walks around to the front of his desk, gives Gia a hug and a light kiss and the same for Oisin, saying,

'Off you go then I have a lot of work to do. I'll inform the government officials of your progress and I'm sure that they will be equally fascinated by your plan'

Gia and Oisin turn round walk to the door open it walk out into the reception area smiling, As they walk past the receptionist, she wonders what they are so happy about'

Chapter 14

Back in Gia's office she looks at Oisin and says, 'I hope we are going to be successful with the plan, otherwise we will not be the President's favourite people and that does worry me!'

Oisin replies, 'Everything will work out fine, Stop worrying and relax, we know that the plan will work. It's an amazing piece of technology and the computers agree with you. You must calm down otherwise it could make your sanity impaired and I would not be happy if that happened!'

'I know, but it is a very big responsibility to have on my shoulders.'

However, I do agree with you and I'm going to be more positive from now on!'

'Good for you,' Oisin replies, as he walks over to Gia, holds her and gives her a big hug and a kiss. 'I must go now as I need to catch up with my own work. I think we should meet for lunch today then we can have another discussion on the technicalities of the plan. Are you happy with that?'

Gia replies, 'Yes, I'm happy with that. Yes I'll be fine. Now off you go. I'll see you at lunch, Thank you Oisin'

He walks to the door, opens it, walks out into the corridor and back to his office thinking to himself, 'I hope Gia will be ok, she has a very big responsibility but I'm sure she will be fine.'

Six months pass quickly Gia and Oisin have been seeing a lot of each other and discussing what the future might bring with regards to this planet Earth. The time has arrived when the two of them must return to planet Earth as scheduled. After a long discussion Gia tells Oisin that she has decided the two of them will leave in twenty four hours for planet Earth, that is, if he is happy with her wishes.

'If you are happy to return to this planet so be it, I'll be very happy to accompany you. I'll make all the arrangements for tomorrow morning. You contact the President and tell him that you are leaving in the morning. Then you let me know. I don't think he will stop us from leaving however you never know. I await your call!'

Chapter 15

Gia leaves a voice mail with the President's office. 'Mr President, Oisin and I are leaving for planet Earth in the morning, if you need me to come to your office now I can accommodate you.

Please call me if I'm needed.'

The President receives Gia's mail listens to it and smiles to himself. Then he sends her a good luck message; 'Take good care of yourself, I'll see you in about two month's time and I hope that your plan will work out as you have anticipated. It's a wonderful plan and I know that it will benefit our two worlds. Good luck and Bon-voyage.'

Chapter 16

The Carney and the Halshram family are hoping for the two families to be united in a matrimonial service in the near future. John Carney is about five-eleven, good-looking and fresh faced. He has a brother JK and a sister Delia. Ciera Halshram is about five-seven, and is very good-looking nice complexion with blue eyes. Ciera is the only child of Mr and Mrs Halshram. They have been engaged and of course to marry soon. The joining of these two families will change the world forever but not immediately. It will take some years before this can happen. This entire development will need the cooperation of the Carney family. However, at this stage the Carney family are not privy to the future of the Earth. The drums of war are beating quite aggressively again on planet Earth. Will the species survive?'

This world, Earth, is heading for an apocalyptic disintegration. If this madness does not cease, it will have dire consequences for all the people of Earth and the Universe. There are outside influences ready to engage in dialogue and technology. People/Aliens are watching. They will be choosing the right time to change that. They are waiting for an opportunity to return to Earth to try to stop this madness of initiating wars and killing indiscriminately. Earth people are very primitive; their brains are big but very little of that brain is used, which makes them unreliable and their stupidity knows no bounds. Some people are born great but some people have greatness thrust upon them at an early age.

There is hope from outside this Earth. But will Earth people engage with a higher, more intelligent being to remedy the situation to save their Earth planet. Hopefully they will see the stupidity they are about to inflict on their Earth, and come to their senses sooner rather than later.

Chapter 17

John and Ciera's wedding reception is well under way. Mr and Mrs Carney are very happy to see their youngest son married to such a lovely young person as Ciera, so are Mr and Mrs Halshram; they are happy to have John as a son in-law. It looks a very good match to them.

JK who is an IT specialist, brother of John is trying to organize things and his sister Delia is helping him.

The sun is out. There is a lovely blue sky, with not a cloud to be seen anywhere. Children are running around and having a good time as children will do. The bouncy castle is in great demand, even some of the adults are having a go on it and the laughter is quite infectious. The photographer is trying to line up the adults for photographs but is having a hard time as cooperation from the adults is not forthcoming and it is proving very difficult to organize. However, he is not going to give up, he has a job to do and he is going to full-fill his contract one-way or another. He goes in search of the bride and groom. After about ten minutes he sees both of them walks over to them and asks in a rather excited and desperate way if the groom could help to round up the guests for photographs while the light is good.

'Yes of course,' replies John. 'Let me give you a hand.'

He looks up and shouts, 'Everyone, the photographer needs your presence for the photos. Could we all pay attention to him while he lines up the different families. Thank you very much.' That little job done, he walks back to his wife and says, 'I think we should go and have our photos done as soon as possible.'

'Yes dear!' she replies. She takes him by the arm and leads him over to the photographer, stands next to him and says. 'We are here now, where do you want us to stand?'

'Good,' replies the photographer. 'That will draw your guests over to us and we can get started!'

Later that afternoon, the photographer is finished with all the guests and he is very happy with his work he turns and says, goodbye to the bride and groom and tells them that the wedding disks will be ready when they arrive back from their honeymoon. He will phone and come to their house for a viewing when it is convenient for them.

Ciera's mum walks over takes her by the hand and says, 'I need to talk to you now please!'

Ciera looks at her mum and asks, 'Is there something wrong?'

'This is not going to be easy but please hear me out. As you know my sister lives in Sidney Australia and she has asked your dad and me to move out there.'

'I'm not going to listen to this nonsense. Mum, are you crazy, why are you going to Australia are you not happy here?' Then she starts to cry uncontrollably turns to walk away.

Her mum places her hand on her shoulder to stop her from walking away saying, 'Please let me explain the situation. Your dad has been head hunted, as you know he is a very good plumber and the work here is not so good at the moment. Come on, Ciera be happy for us it's a very good chance for us, you and John can come for a holiday whenever you like.' She gives her daughter a little smile, 'Please be happy for us.'

Ciera looks at her mum has a little smile gives her a big hug saying, 'Of course I'm happy for you but this is very upsetting for me, you're going to be so far away. She looks at her mum and asks, 'When are you going?'

'We are leaving next week so this is the last time we have together until you and John visit us in Australia.'

Ciera is horrified at this announcement. She looks at her mum in amazement asking, 'You are not telling me everything mum, are you?

'Well this job your dad has taken was only available for two weeks, so he felt that it would too good a great opportunity to miss, he decided to take it. We have sold the house, which will pay for a new house in Australia.'

Ciera jumps back, looks at her, waving her hands in the air, saying, 'I'm not happy about this situation but if you and dad have made a decision to go, then I'm happy for you, I don't like it.' Out of the corner of her eye she sees her dad walking towards her, he takes her hand asking, 'Has mum told you about our move to Australia? We had no option but to tell you today, because you will be on honeymoon when we leave. I know that this move is a very big surprise to you, but I needed to do something, the work was drying up here. We had no other option. We didn't want to leave but the circumstances were such that, I couldn't turn this work down. Please understand Ciera!'

'I'm not happy that you are going to be so far away, However John and I will be happy for you. Hopefully we can come to see you in the future. I'll explain to John and his family after we return from honeymoon. Now let's return to the reception.'

Chapter 18

Two weeks later, John and Ciera are back from their honeymoon and drive to see John's dad and mum, just to let them know that they are back. They knock at the front door and his mum opens the door and sees the honeymooners standing there.

'Come in. How are you both?'

'We're fine,' answers John. 'Just got back so we thought that we would call in for a cup of tea and say that we are very grateful for all the help you gave us.' They walk into the sitting room and dad is sitting in his chair reading his newspaper. He jumps up.

'How are you,' he asks. How was your holiday?'

'Fine,' replies Ciera. 'We had a great time, plenty of sun.'

Mum brings the tea into the sitting room places the tray on the coffee table and says. 'Help yourselves. Would you like a sandwich to eat or something else?'

'No, thank you,' replies Ciera. 'The tea is just fine.' A little later, tea finished, she says. 'Thank you very much, but we must go now to our house because we have a lot of unpacking to do. We should buy some groceries because John is going back to work in the morning and he'll need some sandwiches. I'm going to bed early tonight because I'm shattered and I need some sleep. Come on husband before I fall asleep here.' She jumps up, pulling John with her.

Mum asks, 'Would you like to come for dinner on Sunday?'

'Yes,' replies Ciera. 'We would love to come to dinner on Sunday. That is, if you don't mind?'

'Good. That settles it.' replies mum as she walks to the front door with them. They walk to the car and sit inside, giving a little wave to mum and dad as they are driving away.

Chapter 19

Sunday morning, Ciera is up early, does the housework, all the washing and tidies the house generally. She goes to the bathroom and she has a shower and then goes into the bedroom and calls John, 'Please get up and have a shower 'You do know that we're going to your mum's and we need to be there for one o'clock for dinner?'

'Yes, I know. Do not worry we will be there in plenty of time. You go downstairs and make breakfast. I'll have a quick shower and be down in ten minutes.'

'You promise?'

'Yes, I promise that I'll be down after my shower. Off you go and start breakfast.'

Twelve minutes later John runs down the stairs and into the kitchen and his wife places his breakfast on the table. He thanks her and says. 'Have you had your breakfast?'

'I'm in no mood now to finish my breakfast.' she replies. 'You hurry and finish yours. You know that it will take about three-quarters of an hour to drive to your mum's?'

'I know that dear,' replies John. 'A couple of minutes either way won't hurt. Just take it easy. If we do happen to be late, mum will not mind. She won't place the dinner on the table until we arrive!'

She replies. 'If we're late you can take the blame.'

'We'll be there in plenty of time. So if you're ready we can go now please.'

They both get in the car and John drives away to his dad's house.

On arrival, Ciera is out of the car first, goes to the front door, knocks and waits. The door opens and John's dad is standing there. 'Come in please. Dinner will be ready soon. Ciera, what would you like to drink?'

'I'd like a soft drink please, dad, and what would you like John?'

Wine brandy, whisky or a soft drink?'

'I think I'll have a white wine please.' John replies.

'Shall we go into the sitting room?' Father enquires.

John's mum comes into the sitting room and says, 'Hello everyone, dinner will be ready in about ten minutes. Now tell me how is married life suiting you, how are you and Ciera getting along, is everything all right?

'Yes, Mum. Everything is fine!' John replies. Dad enters the sitting room with the drinks, places them on the coffee table and says, 'Your drinks are ready. Please help yourselves. I must go and help your mum to lay the table with the knives and forks. You just sit down and enjoy yourselves. If you need another drink just help yourselves!'

'Thank you.'

The table is ready for dinner so dad calls John and Ciera. 'Please come and sit at the table. Your mother is just about to place the dinner on it now.'

The dinner is fine and the discussion is about the holiday.

Mum asks. 'What was it like?'

'It was lovely! We had a great time, plenty of sun. We did a lot of snorkelling in the sea and the water was crystal clear it was wonderful. We really enjoyed ourselves, didn't we, Ciera.'

'Yes we did, dear, we had a lovely time.'

Dinner over, Ciera says, 'Let me help you, mum, to do the washing up.'

'No we have a dishwasher so all I have to do is put the dinner plates and cutlery inside and turn on the machine and that's it.'

Dinner over, John and Ciera say their goodbyes to dad and mum, walk to the car and drive away.

Chapter 20

Two month later, Ciera is pregnant and she says to John. 'Would you like to tell your mum and dad that I'm pregnant, and that they are going to be grandparents?

'Ok I'll phone my mum and dad and give them the good news.'

John picks up the phone, dials his dad's number.

His dad answers. 'May I help you?'

'Dad, it's me. Just to tell you and mum that Ciera and I are having a baby!'

'My, that's great news son. Your mum will be over the moon when I tell her!'

'Ciera is only one month gone but I'll keep you and mum up to date on everything. Goodbye for now. Love to you and mum!'

Chapter 21

Gia and Oisin leave their planet Pyseid and head for Planet Earth. Gia's plan needs to be implemented as soon as possible and she is very excited at the possibility of her technology being used to help both her planet and planet Earth. The long journey takes four weeks. On the third week of the journey Oisin decides to cloak the Q.GSC from any prying inquisitive eyes. On arriving in orbit above Earth Gia consults her Quantum computer asking, 'Are there any changes to the Carney family since we were here last time?

'No the family are still living in the same place and Ciera, Mrs Carney, is pregnant, answers the computer.

'Fine thank you, 'She looks at Oisin. 'Oisin I think it is time, will you transport Ciera here please?'

Oisin looks down on the Earth, Ciera's continent is in darkness (night time) and she will be in bed fast asleep. He goes to the Quantum transporter brings it to life moves his hand over the consul the computers find Ciera then he moves his other hand over another consul then Ciera is transported to the Q.GSC. She is still in a deep sleep. She materializes on a very special very advanced apparatus. Gia arrives at her side taps her on the shoulder to wake her up. She wakes up and is quite startled. She looks at Gia and asks, 'Where am I. 'Who are you?'

Gia holds her hand and says, 'Please don't be afraid I will not hurt you!'

Ciera is getting very agitated and distressed. She starts to fight Gia.

Gia places her hand on her shoulder and says, 'Please Ciera, let me explain we are not here to hurt you or your baby. We have come a very long way to help your planet and you have been chosen as its saviour. Well, not, quite, it's your baby we need.'

Ciera starts to fight again. All kinds of questions are running wild in her mind: 'Are they going to take my baby away from me? You hear all kinds of strange things about Aliens coming to Earth and abducting people and babies. Well, they are not going to take my baby from me without a fight.'

Then Oisin goes to Gia's side, 'Please let us explain. We are not going to take your baby away from you. We have very advanced technology which we would like to give to your baby, but we need your cooperation in full. We have been monitoring you for about six months of your Earth time, and, yes, we do know your name and your husband's name as well. Your baby will be able to save your planet and our planet. At the moment we can't go into much detail. Your planet is a very dangerous world to live in. It has very big problems such as wars and the invention of atomic power!'

Ciera looks bewildered and frightened, looks at Gia and Oisin, then she asks, 'Who are you, do you have names?'

'Yes we have names, my name is Gia.' Then she points to Oisin, 'And his name is Oisin, we are from a planet very far away from here called Pyseid!'

Ciera has quietened down but she is still very worried, then she asks, 'How did you arrive here?'

Oisin looks at Gia then says to the computer, 'All around vision please'

Gia takes Ciera's hand, 'Please stand up and look at the vision in our Q.GSC that is your world down there, that's where you come from.'

'I don't believe you, How is that possible? How did I arrive in this.' she waves her hand, 'Q.GSC, as you call it?'

'We left our World five weeks ago, that is five weeks of your time, in this machine of ours. On your world down there,' he points to Earth,' you call this machine a flying saucer or UFO.'

'Oisin transported you here from your bedroom. We are very sorry to have frightened you, Now will you cooperate with me please?'

'I'm not sure. I have a few more questions. Why should I trust complete strangers, who I have never met before in my life, somehow I believe you, something is telling me to trust you, If what your tell me is true then I don't have much option. I can't leave this thing anyway Yes I think I'll trust you,' Ciera Replies

Oisin waves his hand and a door appears in the wall of the Q.GSC. Gia takes Ciera's hand and points to the door, 'May I ask you to enter into the cabinet please?'

Ciera looks at her and asks, 'Nothing funny is going to happen to me' I don't want my baby to come to any harm!'

'Nothing we do will hurt you or your baby. I promise,' as she indicates with her hand. 'Please go inside.'

Ciera looks very apprehensive and asks, 'Are you sure that nothing will happen to me or my baby?'

'Please, we need to make sure that you have not arrived with any bacteria on your person. This unit will make sure that all bacteria are cleansed from your clothing and your person.'

Ciera reluctantly goes inside then a blue light arrives at the top of the cabinet and descends down to the bottom. It takes only one minute to finish the operation. The door opens and Gia beckons her out of the cabinet.

Ciera walks out and asks, 'What happens now?'

Gia looks at Oisin, and asks, 'Can I have the unit up please?'

'Yes, of course,' as he waves his hand. Then, up from nowhere a strange apparatus arrives as if by magic, and stops about two feet high. It has very strange looking writings and lots of lovely colours emitting from the top of it.

Gia looks at Ciera and indicates with her hand to sit on this strange looking apparatus.

She looks at Gia and asks, 'You want me to sit on that thing? It's not going to hurt me is it?'

'Absolutely not, I can assure you it will not harm you or your baby;

Ciera decides to accommodate her. She sits on this strange piece of equipment. Gia indicates to her to make herself comfortable in the horizontal position. She looks at her and she says, 'Please do not worry, nothing will happen to you,' then the sides of this apparatus rise up over the top of her. Then there is a flashing of lights. And the sides descend down.

Gia walks over, looks at her and says, 'Now that didn't hurt did it?' She helps her down off the apparatus. 'The only thing we would like from you. I know that you will think this request is strange. You are not allowed to tell anyone about us, especially where you have been tonight, not even your husband is to know, do you understand!'

'Yes I do, no one would believe me anyway, Can I ask a question?'

'Yes of course you may, what would you like to know?'

'Is all this real, I mean I'm not dreaming, am I?'

'No, Ciera, you're not dreaming, this is for real and I can assure you. We will be back to update the technology from time to time before the baby is born, but we will be very discreet. Your baby will become the most powerful being on your World that I can tell you, and we will become very good friends in the future. We must return you to your bedroom now, so good bye and thank you for being so helpful. One more little bit of information: I can tell you now that you will have an amazing future. Good bye Ciera.'

Before she realises what has happened she is back in her bedroom totally mesmerized. Now her mind is running wild and she is finding it hard to sleep but eventually she nods off.

Next morning she wakes up sweating profusely, she then decides to have a shower. The first thing that flashes into her mind is, was I dreaming last night, did I have an out of body experience? Was I in an Alien space ship last night it looked so real? She is in a quandary as to what is real and what to believe.

Chapter 22

It does not take long for the six and half months to pass and Ciera is in hospital before she knows it. She is having her baby about two weeks early. There are no complications at the birth and everything goes beautifully.

John is by Ciera's side holding her hands.

The nurse holds the baby up. It is a girl. She then hands her to Ciera.

Ciera looks at John and says, 'John, you must phone your mum and dad to tell them that they're grandparents.'

John goes outside. He dials his dad on his mobile phone and tells him that he is a granddad and that the baby is a girl.

'That's fantastic news. Your mum will be very happy at this lovely event. Well done, son!' Dad replies. 'When can we see the baby?'

'You can come tomorrow if you like because I'm at work all day. It will be nice for Ciera to have someone come to see her and the baby.'

'Good. We will be around to see her and the baby tomorrow. I'll phone your brother JK and Delia tells them the good news!' Dad rushes into the sitting room and tells his wife that they are grandparents and that Ciera has just had a baby girl.

'That's fantastic news,' mum replies. 'When can we go and see the baby?' she enquires.

'Tomorrow is fine by me.'

'I'm happy with that arrangement. Tomorrow is fine then. Will you phone JK and Delia let them know. They can come here and we can all go together to the hospital?'

'Sure? Dad dials JK and informs him that he has a niece. Then he phones Delia tells her that Ciera has had a baby girl and that she is an Auntie. 'He tells both of them that, he and his wife are going to the hospital tomorrow to see the new baby. If they would like to go to the hospital he will see them there early afternoon

The next morning JK, the oldest son, gets ready to go to the hospital. He drives into town, buys a large box of chocolates for Ciera, goes to a coffee shop and has a coffee to pass away the time, for an hour.

The grandfather glances at his watch, says to his wife, 'I think it's time to go to the hospital.'

'I'm ready.' his wife replies.

'Good let's go then? The two of them walk out the front door to the car. He sits in the driver's seat, starts the engine waits until his wife sits in the passenger seat and drives off. 'Well I wonder what the new baby looks like.' he asks.

'We'll soon see, replies his wife. 'This traffic is ridiculous. The child will be walking out of the hospital if we don't get a move on.'

'Don't worry. We will be there soon enough, not far to go now. Once we're through these traffic lights we're nearly there.'

Two miles down the road, he turns right into the hospital grounds and looks around for a parking space.

'There's one,' says his wife.

Dad drives into the parking space and tells his wife, 'Will you go and get a parking ticket, please!'

On her return, she places the ticket on the dashboard, and dad gets out, locks the car. The two of them walk to the main entrance of the hospital through the main door, up to the porter at the desk and ask, 'Can you direct me to the maternity ward please?'

Just at that moment JK and Delia walk up behind them. He taps his dad on the shoulder saying, 'Good afternoon, dad and mum. I picked Delia up from her shop, no need to come with two cars, it would be silly. We are here now so let's go and see this baby girl.'

The porter gives them the directions saying, 'Follow the signs!'

Off they go, the four of them following the signs. It is a very big hospital.

Five minutes later, they arrive at the maternity ward, dad asks, 'Which bed is Mrs Ciera Carney in please?'

The nurse points out the bed and says, 'Be quiet, as they are sleeping babies. Do not make too much noise, thank you we like to be quiet in this ward!'

'Thank you, nurse,' replies dad. Then they proceed to the bed.

At the bed side dad's wife enquires, Ciera, are you and the baby all right?'

'Yes we are fine? Replies Ciera. 'Everything is fine!'

'Can we see the baby please?' asks dad.

'Yes of course you can,' says Ciera, as she takes it from the crib. 'Would you like to hold her?'

'I would love to hold her,' replies dad.

Dad puts out his arms and takes the baby from the mother, looks at her, 'What a beautiful child.' Then a very strange feeling comes over him. He is a bit unsteady, so his wife takes the baby from him.

'Are you all right?' she asks.

Yes, I'm fine, no, he replies. 'That was a very funny experience. Something hit me, and I do not know what it was. I can't explain what is happening, but it frightened me. I'll just go out and get some fresh air.'

He starts to walk away but he is getting some very strange thoughts running around in his mind, which is a bit daunting. He does not understand, and he cannot figure out what is going on in his mind. He finds the hospital cafe, goes to the counter, and asks for a cup of tea. He pays for the tea, Walks to a table sits down and is still getting all these strange things in his head.

About two minutes later, JK arrives at his table.

'Are you all right, dad?'

'Sit down, son. Where is your sister? I need to talk to someone, I think that maybe I might be going mad!'

'Delia is staying with mum and of course the baby.'

'Why do you think you are going mad, what do you mean, are you not feeling well?' JK enquires.

'That's the problem. I feel fine. It's just all this strange information is arriving into my brain and I don't know where it's coming from!'

JK looks at him, 'Well you look fine to me. What do you mean all this information in your head, I don't understand. Can you explain what you're talking about?'

His father looks at him and without thinking says, 'Look at that cup?'

It levitates about ten centimetres above the top of the table.

JK jumps up and says. 'Bloody Hell that is amazing. Dad, did you levitate that cup?'

'Well my son let me ask you a question. What do you think? It certainly did not levitate on its own and the only explanation I can think of is perhaps it has something to do with my grand-daughter, maybe it has a mind of its own what do you think. Look at the cup again. I'm going to turn it upside down this time!'

'Dad, you can't do something like that!'

'Well, then watch the cup.'

JK looks at the cup and is amazed as the cup levitates, turns upside down and returns to the saucer.

'Well my son. What do you think?'

'I don't know. This is something beyond me. Are you telling me that all this information is arriving in your mind and you don't know where it's coming from?'

'At this moment in time, that is something I'm thinking about. I don't have an explanation now but we will see what happens. Let's go and find your mother but don't tell her anything you've witnessed so far. It will only upset her and that is the last thing I'd want.'

They go back to the maternity ward and stand next to the crib. The baby is awake she looks up at her granddad and smiles, her eyes are wide open. He looks a very worried man. He sits on a chair to steady himself. Now he knows the baby is communicating with him telepathically, and he is worried. Suddenly, he receives a message from the baby telling him, 'Please do not worry everything will be all right!'

He looks at the baby again and thinks to himself, is this baby telepathically communicating with me or am I just imagining it.'

'No, granddad, I'm for real I can telepathically communicate with you anytime I like!'

Granddad looks at the mother and asks, 'When are you coming home with the baby?'

'I think tomorrow if the doctors allow me.'

'Fine, we'll see you tomorrow at home. Is there anything you need?'

'No, except I'll need a lift from the hospital tomorrow. Could you help me in that area? John's working all day but he is coming in late this afternoon and I'll tell him that you'll pick us up tomorrow and take us home.'

'Yes, of course I can. Give me a ring and I'll come to the hospital to pick you up and drop you home. I'll say goodbye for now.' He looks at the baby and says, 'Bye baby!'

Suddenly the baby answers him, a psychic message at the back of his mind! This message from the baby is. 'See you tomorrow granddad!'

He is now flabbergasted thinks to himself what is going on here. I think that this baby is telepathic. 'Oh my God I think I'm going funny in the head. What am I going to do about this situation? I know; I'll keep my mouth shut for the moment.'

Back at the car, Dad places his ticket in the parking meter, pays the sum required, goes to his car, sit's inside. He drives out of the car park and the hospital.

All the conversation in the car revolves around the new baby.

Anne his wife says. 'It looks like your youngest son.'

Dad says. 'It looks like the mother.'

The grandmother smiles to herself, and says. 'I think maybe you might be right. The genes are in there somewhere, and I hope that she grows up to be a very famous person; maybe a doctor, or a scientist or something like that.'

Dad thinks, 'You don't know the half of it,' aware that she will be very influential, and that she will be very powerful and influence quite a lot of very powerful people and that they will listen. They will try to stop her and even try to kill her. Where is all this information coming from? Is all this information being passed from the baby into my mind, I don't know. This is uncanny. How can a baby be telepathic with me? I am just an ordinary person with no special talents, just a dad and now a grandparent. I'm on my way home and she is still telling me things, but she is still in the hospital.

All this information is arriving too fast and I can't slow the pace down to understand its meaning. I hope that at some future moment in time, I'll be able to make some sense of it all, but there are exciting times ahead, and I hope that I can acclimatize my mind and brain to understand this very strange phenomenon, I seem to have inherited from the baby, but maybe it is all a dream.'

Chapter 23

The next morning granddad is awake early. He has had a very good night's sleep and is very excited about going back to the hospital to pick up the mother and baby and deliver them home.

The phone rings and his wife Anne lifts the phone up, looks over and says. 'It's Ciera. She'd like to know when you're coming to take her and the baby home from the hospital and how long are you likely to be?'

Dad takes the phone from his wife and says, 'Good morning new mum. I'll be there to pick you up in about one hour if that's all right with you?'

'Yes, that's fine,' she replies. 'See you soon.'

'Goodbye for now.' He replaces the phone. He has heard nothing from the baby since yesterday, which is very strange considering all the information he had from her at the hospital yesterday. Maybe it was just a dream or because he was excited about the new baby in the family and the first granddaughter. 'Breakfast is ready, dad, Come and get it! You promised to take the mother and baby home from the hospital and you must not be late!'

Yes, I know and I'll keep my promise.' He sits down to the table for his breakfast. Then it starts a voice in his mind.

'Granddad *I hope you'll be able to come to the hospital this morning and pick us up, that is if you don't mind?'*

He shouts out, 'No, I haven't forgotten!'

His wife looks at him stunned by this sudden outburst. 'Is there something wrong with you?'

'Nothing, I'm just thinking out loud,' he replies.

'Are you going senile?' asks his wife. 'Talking to yourself at your age, finish your breakfast. You'll need to get ready to go to the hospital to pick up Ciera and the baby!'

'Are you coming with me?'

'No. I've a lot to do and I'll have plenty of time to see the baby as she's growing up.'

'Right then, I'll finish my breakfast and go and get ready.' He goes up to the bathroom, has a quick shower, a shave and gets ready. Walks down the stairs and picks up the car keys. He gives the wife a quick kiss on the cheeks and goes out the front door, sits in the car and drives out of the drive. Soon he is on his way to the hospital. Now the excitement is gathering momentum. He can feel a strange urge to get to the hospital, but has heard nothing from the baby yet.

Then it starts.

'We're waiting for you. I know that you're on your way.'

'Fine, I'll be there shortly. Please don't distract me while I'm driving.' He drives into the hospital grounds, finds a parking space, takes a parking ticket from the machine and walks into the hospital. He goes straight to the maternity ward. There he finds the mother and baby ready to leave.

The baby is in her crib but not asleep.

'Let me help you,' says dad. He takes the crib and baby from the mother.

They say their goodbyes to the nurses, the doctor and thank them for all the help they gave while in the hospital. They walk out of the ward, out the front entrance to the car.

Granddad opens the front passenger door for the mother. She gets in. Dad places the crib with the baby on the back seat of the car. Just before he closes the door, he has a quick look at the baby. It is then he receives in his mind a message informing him that they will have plenty of time to communicate with each other in the future.

I know that you're very curious and worried. I'll need you in the near future to protect me. I'll give you the same powers I have. Together, you and I as a team, we will be formidable. You've no idea how powerful I am. Ask a few questions of my mother. She'll know who I am. However, you must be very careful with the questions. Now get in the car and drive us home!

He starts the car and drives out of the car park.

'Granddad, are you all right? You've been very quiet.'

'I'm just very excited.' As he looks at Ciera, 'Do you want to talk about something anything, maybe you'd like to talk about the baby?'

The mother looks at him very suspiciously asking, 'Granddad. What are you suggesting?'

'I'm not suggesting anything, just wondering if everything is alright with the baby!'

'Ciera blurts out, I have to confide in someone about the baby, but I don't know if I can trust you. Nobody knows my secret and it's driving me crazy. Can I trust you?'

'Yes. I know about the baby.'

'What do you mean? You can't know about her. I'm the only one that knows.'

'That's not true. She's been communicating with me since yesterday.'

The mother starts crying. 'What am I going to do? They'll come for her and take her from me.'

'I don't think they'll take her. She's too strong and she has me now to help her and she can expand her power to the rest of the family if she so desires. Can you tell me when did all this happen?'

'Well...when I became pregnant, I was taken by Aliens to some kind of spacecraft, where they examined me in quite a detailed manner. From a standing position on the spacecraft floor deck I was raised unto a very funny looking table then some kind of machine was placed over me, it was amazing lots of lights flashing on and off. They didn't hurt me. I suppose I should be grateful for that. I didn't experience any pain. While I was on the table the woman asked me if I would like to know the sex of the baby, I said no thank you.'

'How many Aliens were there in that spacecraft?'

'I don't know. I was too frightened to look. However, they did communicate with me telepathically, saying to me that my baby would be a very powerful baby and that it would grow up to be a very important person, but that I will need to be on my guard because there's another faction of Aliens who will try to take the baby from me. You could say that the Aliens on the spacecraft are the good Aliens and the other ones will try to abduct me and the baby they are the bad ones.'

'Can't you or they, stop them?'

'They're not allowed. All they can do is to give the baby the power to defend herself and the World. They told me that my baby was a very special baby picked from thousands and thousands of babies to try stop the bad Aliens from taking over the Earth. They told me that, now and then they intervene to maintain the cosmic status quo. Earth people are their descendants and they arrived on this planet thousands of years ago. Every now and then they make a visit to make sure that all is well to make sure that this planet retains its human biology and is not interfered with by other nonhuman Aliens. They are allowed to help but not in a technological way. They are not allowed to give us any advanced weapons, bombs, no ray guns, no technical advancement. Earth people must grow at their own pace but they'll be watching and advising the baby telepathically without interfering with the daily running of her life. If our people can stop fighting, killing and starting wars they would have more resources to live a better life, and advance very quickly into what they call super computers. One other very important thing they told me: You'll need to know, when the baby is born, that Aliens will come to try to take her away from you. She has the power to stop them, and she can increase that power if need be by expanding that power to other family members without effecting any of her own power. Oh and she will make a lot of enemies but do not worry for she will prevail in the end.'

'Now we must plan the next four or five years,' says dad. 'How can we help the baby? Well she'll be able to stop them from interfering, trying to carry out an abduction of any kind, but I think that as a precaution I should be close to the baby, especially at night. May I make a suggestion? I think that you and the baby and of course John, should stay at my home until such time as the baby is in a better position to make these Aliens aware that she's too strong and that they're wasting their time trying to abduct her. They will try their best. They might even try in the daytime. So what do you think of my idea?'

'Well, granddad, I don't want to be a burden on you or mum, but I must make sure that my baby is going to be absolutely safe and free from these Aliens. I'd rather die than give her up to them. I don't have an alternative but to agree to your suggestion. However I must call in at home to pick up some clothes for the baby and myself.'

Right then, let's go to your house. Just a minute, the baby is communicating with me now. She's telling me that they will be trying to abduct her tonight but she doesn't have a time yet but please do not to worry because everything will be all right. She's telling me that when she grows up, things will change for the better, but that they'll try to abduct her many times. By then it will be too late she'll be in a position where she'll be able to control them and that there's nothing they can do about it. Those other Aliens are in league with some world governments and she'll put a stop to that when she's older. At this moment in her early life, she's only a bit worried and the only worry is that she has to grow up naturally, but she knows that you'll look after her and that she loves you very much. Oh, she wants me to tell you that you've a gas leak in your kitchen so be very careful when you enter the house. Don't turn anything on. You might cause an explosion, you must phone the gas people to come out to fix the leak.'

'I'll phone them right now. I have the number in my mobile phone.'

Having arrived at the house they alight from the car.

Ciera opens the front door, goes in and up the stairs. She gets all the clothes for the baby and herself, goes down the stairs into the kitchen, turns off the gas at the mains and goes to the front door. Just as she is about to lock the front door the gas people arrive.

'Mrs Carney?'

'Yes. Are you the gas people?'

'Yes we are. Can we go in and repair your gas leak?'

'Of course you can. Let me show you where the gas main is located.'

They follow her into the house and into the kitchen where she points to the gas meter.

'Thank you. We'll carry on from here if you don't mind. This won't take long to repair.'

Ciera goes back to the car and informs granddad that she will have to wait for the gasmen to finish fixing the gas leak.

'Fine,' granddad replies. 'I'll stay with the baby. I'll phone my wife and tell her that you'd like to stay for a week or two until you feel that you can go home.' He dials his home number. His wife answers.

'I'm at Ciera's house at the moment retrieving some clothes for the baby and the mother. There's a gas leak in the house, but the gas men are here to repair it.'

'You mustn't leave the baby and mother in the house! Now you best bring them over to our house until their house is free of gas. I'm not having my only granddaughter put in danger.' If only she was aware of the danger the baby is in now she would have a fit. 'You tell Ciera what I've said and I'm sure that she'll agree with me.

'Dad replies fine. 'I'll tell her.'

'How long before you leave?'

'I don't know. When the gasmen have repaired the gas leak in the house we'll be on our way home. Goodbye for now.' He shuts the phone down and places it back in his pocket.

Chapter 24

The gasmen appear at the doorway walk towards their van, informing Ciera that they have repaired the gas leak and the house is safe. Then they get back into their van and then drive away.

'Right, Ciera. You go and lock your front door and then we can drive to my house.'

The baby starts to cry and the mother picks her up and starts to breast-feed the baby (it's a human thing.) 'Is your wife happy to have us in your house, I wouldn't want to intrude on your privacy?

No. I've informed her that you and the baby will be staying with us for a while, and she is looking forward to having you and the baby stay, as she hasn't had a baby around for a long time.'

'Good. I'm pleased about that. I was worried in case she might not want us around.'

'Nonsense,' granddad says 'She's very happy that you and the baby are staying with us. Now when we arrive home my wife must not know what is going on, because she would worry her head off especially if the baby might be in danger. Leave that to me. I'll tell her in my own time. If you have finished feeding your baby, please place her back in the crib. We're just about home!' granddad alights from the car, goes around to the passenger's side, opens the door and lets Ciera out. He tells her to take the clothes into the house. 'I'll bring the baby in.'

His wife is standing on the doorstep. 'She then proceeds to the car and tells dad that she will take the baby in herself.

'Fine, granddad replies. 'I'll lock the car and follow you in to the house,'

The grandmother removes her granddaughter from the crib and she is fussing with her in her arms. Now the baby seems to be very happy. 'Ciera, would you like a coffee or tea?'

'Coffee will be fine. With sugar and milk please.'

'Can I make you a sandwich to go with your coffee?'

'Please.'

'What would you like in your sandwich? You can have cheese or ham or both?'

'Whatever you make I'll eat because I'm very hungry!'

Granddad makes up the sandwiches, puts them on a plate and places them on the table.

'Okay Ciera, your sandwiches and coffee are ready and on the table. Help yourself. Now we need to fix you and the baby with a bedroom, would you believe we have a cot as well so if you'll take your clothes up into the bedroom on the right at the top of the stairs after you've had your coffee and sandwich.' He looks over at Ciera and says. Make sure that the cot is at the back wall on the other side of the room away from the window, away from prying eyes.

'I know what to do,' Ciera replies. After she has finished eating the sandwiches and drinking the coffee she says, 'I'll just nip up to the bedroom with the baby's and my clothes if you don't mind.'

Granddad says. 'I'll come up and help you with the cot if you like?'

'That would be nice.' Ciera walks up the stairs and into the bedroom that she and the baby will occupy for the predictable future. She takes her clothes and starts to place them in the wardrobe.

'Shall we move the cot from the window?' dad suggests.

'Yes. It's not very heavy.'

They carry it across to the other side and place it against the back wall.

Granddad advises that all the blankets and covers should be placed in the airing cupboard before placing them back on the cot. 'Perhaps you and the baby would like a nap. You must be tired now?'

'I'm a bit tired. I'll follow you down the stairs pick up the baby and come back to our bedroom. She can sleep with me until we have the blankets back in the cot.'

'Fine,' dad replies. 'You have a nice sleep and I'll call you when dinner is ready.' Granddad goes down the stairs and into the front room sits down and asks his wife for a cup of tea.

'Yes, of course dear.' She goes to the kitchen to make the tea and returns to the sitting room with the tea. 'There you are. It's nice to have Ciera and the baby here for a while!

'It will be nice for me as well,' says dad. 'I'm looking forward to helping with the baby. I'm delighted that the mum and baby are here for a while, but we must try and not be too possessive with the baby. I know that it's our first grandchild but you must let the mother attend to the baby's needs. I'm sure that Ciera will let you mind the baby when she's not feeling too good. Now promise me that you'll be careful and not interfere too much?'

'I promise not to be too dominating, but surely I can give the baby a little cuddle now and again?'

'Yes of course you can but you must be careful how you go about it.'

Chapter 25

The phone rings and granddad picks it up. It is John. 'Good afternoon, son. I suppose you're wondering why your wife and child are not at your house. Well, there was a gas leak in your house and she called the gas people, we waited for them to come out to repair the gas leak. They arrived very quickly and repaired the leak then the gasman made a suggestion, that we should not leave the mum and the baby in the house until all the gas dissipated. He said that it might take a few days so we decided it would be a good idea to stay a few days at my house and that includes you as well. What do you think, son?'

'That's fine with me. So I'm staying at your house as well?'

'Yes you are. Oh, what time can we expect you for dinner tonight?'

'I'll be home about five o'clock!'

'Lovely. I'll tell your mother that you'll be home for dinner. See you then. Incidentally, the baby looks fantastic. Well done, son!'

'See you tonight, dad.'

It is nearly five o'clock.

Granddad says to his wife. 'I think you should go and wake Ciera and tell her that the dinner will be ready soon.' He goes up the stairs, knocks on the bedroom door and says. 'Ciera are you awake? Dinner is nearly ready.'

'Yes, I'm awake. I'll be down shortly. Thank you, granddad' she replies.

He goes down the stairs into the kitchen to help his wife with the dinner.

After about twenty minutes have passed, John comes in the front door walks to the kitchen.

'Good evening, son. Dinner will be ready soon. You go and see your wife and baby. Have a quick shower and come down when you're ready!'

'Hello mum. Thanks for having us for a few days. It's very nice of you and dad. You're so kind. Well I'll go and see my wife and baby and then have a shower. See you soon.'

He runs up the stairs and into the bedroom, gives his wife a cuddle and enquires if the little baby is all right.

'She's fine,' replies his wife.

'Fine, I'll go and have a quick shower and then we can go down to dinner. You'll like mum's cooking!'

'I'm sure I will. You go and have your shower and I'll get the baby ready.'

Granddad and wife are just getting ready to put the dinner on the table, when his son, his wife and baby arrive in the sitting room.

Granddad says, 'Sit at the table and we'll bring the dinner for you!'

Dinner on the table, everyone takes their places.

'Well, my son. How was your day at work?'

'Not very good we have a lot of problems with the computers. I hope that they're up and running by tomorrow. We have a lot of technical work to do. I'd rather forget about work at the moment and concentrate on dinner!'

'Sure, let's just get on with dinner. How is your dinner, Ciera?'

'Fine, it's just right, nice, and as good as ever. I always look forward to coming to dinner here. The food is always good.'

'So glad you like your dinners,' says mum. 'We love having you here and now with the baby we might see you more often.

'Not for me,' says granddad.

'Nor me,' replies his son.

'What about you, Ciera?'

'No, I'm too full. I couldn't eat another thing. The dinner was fantastic. I'd better attend to the baby, she is due a feed about now, excuse me.' She gets up from the dinner table. She goes to the crib and lifts the baby out and goes into the front room and breast feeds the baby who appears to be a bit upset, however she settles down and takes her feed, then falls asleep again. Ciera puts her back in the crib and settles her down, knowing that the night is going to be very difficult indeed. She leaves the baby in the front room, walks into the dining room sits next to her husband and has a little cuddle.

Mum and granddad look at them and have a little smile.

'Anyone for television?' asks dad.

'Don't mind, dad,' replies his son.

'Well, what about World Forests? That's a very interesting program.'

'Sure,' replies John. 'That might be very good.'

'Okay then.' All say yes except Ciera, as she is asleep.

Granddad looks over and says. 'We'll keep the sound down!'

Before the program finishes everyone falls asleep.

About an hour later, granddad wakes up, calls Ciera and tells her to take the baby up to the bedroom as soon as possible. He then wakes his wife and tells her it is time to go to bed. She lifts herself up off the settee, says goodnight to everyone and trots up the stairs to bed.

John is just about to say that he is off to bed, when his dad says, 'I need to talk to you now.'

'What do you want to talk about dad?' 'Remember yesterday when I was at the hospital with your brother JK and Delia. I made a very big impression on him. I levitated a cup and I said to him that I didn't know what was happening. Well, that wasn't quite true?'

'What do you mean dad, He looks at his father very intently and looks very worried.

'You've a very special baby and she is one in billions. Now I don't want to frighten you but I'll need your help tonight with the baby!'

'Come on, dad. What do you mean?'

'She's different from any other baby on the planet. She has special powers enabling me to do things like JK saw me perform at the hospital yesterday.'

'Oh come on, dad! Do you think that I'm an idiot?'

'No, son, I don't. Can I trust you with a little secret?'

'Okay, fire away. Let me have the whole story.'

'Right, please place your hand in mine.'

Reluctantly, John places his hand in his dad's hand and a powerful burst of power goes up his hand. After about two seconds, it stops and he is quite shocked. 'Bloody hell dad! What did you do to me?'

'Look at the television. Switch it off.'

'But...that's never going to happen.'

'Just look at it. Concentrate.'

'I'm going to look a right idiot but I'll look at it!' John turns round and looks at the television and it switches itself off. 'You have the remote behind your back!'

'Look. It's there on the table over by you. Now look at the television again and switch it on.'

John turns again and looks at the television.

It switches itself on.

'No! I don't believe that me looking at the television switches it on!'

'Fine,' his dad says. Look at the remote.' John turns and looks at the remote whereupon it levitates up from the table.

'I'm trying to tell you, son, that you have a very special child who has exceptional powers far beyond my comprehension.'

'Oh my God, dad, what have you done to me?'

All we can do is to carry out her wishes. Now do you believe me?'

'I don't know but I suppose I'll have to believe what I see.'

'Now I can tell you about the hard bit. Sometime tonight, or early morning we'll have visitors come from another planet and they will try and take your daughter away!'

'Hang on a minute! Don't you think that we should phone the police or the army or the RAF?'

'No! She doesn't want anybody outside of this family to know about us at the moment but don't worry, your daughter is a hundred times more powerful than the Aliens, but to make sure she has given me the power as well, and I have given it to you. Your daughter talks to me and I know exactly what's in her mind. I know that this is hard for you to understand, but everything I've told you is true. Also, your wife knows everything about the baby, and I mean everything there is to know. Now, I need your help tonight. We'll be staying in the baby's bedroom until everything is okay, but you must not mention anything to your mother. I don't want to worry her. What is the time now? It's just coming up to half-past eleven. When we are in the room with the baby, we must hold hands until your daughter tells us to drop our hands, because she will use her power through us but she will be in communication with us throughout the night so we'll have to be very diligent. Are you ready to fight for your daughter?'

'I am!'

'Then let's go and protect her. You go up the stairs and I'll follow you in a minute. I suspect that your wife and the baby will be awake so don't be afraid if she talks to you. She knows that I've given you the power to help her. Whatever she tells you to do, you do it without question. Do you understand?'

'Yes, I understand dad.'

'Okay. Now I can't emphasize too strongly the fact that your daughter will depend on us to help her. Off you go up to the bedroom. Don't you worry about making a noise going up the stairs your mother will be sound asleep by now!'

Chapter 26

Dad goes up the stairs and into the bedroom to ask if everyone is all right.

'Yes,' his son and his wife reply, and so too does the baby and for the first time John receives a communication from his daughter, She asks her dad if he is comfortable being in here. He is about to answer when she communicates again and says. *'Dad you only have to think about what you are going to say.'*

'Ok. I'll listen to you and do what you say.'

'That is splendid,' says the baby. 'Things will get very futuristic, there will be lots of very baffling, mystifying, and confusing happenings tonight but I'm here to make sure that we convince these Aliens that we will not tolerate them coming to our world. When they arrive, it will happen suddenly so be aware. I'll place a strong protective shield around the house. When they materialize, I'll then place a barrier around them so that they can't get out and then *we* decide what we do with them. Is everybody ready? I sense them getting nearer. They're already in Earth's orbit and as long as we only communicate telepathically, they'll not be able to hear us. So for time being we only communicate in the mind. Dad, you do understand?'

'I understand!' he replies in his mind.

'Okay, everyone settle down. I'll tell you when they are about to enter the room. They will try and enter your minds; you throw it back as hard as you can. That will confuse them. Then they will be trapped and I will deal with them. They're on their way. Dad and granddad please join hands.'

A flash of azure light and the Aliens materialize in the room. There are two of them.

Granddad and John look at them and they are surprised at what they see. They are very little people, blue gray in colour with large dark eyes. Their heads are rather large, long arms with thin fingers, thin legs and small feet. These Aliens have a very strange look about them. There is a sad, worried look on their faces, because this is probably the first time that an abduction of any human being on this planet is going to be prohibited and this will stop them from achieving their goal, now they are very confused. They do not know what to do and they are beginning to panic, trying to beam out, but they are not able to penetrate the two shields. They have a dilemma. This is the first time that they have been thwarted taking a human being by force, that has them worried, and they don't like what is happening to them. This is fascinating. Fancy all the power they have and they are stuck in this house unable to leave. If it was not so serious you would laugh, but this is very serious for these Aliens have been causing havoc on Earth for generations and now they do not know what is happening to them. They are having a telepathic conversation between themselves and their spacecraft, throughout their conversation the baby is listening. She is able to learn any language instantly because of her technology. They are looking at the possibility of sending more Aliens down but the leader is worried in case they would not be able to beam back to their ship. It is panic stations aboard the craft. They are running around like headless chickens trying to figure out what to do. They are even thinking of coming down and landing near the house, but they are very afraid. They really do not know if they can chance coming down. All that technology and science on their craft and they are in a state of panic.

The baby sends out her psychic thoughts. 'We have them trapped. It's crucial that we retain the upper hand. Granddad, would you like to interrogate them?'

'Yes I would. Thank you.'

'They are telepathic. You can talk to them now.'

Grand-dad looks at them. 'Why have you come to this particular house?'

The answer comes back. 'We are here for the baby!'

'Well you can't have her. Now what are you going to do about it?'

'We *will* take her!'

'You can try!'

Then the baby has her input: 'I could vaporize the two of you now if I wish but I'll give you four options. One; I could keep you here. Two; I could call the military. Three I could vaporize your spacecraft in orbit around our world...yes I could, and four: the worst scenario for you would be if I take your craft out of orbit and land it in a field near here. You have four options. Which one will you take?'

'We are here to take the baby!'

'Ask your crew what is happening with your craft?'

A couple of seconds go by.

'It's out of control. What do you want from us?' ask the Aliens.

'Granddad asks, 'what do you think we should do now?'

'Well, they can't escape otherwise they'd have left and taken the baby, so they are at our mercy. I don't trust them. I say vaporize them now and their craft, otherwise they'll come back.'

'Okay, minds together, now project your thoughts to the craft. I'll show you in your mind where it is, hit it with all your power. The craft is now vaporized dad and granddad. What would you like to do with the two little Aliens, we have before us? They can't return to their craft because it does

not exist. I'll place them somewhere safe for the time being. I might need them later in my life but for now they are in a very secure place!'

'They are no good to us, so vaporize them,' dad replies. But if you should need them sometime later in your life for whatever reason that's fine by us!'

'Right then leave them to me. Shields off and they are gone. Now we can have some sleep, and my mother has slept through it all. There will be a next time but we are ready for them now. Dad and granddad, you are not to display your abilities in public because I'm not quite ready yet to make my announcement and entrance to the world. Anyway off to bed, granddad, see you in the morning. Dad you can go to bed as well please. Oh I'll need a name but don't worry as I have chosen a name I like, so if you and mum don't mind I wish to have the name Leila, What do you think? If that is the name you want that's fine by me I'll inform your mother in the morning, *good night dad!'*

In the morning Ciera asks, 'Did everything go well last night?'

'Yes,' replies John. 'In fact everything was very satisfactory, and yes the Aliens did come for Leila, but your little daughter won the day or, if you like, the night. It was just amazing. Our daughter is just awesome, something beyond belief. She has the wow, wow, wow factor. She is extremely powerful and she tells me that she will be even more powerful as she gets older. Every day she can keep the Aliens at bay is a plus for Earth!' 'Incidentally your daughter has chosen a name for herself. John looks at his wife and says, 'she likes the name Leila, what do you think? 'Well if that is the name she wants to be known by, so be it, that's what we will call her. Leila is a very nice name I like it, yes I think that is fine by me.' 'Good.' John replies.

Three months go by and all is well in the Carney house. The mother and the baby named Leila are doing fine.

Leila is worried because she was expecting another visit from the bad Aliens. She contacts granddad telepathically. 'I'm worried we haven't heard from the Aliens. I'm sure that they're planning something. We will need to be on our guard, they will try again and spring a surprise on us sooner then we think. I'm monitoring outer space all the time. When they try to sneak a blind visit to our planet I'll know when they are on their way. I should be able to tell when they pass Jupiter. That will give you time to come to our house before they arrive. It will probably be night time when they arrive. However I'm a lot stronger now but they don't know that and they're in for a bigger surprise than before. The first Aliens will have sent a message to their home planet about us and they will have a new plan. They will come with two or more craft and try to abduct me, but don't worry I'll be ready for them. I might try to take one of their craft out. I can certainly

54

make one or two of the craft wobble and that should slow them down because they'll have to check everything and try to figure out what's wrong. They'll not associate me with the problems, so they will carry on to Earth. That will give you time to arrive here at my house. With the three of us here, there will not be any problems. They'll be a lot more careful now and they know that it will not be easy to abduct me so they'll be mob-handed. I'll try to abduct their leader before they realise what's happened. I can take him from the craft in space to my room and shield him and the house. I can make a stronger shield now and they'll not be able to penetrate it!'

Another month passes by and no sign of the Aliens. Leila is just beginning to crawl about the house is able to sit up and learning to be a pain, but in a nice way. They are due a visit to granddad's house for Sunday dinner. Ciera is looking forward to being with the in-laws for a change and a nice dinner would go down very nicely and of course save her the cooking at home. Ciera is very contented now at least for the present, but she knows in her heart that things will change with regard to her daughter. She knows that the Aliens will come again and try to abduct her. She has consoled herself with the knowledge that Leila has the power to stop the Aliens in their tracks, while hoping by making them realise they are wasting their time trying to abduct her. They will pay a high price for trying, but she knows that they will never give up. They want this child but not at any cost. They know that she is not just an ordinary child. They will employ all their technology and science in an attempt to abduct her. They also know that as she grows older she will be stronger. Then the whole scenario will change; she will be able to control them and they will not like that, but they will have to choose between staying alive or dying.

Chapter 27

Sunday morning Ciera goes to the bedroom asking, 'John, you are going to have a shower and come down for your breakfast?'

'Give me two minutes and I'll go in the shower.'

'I'll go down to the kitchen and start making breakfast. Don't be too long, I'll feed the baby first and then have your breakfast ready when you come downstairs.'

'That's fine with me love. I'll go in the shower now.'

'Your breakfast is on the table!' Ciera shouts.

'Okay. I'm coming,' replies John as he ambles down the stairs into the kitchen and sits at the table.

His wife places the breakfast in front of him. 'Shall I pour your coffee now?'

'Please. Do you need any help packing the car?'

'No. I've packed it all. You just get on with your breakfast.'

The journey takes about one hour to his parent's house.

Ciera gets out of the car, goes to the back seat and takes the crib and the baby out. She goes to the front door where the grandmother is waiting.

'Let me take the crib please. How is the little baby?' she asks.

'She's fine,' replies the mother. 'She slept all the way here!'

'Good. Shall we go in?'

'Yes, please,' replies Ciera. She turns round and says. 'John, you are coming in now?'

'Yes. Just leave the front door open.'

Inside in sitting room the grandmother asks: 'Ciera, can I make you a coffee?'

'Yes please, that would be lovely.'

'Now, tell me all the news about the baby. She's grown a lot since I saw her last.'

'She's just beginning to crawl as well and she's a right little devil.'

'Well all children are like that. They're just learning. Everything is new to them and their little brain is absorbing all kinds of information, hopefully the right kind!' Little does she know that Leila is not your average child, but that is sometime in the future, Leila is looking forward to it.

'Is granddad about?'

'He's in the garden. I'll go and call him. You finish your coffee.' She opens the back door and calls dad, informing him that Ciera, John and the baby are here.

'Just coming!' he replies having just dug up some new potatoes for dinner.

Then they have another visitor and it is JK just coming down the hallway.

Mum says. 'Well now look who's here! It's our JK.'

JK strides into the kitchen. 'Where's dad?'

'He's gone down the garden to get some new potatoes for dinner. Will you be staying for dinner JK?'

'Well, if you have enough I'll stay. How's the baby?' JK asks Ciera.

'She's fine, growing up fast. It's now four months since she was born she's just beginning to crawl as well, just a little bit!'

'Why, that's fantastic. I bet she's a right little devil. JK replies. 'I'll just go and see dad in the garden! He turns and walks out the back door.

Dad looks up and replies. 'Hello son! How are you? Are you staying for dinner?'

'Yes, I'm here for dinner. How are you keeping, dad?'

'I've been meaning to have a talk with you about what we discussed in the hospital, but there was always someone around, and I didn't want to talk about it when mum was about. So can we have a discussion now?'

'What do you want to tell me?'

'Well, about the baby. The time has arrived when patience becomes a crime and mayhem appears garbed in the mantle of virtue.'

'What are you talking about dad?' Well that is a very old quote I read it somewhere some years ago and it remains in my mind I don't know why!'

'Anyway since the hospital incident, I was hoping you could bring me up to the present regarding the baby.'

'Well, we had visitors from space a while back, but the baby was able to send them packing!'

'What do you mean? They didn't harm the baby, did they?'

'No. When the baby came here from the hospital that night they came to take her away. We fought them off with the help of the baby. They were no match for the three of us. I gave John the power, but we're expecting them back soon!'

'So, my little brother has the power as well?'

'Yes. You weren't available at the time so I had to take him into my confidence as a backup. Will you be staying the night or are you going away again?'

'No. I'm staying for a couple of days if I can. That's if you and mum don't mind?'

'That's fine. I'll tell your mother. I'm sure that she'll be very pleased to have the whole family here for dinner. I'll not tell her why, it might worry her. I must take the new potatoes to your mother for the dinner. You stay here and I'll ask your brother out into the garden where we can have a good talk about the baby. Is that all right by you?'

'Of course,' JK replies. I'll just sit on the bench and wait.'

A few minutes go by and dad and John emerge through the door. They come down the path and the two of them sit on the bench with JK.

Dad looks at John and tells him that JK is in possession of the power as well, that it was given to him in the hospital by his daughter!

John shrugs his shoulders and says. 'That's fine by me.'

'Good! Then shall we go in and have a drink?'

'Yes,' say the two sons in unison. 'Let's go.'

The three of them walk up the path and in the door and dad asks. 'What would you like to drink JK?'

'I'll have a glass of white wine please.'

'What will you have, John?'

'I'll have a red wine, please!

'Ciera, what would you like?'

'I'll just have an orange juice!

'I'll have a small brandy!' Dad says to himself.

'What would you like, mum?'

'I'll have a small white wine, please. Oh, and the dinner will be ready in twenty minutes. Ciera the baby is crying. I think that she might be hungry?'

'I'll see to her now.' Ciera goes and picks the baby up and walks into the sitting room and feeds her.

'Is there anything I can do to help you?' asks dad.

'No. I can manage. You go and have a talk with your sons. It's been a long time since we have all been together and I'm sure they've a lot to catch up with.'

Twenty minutes pass and mum shouts: 'Dinner is ready everyone. Please come and sit down!'

Dinner over, dad asks his sons if they would like to help to do the washing up.

'Yes!' they reply. 'No problem. We would love to help, and the ladies can retire to the sitting room and look after the baby.'

'Well boys, what do you think of what I've told you about the baby?' says dad.

'Well,' JK replies. 'I find it very hard to get my brain around it. It sounds very sinister to me. What about you, John?'

'Well, I'm perplexed as to what to do or say. This is way above my intellectual level and I still think that all this is a dream and after that vision when I stayed here the last time of the two Aliens in the bedroom, I find it amazing that my daughter has this powerful effect on the Aliens and can control almost anything that she wants.'

'Well, I don't think we know the half of it!' Dad replies. 'I mean, where is it going from here and how should we prepare ourselves for all that will happen when we don't know? I'm sure that we've not heard the last of it. These Aliens are not fools and are intellectually way above us. On our own that is the two of us, you and me, are no match for them, but the baby is more than equal. She is on a much higher intellectual plane. I think that she could, if she wished, be very difficult to defeat, She will definitely get stronger as she grows up. I wouldn't like to go against her at any time in the future. She's very special and we will need to put our lives in her hands. I know that's a strange thing to say, but I have a very strong feeling that we will be going on some wonderful adventures in the future. What do you think JK?'

'From what I've seen so far I have to agree with you, dad. There's nothing else that we can do; only support her.'

'What about you, John?'

'Well she's my daughter. I know that what I've witnessed up in the bedroom is very hard to believe and if the worst comes to the worst I'd certainly lay down my life for her. I do get the feeling that she's just biding her time until she's ready to do whatever it is she's here for.'

All three of them receive a message from the baby at the same time, *telling them that they will be having visitors sometime tonight, not to worry because they are her godparents. They are coming to see her and enquire how she's getting on. They already know what happened to the Aliens and their craft. It is just to check up on her and maybe give her a telling off. They will materialize in the sitting room and they will need to meet the family not mother or grandmother. She will explain later. They are to be very courteous and considerate at all times. These particular Aliens are the good ones and she is sure that everyone will be very polite in their presence. They will need authorization before they ask questions if they wish, but she does not know if they will be given, the answers they might require. Do not try to intimidate,'* she cautions, *'because they are far superior and untouchable. They will talk verbally and they are very nice people so be very careful what you say and do not have a pre-emptive strategy because they will know. Lastly, know your place. They are probably six or ten thousand years ahead of us. They will tell you what they want and how to manage the powers you have now. Is everyone clear on what I've said?'*

All three answer together: 'Yes, we understand.'

Chapter 28

'JK, you didn't participate in the last visit of the Aliens,' says John. 'Let me tell you they're very dangerous, manipulating, and controlling freaks. They've impinged upon the human race for hundreds of years and very probably taken some hundreds of Earth people to other planets. What has become of those people or where they are now only God knows. They seem to be able to come and go as they please, there was nothing we could do until now. We're just about to make some headway against these Aliens with the help of Leila with the help of her godparents as she calls them. They are Aliens but I think that they're good Aliens. At least I hope so. The other Aliens, shall we call them the bad Aliens, they have instant transportation techniques that we aren't capable of or even near or perfecting. Our scientists aren't even close. We're years behind. Very realistically, two or three hundred years away from perfecting it, unless we're given help and make a breakthrough. I can't see it happening in my lifetime, perhaps in the baby's lifetime. Oh, I think that we should stop saying the baby and let her have the name she likes – which is Leila.'

'That's a lovely name,' replies JK. 'Where did that come from?'

'Leila selected the name herself. She said that she likes that name so that's what we're going to call her.'

'All right then, everything washed and cleaned and put in their right places?'

'Yes,' reply the two sons.

'Okay then. Let's go into the sitting room and see how Leila and her mother are getting on. Is our little grand-daughter okay?' asks dad.

'Fine,' replies Ciera. 'She's just gone back to sleep again.'

'Isn't it amazing how babies sleep most of their time? What a life! I suppose that's their nature. Well the boys and I have finished the washing up the dinner dishes and everything is back where it belongs. Mum, JK's staying the night.'

'Yes, of course. I'll go and see to that now.'

'Just for one night, mum, I'll be away in the morning. I can't miss tomorrow as I've a lot to do. We're very busy and I don't want to get behind with my work.'

'Ok. I'll make you some breakfast in the morning.'

'Thanks mum. Just a light meal if you don't mind.'

Now dad grabs the chance to relay to Ciera. 'We have had a discussion with the baby.'

Ciera enquires. 'What are you saying dad?'

Dad replies: 'Your Alien friends are coming tonight!'

'What do they want?' asks Ciera.

'Just to see the baby and make sure that everything is okay. I'm sure that we've nothing to worry about because Leila is quite happy and looking forward to meeting them again. Shall we watch some television? What about a nice movie shall we have a look at the television schedule? I'm sure that JK and John will watch. Anyway, there's nothing else on at the moment, only the usual rubbish.'

Leila wakes and starts to cry and wakes her mother. She takes her out of the crib starts to feeds her looks at the time and says. 'Goodness, is that the time?'

Dad replies: 'It's nearly half-past six. It's about supper time.' He wakes his wife and she enquires. 'Would you like me to set the supper table?'

'Yes, please, if you don't mind. That would be nice!'

'Is there anything we can do?' their two sons ask.

'You can lay the table and put out the cutlery. I'll cut the meat, do the greens and make the tea!'

Five minutes pass and dad lets everyone know that supper is ready.

Ciera leaves Leila in the sitting room and walks into the dining room. She sits next to John.

'Please help yourself to whatever is your preference!' Dad says.

'Anyone for a drink?' asks JK.

'I'll have a white wine,' replies Ciera.

'Dad, what would you like?'

'I'll have a red wine.'

'Mum, what would you like?'

'Well, I think I deserve a brandy.'

'Fine, then, I'll have a brandy as well,' says dad. 'I'll go and pour all the drinks. He walks to the drinks cabinet, takes out three wine glasses and two brandy glasses, dispenses the white and red wines and dispenses the brandy into the brandy glasses. He places them on a tray, turns round, and walks back to the table and states: 'Help yourself to your drinks,' and sits down.

Dad enquires if everyone has had enough food.

Everyone replies at the same time. 'Yes, we're all full! Thank you, mum and dad!'

Ciera replies: 'Yes, that was a fantastic supper. Oh dear, Leila is awake. I'd better go and feed her.'

'Ok boys. I think that you can again do the washing up.'

'Yes!' the two sons reply. They jump and take the dishes out to the kitchen.

Washing up finished and everything in its proper place, the three of them walk back into the dining room.

'I'm going into the sitting room to relax and have another drink. What about you two boys?' Dad asks

'I'll have another wine!' JK replies

'I'll have a wine as well, please!' says John

'Mum, what would you like?'

'I'll have another brandy if you don't mind. Thank you very much.'

'And you, Ciera? What would you like?'

'I'm fine. I've had enough drink and food to last me a lifetime, thank you very much!'

Dad walks to the drinks cabinet. 'He places them on a tray returns to the sitting room places them on the coffee table, tells everyone to help themselves to their respective drinks.

Everyone is just reminiscing about jobs, work, cars and houses and the nice holidays they had when they were young. Time is ticking on now.

'I'm a little tired now!' Mum says. 'I think I'll retire to bed. Good night to everyone!' She leaves the sitting room and walks up the stairs to her bedroom, goes inside and gets ready for bed.

Chapter 29

Down in the sitting room, all are anticipating the return of their Alien friends and Ciera decides to stay and wait.

Leila wakes up and sends a message to everyone in the room: *'Our visitors will be here very soon. Are we all ready to receive them?'*

'Yes,' answers everyone. 'We're ready to receive them!'

'Relax, everyone, no harm will come to you for these are nice people!'

A flash of light and two Aliens are in the sitting room and even though they are expected, everyone is very surprised because standing in front of them are a man and a woman. They are very good-looking, about six-foot tall, very slim with one-piece androgynous suits; white in colour and they say. 'Greetings to everyone please don't be afraid. We're not here to harm you. We're here to talk to you about your baby and the danger she might be in – at least until she grows up. We will now talk to you in your own language. Yes, we can communicate verbally, so there is no need to read your minds.'

'Please, sit down,' says dad.

'Thank you very much. My name is Óisin (pronounced O-she-in) this is Gia' as he points to her, 'my partner. We are from a World many light years from this planet. May I please have a word with the baby? Oh, she is telling me that her name is Leila. That's a very nice name, and that she has chosen the name herself. Well, we're here to make sure that everything is all right with Leila but I must first ask a very small favour. We need to transport Leila to our spacecraft for a few new updates on our science. Shall we say software – that's the easiest way we can explain it. We couldn't place all the information in Leila's brain in one go the last time we had her in the craft. So, if we ask all four of you and Leila to transport up to our craft – we're in orbit around your world, would you be in agreement? Incidentally we are cloaked, that is to keep prying eyes on this planet from seeing us

Leila sends a message to everyone including Óisin and Gia: *'Please, let them transport us to their craft. Everything will be fine. I can vouch for them, after all they are my godparents and I won't let anything happen to you.'*

'Ok,' replies dad. 'If that's what you want, then all of us agree.'

'Good!' replies Óisin. 'We will transport everyone from the house to the spacecraft in an instance.'

On arriving into the spacecraft, they feel a bit groggy.

Óisin smiles and says, 'Gia and I will need to place all of you through our cleansing anatomical and cytological technology equipment. Don't worry for it will not harm any one of you. We have to do this because you might bring harmful bacteria or bugs into the craft from which we could have problems. He waves his hand a door opens up in the wall inside the craft and he waves them to go inside a cabinet.

Ciera takes the baby. Dad and his two sons follow in behind them. The door closes behind them. They then hear a low buzzing noise and a blue light arrives at the top of the cabinet they are in and encapsulates them. Then it moves slowly down around everyone until it reaches the bottom of the cabinet and rises back up again.

The door opens and Óisin beckons everyone out and says. 'Everything is fine now. You are all cleaned and debugged. Apologies for any discomfort you may have had in the cabinet but it was very necessary in the circumstances. I'm sure that you will forgive me. Now, everyone please sit down!' He waves his hands and points to some very strange looking armchairs, which as if by magic, appear from nowhere. 'You can watch if you like.'

Everyone looks at each other and they decide to sit down.

Dad says. 'My goodness, these are very comfortable! They encompass the body! Oh yes, I do like these chairs!'

In the middle of the room is a strange future looking technological apparatus with lots of lights and scientific equipment, There are no legs to be seen holding it up and it could be assumed that it is floating on air nothing visible holding it up. It has a white glow about it and it is about twelve feet long, next to this strange looking apparatus stands a long console with lots of signs and little squares indented in the console with internal letters but what they mean is anybody's guess. There are no visible switches no buttons of any kind, no levers or anything that could be identifiable by humans. It looks very futuristic way beyond our technology. This whole room has no visible lighting but it has a lovely glow about it, no switches visible on the walls no lighting in the roof. There are no windows and no doors the whole room feels warm, comfortable and friendly.

Chapter 30

Dad says to JK. 'What do you think of all this scientific apparatus? It looks very futuristic. Is there anything familiar you see on the table or on that long thing at the side of the table?'

'I don't know, dad. It's all above me. I don't recognise anything. It's all very highly technically advanced. I would assume that it is run with very sophisticated software. This is all beyond anything I've ever seen in my life. I wouldn't know where to begin. I'm mesmerised. It looks so advanced and technical and I can't imagine where I might start.'

Óisin looks at JK, beckons him to the table and points to one of the squares on the console. He tells JK to place his index finger on it and the whole room lights up in a shape of Euclidean geometry – a complete circle.

JK recognises that he is looking down on the world. He inquires: 'Is that our Earth?'

'Yes, and your human race is hell-bent on destroying that beautiful world,' answers Óisin. 'Earth people are very violent, greedy, domineering and very stupid. You have been at war for thousands of years. Now if you were to blow up your Earth, it could have grave consequences for the whole Universe. You're a taxonomic unit of biological classification: a species heading for oblivion. We can't allow that to happen. That is why we are here. There is one problem; we as Aliens are not allowed to interfere in a physical way or how the Governments run you're Planet, but we are allowed to help, and that is why Leila is so important. We will give her the technology because she is of your Earth. There is no pain but there is a lot of gain, and if she decides that her family can help, that is perfectly agreeable with us. Would you please let me have Leila, Ciera, we are ready now to upgrade our technology into her brain and mind.'

Ciera looks bemused and she is a little frightened, but reassuring messages from Leila have placed her at ease. She hands Leila to Óisin.

He then beckons the rest of the family over to the table. 'Let me explain this procedure. I think the best way is if you think of BIO/DNA as a science except that ours is about six thousand years older than any technology you have on your Planet. The technology we use in this case is BIO/DNA technology. It's the science of the future and it will be used in computers. That is all the information I'm allowed to give you, because we would be in big trouble when we return to our own planet. This planet does not have that kind of technology yet, and it will take a long time to bring it to its optimum use. We know that some of the Earth governments are trying to make the technology more effective and the scientists of your world are working on that futuristic science, but I can tell you that they have a long way to go yet before it will work for your human race. The technology they have is too big and clumsy and it will take many years to refine it, and I am not going to tell you how to do that. You must realise that babies in the womb are not equipped with any kind of intelligence but do have instincts like feeding and crying. That is why we are able to instil our technology before the baby could have her mind and brain contaminated with other useless information. That way we can return to increase the learning capacity of her brain from time to time so that she will be able to have a fully functioning brain and intelligence to match. That is why we can't give grown-up people this intelligence because it would not function properly and there would be lots of problems and unanswerable questions which your scientists or doctors would not be able to diagnose. We could not do that to the human race. That is why we choose Leila over billions of other babies for this new infusion of our technology. We think that this is the right time to give this technology to the human race and we know that Leila will not abuse it. It will not solve all of your problems but it will certainly help to bring the human race to their senses.'

With that out of the way, he places Leila on the table, runs his hand over one of the squares with a light shining through, then the sides of the table rise up vertically over the top of Leila. He then runs his other hand over another square; there is a lot of lighting in the apparatus. An infusion of BIO/DNA technology is transferred into Leila's brain in waves, no pain or uncomfortable after effects. About twenty seconds later the cover opens up and descends back down to where it came from.

Óisin picks Leila up from the table and hands her back to her mother: 'She will be a lot better now. She is even more powerful than Gia or I. The reason we picked your child for this wonderful technology is she couldn't be intimidated or manipulated in the womb, until we have educated her our way. She is not quite ready yet but she is very close. JK, I know that you are very interested in technology, science and computers; you have something very interesting in your brain. All you have to do is find it and I am sure that it will be very useful to your species. I will give you something new to work on but it will have gates on the software so that when you reach each gate you will need to break the code and then move on to the next gate. It has twenty gates where you have to break the code but I am sure that you will excel in this very hard challenge and if you can figure this out you will receive another one. It is what we call refreshing the brain with complex software.

We have helped your species many times before but we have to be very careful the species we select. You will never be as powerful as your Leila, she is a one off. You are too old now. I don't mean this in a derogatory way and I hope I'm not offending you in any way. The technology that Leila has would be too powerful for your brain. It would damage you exponentially and we would not be so callus as to do that to you. We think that you will make a good candidate so that is why we will trust you. Humans only use about half the capacity their brain or mind we use all of our brain. That is why it will be quite a long time before the human race will travel the Universe. We have explored many planets and have done for many millennia. You or your family will never be able to travel in space because the technology your Planet needs on space travel has not been invented yet, I do not see any progress being made at the present. We are that is Gia and I are not authorized by our planet to give you any help with our technology, as that would be detrimental to this world. The technology you need will take some years to bring to fruition, so your scientists must up the stakes in your own technology. Your scientists will have to develop that jump in technology sometime in the future. We have seen some of your technology and we have analyzed some of the contents of what you call rockets and space stations; very primitive and dangerous but it is a start. The only information I can to give you is that you have to stop all these rockets going into the space above your planet and all the rubbish that goes with them. Turn to your Supercomputer software and develop your own technology but that will take time, that is the science that will be to your advantage.

Maybe when we come back the next time, I might ask for permission to take you and your family for a round trip to your Moon. Would you like that?'

'Yes,' replies JK. 'That would make my family very happy.'

'However, you are not allowed to tell anyone on your Earth, not even your friends. Shall we say that all the information we are giving you now is secret. You will be tempted to tell your friends but you must not go beyond the limits we have allowed you otherwise we might remove that information from your brain indefinitely. Do I make myself quite clear?'

'Yes,' replies JK and all the family nod their approval.

'Very good,' replies Óisin. 'I will take your word on that but be very diligent. We will keep an eye on you and see how you manage this amazing software, and as you figure out each part it will drive you on to finish it.'

For dad and John everything they have seen has gone right over their heads leaving them totally bemused by everything that they have witnessed.

'How big is this craft?' enquires dad.

'That is a good question and it requires a good answer,' replies Óisin. 'In your measurements this ship is about three hundred square meters. This is a small ship compared to some of our big ones. We do have smaller ships as well. We have some twice as big as this one.'

'Could you give us a tour around this ship?' enquires dad.

'I do not think so. We are bending the rules as it is,' replies Óisin. 'We have let you see too much now, so be very thankful for that. Maybe in the future we might concede to your requests.'

'How is this technology transferred to Leila?' JK asks.

Óisin looks at Gia smiles. 'The answer to that question, JK is you will never be able to grasp the significance of its technical and scientific logic. It is way beyond the capacity any of your own world scientists' intellectual ability. This technology is some thousand years old. Gia's great, great, great grandfather was the first to develop this amazing technology then passed it down to her great, great grandfather then down to her father and then down to Gia. It would take years to give you some idea of its basic workings and you would not live long enough to see it finished. It's a very complicated, far advanced technology for your mind. I hope I haven't offended you in any way, you asked the question and I have given you my answer!'

'I think I understand!' replies JK.

'As long as you are happy that is fine by me JK!' Óisin replies.

As for Ciera, she is in a different world all together. She has no idea what has happened. She is just standing there totally bemused and has not said a word.

John walks over to her and says, 'I know what you're thinking. I have the same feeling but everything will be fine!

Then a new message comes from Leila. *'We need the long-range sensors on. We have about thirty-five minutes before the visiting Aliens can try to scan us and they're not very friendly so we need to cloak our craft and place a shield around it as well. I'll do that.'* Leila tells Óisin not to worry as she had fixed everything. *'No talking from now on. Just mind-reading if you please.'* She communicates with Óisin: *'What would you like me to do?'*

'Can you take their leader from their flag ship and transfer him here?'

'Yes, of course I will and I can stop him from beaming back to his ship. That is no problem now.'

'What do they want?' asks Gia.

'They want to take me but they don't know that I'm scanning them now, and when they arrive they will not be able to find me on the planet. They are going to fall into a trap and I'm beginning to love this power but don't worry. I know all the technology in their space ships. I'll deal with them!'

'How many ships are coming?' enquires Óisin.

'*Six,*' *replies Leila.*

'Oh dear!' replies Óisin. 'I do not know if we are ready for them. Two ships we can deal with but six? I'm a bit worried about that. You're sure that you will be able to manage these six ships, Leila?'

'*Of course I'm sure. You just wait and see what's about to happen. They're within scanning distance now. Óisin, can we have the front screen on please?*'

Óisin places his right hand on one of the squares of the desk. The front screen on the craft is switched on. The view is amazing. The lucidity is something else and all the family shocked at what appears in front of them.

'*Óisin asks, 'Is our ship scanning their ship now?*'

'*Yes!*' *relates Leila*

'*Keep your eye on the screen. You should see them any second now. They're still a very long distance away but it won't be long before they arrive above the Earth and start scanning to locate me. However, I'm more than ready for them.*'

'Are you sure?' Óisin enquires. 'You get it wrong and we could be in very serious trouble!'

'*Don't fret. I know that they're not aware we're waiting for them. They're trying to scan now but there's nothing for them to find. Right, I'm going to move our craft away some two hundred miles from the Earth so that I can keep an eye on their movements.*'

'Are you sure that you are able to intermingle with the craft?'

'*Yes, of course I can. I can even intermingle with all the other Alien crafts at the same time if I so wish. This new intelligence is amazing. The BIO/DNA technology I have now is ahead all the advanced scientific knowledge on Earth but I'm not complaining. Oh, I do wish I could grow up more quickly, but I know that it might interfere with my growing up normally. I must allow myself to grow slowly as a child, and then I'll understand all the technical knowledge you have given me and use it for the benefit of the human beings on my planet. The secret documents held by all governments on Earth. I'll be able to scan them no matter where they hide them!*'

Chapter 31

'The Alien crafts are almost here! Óisin and Gia don't intermingle with our craft! I'll carry out all the necessary adjustments and I'll try to placate the Aliens; tell them to go and leave us alone and if not, I'll then decide what to do with them. Óisin and Gia, you're not to interfere at any stage of this encounter. I'll deal with the whole situation as it arises. Please don't try to override me. You now know that's impossible since the new infusion of Physics of Tera and Bio/Dna that I've received. However, if you think that I'm being too aggressive you're in your rights to ask me to stop, I'm honour bound to listen to you and review the whole situation to find another way to could suit you both. Are you happy with that explanation or have you other issues to discuss relating to our present situation?'

'No,' replies Óisin. 'I do not think that there might be a problem. I am hoping you know what is right or wrong but I will keep an eye on the situation. Gia what about you what are your thoughts on the situation we are about to have to deal with?'

'I'm quite happy at the moment. My worry is if the Aliens are able to over-ride you, then we might not be able to intervene. They might be too strong for us.'

'I've told you they're not able to over-ride me now,' replies Leila. 'I know every move that they might try. This is like a chess game except I know all the moves before they even played them, and whatever move they make I'll stop them. They'll not know what is happening because I'll just keep confusing them, and over-riding all technology on their crafts. They will not leave orbit without trying to locate me. I'll try to convince them to leave peacefully but if the worst comes to the worst then I'll need your cooperation and input. Granddad, dad, mum, JK, have you any thoughts on this subject?'

They all look at each other and just shrug their shoulders.

'Ok then I'll shoulder the responsibility of this situation with the help of Óisin and Gia. As you will observe the Alien spacecraft are just about to drop in orbit and they're discussing what to do between the crafts. They're looking for me on Earth but can't find me and they're very confused and don't know what to do. The leader is getting very upset and he's demanding that they find me soon or there will be serious trouble. I'm just about to transfer him here.'

There is a sudden flash of bright light, everyone shields their eyes and the Alien is standing in the craft with a shield placed around him. All communications from his craft are isolated from him. Now he is alone.

The panic has started because the crafts' intercommunications are trying to find their Commander but they are having some amazing discussions wondering where he has gone, what has happened to him, why can't they find him. What are they going to do without him? They are very worried what if he can't be located in the craft.

The second-in-command says. 'He must be somewhere. Find him and report back to me at once!'

In Óisin and Gia's craft, the Alien is about to be questioned by Leila.

'We would like to know your name and what you're doing here.'

'That is none of your business and anyway, I'm in communication with someone. Where am I?' asks the Alien in a highly excited fashion.

'You're in communication with me, the baby you've come to abduct and you're in my craft!'

'That's a lie!' the Commander retorts. 'If that is so, why can't we see you in orbit?'

'Maybe we're not in orbit. We could be anywhere on the moon or any of the other planets. We are not here to discuss where we are but to stop you from abducting the people on Earth and me. Why are you trying to abduct me? What's so special about me?'

'I don't know. I was given orders to find you and take you back to our planet and that's what I'm going to do!'

'How do you think you're going to accomplish that? Your second-in-command doesn't know where you are and he is now in a right panic and thinks that there's a conspiracy to kill you. Your whole abduction is now in jeopardy and he's not willing to return to his planet without you because his life will be forfeit and in his brain is telling him you're the one he blames. He's extremely worried about this situation, but that is not my concern. I need you to tell me your name and rank and what you might do when you can't abduct me to your planet?'

'I'm not going to tell you my name and you can't make me tell you. So what are you going to do about that?'

'If you do not tell me, I'll hurt you and make you tell me.'

'You're not strong enough to challenge me.'

'Look at your arms. What do you see?'

'They look fine to me.'

'Look again. Now what do you see?'

The Alien looks again and nearly faints. Both his arms are on the floor and one leg is where his arm was!

'Now would you like to convey to me your name?'

'No! I don't believe what you're doing to me. It's all an illusion. That does not frighten me!'

Leila now penetrates the Alien's mind and has a good look around. She now knows that he will not return to his planet without her but he is looking for a way to break the shield around him. He is not being very successful for he has never come up against this kind of shield before and is completely perplexed. *'Your name is Guber, and you are from the planet Xyren and now I'm your keeper and you can't do anything about it!'* She tries to defuse the situation but the Alien is having none of it. *'I'm fed up with you. I'm going to transfer you to one of the secret places on Earth where you will be not so welcome. You will not like their methods of interrogation which are not so endearing, especially when they know what you are and where you come from!'*

'You're bluffing. You can't transfer me to ground level because you don't have the power.'

'Yes I do. Commander Guber, I would like to know how many craft are in your flotilla.'

'I'm not telling you the exact number. Shall we say about one hundred spacecraft?'

'All I can see are six ships.'

Guber looks decidedly worried and thinks to himself. *She is very clever. What can I do?* 'Commander Guber, you're entering a very difficult phase of your life. You can make this easy on yourself if you leave orbit and return to your planet. I'm asking you very politely. If you don't comply I'll vaporise one of your ships.'*

'You're not powerful enough to do that!'

Leila wills the front screen on and says. *'Commander, take a look at the screen. Which ship would you like me to vaporise?'*

'It does not matter to me as I don't think you can.'

'In that case I would like you to watch.' There is an explosion and one of the ships is vaporised. *'Now, Commander, I don't want to do any more damage to your ships, but I need to know if you're going to insist on going against me and trying to abduct me from Earth. Please, may I have your answer now I'm waiting, be very careful how you answer because my patience is not going to hold forever. I'm not playing this silly game anymore with you. What is your advice on this situation, Óisin and Gia? You've listened to everything. I've tried to be pleasant but maybe I'll give him one more chance. Commander, what are you here for?'*

'I'm here for *you* and I will not leave without you.'

'Óisin and Gia, may I have your advice please. What can I do? Are you going to let him abduct me?'

'We are in agreement on this issue. If we were to agree to his demands, it could be difficult for us to return to our planet. This situation has to be resolved!'

'Very well then I'll do what's necessary. Commander, I've tried to be pleasant with you but to no avail. You don't seem to understand that we don't want you coming to Earth abducting humans with no sympathy or remorse for the families and friends left behind. You're a despicable race of beings and I for one will not tolerate it. I'm not able to accede to your demands. Consequently, you can say goodbye to your ships.'

One by one, they are vaporised.

Now all the six ships are gone and the Commander is very upset. He feels very alone and says. 'That message will have been sent back to my planet, telling them that you are too strong for us. My colleagues will have asked for assistance!'

'I don't think so. I've been monitoring all the frequencies on all of your ships I must tell you that there will be no assistance from your planet on your behalf. You will spend the rest of your life down there on Earth, put in total isolation and in hibernation so that you will not be able to communicate with any of your beings if they were to return to Earth, looking for you and your ships. The trouble with you is too much power and abusing it without thinking of the consequences but fortunately I'm able to remove your powers for now or until I decide when I need more information from you. I'm now going to test your recollection of what you're doing here. Please answer the question!'

'I don't know,' replies Guber.

'What is your title or name?'

The Alien looks perplexed. 'I don't know.'

'Which planet are you from?'

The Alien is having a terrible time with this question and replies: 'I think I should know but I can't bring it to mind right now.'

Óisin intervenes and asks. 'Have you any idea where you come from?'

'No, I don't know anything,' he replies and is looking rather distraught and is looking quite distressed and worried.

Leila has been monitoring Guber's response to all the questions and answers, she is very happy that she has removed all information from Guber's brain and mind and wipe it clean appertaining to his visit to Earth. 'Óisin, you are happy with the present situation?'

'Yes, I'm very happy.'

'What about you, Gia?'

'Well, I have to agree with Óisin. I'm completely flabbergasted with your power. It's awesome. We've being looking forward to this day for many long years. It has been of particular interest to me because my great, great, great, grandparents, my grandparents, and my parents, were all part of this technology and I followed on from them.

I then carried on their scientific investigation into Quantum computers, Supercomputers, Cryptology, Cryptography and Nanotechnology. They were the two scientists that started and I perfected this Bio/Dna science some two hundred years ago. You, Leila, are the first baby on the Earth to have had placed scientifically into her mind and brain this fantastic and futuristic innovation of science, which will greatly enhance your ability to persuade all governments of all countries to listen and take notice of what you need from them. It will be extremely difficult for them to understand. However, there will be dissenters. A statuary referendum of all Earth people will be cited, then made world law and be on the statute book. Voting will be compulsory for everyone. This whole voting system will be located on a world computer system and will have one member from each country to supervise all voting. Each country will make provisions for a change of their voting member every five years.'

Óisin enquires from Leila's family if they will be able to face up to this gargantuan task before them and elicits from granddad if he is willing to continue as first choice of his lifetime protection of Leila. 'There will be times when Leila will make her own choices especially when she is a teenager but you will be tempted to interfere. Don't worry, because she's technically years ahead of you and when she needs your help, she will give you that extra power when you need it. A couple of things that you'll need to know; that is you'll not be able to abuse this gift. The family will be rich and you are not to abuse that concession. It's not all about being rich it's about saving your Earth from destruction. We don't understand why humans are so aggressive and greedy to their fellow humans. It's not necessary and here is the message: we will not tolerate it. That is why we have chosen a baby to stop this slaughter among humans. When our ancestors first visited you planet over three thousand millennia ago it was very primitive even then humans were more tolerant but could be violent. Down the years, we have been watching the progress made but somehow it has lost the balance of camaraderie and friendship. Optimistically for the future of your planet, you have a new guiding figure from now in Leila. She has the power to go anywhere she needs and make the necessary changes in any government on your Earth and they'll find her a very hard bargaining person. She'll be able to read their minds and do amazing things that even we are not capable of doing because our brains are not able to digest what Leila's brain is able to process. Even computers will not be able to decipher her powers. She is now able to communicate with all computers on Earth. She is one of a kind for now. We might take another baby and give her or him the same knowledge sometime in the future, but we will need to be very careful because there might be a conflict of personalities between Leila and the new baby, and that might make things worse but that is in the future. We have finished our mission here, and all we have to say is goodbye for now, but we will see you in the future if Leila might need us we will be at hand for her. Our last words are to Leila. What are you going to do with Guber?'

'I'll consign him to a secure environment on Earth where I can keep in touch with him!' Leila replies.

Before you could blink an eye, the whole family are back in their own front sitting room, and Óisin and Gia are on their way to their home Planet (Pyseid) hoping they have done the right thing

It is five o'clock in the morning and Ciera says, 'I'm going to feed Leila.'

'I'm going to make tea,' Granddad replies.

JK and John are shattered. They say. 'We'll have tea as well please!'

JK says. 'What a night. I can't believe what we've seen and heard. It's out of this world!'

John looks bewildered and replies. 'That was some adventure! I still can't believe that we were in orbit around the Earth and the spacecraft; that was awesome! It was like something out of a science fiction movie. I just can't get my mind around it!'

'Ciera, what's your view on the situation,' asks JK.

'I don't know. I'm only Leila's mother. It's all above me. I'm afraid I'll wake up and think that it was all a dream!'

JK asks dad. 'What are your views?'

'Well, son, that's a very interesting question. This family is never again going to be the same. We now have great responsibility to this family and to mankind and with our help Leila will be able to make a positive contribution to Earth and its people, but how it's going to come about I don't know. Only Leila knows that, how she's going to evaluate and analyze all these permutations.

'Óisin says that she has infinite power to do anything she wants!' says JK.

'I'm not going to disagree with him. Of course I'm not, that would be silly. We'll just have to wait to see the outcome and how the future unfolds but I'm sure that there will be lots of danger ahead and attempts on all our lives. We'll have to face up to these dangers together whatever happens. We don't drop our sentinel duty to each other!'

The sitting room door opens and in walks mum. She looks around. 'What's going on here? Why is everyone up at this hour of the morning?'

'Well,' dad replies. JK and John have to go to work and the baby needed feeding so we all ended up in the sitting room having tea. Is that right, JK?'

'Yes, dad,' replies JK, just having a cup of tea.

'I'm fine,' replies Ciera. 'I'm not hungry now, perhaps later.'

Dad says, 'I'm not hungry at the moment. But I'll just have a cup of tea please.'

Chapter 32

The next four years pass rather quietly in the Carney household, nothing exciting just the everyday chores for Ciera and Leila, just keeping Leila occupied which is hard work when you think of what she could do. Leila is growing up rather quickly now and because of the influence of Óisin and Gia, her godparents, she has been very vigilant. Leila has now reached the age where she is required to go to school. Her mother knows that there will be problems, because the school is not privy to anything regarding Leila, and are they in for an awakening when she pretends to learn. Optimistically, she will conform to the philosophical ethics and moral principles of the human race but that could be a problem for Leila, as she is in a great hurry to grow up. Her future on this planet is as intended. Learning will not be a problem for her. With a bit of luck she will be careful how she manages her life. It will be very eventful and stressful for the family but there is no alternative – she will have to make big decisions whether she likes it or not. Ciera may not be able to explain to the school how Leila is so gifted, which leaves her in a state of perplexity, but what can she do? Of course, there is another big problem: Leila is able to talk in several languages. How does Ciera explain that to the teachers?'

'Leila, we need to talk.'

'I know, mother, I can read your mind.'

'You must not do that because it's very frustrating for me. I need to keep my thoughts to myself. Do you understand?'

'I'm sorry mum, I do understand, I'll try not to interfere with your inner thoughts again. I know that they are private but it's very difficult. Can we talk about school please, mum? I know that I'll have to go to school but I can be as dumb or as bright as you want me to be.'

'Listen, I want you to be someone we can look up to at all times. I think that we should invite the whole family into this discussion including your grandmother. We can't leave her out. She might think that we're keeping something from her. That might upset her and that wouldn't be fair. We all know about you, I think that your grandma should have some say and given consideration, in any discussion about your future, but when, that is the question. The school secretary has asked me to go to the school next week to discuss when they will induct you into the school curriculum and give me a start date. How do you feel about that, Leila?'

Leila decides to talk normally now as she looks at her mother 'I'm happy with whatever you decide to do. This schooling doesn't bother me in any way what so ever as you well know. I can adjust to the school curriculum with no problem at all.'

'I know that you will be tempted to show off. I know I would be. You'll have a very good life and I do know that nothing fazes you but I do worry. I'm your mother after all. It's only right that I should worry.'

'I know our lives will never be the same again because of my powers, but there's nothing we can do about it. I know my destiny is already half planned. I'll have to go through with it. I think it will be a very exciting and eventful time for all the family.'

'I'll talk to your dad tonight about the school and I'm sure that he'll agree to let you start your education. Not that you'll need it but it will be nice for you to meet other children and have some friends and maybe ask some of them to your house for tea.'

'I'm looking forward to school. I need to mingle with children my own age and learn about what they like without interfering in their lives. This is a completely new experience for me. I'm going to be out there learning about our world with all its problems.'

Ciera is very happy that her daughter is starting school in the new term, a little sad but very happy. She will miss her about the house but it is a requirement in law that all children have an education. The rest of the week is used up shopping for suitable clothes for Leila for school. Eventually they agree on the clothes and the school uniform and mum is ecstatic that Leila has finally settled on her school clothes. She is worn-out running from shop to shop and is happy to be going home.

Monday morning and Ciera is up very early to make sure that Leila is not late for her first day at school. She goes up the stairs, knocks on Leila's bedroom door.

'Yes, mum, just coming. Can I have a shower?'

'Yes of course you can but don't take too long. I'll place your school clothes on your bed while you're in the shower. She goes up and places the school uniform on the bed, goes back down the stairs 'Leila, your breakfast is nearly ready. Please hurry up. You don't want to be late for your first day at school.' Ten minutes pass she runs down the stairs. 'I'm ready for my breakfast mum.'

'Yes of course. I'll just take it from the oven.' She places it on the table in front of Leila. 'There you are my pretty one. You do look very nice in your school uniform. I hope you like it.'

'Yes, I do. It feels nice and comfortable and I like the colour!'

'Good. I'm pleased that you like it. Your lunch box is on the top of the fridge. I'll go and start the car and warm it up. It's a bit cold this morning.' She leaves the car running and goes back inside, has a quick cup of tea. 'She looks at Leila and asks. 'Are you ready to go?'

'I'm ready now. I'll just get my lunch.'

'Then let's go,' replies mum. Out the front door to the car, mum drives away to the school. Ciera is feeling a bit overwhelmed but she is not going to cry. She knows she has to be strong. Up until today she has had Leila to herself, she knows that she has to share her with all the other children at the school. The first day was always going to be difficult anyway. They arrive at the school.

Leila gets out and mum follows her to the school gates. She gives her mum a great big kiss on the side of her face and says. 'I love you, mum. Don't worry. I'll be home after school and I'll tell you what I've done at school.'

'Fine then, off you go. I'll see you later!'

Leila is a bit apprehensive but does not let on that she is a bit worried. Off she goes in the gate, turns round and waves to her mum.

She waves back, 'That is it' she says to herself.

Off she drives and she can hardly keep herself from having a little cry, but she knows that she must be strong. This is the way it is going to be from now on. She stops at the shops in the high street, does a little bit of shopping and is thinking, 'I hope that Leila is ok.'

The girl on the till asks. 'Are you all right?'

'Yes I'm fine now. I just dropped off my little girl to school. It's her first day and I'm just not myself. But I'll be fine!'

'I was the same when my little boy went to school for the first time. It was terrible. He was crying. I was crying as well. He didn't want to go but he went in the end. I was distraught. That was a bad day for me however, he loves going to school now and I'm sure that your little girl will be fine.'

Ciera gives her the cash for the groceries and says. 'That's fine! Thank you very much. I feel a lot better now.' She walks out to her car, gets in and drives out of the car park. She gets home, parks the car in the drive, goes inside and puts the kettle on, makes a cup of coffee and decides to go mad and have a good spring clean to keep her mind clear. But it is going to be a long day until she drives back to the school to pick up Leila.

Ciera keeps an eye on the clock because she needs to be at the school to pick Leila up when she comes out of school.

She waits patiently at the gate for Leila when she emerges. Ciera waves her hands to attract Leila's attention.

Leila sees her mum, runs to her and gives her a big hug. 'I liked school today!'

'Good. I hoped that would be the case,' Ciera replies. 'I was very worried for you.'

'I really enjoyed today, mum. Everyone is so friendly. I think I'm going to enjoy going to school.'

Chapter 33

Everything is going fine at school with Leila. Her mum is happy at just being a mum and having long conversations with Leila; what she is learning at school and the usual things that a mother and daughter would be interested in – fashion and science for Leila. Leila has been at school about six months now and boredom is beginning to set in. One of her school friends is a boy. Her friendship with him is beginning to wane. He is taking advantage of her because she is a girl and has started pulling her hair. She has asked him to stop pulling her hair but he has continued in spite of her request, so she is going to teach him a lesson in manners.

Playtime in the school playground and again he runs over behind her back and pulls her hair. She turns round and looks at him. He runs away. She then runs after him. He stops and she already knows that he is petrified of lions, so she gives him an illusion of a lion running after him and he falls over hits the ground with his hands over his head, shouting: 'Please don't feed me to the lion!'

Leila catches up with him and is standing over him. She puts out her hand to help him up when one of the teachers says, 'I'll pick him up.'

Leila steps back and smiles at him but he has lost it. He starts to fight with the teacher and becomes very aggressive towards her, Then another teacher runs over and between them they try to lift him up and he shouts out: 'There's a lion in the playground and he tried to kill me!'

The teachers look at each other shrug their shoulders then lift him up but he is still struggling with the teachers. Eventually they take him back into the school to the headmaster's study and sit him down. He is now a lot quieter.

His teacher asks him. 'What is this all about?'

The boy looks mystified and says that a lion was running after him and he ran away and fell over and he thought that the lion was going to eat him

Now the teachers are worried, so they phone the boy's mother to come to the school as they would like to talk to her about her son.

Ten minutes later the young man's mother arrives at the school, one of the teachers quickly escorts her to the headmaster's study and her son runs over to her and says, 'Mum, a lion ran after me in the playground and he was going to eat me!'

She looks at him and then glances at the teachers and they shrug their shoulders.

One of the teachers takes the mother to one side and asks. 'Does your boy have funny dreams at night time?'

'Not to my knowledge. What was he doing when all this happened?' enquires the mother.

'Well, as far as we know he was playing with a little girl in the playground.'

'Can I please have a word with her? Maybe she might know what happened.'

'Yes of course you can. I'll send one of the children to fetch her.' The teacher goes out of the headmaster's study and finds one of the children in the hallway. 'Go and find Leila and ask her to come to the headmaster's studio as soon as she can.'

The boy runs out into the playground and looks around. He sees Leila and calls her over to him, tells her to go the headmaster's study now because the teachers are waiting for her.

'What do they want from me?' asks Leila looking totally bemused. She knows why the teachers want to talk about but she is going to keep it a secret. 'Fine,' she replies and trots off to see the teachers.

As she walks up the hallway one of the teachers is standing by the headmaster's door and asks Leila. 'Do you know anything about your friend? He says that he saw a lion in the playground and he ran away because he thought that it was going to eat him. Did he say anything to you Leila?'

'No. The only thing I can tell you is he's always pulling my hair and he ran up behind me again, pulled my hair and then ran away. I ran after him to tell him off but he fell over and I went to pick him up. That was when you came and told me to leave him and you picked him up.'

'All right, can you please come with me?' asks the teacher.' She then opens the headmaster's door and ushers Leila inside.

The other teacher calls Leila over and says. 'Don't worry. We're not going to reprimand you. We would like to ask you – did you see a lion in the playground?'

Leila replies of course not. 'What would a lion be doing in our playground? Everyone would see it and we all would run away!'

'Fine, Leila. You can go back to the playground and play.'

'Thank you,' replies Leila and opens the door and walks out into the hallway and proceeds out to the playground and has a little laugh, knowing full well what the boy thought he had seen.

The teacher calls the mother, tells her that maybe she should take her son to see a doctor just in case there might be something going on in his head. 'I'm not saying that there is zilch wrong with him, but to be safe it might be a good idea. You can take him home now if you like. He can have the rest of the day off. He can come back to school in the morning. I'll tell the head-master what's happened.'

'Fine,' replies the boy's mother she beckons her son over and says; 'We're going home for the rest of the day and if you're all right in the morning you can return to school.'

Chapter 34

Leila is very happy now and is hoping that the boy has learned his lesson because she does not want to frighten him again. The teachers might realise that something is going on. She needs to be on her guard now but she is not too worried. On her way home from school as she is sitting in the car she tells her mother what happened and the mother looks at her and says, 'Leila, You must be a bit more careful in the future. You know that you must keep your secrets to yourself!'

'I know, mum, but the illusion I created in the boy's mind was only in his mind. He thought that a lion was going to attack him but he was the only one in the playground to see it so there's no problem, just a very confused boy and I think that he'll not be so quick to pull my hair again!'

'Fine, if that's all that happened and none of the teachers know the full story then I think that might be okay but you must be a bit more careful in future. We don't want any idle blether at the school because the authorities might hear about it and that could invite problems of all kinds. Now we don't want that, do we, Leila?'

'No, mum,' she replies. I quite agree. I'll try and be a little more careful in the future!'

'You must phone your granddad when you get home.'

'Why must I phone granddad? I can talk to him anytime I like'

'Yes, but you must not get into a position where you're too lazy to use your vocal cords to communicate with people, especially your own family'

'I know, mum. Sometimes I don't think. I just automatically use my telepathic powers because it's easier for me because I can do other things at the same time. I suppose you could call it multi-tasking.' On arriving home, Leila runs into the house picks up the phone in the hallway and dials granddad's number, waits a minute and her grandmother picks it up at the other end and enquires: 'Yes, can I help you?'

'Gran, its Leila, how are you? I've just come in from school and I thought I'd phone and ask if you're all right?'

'Well that's a very nice gesture on your part and how are you doing at school?

'I like it very much and I'm behaving myself!

Can I talk to granddad please?'

'Of course you can, my dear just a minute and I'll call him.' She calls out to granddad. 'Leila is on the phone for you. He's just coming, dear. Goodbye for now, Leila. Hope to see you soon.'

'Hello Leila! Is there something wrong? I'd have thought you would've communicated with me telepathically?'

'No. Mum said that I must communicate by telephone and have verbal talking with people in future.'

'Well I think that would be a very good idea because you'll need your vocal cords in the future so you must exercise them as much as possible.'

'Well I do. I talk a lot at school and in the playground, but if that's what's needed then I shall do that!

'Good for you. I know that you'll do the right thing. Now, how are you getting on at school?'

'Well I used my powers at school today!

'What did you do?'

'Well, one of the boys at school is always pulling my hair and I don't like it so I made him see a lion running at him and he nearly had a fit. I was summoned to the headmaster's office to explain myself. He asked me if I had seen a lion and I said no. He seemed to be happy with that explanation. It was all an illusion and nobody else saw the lion only the boy but I didn't tell the teacher that or the headmaster. Are you cross with me granddad?'

'No of course I'm not. I know that whatever you do will be very discreet. Now when are you coming for dinner?'

I'll ask mum. Just wait a minute I'll go and find her.'

Ciera arrives at the phone and says. 'Hello granddad, how are you keeping?'

'I'm fine, Ciera. Leila was just telling me about the little episode at school today. Did she tell you about it?'

'Yes she did and I had a word with her, but it would appear that it's just between her and the boy. I don't think that there was any damage in any way. It appears nobody else saw this lion illusion. Now about dinner, I'll ask John when he comes home tonight and ask him to give you a ring and confirm a date. Is that all right with you and grandma?'

'Yes of course. I look forward to hearing from him later.'

John arrives home about six o'clock that evening.

Ciera sits him down on the settee and informs him that there was an altercation at school with a boy and Leila created an illusion of a lion to frighten the boy because he would not stop pulling her hair. 'To be fair to her she did ask him nicely to stop pulling her hair but he declined and carried on assaulting her so she created an illusion of a lion, which gave him a big fright. Then Leila had to go to the headmaster's studio and explain herself to the headmaster and her teacher but there was nothing to clarify the boy was the only person to see it. She did very well considering the provocation and strain she had to encounter.'

John looks around sees Leila is standing in the doorway and he says. 'Come and sit down Leila. I'm not going to tell you off, but I'm a little bit worried. I'm not condoning what this boy has done to you and I'm sure that you made sure that the illusion was purely to teach him a lesson and I agree with you, but you must make sure that whatever action you might take in the future has to be, shall we say, of an invisible nature. That way we can keep you cocooned in secret until you decide it's time to let you do what you've been singled out to do and present yourself to the world. As long as we know that you'll be very discreet from now on, your mum and I are quite happy. We will explain to JK and granddad with any luck we all will be in accord about Leila. Now let's have dinner. I'm rather hungry, so mum, if you're ready you can place the dinner on the table.'

'Do you think that the time is right to bring grandmother into our confidence, Leila?'

'Yes I do. We can't carry on keeping her in the dark. It's not fair and it would be best to tell her sooner rather than later.'

'John, we're going to your dad's for dinner on Sunday. That is, if you don't mind.'

'That's fine with me. Maybe we can put our cards on the table and ask dad to convey all we know about Leila to grandma with everyone present including JK. She might need time to absorb all we tell her. She might think that we're trying to fool her. I think it might be a good idea if we could make it a question and answer session and hopefully she'll be able to grasp the whole situation.'

Dinner finished, Leila goes about her school homework, which is very easy for her. Dad helps mum with the washing up.

Ciera looks at John. 'Would you phone your dad, and let him know that we would love to come to dinner on Sunday?'

'Yes I'll do that as soon as we've finished the washing up. Is that all right with you?'

'Yes of course it is. I'll make the tea and take it to the sitting room then you go and phone your dad and make sure he knows what we talked about with Leila, and about letting your mum know the whole situation about the Aliens and what's going on.'

John takes his mobile from his pocket dials his dad's number and waits.

His dad picks up his phone.

'Dad, it's John, you're on your own at the moment?'

'Yes, I am why?'

John asks. 'Where is mum?'

'She's in the kitchen. Why?'

'Well, I don't want her too close to you at the moment. I need to tell you something.'

'Ok. What do you want to tell me?' enquires dad.

'Well, we think that mum should be told about the Aliens and Leila.'

'Why?' replies dad.

'It's Leila's and Ciera's request. They think that it's not fair on mum, when we all know what's going on, and as we're coming to dinner on Sunday it might be a good time to take her onboard and explain everything to her about the Aliens. What do you think, dad?'

'I don't know, son. It might have a detrimental effect. If you think it needs to be talked about, I'm fine about that. Who's going to tell her?'

'Perhaps we could let Leila do the talking. She might be the right person to deal with this exceptional situation. It's not every day that a family has a talk about Aliens being friends with the family,' replies John.

'I don't know. It's a big responsibility for a child, son.'

'I don't think that it's a problem. After all, she's more educated than all of us together.'

'Fine, my son, maybe I'm a bit uneasy about a child giving a lecture on Alien technology. It might actually be just the right thing to do. Leila can sit down next to her and explain everything and I'm sure that she'll listen to Leila. She'll listen to Leila but she might not be able to take it all in one go. I'm sure that in time she'll understand what's going on. Your mum is no fool son. She's very bright and had a good education so I'm happy to give it a go.'

'Good. I'll get in touch with JK and arrange for him to be available for dinner on Sunday,' replies John.

'Ok son. See you and the family on Sunday. I'll tell your mum to expect the whole family for dinner on Sunday and JK as well.'

John phones JK and asks if he would be available to come to dinner on Sunday because they might have a little problem.'

'What problem?' JK inquires.

'Well, we're having the whole family over to dads for dinner on Sunday and we hope that you can be available as well because Leila would like to inform our mum about our Alien friends so it might be nice to have all the family there to support her.'

'Do you think that's a good idea, John?' enquires JK.

'That's not for me to say. If Leila says that she can handle the situation I'm fine with that.'

'Ok. Then in that case I'll go along with that,' replies JK.

'Good, we agree then and you'll come to dinner on Sunday. I'll arrange everything with mum and dad.'

'Yes, yes. I'll be there don't worry. This will be some get together. I can't wait to see how mum's going to respond. It should be amazing. She'll be astonished at what she hears. I can't wait to see her face, but I do hope that she doesn't have an adverse feeling about this, and as Leila is going to inform her about everything I don't see a problem as long as everybody is present when this education takes place.'

'That's fine then. We'll see you on Sunday about one o'clock. Goodbye,' replies John and shuts his phone down.

Leila has gone to bed and now is the time for John to question Ciera about the confrontation at the school today.

'Now my dear Ciera, can you bring me up to date about today?'

'Well to be honest, I've told you everything, nothing really happened. Leila made sure that this event was only seen by the boy so as far as I'm concerned it's over and done with.'

'Good. We'll not discuss this particular episode again.'

'Okay then. I'm going to bed. I've a lot to do tomorrow so the rest tonight will do me good. What about you?'

'I'll come to bed soon. I'm just going to clean up and do a bit of washing before I come to bed.'

'Goodnight dear,' replies John as he walks out of the sitting room. He walks up the stairs and has a look in Leila's bedroom to make sure that she is all right. *Dad goodnight* is the message Leila sends him telepathically which amuses him greatly and he smiles very gently while running over in his mind what wonders he is going to see in the future, puts on his pyjamas, goes into the bathroom, cleans his teeth goes into his bed and falls asleep very quickly.

Next morning, up nice and early he has a quick shower, gets dressed, goes down the stairs into the kitchen, has a quick cup of coffee, gives his wife a quick kiss on the cheeks, goes out the front door into his car and drives to work.

Chapter 35

Sunday morning. Leila is up very early and is quite excited about going to granddad's for dinner. She is running up and down the stairs and disturbs her mum and dad who are not too happy, especially at this hour of the morning.

Dad shouts out to Leila, 'what are you doing running up and down the stairs, Leila?'

'I'm sorry dad but I'm very excited today because we're going to dinner at granddads and I'm looking forward to seeing them as we haven't seen them for awhile. It's going to be very exciting. I can't wait to see granny's face when I talk to her about our little adventure with the Aliens!'

'Good. Find something a little quieter to do please and stop running up and down the stairs.'

'Sorry. I didn't mean to wake you up. I'm sorry, dad. Then I'll go downstairs and find something quiet to get involved with.'

An hour passes and her mum walks down the stairs and into the sitting room where she finds Leila *levitating about two foot above the floor and singing to herself some new song she picked up on the television.'*

Mum looks at her and says. 'Leila! Please put your feet on the floor. I know that you're able to do anything that you want but what would happen if someone were to see you through the window? We could be in trouble with the police. They would not understand and you're not quite ready to make your entrance to the world yet so you must be very careful with your special gifts. Have you decided how you're going to explain to granny about your gifts?'

'I think that I'll just wing it and see what happens. There's no easy way of doing this, unless you can think of something.'

'Well then, you'll have to wing it and see how it pans out. I'm sure that you'll find the right way of making her understand. It'll be difficult but I'm sure you'll find a way and with a little bit of luck she'll understand. The whole family will be in the sitting room to keep an eye on her and when she asks questions about what she's looking at we'll try to explain the situation what's going to happen in the future. You've a very exciting time ahead of you young lady so don't try to make it happen too soon. It will have long term problems for the whole family but I'm sure that we'll come through it together.'

Ciera goes to the bottom of the stairs and shouts: 'John I'm going to make your breakfast. How long will you be?'

'I'm just going into the shower. I'll be about ten minutes. Then I'll get dressed and come down.'

'That's fine. We'll see you in about ten minutes.'

Ten minutes pass.

Ciera hears John coming down the stairs, goes and retrieves his breakfast from under the grill and places it on the table.

He sits down; his wife pours him a cup of coffee he says. 'Good morning to everyone.'

Ciera and Leila reply. 'Good morning dad!'

Ciera says that she is going to pack the car and asks Leila to help her.

'Yes, I'll help,' replies Leila. 'What would you like me to do mum?'

'If you can bring out some of the small items please that will be fine,' replies mum.

Half an hour later, the car is packed and ready. All they require now is dad to drive, so mum tells Leila to go tell her dad everything is ready in the boot of the car and that all they need now is the driver.

Leila goes to her dad. 'We're ready to go to granddads.' As she runs into the hallway and shouts: 'Dad! Mum's waiting to go! Come on please.'

'I'm on my way!' He walks down the hallway to the front door, pulls the door and closes it, making sure that it is secure and walks to the car, sits in the driver's side and says. 'Right then, off we go to granddads!'

Chapter 36

It takes about an hour to reach granddad's house and Leila is out of the car like a bat out of hell, in the front door and runs up to granny and gives her a great big hug.

'Well that was a very big hug, Leila! What's all that about?'

'I've not seen you for a long time so I thought I'd give you a nice big hug!'

'Well now, let me see you. You look very well. You're growing up very quick. You're getting very tall. You're quite a young lady.'

'Where's my granddad?'

'He's down the garden. You go and find him while I have a talk to your mum and dad. Well, my son, how are things at work?

'Everything is okay at work, and at home mum,' John and Ciera both look at each other and answer together, expressing to her that everything is fine and that Leila is doing very well at school. John is wondering if he should tell her about the little incident at the school, but he decides against it.

Leila is running down the garden path, sees her granddad, jumps up and gives him a big hug and a kiss.

He is very surprised and says, 'You didn't communicate with me telepathically.'

'I don't need to anymore because I can keep it under control now and use it only when I need to communicate if an emergency crops up. On the outside, I look as normal as anyone but my brain and mind are learning all the time. What are you doing in the garden now?'

'Well I'm going to dig up some potatoes and greens for dinner, why?'

'Just watch,' replies Leila. 'Have your container ready. I want to show you something.' She looks at granddad and the potatoes rise up out of the ground and into granddad's container and that does surprise him. She asks, 'How many potatoes will be needed for dinner.

'About twenty-four will do thank you.'

'Please count them? Leila replies.

Granddad counts the potatoes in the container and sure twenty-four of them are in the container. He is not surprised because he knows that Leila's powers are getting stronger all the time and he is relishing the time when she announces to the world that there are going to be masses of changes.

'What greens would you like in the container?' Leila asks.

'Some carrots and parsnips will do nicely.'

Up come some carrots and parsnips. They drop into the container.

'I wish I could do that,' remarks granddad.

'But you can. Just think about it,' replies Leila. 'Why don't you pick a cabbage? Go on try.'

He looks at a cabbage. It elevates out of the ground shakes all the earth off and falls into his container. 'Leila, you made that happen didn't you?'

'No I did not! You did that yourself.'

'Anyway, let's take all these vegetables to your granny. Can I ask how you are performing at school? I hope you're doing well?'

'Why yes of course I'm doing well. No problems at all.'

They walk up the garden path together and into the kitchen and granddad places the container on the side of the water taps for washing and cleaning. He goes into the sitting room and tells his wife that the fresh vegetables are in the kitchen for dinner.

'Thank you,' his wife replies as she rises up from the sofa and goes to the kitchen.

'Well now, what shall we do?' asks Ciera

Leila asks. 'Why don't we go to the playground?'

Good idea, 'I'll come with you as well, granddad replies. 'We can walk there. It's just around the corner.' He looks into the kitchen and enquires from his wife when dinner is likely to be ready.

'Why?' asks his wife.

'Because, Leila wants to go to the playground with her mum and dad and I'm going with them as well. We will leave you in piece for a while.'

'Give me an hour or so, please.'

'Fine,' granddad replies. 'We'll carry on and be back in an hour. Come on let's go everyone, put your coats on please as it's a bit cold outside!'

Chapter 37

They walk out the front door, up the road and into the playground. The first thing Leila wants to try are the swings but they are all taken by older boys so she goes to the slides and they follow her, and hassle her, so she goes back to the swings. Granddad is looking on and knows that there is going to be trouble he communicates telepathically with Leila, asking, *will you be all right?*

She answers back: *'Don't worry granddad, I'll take care of these boys. You stay out of it. Just leave it to me.'*

'Ok! You do what you have to do, but make sure you are very careful. I'll just watch.'

Leila sits on one of the swings and they follow her back to the swings.

Ciera asks granddad: 'I think those boys are giving Leila a hard time.'

'Don't you worry one little bit, Just watch!' 'She's well able to look after herself!' 'Now you just watch what happens. That goes for you too John!'

'No worries,' John replies. This could be fun!'

Behind the swings, about ten metres, is a muddy stream and Leila has clocked it in her mind.

The tallest one orders Leila off the swing and she tells the boy that there are three other swings so why do they not try them.

He says, 'There are four of us so we need the four swings!'

Leila jumps off and stands by the swings, watching the four boys having a wonderful time swinging very dangerously high. Leila decides to experiment with her powers. She is not sure what to do about those boys. She needs to be very careful not to hurt anyone of the boys or doing anything physical that might attract the attention of the public. Now she is beginning to understand her amazing powers. Leila looks at the boys then decides to dump them in the muddy water. All four of them go over the top of the swings and land in the messy muddy water. She then rolls them about in the water, making sure that they are well covered in mud and they are wet through and through, she walks back to her mum dad and granddad, but keeping an eye on the boys in the mud rolling about. It looks like they are having a very good time. However this playful time the boys are having is about to end.

They are falling over one another and are beginning to fight amongst themselves. She keeps them in the mud a little longer. She looks at her granddad and smiles at him. He doesn't say a word just wonders what she is going to do next. She levitates them up splashes them down again and again, making sure that they are absolutely covered in lots of mud and of course all the people and the children in the playground are laughing their heads off and pointing their fingers at them.

She decides to play with them a bit longer. Every time they are just about to climb out of the muddy water, she makes them fall back in again. Now there is quite a crowd of people gathered round and all are having a wonderful time laughing, when out of the crowd walks one of the boy's mothers. She puts her hand out to her son – at least she thinks it is her son. He reaches up and takes her hand. Regrettably he slips pulls her into the muddy water, which is now a pond. Now the people in the park are taking photographs. It is like the keystone cops. The mother is trying to get out and the boys are pulling her back in!

Leila has had enough, so she takes them out one by one then she makes them go down on their chests there she pushes them along on the grass trying to clean themselves just like dogs. Then she makes them turn over on their backs and start rolling about. Oh, what a sight and everyone thinks that this is just a stunt

Now a television crew has arrived. Someone must have phoned and told them what was going on. The mother plus her son and the three other boys proceeded to roll around in the sand, now their clothes and the four of them are covered in grass and mud from head to toe. There are a few dogs playing with them and rolling about with the boys and the mother in the sand as well.

Ciera, John, and granddad cannot stop laughing.

By now there must be about fifty or sixty people about, all watching the antics. Little do they realise that Leila is the key to this madness and the television people are making sure that they are getting all this for the evening news. Even the television crew cannot stop laughing.

Leila stops and lets them stand up. The television crew go over to them and ask what is going on. The mouthy one throws a punch at the television man. However, a community police officer is watching all this going on so he phones the station asks for assistance and a van, gives the address and goes into the playground. He tries to find a way in between the boy and the television man but keeping at arm's length, so that he does not fall in the mud, and asks. 'What's going on here?'

The television man replies, I had a phone call saying that there was something going on in the playground and as he had nothing else to do he decided to cover it. 'Then this boy started to punch me, 'So I defended myself. I didn't strike or hit him!'

The police van and a response car have arrived with four police constables. They run inside and break up the fracas and without warning, place all the boys and the mother in the van. The police take statements from some of the people asking, 'Can you tell me what is this all about.' One of the police officers looks over at John and Ciera, sees that they are still laughing and decides to have a word with them.

He walks over to them and enquires: 'What's so funny?'

'Oh, nothing officer!' replies John.

'What's your name?' enquires the police officer

Then Leila says. 'I can show you what happened, sir.'

'Can you?' enquires the policeman with a mile. Will you show me what this is all about?'

Leila catches him by the hand leads him over to the mud pond, saying, the boys fell into the mud and were fooling around and everyone was laughing at them. 'If you go a bit closer, you'll see what I mean.'

She turns around and starts to walk back to her mum. The police man jumps into the muddy pond he does not know why, starts rolling about for no reason, so Leila decides to make him levitate and dumps him back in the mud again. As she arrives back at her mum's side, she says. 'That'll teach him a lesson in manners. He won't be so cocky in future.' Then the other police officers run across to help him to get out of the mud pond, so she decides to dump them in as well.

The television people are having a marvellous time, plenty of good professional visual news for that evening. Leila is very pleased with herself. She hasn't hurt anyone just their dignity. She is beginning to understand the powers she has acquired from Óisin and Gia

'Come on, mum, dad and granddad, let's go home to dinner. I've had my fun.'

Her granddad looks at her saying, 'Leila, you are a little devil but we enjoyed the circus.'

'Well that's the first time I've tried my power. Just a very tiny bit I don't think that they knew what was going on and anyway who's going to believe them? They'll look right twits when they return to their police station with mud caked on their uniforms. I can't wait for the news tonight. It's going to be hilarious,' says Leila.

Dad is still laughing and says. 'That's the funniest thing I've ever seen. It was amazing to watch!' Leila is very pleased with herself. She has refrained from hurting anyone and she is learning to control her powers.

The four of them walk out of the playground and up the road.

Leila looks back at the police officers and nods her head. They climb out of the mud, up onto the grass, drop down on their knees and act like dogs pushing along on their chests and into the sand pit. They too are now in a terrible mess in wet mud and sand, so she decides to let them stand up. They are completely bewildered at what they have been doing and do not understand what has happened.

One of the police officers looks at himself and says. 'We'll be reprimanded. This is going to be hard to explain to the inspector!'

Dad is still laughing and says. 'I can't stop. What a day! It's been marvellous!' He opens the front door and everyone goes inside the house.

Granddad asks, 'who would like a drink as he goes into the sitting room where JK is sitting on the sofa. 'Well, look who's here. JK, you missed the funniest thing of your life.'

'What did I miss?' enquires JK.

'You wait until the news tonight and you'll see. Right, who's for a drink? I need one anyway.'

'I'll have a red wine, please,' replies JK.

'I'll have a white wine,' replies Ciera.

'What about you, John?'

'I'll have a white wine as well,' replies John.

Dad goes into the kitchen and asks his wife what she would like.

'May I have a brandy please? The dinner is ready. Can you place the condiments and the knives and forks on the table please?'

'Yes of course I will.' He goes back into the sitting room and pours the drinks for everyone and passes them round, gets a brandy for his wife and a brandy for himself. He then goes back into the kitchen, leaves his wife's brandy on the side 'Right, everyone, can you please take your places; the dinner will be served shortly.'

The rest of the family retreat to the dining room take their places and sit down.

Mother brings all the food out of the kitchen places it on the table and says. 'Please help yourselves.' She goes back into the kitchen picks up her brandy returns to the dining room and takes her place at the table.

'Right, I'll cut the meat,' says granddad. 'You just help yourselves to whatever you want. Ciera, would you like to give Leila her dinner please?'

John is still laughing so he says. 'Please excuse me I'll be okay in a minute.'

JK looks at him and says. 'Are you all right?'

'I'm fine,' he replies. 'Just thinking about what happened today.'

'Well it must have been very funny,' replies JK.

'Please can we get on with our dinner?' enquires mother.

'Yes of course,' replies granddad. 'John, please, you must concentrate on eating your dinner!'

Dinner over, the three men remove all the plates, knives, forks, condiments, and dishes from the table out to the kitchen and place them in the dishwashing machine.

In the sitting room, everyone is in a jovial mood and granddad is making sure everyone has a drink.

'How's the schooling going, Leila?' JK enquires.

'I'm having a great time, lots of friends. Learning lots of unwanted information but I'm not going to complain. I don't want the teachers to know what I'm capable of so I just carry on learning.'

'That's good.' Replies JK. 'Have you done anything unusual lately?'

Leila looks at her mum and she nods as much as to say it is all right. She looks at JK and says. 'I made one of boys at my school see a lion and he nearly had a fit but no one else saw it, not even the teachers. I was very discreet.'

'Well I suppose it was bound to happen. All that power is no good unless you can use it. As long as it's used properly,' replies JK.

Granny enters the sitting room and sits down but she is unaware the family have been talking about Leila's powers. Leila goes and sits by her side. Leila has decided to tell granny a very interesting fact about what she is capable of doing. Leila takes granny's hand and says. 'I'm going to tell you something fantastic but I don't want you to worry. It's nothing bad so if you are ready, I will begin.' Leila gets off the sofa and lies flat on her back on the floor.

Granny is watching her very intently wondering what she is going to do.

Leila is levitating about three foot above the sitting room floor.

Granny jumps up in total amazement, looks around and asks. 'What is going on here?'

Nobody says a word, in a flash Leila has disappeared. Now granny is very confused. She sits back down on the sofa.

Ciera says to granny. 'Look behind you please, granny.'

Granny looks behind. Leila is standing behind the sofa!

'Well I don't know. That's quite a trick, Leila!' says granny.

'No, it's not a trick. I'm able to do anything I put my mind to. Look outside on the veranda. Who do you see?'

'Well I can see JK and John. How did they get out there because they were in here a second ago?'

'That's what I'm trying to tell you! I have very special powers given to me by Aliens, granny. Where are John and JK now?'

'I don't know,' replies granny. 'I don't see them in the veranda now.'

'Look behind you. Can you see them now?'

'Yes I can. That's amazing! How do you do that, Leila?'

'I've told you I have powers you can only imagine in your wildest dreams. I know that I have to go to school and behave in an orderly fashion and learn all about this World, this Earth, this Planet. Today, I've only used an infinitesimal part of my brain or my mind, if you like. I'm of this Earth and I'm human. I'm your granddaughter. Nothing can or will ever change that. Give me your hand please.' Leila takes granny's hand and places it on her chest. 'Now, I don't want you to worry about what I'm going to do.' Leila takes a step forward and granny's hand goes straight through Leila's chest. 'Now withdraw your hand please.'

Granny pulls her hand out of Leila's chest. As she withdraws her hand she looks at Leila and is decidedly worried.

'Now place your two hands on my shoulders.' This time Leila levitates granny and herself one metre off the ground. About a minute goes by she drops down slowly to the floor again.

'I can't believe what I've just done. Please; someone tell me that this was all an illusion, a dream. John, JK, Ciera, Dad, I'm seeing things?'

No,' granddad replies. 'It's all true. We couldn't tell you before because it might have frightened you we decided that all of us should be present when Leila would explain to you her wonderful technology she has in her brain. We're not allowed to use that technology except when necessary.'

'Are you telling me that you have that technology in your brain as well?'

'Yes, but Leila holds the key to that technology. We'll never be as powerful as Leila but she'll need us from time to time and we'll be there to help her.'

Leila places her hand on granny's arm and a surge of wisdom flows up her arm and into her brain. 'Now you know what I've told you. It is in fact true because you can do things other people can only dream of doing. I want you to look at the television and think of switching it on. Go on, look at the television.'

Granny looks at it and it turns itself on as if by magic. 'No, I don't believe it! That's just impossible!'

'Okay, then look at the remote control. Lift it up!' She looks and it levitates about six inches above the coffee table!

'This is too much for me. I can't take all this in.'

'Ok. You just take your time over the next few days and I'm sure that you'll be able to grasp what I've been telling you, is absolutely and honestly true,' replies Leila.

Dad looks at his watch and says. 'It's time for the news. Go on mother, turn on the television.'

Mother looks around, smiles and looks at the television and it switches itself on.

'Right, JK, you just watch this and if you don't laugh I'll buy you a pint sometime. Right, here it comes now.'

The person reading the news starts to laugh and says. 'Don't switch off the television.' She is still laughing saying: 'This was recorded this early this afternoon.'

Then it switches over; the boys in the playground that were pestering Leila are flying in the air from the swings, landing in the pond and they are rolling about in the mud. They cannot get out of the mud at least they are trying to get out. Leila helps them to crawl out and then she makes them crawl on their chests on the grass and roll around like dogs, trying to remove the mud from their clothes. One of the boy's mums is doing the same as the boys.

JK is rolling around on the floor asking: 'Please, turn it off, please!'

Now they are in the sand pit.

JK says. 'I can't stand this any longer. I'm going outside for some fresh air,' He crawls away on his knees.

'JK this is the best bit. Just watch!'

In come the police, the Keystone cops. When Leila has finished with them they are rolling about in the mud and sand as well.

The person reading the news begins laughing her head off again her colleague has to apologise and finish the news bulletin.

Leila continues her explanation:

'When I was conceived, mum was taken to a spaceship. I was in my mum's tummy. They gave me these powers and they have been back to make sure that I'm going on fine and they will be back again. I don't know when, but I suspect it will happen sooner rather than later. The next time we get a visit we'll take you with us, when you'll be in a better frame of mind.'

'Now children, we'll have some supper and I think that our two sons will do us the honour of setting out the table,'

John says. 'JK, you owe me a pint, if you don't mind.'

'I'll gladly pay up. That was amazing!'

Leila tells granny: 'I'm not allowed to show my power outside of the house unless there's an emergency. Do you understand, granny?'

'Yes, of course I understand,' she replies. 'At least I think so.' She is totally bemused

'Okay, who is going to lay the table?' asks dad.

'I'll do that,' replies Ciera.

Leila says. 'I'll help as well.'

Supper finished, dad says. 'What a day, very enjoyable. I think that Leila deserves all the credit for that spectacular piece of genius and laughter we had today. I didn't know or see her perform any of her powers on that scale before but I must say that it's an astounding feat of the mind and I'm sure that we'll be having a wonderful time with Leila in the future.'

The discussion goes on during tea about where and when things will change in their lives, but of course only Leila knows that and she is not about to give any hint to what that might be, because it would put a very big strain on the family.

'John, could you place all our things in the car please?' asks Ciera.

'Yes of course, dear. No problem,' he replies. John finds all the items, gathers them up and takes them out to the car and places them in the boot of the car. He walks back into the house. 'Come on, Leila. You've school in the morning!' Ciera gives granddad and granny a kiss and a hug.

Leila says goodbye and gives a kiss to granddad, a kiss and a hug to granny, not forgetting JK. He has a kiss and a hug as well

'That's it then, away we go to the car.' John says goodbye to his dad and his mother and he walks out to the car, sits in the driver's seat, starts the engine, and then all the family wave as they drive away.

Chapter 38

Leila is now approaching eight years old and school is going very well. All of her teachers are amazed at Leila's intellectual learning, and skills. The headmaster is considering placing her up to a higher grade in the school, but he is a bit worried. He cannot put his finger on it but this child is very special. He knows that she is way above the rest of the school from a learning point of view that is all the children in the school. In all frankness she is ready for University. He keeps an eye on her progress for another year. What he must not do is to let her ability and her academic skills fall away. He thinks that maybe the best thing to do would be to talk to her parents about it. He phones the school secretary and asks her to prepare a letter requesting Leila's parents to come to the school in order to discuss Leila's future. 'When you have the letter ready please come to my office and I'll sign it. Thank you very much.'

A couple of days later, Ciera receives a letter from the school, so she places it on the sideboard until John comes home and decides she will give it to him that evening.

John arrives home about six o'clock,   Ciera arrives in from the kitchen, goes to the sideboard, picks up the letter and hands it to John saying. 'I had this letter from the school this morning. I didn't open it. I've left it for you.'

'Where's Leila?' John asks.

'She's up in her bedroom, doing her homework!'

'Please call her down. She might like to know what this letter is all about.' Ciera goes the bottom of the stairs. 'Dad's home Leila and he would like to see you, to have a talk about the school letter!'

'I'm coming mum. I'll be down in a minute!'

'Please hurry up. I'll put the dinner on the table. You go and wash your hands,' replies Ciera.

A minute later, Leila runs down the stairs into the sitting room, gives her dad a big kiss and a hug and asks. 'So, what do you want?'

'I've had a letter from the school. Before I open it, is there anything I should know? You've been behaving at school?'

'Yes. I'm very good at school. I don't have any trouble with anyone. Incidentally, I can tell you what's in that letter you have in your hand dad.'

'Well, we'll see.' He opens it, looks at Leila and asks. 'Okay, tell me what it says.'

'It's from the headmaster and it says. 'Dear Mr and Mrs Carney, I would like the two of you to come to the school to have a talk about Leila on such a date and time. I'm right, dad?'

'Yes of course you are. I don't know why I asked. Ciera, the headmaster is asking if we can go to the school next week and he has given the time and date. He would like to discuss with us the future of Leila.'

'I don't have a problem with the date or time, so you can write back to him and say that we will come to the school next week and discuss Leila's future,'

Is that all right with you, Leila?'

'Of course it's alright mum. I'm happy with whatever you decide for my future. It's best if we go along with whatever the headmaster discusses with you but it'll not make any difference to me.

'Good then,' replies dad. 'So let's have dinner.'

Ciera sets the food on the table and says. 'Please have what you want.'

Dad asks Leila. 'Are you worried about your future? Do you have second thoughts about it?'

'Absolutely not I'm looking forward to my life in the future. I can't wait. It's going to be a very exciting time for all of us. What do you think, dad and mum?'

Dad looks at Ciera and replies: 'Leila, if you're to have us to help you we'll be very happy. I know that there will be dangerous times in the future in front of us but I'm sure that with your help we'll overcome anything that might be difficult. We'll meet these challenges as and when they come, of that, I'm certainly sure. No question about it whatsoever. I take it, Ciera, that you agree with me and I hope you're not having second thoughts about this whole situation, are you?'

'Of course not, we're in very good hands and I'm sure that our daughter will not let anything happen to us or any of the family.'

'Then we agree to carry on with our lives for the present.'

Chapter 39

The following week at the date and time, John and Ciera go to see the headmaster in the school. The headmaster has left a message with the secretary to take Mr and Mrs Carney to his office when they arrive at the school. They park the car in the car park at the school, walk to the secretary's office, announcing that they are here to meet the headmaster.

The secretary gets up from her desk and says. 'Follow me please.'

They walk after her down the hallway to the headmaster's office, she opens the door and ushers them inside.

Mr Carney says, 'Thank you' and his wife and himself proceed to the headmaster's desk.

The headmaster welcomes them to the school and indicates them to sit down in the chairs provided, and asks. 'Would you like a cup of tea or coffee?'

'No, thank you very much,' replies Mr Carney. 'We are fine.'

'Good then. Let's begin,' replies the headmaster. 'Now as you probably already know you have a very gifted child in Leila. I think that she's very much ahead of her time and it worries me, not in a bad way, but I need some input from you concerning her future. I would like to send her to university at the end of this school term. I know that she'll have no problem sitting the entrance exams. She's so bright it is unbelievable. Have you any idea where this comes from?' Maybe she's just one of those gifted children that come along now and again and astounds everyone that meets with her. She amazes me in everything she does; she does not seem to have to work on it. It's my opinion that she should try for university and I'm sure that anyone of the top ones would only be too glad to enrol her. What do you think, Mr and Mrs Carney?'

'Well if you think that's the best for Leila you have our permission to make the provisions for university and whatever paper work needs signing, we'll only be too happy to sign,' says John.

'Good. I'll attend to that this week,' replies the headmaster. 'Any preference of university you would like for Leila?'

'We'll trust you to place her in the best university as long as it's not too far away. What would you like her to study?' John asks.

'Well perhaps science, politics, and computers might suit her,' says Ciera.

'Well strangely enough, that's what I was going to suggest,' replies the headmaster. 'Leila's a very gifted child as you already know. I know that she'll excel in all of these categories. Right then, if you're happy with that we can end this meeting and leave the rest to Leila. It was lovely to have met you. I'm sure that we will meet again.' The headmaster rises from his chair and shakes the hands of Mr and Mrs Carney. He goes to the door and lets them out into the corridor. Then they walk out of the school and go to their car, get in and drive out through the school gates. On their way home in the car they discuss the topic which is about the university situation regarding Leila. Having conditioned themselves to the fact that she will be at university for some years to come but they are delighted that she will have that chance, not that she will need it but it will give her the opportunity to sharpen her brain and be able to hold a conversation with anyone from an intellectual point of view.

That afternoon, they decide to tell Leila about the meeting they had with the headmaster about university.

As usual Leila comes bounding in the door after school and walks straight into the sitting room and looks at her mum and dad and says: 'Did you have a good meeting with the headmaster today? Don't look so surprised, mum, dad, you know that I know everything that goes on in the family. I'm very happy to go to university when the time comes!'

'Good,' replies dad. 'As long as you're happy, that's fine with us. We know that you're not in need of education but we must make sure that you're sheltered from the world for some time to come. It might cause problems for your family. We'll just have to wait for the return of your godparents. Have you any idea when they might come back to Earth?'

'I'm expecting to communicate with them soon. It's been a long time since they visited us but I'm sure that we'll see them sooner rather than later!'

'How are you feeling in yourself? Are you worried about anything, I mean in your mind?'

'Of course not, nothing wrong there. In fact, it's getting better every day.'

The headmaster gets all the paper work for Leila's exams. The next day he requests Leila to come to his office at lunch time. He has some very important issues he needs to talk to her about.

She arrives at the door of his office and knocks. 'Please come in.'

Leila opens the door and walks inside.

He looks up from his desk, 'Ah! Leila nice to see you I'm sorry that I requested that I wanted to see you in my office at lunch time. I'm going to let you sit your exams for university, at the end of term. That is if you don't mind. I know that you are very young, but I'm sure that you are ready for university.'

She answers, 'Well sir, if you think that I'm capable, I'm happy to take the exams. It's a great honour, sir that you have such confidence in me and I hope that I will not let you down.'

'Leila, 'May I ask you a few questions?'

'Yes sir, you can.'

'What are you thinking about, now, I mean in your mind?'

'What do you mean sir, can you be more specific?' Leila knows where this conversation is going. *She is going to need to watch what she answers to the headmaster*

'Where do you get all this intelligence from? You are quite unique from my point of view. You are very different from the rest of the children in this school. All of your teachers tell me that they can't keep up with you in class. You don't seem to have a problem of any kind with your work ethics; everything seems to be very easy for you. What I mean is you are way ahead of your time with the   education you are having at this school. Is there something we don't know about you?'

'What do you mean sir?'

'I don't know, Leila. I can't really put my finger on it. It's weird. There is something very special about you. I'm looking forward to seeing you in the future. I'm sure that you will be very famous, and that you will return to see us when you have left university. When you have finished your exams, I'll personally send them to Balliol College for the attention of Professor Michael Barlow, he is a very good friend of mine. I'm sure that he will be as fascinated as I am, with that very special gift of yours. He will write back to me when he receives my recommendation. That is if you pass all these exams at the end of term. I am sure that you will pass with flying colours. Now, Leila, do not let me down please.'

I promise sir that I'll do my very best. This is a very great opportunity for me and my family, I hope that I'll make this school very proud of me sir.'

'You may return to your class now Leila. There is no need to tell anyone about our discussion that is between you and me for the moment. Oh you may tell your parents about what we discussed and that I'll be in touch with your dad as soon as I have any information from Professor Michael Barlow. Good bye. Leila walks down the corridor to her class. He sits down at his desk, his mind is running wild. All he can think about is Leila and how brilliant she is. Where does she get this very impressive mind from, the parents don't seem to be above average intelligence, They are very nice people, However my remit at the moment is to make sure that Leila passes her end of term exams, and then university. I'm sure that Professor Michael will be very impressed when he reads and digests the potential of Leila.'

Three weeks later Leila has finished her end of term exams. It was no big deal to her. She didn't hurry through the exam papers. She just made it look as if she was struggling with some of the questions, trying to make it look as if it was difficult.

The head master is waiting outside the exam room until the exam is finished. The teachers walk around the room picking up all the exam papers. The head master walks into the room saying, 'Children that is it, you may go home now, and I hope that all of you have passed your exams.'

All the exam papers are taken to the head masters office where he singles out Leila papers. Somehow he knows that all the questions on Leila's papers are correct which fascinates him. He has already prepared a letter to send to Professor Michael, explaining Leila's qualities. He does not look at her papers he knows that there is no need. He copies them. He then places the copies with the letter in a large envelope, addressed to Professor Michael Barlow, Balliol College Oxford.'

He takes the envelope to his secretary saying, 'Will you please make sure that this envelope goes in the post as soon as you can, it's a very important document.'

Two days later his phone rings he picks it up. It's his secretary. Sir, I have a Professor Michael Barlow on the phone for you.'

'Put him through please.' He picks the phone up saying. 'Michael I wasn't expecting to hear from you so quick. I'm assuming that you want to ask me about Leila.'

'Who is this child Edmund? She is amazing in all my years in teaching at college and university; I have never seen such amazing results in an end of term exam. She is ready for university now. Her grasp of all the exam subjects has over whelmed me. I have never seen such well structured answered. It's too good to be true. Have you looked at her answers Edmund?'

No, Michael, I didn't want to look at them, I just knew that she would pass with flying colours. Well do you want her at Balliol or not? I'm on tender hooks. I need to know now. Please Michael tell me that you will enrol her now.'

'Edmund you know as well as me that it not easy to jump the queue, only in exceptional circumstances is that allowed. Tell you what, I'll enrol her now and hope that she passes. Edmund I'm placing my career on the line for Leila, I hope I'm not making a mistake.'

'Michael, this is like winning the Derby, she is that good. Her intelligence is astounding. I know that you'll be very proud of her in the future.'

Six weeks later, John receives a phone call from the headmaster. 'Good news Mr Carney. I wish to inform you that Leila will be going as a student for the rest of her education into Oxford University. – Balliol College founded in the year 1263. That is a very prestigious college, one of the best.'

'Wonderful,' replies Mr Carney. I'm sure that Leila will be thrilled to bits at the news!'

'Yes, but will she go to university?' asks the headmaster.

'Of course she will. I know that she's looking forward to it and I'm sure that she'll excel in everything she does!'

'Well, then, John. You'll need to contact Professor Michael Barlow at Balliol College to make sure that she's an under-graduate and see to any accommodation she might need during her time at college. We're ecstatic at the school but a little sad because she's a very interesting child and a very good listener. All the teachers are very fond of her and she's the most intelligent, bright, gifted child we've ever had. We'll miss her greatly, and I hope that she'll not forget her first school, and come back to see us when she comes home on holiday. Incidentally, the college will write to you and send you the papers to sign.'

'I'm sure that she'll not forget her school, and don't worry, she'll want to return to see all of her past teachers and her school friends of course. Thank you headmaster, for all the help you have given Leila and I'm sure that she'll appreciate all you've done for her. Goodbye for now.' John phones his wife and relays the message he received from the headmaster about Leila going to Balliol College in Oxford.

She replies, 'That's absolutely fantastic news! I can't wait until Leila comes home to tell her the good news.'

Dad says, 'Leila will know this even before you and I were given this information. You know that she's capable of picking up on anything about her, whether at school or at home. She'll be able to relate word for word exactly about the letter the headmaster had from the college. Try and be happy when she comes home and I'll see you later.'

'Thank you, dear,' replies Ciera and hangs up the phone.

Leila arrives home from school and runs into the sitting room where her mum is sitting on the sofa and says. 'You know the news about the college at Oxford?'

'Yes I do.' Leila replies.

'Your dad phoned me and relayed what the headmaster said to him. It is fantastic news; anyway we're very pleased for you. It's going to be very quiet when you go to college and I'm sure that you'll be happy there. I'm also sure that you'll excel there in all your subjects.'

'Just a minute, mum, I'm receiving a communication from Óisin. They're on their way to see me but they are prisoners on their space craft and I'm to be extremely careful and be on my guard at all times.'

'This communication is not being intercepted by my captors,' says Óisin. 'I'll explain when you come aboard the ship. Please help us to take our ship back.'

'Óisin's in trouble mum and I'm going to have to help him when the ship arrives.'

'When do you think they'll arrive?' asks mum.

'At the moment I don't know but I'll know when they're in orbit around the Earth and I'll be ready for them so don't worry. I know what I'm going to do.' She communicates with granddad and relates to him what Óisin has told her and asks if he will come to her house tonight and stay until the abduction of Óisin and Gia is thwarted. 'I'll give you the plan when you come here later. Thanks granddad. See you soon.'

Chapter 40

Granddad arrives about seven that night. Leila goes and lets him in and they go into the sitting room.

Granddad looks worried and asks Leila if she is going to be able to release Óisin and Gia.

'Of course I can. My powers have greatly increased since the last time we were aboard the spacecraft. In truth I know I'm nearly at my full power, now the technology is improving all the time. Whatever happens in the spacecraft, I'll ready and able to compensate any variation that they might be trying to overpower me. It'll not matter how many people are aboard trying to overpower me. It's not going to happen.'

'Well that's all I need to know,' replies granddad. 'I'm not here to question your ability. I'm here to help and whatever you ask me to do I'll be only too glad to stand by your side!'

'That's absolutely fine with me,' replies Leila. 'Mum you look worried. What's the matter?'

'I don't know. This is a big step forward in your life,' replies mum. 'And of course I'm going to worry. You're my child and I feel helpless!'

'Mum, nothing will happen to me now. My technology is far superior to anyone on the spacecraft. Please believe me I know what I'm talking about nothing will happen to me now!' The people on the craft don't have a chance against me, of that I'm sure. Granddad, when the time comes I'll blend into your body and we'll be as one. There's no pain or discomfort. You'll not know that I'm in your body so you're not to worry. I'll detect the spacecraft when it is in orbit above our planet I'll merge with you because they will be trying to locate me. They will not be able locate me, they will panic, then they'll take you instead. I'll make sure of that. Now, everybody, just stay calm please. I'll give you plenty of time and mum, I'll cloak you just in case they try to abduct you instead of granddad. Dad's just coming to the front door. I'll go and let him in.' She opens the door and she implants all the information she has given to mum and granddad so that he understands the whole situation before he goes into the sitting room.

Ciera looks at John and asks. 'Are you ready for your dinner?'

'Yes, I'm ready. I'm hungry. I've had a bad day at work but there are more important things to worry about and yes, I know what's about to transpire. Leila has told me everything by telecommunication. I'll have my dinner now.'

'Give me a minute and I'll fetch it.' She arrives back with dad's dinner and places it on the table.'

'Well, all we can do now is to wait until Leila senses when the spacecraft is in orbit,' says granddad.

'What about JK?' John asks. 'Surely he needs to know.'

'No problem,' replies Leila. 'I'll communicate with him now and explain the situation. We will not need him but if it does happen that we need his presence, I can locate him then transport him to the spacecraft. Now just settle down, we have a bit of time to relax.'

Time is moving on and no sign of the craft yet.

'I think I'll phone my wife,' says granddad. 'And tell her that I'll be late tonight because Leila needs us to be near.' He takes the phone from his pocket, dials the number.

She picks her phone up and answers, 'is that you, granddad?'

'Yes, it's me, just to tell you that I'll be a bit late tonight.'

'What's wrong, dear?'

'I'm staying for a little while at John's tonight if you don't mind. Leila's expecting a bit of trouble so we need to be available if she needs us.'

'What kind of trouble are you talking about?'

'Nothing for you to worry about,' dad replies. 'Just a little bit of tidying up to do. I'll see you later. Goodbye for now.'

Chapter 41

Everything is at a standstill in the Carney household, waiting for Leila to detect the spacecraft when it arrives in orbit. The tension is quite high as you would expect in this kind of situation, but Leila does not appear to be too worried about it. She seems to be very calm and is obviously planning her strategy for the forthcoming clash with the new Aliens on Óisin and Gia's craft. How dare they subject her godparents to any form of treachery – the question is why?

Leila is well versed in all kinds of wilful betrayal of trust and perfidy, and she is not going to let her godparents suffer any kind of indignity or harassment perpetrated by the Aliens whoever they might be. The problem is probably about her as she is a very technically advanced being and there are Aliens somewhere out in the Universe who would give anything to get their hands on her, but they could be in for a very big surprise. What they do not know is that the power she has now is way above their intellectual capacity. The nanotechnology BIO/DNA software is futuristically so advanced now that she is of the opinion that is why she is so valuable, and she knows that she is making technical advances all the time. She is updating information from all sources and processing accordingly. All of a sudden, she jumps up and says. 'Granddad, I need your body *now*! The space craft is just about to orbit the earth, but first I'll cloak mum and dad, JK, Delia and granny.'

'Can you do all that, even when they're not here?' asks granddad.

'Of course I can. I need them to think that I'm not on the Earth and the only one they can transport is granddad. They'll be frustrated when they can't find me. Because granddad is the oldest one, they'll take him instead. Granddad and I will be as one when they transport us up to their craft. Now granddad, I'm going to remove anything you know about me from your brain so that you'll be unable to give any information about me, but I'll restore it when I've finished with the Aliens. Are you happy with that?'

'Yes of course. I'm happy with whatever you think is going to facilitate helping Óisin and Gia!'

Leila walks over to granddad and they are coalesced together as one person.

The bait is now set in motion for the Aliens orbiting the Earth.

Leila knows that they are not able to locate her anywhere so they go for granddad instead and beam him up to the craft. He materializes in the control deck. There are four Aliens standing in front of him. This lot are a lot different, they are from a planet called Esmyic and they are very

109

dangerous. They look human but not a friendly race by any means. They teleported aboard Oisin's craft from their own craft, as Oisin left Pyseid. Then they placed Oisin and Gia in security.

Oisin demands to know what they are doing on his craft.

'All in good time, we understand that you are going to a planet called Earth. Well we have business there and as you are going there we decided to commandeer your craft.'

Oisin asks, 'Why our craft? Who are you?'

'You don't need to know now, all will be explained when we arrive at planet Earth.' The one giving the orders is wearing an androgynous suit similar to Óisin and Gia; white in colour. The other three are wearing the same kind of suit but the colours are different.'

'Oisin's mind is running wild. They look the same as us. Then it hits him, 'I know what they want, they want Leila.'

Granddad thinks that the one in the white suit is the leader. 'Who are you?' he asks.

'We ask the questions here!' replies one of the Aliens. 'And if you do not cooperate we will subject you to a lot of pain!'

'You're not able. I can stop you.'

'I don't think so. We know what Earth people are like. Very little brain and all talk. Now you're in our power all we would like from you is information about Leila. All we want is Leila and then we can leave.'

'I don't know what you're talking about,' replies granddad. 'I don't know anybody of that name.'

'We will make you tell us.'

'No you won't!' Leila is standing in front of the four Aliens and they are flabbergasted at the sudden appearance of her in the craft.

'Where did you come from?'

'You'd like to know, wouldn't you?' replies Leila.

'We are more technically powerful than you,' one of the Aliens says.

'No you're not. I'll show you what power is.' She moves her hand in a circular movement and the four Aliens are back against the inside of the craft as if by magic. The four Aliens are desperately trying to detach themselves but are unable to break away. 'I'd stop trying to escape from me. You're not capable or strong enough to override me. Where are Óisin and Gia?'

'We don't know and if we did, we would not tell you.'

'Okay. Tell you what, which one of you would like to be transferred to the outside of this craft?'

The mouthy one says, 'You are not able to do that!'

Leila waves her hand. He is situated on the outside of the craft. She then switches on the viewing at the front of the craft there he is hanging on to the craft and looking quite worried, she asks him telepathically: 'Would you like to come back in?'

'Yes, yes please. Take me back inside!'

'Now you will cooperate?'

'Yes, yes just bring me in,' replies the mouthy one.

Leila waves her hand again, As if by trickery he is back in the craft but held flat against the inside of the craft. 'Please be very careful what you say from now on because the next time you give the wrong answer, all four of you will be transported outside.' Then she gives the four of them a vision of lions running towards them and it is panic stations. As the lions are closing on the four of them, she allows them to break free.

If it weren't so funny, it would be sad. The four of them are running around in circles trying to get out of each other's way, so she decides to make the lions vanish. They are now in a state of shock and are huddling together on the floor.

'I would like to know what you've done with Óisin and Gia,' asks Leila. No answer from the four, but she has now gained complete control of their minds. 'It does not matter. I know where they are. Granddad, I'm going to find Óisin and Gia. You stay and watch them!'

'Are you sure I'm the right person to watch that lot?'

'Yes, they will not give you any trouble now. I have complete control of their minds. They're unable to function by themselves without my command.'

Off she goes, telepathically communicating with Óisin. She teleports to the destination where Óisin and Gia are confined, waves her hand and the security panel is disengaged so that they are visible. They look very worried.

'Good evening to both of you. How did you get yourself in this situation?' She runs to them and gives them a big kiss and a hug, saying: 'It's lovely to see you again!

'Leila, we were wondering if you were going to be able to overpower and control the others on the control deck.'

'Of course I'm able. They were no match for me.' She looks then she gives them a very devilish look.

'What do you mean?' They look at each other. 'We were worried for you. We didn't know if you would be able to stop them from abducting you. We were powerless against them. They were able to overpower us.'

'How did this happen?' Leila asks, 'how did they take over your craft?'

'We left our planet and when we were just outside in orbit, these Aliens transferred from their craft to our craft. They must have been in waiting with their craft. Our computers did not pick it up, and before we could do anything they were inside our craft, and that is how we were taken prisoners. They did tell us what they wanted, and that it was you there were after. Someone on our planet must have been in touch with them, and for whatever reason they decided that you were their priority for the technology you process.'

'Well everything is fine now. Where would you like to go?'

'We would like to return to the control deck.'

'Both of you hold my hand, please.'

In a split second all of them are on the control deck. They are absolutely amazed and look around to make sure that they are really there in the control deck.

'Did you do that, Leila?' inquires Óisin.

'Yes of course it was me. I'm now almost at full power with my mind and it's getting better every minute.'

Óisin and Gia look a bit worried they are shaking in anticipation of what they are going to find when Leila has the rest of the upgrade of the technology placed in her brain and mind.

'What would you like me to do with the four on the floor?' asks Leila.

Gia replies: 'I think that you should place them in the security section where we were.'

'That is done! Leila replies.

Gia looks at Leila. 'But you didn't leave the control deck and the four other Aliens are gone!'

'I don't need to but I can show you from here that they're in the security section if you like.'

'Yes, I would like to see them if you don't mind?

Leila waves her hand and says, 'There you are.' The vision in the security section is as clear as if they were in the room with them. Leila levitates herself up on to the technological apparatus that she remembers from the last time she was here.

Óisin walks over and for the first time in his life is afraid to do anything, so he calls Gia over, looks at her and says, 'Can you take over? You know more about this apparatus than I do. I don't know what might happen. What if I should damage Leila?' I would never forgive myself for losing the most precious technology that was ever developed and Leila as well. We could be in very big trouble when we arrive back to our own planet!'

'Look, just switch it on. I'll do the rest myself,' Leila advices.

Gia looks at Leila, places her right hand over the console places her left hand at one of the squares. The sides of the table rise up and cover Leila. Twenty seconds later, they open up and descend. Gia takes a small, oblong, thin-looking piece of very futuristic apparatus in her hand. It looks like a small computer. She runs her hand over the top of it and then looks at Leila.

'Leila, you've evolved so quickly you're no longer in need of our help. We could do with some of your technology now that you're so far advanced. I don't know what to say. I knew that it was good but this is something else. You're now superior to all the technology we have at our disposal. You're way ahead of it all, probably by three thousand years. I wasn't aware that this technology was so highly developed. Óisin, what do you think?'

'I'm so pleased that it's working but is it going to have a detrimental effect on Leila?' enquires Óisin.

Leila is now standing by the table and replies: 'I'm in total control. I can slow the technology down if I want to so don't worry!'

Óisin and Gia have a long look at each other and decide that Leila is the only person to control the technology, so they have to believe her and accept her word but very reluctantly.

'I have an idea,' says Óisin. 'Gia and I think if Leila would agree to come to our planet we will be able to give her a more in depth examination. No strings attached. What do you think, Leila?'

'Well first of all, I now know that I'm way ahead of all your technology and the nanotechnology you have on your planet and I'm way ahead of your thinking as well. I'm not against helping you. I was hoping that I could go and help your planet. We need each other. You gave me the technology, so why shouldn't I help you? I have to ask my parents if I can go. I could take a holiday gap for a year because I have been inducted into college now and it would only be right to ask for the time off. Then I can return and finish my education. I know that it doesn't matter about education. I don't really need it. When I return I'll then decide whether I should be involved in world affairs. Now I must remove all the cloaks around my family before we do anything else. Granddad, I think it's time to return you to my house, and Granddad, you've done a wonderful job here. I thank you for all the assistance. Please tell my mum that I'll be home as soon as possible and you may tell her and dad that everything's fine. Goodbye for now!' She waves her hand and granddad is immediately in Leila's house on Earth. 'One question for Óisin: what are you going to do with the prisoners?'

'We will return them to our planet and question them as to why they wanted you!'

'I could find out now if you like?' replies Leila.

'No. I think it's only right that my people question the four of them,' replies Óisin.

'Okay. That's all right with me,' replies Leila. 'I'll give them back their minds so that you can glean all the information you may need and find out why I'm so important to them. Well, I know why, but who wants to abduct me? That's the question.'

Chapter 42

'Well, I think that we've done very well tonight but I must return home.' Leila walks over to Óisin and Gia, gives Óisin a big kiss and a hug, saying: 'I love you.' She then goes to Gia and gives her a very special kiss and a hug saying: 'I love you, too. You two are very special to me. I've named you my godparents because you've looked after me extremely well and I'll be forever grateful to you for all the technology BIO/DNA you've installed in my mind and whatever happens, I'll always be at your beck and call. You only need to contact me at any time and I'll be at your side.'

Óisin and Gia look bemused by this statement and enquire what does that mean?

'It's simple. You think of me. I'll receive your message and I'll come to you.'

'But that's impossible,' replies Óisin as he looks at Gia.

'Not any more. I can go anywhere I like in the Universe. You do understand what I'm telling you?'

'Yes,' Gia replies.

'As we speak I'm upgrading the technology BIO/DNA to transport me to your planet now if I so wish.'

'Unbelievable I'm astounded, Leila. You're one very powerful young lady,' replies Gia.

Leila looks at Gia, 'Now I must tell you that you'll need to be very careful when you arrive back on your own planet. There are some very powerful people on your planet. You'll need to be very careful of them. They're waiting for you when you arrive back. They're your immediate senior scientists, very high up in your department and they'll stop at nothing to try to extract as much information out of you as they need and then try to discredit you. There are still some very greedy people on your planet, so be very careful. These scientists are not your friends. You must contact me when you need me and I'll deal with them. I'm sorry that I needed to give you this information but I couldn't let you walk into a trap. As I've said, you're my godparents and I'll protect you, whatever the cost to me.'

Óisin is having a hard time believing what Leila has told them. He looks at Gia and enquires: 'What do you think of this information?'

'I don't know. I would never have thought that we've any enemies on our own planet!'

'I'm sorry, but technology is a very powerful, mesmerizing and appealing science. I can assure you that they're waiting for you,' Leila replies. 'They want me and that's why they sent the four other people to make sure that I'd be taken prisoner and returned for experimentation on your home planet.'

'Where does that leave us now.' enquires Gia.

'Can I look inside your mind, Gia?' asks Leila.

'Why?' replies Gia.

'I need your star chart for that part of the Universe so that I'll know where to go if you need me.'

'Okay, if you must,' Gia replies.

Leila looks at Gia and takes all the information she needs, and she knows that she will need that information very soon. 'All you have to do is return and see what happens, but be very careful and don't forget I'm on your side. Any trouble, you must communicate with me and I'll be at your side quicker than you think. Please trust me. I must go now.' In a twinkle of an eye, she has gone home. She arrives in the sitting room and her mum is asleep on the sofa, so Leila goes over and taps her on the shoulder. 'Mum, I'm home now. You can go to bed if you like!'

Ciera nearly jumps out of her skin. She looks at Leila and cries, cuddles Leila intently and says. 'I thought that I was never going to see you again.'

'Don't be silly, mum. I'm not going to leave you. I'll have to go from time to time but I'll always come home. Shall we go to bed now?'

'Yes of course. You know that I was very worried about your well being,' replies Ciera.

'Yes, mum. Oh mum, are you going to tell dad that you are pregnant again?'

She looks at Leila and says, please, you are making me blush. I'm not sure if I'm pregnant, I am going to see the doctor tomorrow morning and hopefully everything will be fine. Shall we talk all about it tomorrow?' Oh I don't want to know whether it's a boy or a girl

'Okay. That's all right by me.'

They go up the stairs together and into their own rooms and get ready for bed. It is a bit late so Leila gets into bed and falls asleep very quickly and thinks to herself, 'What a night!'

The next morning Leila is up very early and eating her breakfast in the kitchen so that she can meet her dad before he goes to work and have a little chat with him. About five minutes go by and he comes into the kitchen saying to Leila: 'You're back then?'

'Yes, I'm back dad. I'm sorry but you were in bed when I arrived home last night. I didn't want to wake you up so thought I'd leave it until now to talk to you before mum comes down for her breakfast. Is that all right with you?'

'Yes of course. We were very worried about you but granddad told us what happened up in the craft. I hope you were all right; no adverse problems then?' replies dad.

'Look, dad. I may have to go away from time to time. I think Óisin and Gia might be having problems on their own planet and I must help.'

Dad looks at Leila and asks. 'How are you going to do that? How are you going to get there?'

'I'll teleport there. It's not a problem for me now. I don't need a spacecraft. It's part of my technology. All I have to do is believe about teleporting.'

'That's impossible! You can't be that far advanced!'

'Yes I am, dad. Let me show you what I can do. Tell me what you would like for your breakfast.'

'Well, let me see. I don't believe you but I'll go along with your request. I'd like two fried eggs, one rasher and two sausages please.'

In an instant, as if by magic his breakfast materializes in front of him just as he requested.

Leila looks at her dad and smiles.

Dad looks bemused looks at Leila and says. 'Thank you.' He looks again at Leila and says. 'I'm not going to say anything but I'm very proud of you. Your mum and I know that you'll leave us sometime in the future and we'll miss you very much. All we ask is please don't forget us and do come to see us from time to time, just keep in touch!'

'Don't be silly, dad. I'll never forget you or mum. You're my biological parents and I'll always be there for you no matter what the circumstances might be. From time to time, I'll leave to negotiate with the different governments around the world and try to reason with them. They'll try to talk me down and try to be clever but I'll win them over in the end. I don't have a worry about that situation. My worry at this moment in time is Óisin and Gia. They might be in trouble on their own planet.'

'Why do you think that might be a problem, Leila?'

'It was something I learned on the craft,' replies Leila.

'Can I ask you what you mean?' enquires dad.

'It's a bit complicated and I'm not sure at the moment. However I'll know very soon and when I receive a message from Óisin or Gia, I'll have to leave for a while but I'll be in communication with you and mum I'll keep you informed at all times.'

Ciera arrives in the dining room and asks Leila if she has had her breakfast.

'Not yet,' replies Leila.

'What would you like for your breakfast then?'

'May I have a bowl of cornflakes and coffee please mum?'

'What would you like for your breakfast, Dad?'

'I've had my breakfast. Leila made it for me but I'd like another cup of coffee please.'

Ciera looks at dad and asks. 'How did she do that?'

'You have a very talented daughter she just magically drew it from the air. I don't know how, but it was a lovely breakfast, I think she was trying to impress me.' He gets up from the table. 'I must go now. I don't want to be late for work.' He gives a kiss to his wife and Leila, picks up the keys for the car from the table, walks out the front door to his car, sits in the driver's seat, and drives off to work.

'What kind of breakfast did you give your dad, Leila?'

'Exactly the same as you would make it. I gave him two eggs, bacon and sausages. I needed to talk to him before he went to work so I made him breakfast to impress him. I hope I didn't upset you, mum.'

'Of course not I know that you're a good girl and I accept that you'll do these little magic tricks from time to time. That's fine by me, Leila but be very careful please!'

'Of course, mum. I'll try and be very discreet,' replies Leila.

'Look at the time, Leila. We need to go now or you'll be late for school.'

'Don't worry, mum, It only takes about ten minutes to get to the school,' replies Leila.

'Pick up your school bag and sandwich box, Leila, and go to the car and wait for me. I'll follow you out and lock the front door.'

'Okay, mum. See you at the car.' Leila hops down the hallway, out the front door stands by the car and waits for her mum.

Ciera follows her out the front door, locks it and walks to the car. Then she unlocks the driver's door.

Leila opens the passenger door and sits in the front seat.

Mum looks over and asks. 'You've everything you need for school?'

'Yes, mum. I have everything I need. 'Can we go now please?'

Chapter 43

Leila has moved up two grades at her school, 'That will suit her fine. The children here are a bit more mature. On arriving at the school gates, Leila jumps out of the car, closes the door behind her, waves to mum and darts inside the school playground to meet her friends. Mum looks at her daughter and wonders what will the future bring, and for the first time in her life, she feels sad, because she knows that Leila will leave sometime soon. She will need to be very strong and her only hope is that Leila will make a big contribution to world peace. As she drives away from the school, she dries a little tear in her eye.

The school bell rings and all the children line up in their respective places walk into their classrooms and sit down. In Leila's class room there is a lot of talking until the teacher enters the room. She looks around to make sure all the children are present and says. 'Good morning children.'

The children answer back: 'Good morning, Miss!'

The teacher walks to her desk looks around and says. 'Leila, would you go to the head master's office please? He would like to talk to you. Off you go.'

Leila gets up from her desk walks out the door down the hallway to the headmaster's office and knocks at his door.

Mr Edmund Scarry is headmaster; a tall person, immaculately well dressed, clean shaven, has a look of authority about him. He gets up, answers the door, opens it and says. 'Leila, please, if you will?' He indicates to Leila to sit down and says. 'I suppose you're wondering why I've sent for you. Don't you worry about it, just to ask if you're happy to be going to university?' I hope that I'm not putting too much pressure on you.'

'Of course not,' replies Leila. 'I'm looking forward to going there. All of a sudden Leila receives a communication from Gia.' *'We are in need of your help, Please come as soon as you can Gia.'*

Leila sends one back: *I'm on my way. I'll make contact you with when I arrive.* 'Headmaster, what you're about to see must not be communicated to anyone outside this office. I'll explain when I arrive back. If my teacher inquires just keep her happy. Will you do that for me please? I'll inform my mum and dad by telepathy.'

The headmaster looks at Leila and enquires: 'What are you talking about, Leila?'

'I can't tell you everything now. I'll try to explain when I return. Trust me, please,' replies Leila. In a flash, Leila turns into pure energy and is gone.

The headmaster is looking around the office trying to find Leila when he receives a communication from Leila.

'Please don't worry. I'm not in your office. I'm a long way from your office now.' Leila makes contact with her mum, and tells her that she is on her way to help Óisin and Gia. 'I'll be back for tea as soon as I can. I do love you and dad.'

The headmaster is truly perplexed and sits down in his chair. His mind is running wild and he says to himself. 'I knew that this child was different from the rest of the children in the school. My God, what have I witnessed? Who is this child? Where has she come from? What is she doing here in this world? What does she want here? All this information is flying around in his brain. He says to himself. 'I can't make head or tail of it.' There is a knock on his door, he gets up and opens the door.

Leila's teacher is standing in front of him asking. 'Are you all right, sir?'

'I'm fine. What do you want?'

'I just wondered if Leila is alright to come back to her class with me,' replies the teacher.

'She's fine. He has to think fast and then replies. 'Her dad came and picked her up. Apparently her mum has been taken sick so her dad has taken her home.'

'Will she be back to school tomorrow?' enquires the teacher.

'I hope so,' replies the headmaster under his breath.'

'Sir, are you sure you are all right?'

'I'm fine nothing to worry about. You just go back to your class!'

The headmaster is still not sure what happened he is confused and bemused by this whole episode,' Am I dreaming is this a real dream. He decides to have a brandy. He pours himself the drink, his hand is shaking profusely he goes and sits behind his desk and ponders about...what? He does not have any idea what is going on in his mind. Did he imagine the whole thing or is she more even gifted than he had realised?'

Chapter 44

Because Leila is pure energy, she can travel at speeds ten times faster than the speed of light. Her transportation is such that there is no restriction or limit to the speed she is able to achieve in the Universe. Bio/Dna technology Quantum physics enables her to travel as fast as she likes and she is in a hurry to rescue Gia and Óisin. She makes telepathic communication with Gia. 'Keep in communication with me and tell me where you are on your world!'

'We are prisoners in the science department, two hundred metres underground and we're being forcibly held and tied down,' Gia replies. 'They know that you'll try and rescue us. What they don't know is when you'll arrive and how you're coming to rescue us. Your power is far greater than they realise and they'll try and stop you, so be very careful!'

'Don't worry. You and Óisin will be free as soon as I arrive on your planet. I know the extent of their power and I'll neutralise that power before I arrive. Look forward to seeing you soon and give my regards to Óisin. Bye for now, Gia.' Leila is now out of her Galaxy and into the Physerus Galaxy, which has taken her about ten minutes and is closing in fast on Gia's Planet.

Five minutes pass, she is in orbit and has a fix on Gia. She goes straight down to ground level. Down through the ground, two hundred metres, where Gia and Óisin are being held and into the science department in the security section.

Óisin and Gia are behind a shield.

Leila materializes in front of Gia and Óisin. Six security guards with strange looking weapons surround her. It takes about two seconds for Leila to neutralize the weapons and make them too heavy to hold up. She waves her hand over the shield and removes it, then the restraining bonds holding them.

Gia and Óisin stand up.

Leila hugs them both and asks. 'Everything will be all right?'

'Good,' replies Gia. 'We're fine now that you're here.'

'Where are the people I need to talk to?' enquires Leila.

'Follow us,' replies Gia.

The three of them walk out into the corridor and there are more security guards waiting for them.

Leila waves her hand and brushes them aside like feathers, at the same time neutralizing the weapons in their hands. 'Where are the perpetrators of your imprisonment?'

'Right in front of you behind that big door,' replies Óisin.

'What's behind that door?' enquires Leila.

'Special high power weapons,' replies Gia.

They are in front of the door and Leila puts out her hands, telling Óisin and Gia to hold her hand, one each. 'Don't you worry when we arrive at the other side of the door we'll be shielded.'

'How are we going to get to the other side of the door?' asks Gia.

'I'll take you there. Hold on tight. Now just walk. Please trust me.'

The three of them walk through the door, into the room behind with the shield surrounding them all hell breaks loose with a barrage of laser beams.

Leila waves her hand and they switch off with immediate effect. The people in the room are frantically trying to start them again but to no avail. 'Gia, please point out the people that were behind your abduction.'

'The two behind that laser gun,' as she points her hand in their direction,'

Leila points towards them. They levitate and move towards her. Three of the other guards make to rush Leila, but she has anticipated their movement and again waves a hand that sends them flying through the air. They hit the wall and drop down, unconscious. 'Now, Mr Scientists let me ask you something. Do you think that you're more powerful than me I'd like to know, did you think that you could interrogate Óisin and Gia without my knowing about it? Have you lost your speech? Nothing to say, please give me the information I need. I will look in your minds if I need to, in order to glean that information. Gia, can we go and see your government officials please?'

'I'm not sure if they will see you,' Gia replies.

'They'll see me whether they like it or not!' Leila says.

'What about these two scientists?' Gia asks.

'Don't worry about them. I'll place a shield round them. If I need them to answer question I'll transport them. Can you get in touch with someone you know in your government and find out where your President is? I would like to have a conversation with him, now?'

'Yes of course,' replies Gia as she communicates with her friend, tells him about their abduction, and says to her friend: 'We need to arrange a meeting with the President. Now, please.'

Leila is listening in on the conversation. The answer she is receiving is the President is very busy now, maybe this afternoon. She breaks into the communication and tells Gia's friend: 'I want to know where the President is now!'

'Who are you and why are you demanding to see the President?'

'My name is Leila and I'm from Planet Earth!'

'You can't be from Earth. How did you get here?'

'That's not important at this particular time. All I need to know is will you tell me where he is please?'

'I can't tell you that. I'm not allowed to give out that kind of information to strangers!'

Gia enters the communication. 'Please tell Leila where the President is now. Where are you now?'

'I'm in the Presidential Hall. Why?'

'Good. We'll see you shortly.'

Leila asks. 'Gia, do you know where the Presidential Hall is?'

'Yes I do.'

'May I look into your mind, Gia?'

'Yes of course you can,' Gia replies.

'Right Gia and Óisin, please hold my hands!'

Óisin and Gia look at each other and nod.

The three of them hold hands in seconds they transport into the Great Hall, right next to Gia's friend.

'Leila, this is my friend Zea!'

'Nice to meet you, Zea I'm sorry if we frightened you but I need to see the President now, please.'

'How did you arrive here?'

'That does not matter at this time. Are you willing to tell me where I might meet the President, please?'

'No. I don't think I can. I would be in very serious trouble if I were to give you that information.'

Gia pleads with Zea. 'Please give Leila the information she needs.'

'But she is only a child. What can she do if I don't give her that information?'

'You don't want to challenge her! You're no match for her. She's too powerful for you,' Gia replies.

'I don't believe you. Where would she glean that technology from?'

'From me,' Gia replies.

Zea looks perplexed but is still of the opinion that she should not give Leila any information on the whereabouts of the President.

Leila looks at Zea. 'I don't need you now. I know where the President is. He's in his office, just reading. I think that you, Gia and Óisin and I will transport to his office.'

'How do you think you're going to do that?' He's surrounded with security guards. You will not be allowed through!'

'Can we all hold hands, please?' Leila enquires.

Gia places her hand in Zea's hand then all four of them hold hands together.

It only takes one second to reappear inside the President's office.

He is completely astounded and surprised by this intrusion into his office and calls the security guards but they are not able to open the office door. The President is shouting as loud as he can. He is running around like a headless chicken.

Leila waves her hand, places him in his chair and stops him from getting up. She walks over to him and says. 'Mr President. I don't have the time to play around, so I'll come straight to the point.'

Zea runs to protect his President but he is stationary and feels like a statue. He cannot move. The President is sweating copiously and he is very much afraid.

'Please, sir. Don't be afraid. I'm not here to hurt you. I'm here to help you. Gia and Óisin are my godparents. I'm from planet Earth and I'm very pleased to meet you.' She holds out her hand to the President. He takes Leila's hand and she says. 'I'm very happy to be in your world. Gia and Óisin will explain the situation to you if you're willing to listen!'

'Yes, yes of course. I'll pay attention,' the President replies. He invites them to sit down and relay to what he has just witnessed.

Gia and Óisin walk over to the President's desk and sit down.

Leila has put his mind at rest so he says. 'Okay Gia and Óisin, please tell me that I'm not dreaming?'

'No sir, you're not dreaming and yes this little girl is from Earth. As you know my great, great, great, grandfather, my father and I, have been working on a long-term project. We've been to planet Earth with the new technology and we've tested it on Leila as requested by the high commission guardians and signed by you, sir.'

'Yes I do remember and we were very excited to see if it was as good as you said it would be, but why are you in my office?'

'We were taken prisoners when we returned from the last voyage by the superior scientists of our department and here's the best part; we communicated with Leila from here to her world. She left Earth less than fifteen minutes ago! You do understand what I'm telling you sir? She didn't travel by spacecraft! She can dissolve into pure energy and travel anywhere she likes at whatever speed she needs!'

'That's amazing! I hope you're not trying to fool me. This child is from Earth?' He points to Leila. 'How advanced is she?'

'Her power is infinite. She could tear this world apart if she needed. Ask her to do something special for you, sir.'

The President looks at Leila and says. 'Show me something daring and out of this world?'

Leila walks to the President says. 'Sir, please hold my hand.'

The President holds out his hand. Leila grasps it firmly and in a twinkle of an eye, Leila transports them one hundred miles above the planet, cocooned in a shield with plenty of air to breathe, looking down on the President's planet.

Leila asks the President. 'What do you think, sir?'

'I don't know. This technology is way above anything our scientists can do. How good are you with this technology?'

'It's upgrading itself even as I speak, sir. I have to tell you that this technology is extremely dangerous. I would suggest that we should consider if it might be in the interest of all that you and I wipe it from Gia's Bio/Dna Quantum computer as soon as possible before other Aliens get their hands on it. There has been an attempt to abduct me on Earth on two occasions but I was able to stop them. I'm sure that there will be other attempts. Your two top scientists have tried to gain unlawful access to this technology. If I hadn't stopped them it would've been very serious.'

'Why did they want this technology? What were they going to do with it?'

'I think you should have those two scientists interrogated as soon as possible. There are other Alien races out there looking to dominate other people and Aliens. We don't want that to happen, sir. That would be very dangerous. I'm sure that you would not want that situation on your conscience. It could have a detrimental effect on the future of your planet and your people. I'll be the protector of your planet. As long as this technology is made safe and in secure hands, I could modify or make it impossible for anyone else to gain access from Gia's technology. I need to tell you that if this technology is hacked from Gia it can never be more powerful than me; I will then give up my interest in your planet. I'll only protect my planet if you and I can agree to make it impossible for other Aliens to steal it. Do I make myself clear, sir?'

'Yes I understand. I think that we should return to my office and discuss the situation with Gia and Óisin.'

'Good!' replies Leila.

President is back in his office in a flash.

Chapter 45

Back in the President's office, Gia and Óisin are waiting in anticipation of the President's ordeal. 'Where did Leila take you, sir? We'd like to know please. That is, if you don't mind?' they ask.

'We were in space, in orbit around our planet. We had a discussion on your technology and we decided to ask your advice on what to do with it. Would it be prudent to ask you if you would consider deleting this particular technology from your computers?'

Gia looks astonished, in fact totally bemused, and asks, 'Why?'

The President looks at Leila and suggests that she tells Gia her view of the technology.

'Please, Gia! This technology is very risky, as you know there have been two attempts to abduct me. It will happen again. You must be aware that it will happen. I can handle any situation with ease of course. There are your two scientist friends and they tried to extract this technology from you. The President and I decided in the interests of all humanity, it would be best to make this technology safe, unless we can come up with another solution by which we can protect Gia's technology, I will still protect your planet from all attempts to steal your technology. What do you think, Gia? You'll have to decide. It's your technology.'

'I don't know,' Gia replies. 'It's taken thousands of years to assemble this quite complex technology and I'm very reluctant to delete it from my computers.'

'What about you, Óisin? What are your thoughts on this dilemma?' the President asks.

'It would be very stupid to discard such advanced technology because it might fall into the hands of unscrupulous scientists or other Aliens. You can be sure that at some time the chances are it could be made to topple governments, planets and worlds, which could have a detrimental effect on this planet. There must be a way to keep this technology safe. Leila. What do you think we should do? You are the most advanced person in the Universe. You must have an idea how to protect this technology?' says Óisin.

'There is a way,' Leila replies. 'We can't allow this technology to be handed out indiscriminately throughout the Universe but we can place a dead end by which the formula can be made to scramble itself. We can send it in a loop twice then it shuts itself down. We can send it into dead mode and I can be the key. That way Gia's technology can be saved.'

'Gia, what's your thinking on Leila's proposal?' the President asks.

'I think that it's a very good idea, but how will we make it safe and secure?'

'I can do that.' Leila replies. 'It's very simple for me to place this in a secure mode Gia. I'll remotely look into your computer and make the necessary changes. Gia and Óisin will need to communicate with me when it's necessary to activate the technology. You'll need a security code when you make contact with me that will make this technology un-operational unless I make sure that it's safe. That code is now in your mind and the only one able to retrieve it is yourself. It's impossible for anyone to access it unless I allow it. If this is agreeable to all in this room then I think my mission here is finished. One other thing, it would not be a good thing having thousands of children in this Universe or any Universe with this technology for it would be abused it would cause very big problems. Thank you very much for your time and courtesy, Mr President. I hope to see you in the future, sir.' She goes over to him and gives him a big hug. Looks at Gia and Óisin, walks over to Gia first, she gives Gia a kiss and a big hug and says. 'I love you very much.' Then she gives Óisin a hug, steps back and she is gone.

'What a lovely child,' the President says.

'Yes sir. We agree,' Gia replies. 'What do we do with our scientists?'

'I'll deal with them. Don't worry,' the President replies. 'Right, you can return to your science lab and carry on with whatever is your choice. Keep me up to date on everything you do from now on. Is that clear?'

'Yes, sir,' replies Gia and Óisin.

'Off you go then!'

Leila is returning to Planet Earth and she is wondering if she has done the right thing with Gia's technology. She decides not to return to her school but go home to her mum where she materializes in her front sitting room. She hears her mum in the kitchen cooking so she calls mum and says. 'I'm home, mum!'

Into the sitting room Ciera rushes, saying. 'I'm so glad you're back. I was nearly out of my mind worrying about you!'

'I'm sorry, mum, but Gia and Óisin were in very serious trouble so I had to go and release them from their captors. I did meet the President of their world. He's a nice person, a tall man pleasant and very good-looking. The only thing; I had to dematerialise in the headmaster's office and I think I might've frightened him. I'll fix that tomorrow when I return to school. I had no choice. I had to go, mum. Please understand.'

'I do understand. I know that you were not showing off. It was an emergency, so we'll say no more about it, as long as you talk to the headmaster in the morning and make him understand that the world is not ready to receive you yet.'

'Yes, mum. Can I have something to eat please? I'm very hungry.'

'Of course you can. I'll do something special for you.'

Mum goes back into the kitchen, makes a pizza, places it on a plate, and takes it into the sitting room, 'Look, I made a pizza for you, Leila.'

Leila looks up says. 'Thank you, mum. I do appreciate you very much and I do love you and dad.'

'I know; Leila and we love you too! Mum replies. 'Have you any homework from school?'

'No mum. I'll do it tomorrow when I see the headmaster. I'm sure he'll understand the circumstances. I think he is confused and amused by all this technology. I don't think anyone will believe him.' He'll not want to look a fool so he'll keep his mouth closed. I'm very tired, mum, so if you don't mind I'll go to bed.'

'Goodnight dear. I'll see you in the morning,' mum replies.

The next morning Leila is up nice and early, has a shower, gets dressed, goes down the stairs into the sitting room.

Mum is already making breakfast so she asks Leila. 'Can I make you some breakfast, Leila?'

'Yes please, mum. Can I have some cornflakes and coffee thank you, mum?' Leila is contemplating what she is going to say to the headmaster.

'There you are. Please don't let it go cold.'

Dad arrives at the table and enquires: 'Well young lady, what have you been up to?'

'Not a lot dad, just helping out Gia and Óisin.'

'Good. You're not giving me any information. Can you elaborate a bit more so that I can assimilate something in my mind about where you've been?'

Leila looks at her dad and says, 'I've been to the Physerus Galaxy which is a very long way from here.'

'How did you get there?' Dad enquires.

'That was very easy,' Leila replies.

'You're not telling me a lot about your adventure.'

'I'm sorry, Dad. I didn't mean to ignore you,' Leila replies.

'I'm your dad and I'm very interested in anything you do, so please give me a little more information.'

'As you know, I'm able to do anything I like, so to help Gia and Óisin I changed into pure energy. I can travel at any speed I like, ten times faster than the speed of light. I know in your mind that's impossible but it's true, dad. Speed's not a problem for me. You do understand, Dad?'

'I don't know. It sounds impossible but if you say you can do these speeds, I believe you.'

'Dad, let me show you something. Hold my hand, please. We'll be back very soon, Mum. Don't worry.' She winks her eye.

Dad places his hand in Leila's hand in a split second the two of them are in orbit above the Earth cocooned in a shield and with plenty of air. Dad hangs onto Leila and says. 'Are we safe up here?'

'Yes, of course we are. I just wanted you to see the power I have. I didn't do this to frighten you. I wanted you to understand how far I've come with Gia's technology. What do you think of the view up here?'

'It's quite frightening. Can we go back to the house now, please?

'Sure,' Leila replies. In the twinkling of an eye, they are back in their house.

Ciera asks dad, 'How did you like your trip?'

He looks at her and says. 'I enjoyed it very much. It was very interesting but intimidating to say the least.' He has a little smile to himself.

'Good. Now what would you like for your breakfast dear?'

'I think I'll have two slices of bacon, one egg, and one sausage and coffee.'

'Mother turns and walks into the kitchen. After about five minutes, she returns with dad's breakfast, 'There you are. Don't let it go cold!'

'Thank you,' dad replies.

Leila finishes her breakfast, takes her cup and dish and walks to the kitchen, gives her mum a hug and a kiss then picks up her school bag and lunch. 'Bye mum. I'll walk to school today if you don't mind.'

Mum looks at her and says. 'Are you sure you want to walk to school, Leila?'

'Yes, mum. I'll be fine. Don't worry!'

As Leila walks into her school playground, her teacher sees her.

She tells Leila that the headmaster would like to see her as soon as she arrives inside the school grounds

'Yes, Miss,' says Leila. 'I'll go and see him now.'

'I'll take you,' says the teacher. 'Follow me!' She walks into the corridor and down to the headmaster's office, knocks on the office door and they both wait.

The door opens. The headmaster is standing there and says. 'Thank you. I'll take it from here. Come in, Leila, and please sit down. Can I talk to you about yesterday, please?'

'Yes of course you can. What would you like to talk about, sir?'

'Well, I'm a bit perplexed about yesterday. Could you explain what happened? Can you explain to me who you are and why you're in my school?'

'Why. Have I done something wrong, sir?'

'No,' the headmaster replies. 'You're not like other children, are you?'

'No sir. I know that I'm different from the other children, and I'm not able to provide you with any information, I'm authorized to tell you that my powers are infinite. Let me give you a demonstration of my powers.' She puts out her hand and says. 'Please place your hand in mine, sir. Don't be afraid.'

The headmaster duly obliges.

Leila enquires. 'Is there anywhere in the world you would like to see?'

I would love to see the Pyramids in Egypt,' the headmaster replies.

'Hold on tight, sir.' In a twinkle of an eye, the two of them have transported to Egypt, standing in front of the Pyramids.

The headmaster looks. 'Where are we now?'

'We're in Egypt, sir. Don't you recognize the Pyramids?'

'Well, I can see them. But are they real?'

'Yes, of course they're real. Touch them and see for yourself.'

Over he goes, touches the foot of one the Pyramids, looks back at Leila and says, 'Can this be true, Leila?'

'Yes sir. It's completely true. You're in Egypt, which was your wish. We must return now to the school because there's a teacher walking down the corridor to your office.'

In a flash the headmaster and Leila are back in his office.

The teacher knocks on the door and the headmaster goes and opens it, says. 'Yes, what can I do for you, teacher?'

'Just wondering when Leila is returning to her class, sir?'

'She'll be right there soon. I'll take her there myself, you can go now. What am I going to do with you, Leila? I can't negate what I've seen. It's too powerful a memory to ignore.'

'Don't worry, sir. Just take my hand, please.'

He again takes her hand all that he has witnessed today is now isolated from his mind.

Leila drops her hand.

The headmaster shakes his head and says. 'Now, Leila. What are you doing here?'

'You sent for me sir,' she replies.

'Did I? Well whatever you came for, I can't remember. So you can go back to your class.'

'Thank you, sir.' Leila walks out of his office, back to her class.

The headmaster is totally bemused. He is trying to remember something but he is not able to retrieve it from his mind. He speaks out talking to himself, 'Is it important? I don't think so. Otherwise I would remember, I think.'

Leila returns to her class.

Teacher asks. 'Is your mum all right, Leila?'

'Yes, she's fine now,' replies Leila.

Leila has just received a communication from her mum saying, 'Leila you have a new baby brother, see you when you come home.'

She is ecstatic and very excited. About one hour later she arrives home and the first thing she wants to do is see the baby. She rushes up the stairs into her mum's bedroom asking, 'Can I see the baby now please?'

'Yes of course you can, he is in the crib.

She is highly amused at this tiny little baby, she asks her mum, 'Was I as small as that?' as she touches the baby on the hand with her index finger and smiles.

'Yes you were, and a right little devil you were. You do like your little brother?'

'Yes of course I do but he is so small and fragile. May I pick him up?'

'Off course you can. Be very careful.'

Leila lifts the baby into her arms looks at him saying. He is lovely, very cute and cuddly. He looks very much like you mum.'

'Well I hope so. He is my flesh and blood, and yours as well, Leila. Okay place him back in his crib carefully and cover him up.'

'Can I hold him a little bit longer, mum, please?'

Mum looks Leila, decides to grant her little more time holding the baby.

'He's so lovely, so cute cuddly and warm, I want to hold him forever. What are you going to call him?'

'Well you picked your name, so dad and I thought 'Alfie might be a nice name.'

'Yes I think that's a nice name. Okay, that's it then. Alfie it is.' She places the baby back in his crib.

Chapter 46

Another year passes by and Leila is at university and is doing very well. She has made some nice friends and life is looking very good.

At one of her tutorial's her tutor says. 'I would like to discuss with you your progress in science and computers and world politics, Leila.'

'Yes of course, sir. When would you like to see me?'

'I'll see you in my study. Shall we say four this afternoon?'

'Yes, that will be fine, sir,' Leila replies and walks away. Out in the quad she finds a quiet spot and sits down to gather her thoughts. She has had no communication with Gia or Óisin for over a year and she is beginning to worry. She sends a communication asking if everything is okay. As time marches on, she receives a message from Óisin saying that Gia is dying, she is very sick and she is asking for you. Leila is now very worried and she is feeling sick because of Gia. She looks at her watch. It is nearly four o'clock. She has a meeting with her tutor in ten minutes so she decides to go early. At the tutor's door, she knocks, the door opens and it is her tutor.

'Come in, please, Leila, and sit down. I'd like to have a discussion with you about your progress here at university.'

She has not the time for a discussion now but in order to defer this meeting she will need a very delicate touch indeed. She decides to tell the tutor that she is not feeling well and could she make another appointment for tomorrow?

The tutor looks a bit bemused and says. 'Yes, we can make another appointment for tomorrow if you wish. Is that all right with you?'

'Yes sir. That will be lovely. Can I go now? I'm feeling a bit sick.'

'Yes of course you may go now. Don't forget I'll see you tomorrow afternoon. Goodbye, Leila.'

She cannot get out of there quickly enough. She is extremely worried about Gia and needs to go to her as soon as possible. The first thing she needs to do is communicate with her mum. She sends a communication to her mum saying: *'Gia is very sick and I need to go to her now mum. I don't know how long I'll be away. If I'm not back for university tomorrow will you please phone my tutor tell him that I'm not very well and I'll catch up with my studies when I'm back. Thank you, mum See you soon.'*

Chapter 47

Leila is on her way to the Physerus Galaxy. Ten minutes in space and she is almost there. She makes contact with Óisin and lets him know that she will be on his planet in about five minutes. Five minutes later and she is in orbit above the planet. She contacts Óisin again, marks his position and drops down to where he is waiting. She materializes next to him, does not surprise him and says: 'Okay! Hold my hand!' At the same time, she probes his mind to find out where Gia is. In a twinkling of an eye, the two of them are standing next to Gia's bed. Leila bends down and whispers in Gia's ear. 'Don't worry. I'll look inside you and see what the problem is and fix it.'

Gia looks up, starts to cry and hugs Leila, saying. 'I'm dying. I don't think you can do anything for me but I'm glad you're here with me.'

Leila places both arms around Gia and holds her tight. She looks inside her body then decides to make her better. As she is holding Gia, the whole room lights up in brilliant colours. There is an exchange of energy from Leila to Gia. It takes about one minute then the lights dim back down. Leila is still holding Gia. The wonder of wonders has happened.

Gia looks at Leila and says, 'I feel absolutely fine now. How did you do that, Leila?'

'I only used the technology you gave me. You'll be fine in the morning, just rest.'

Óisin is overwhelmed with emotion and is beside himself with happiness. He goes over and hugs Gia, then turns and hugs Leila. He starts to cry.

Leila wipes the tears from his face and says, 'That's what this technology is all about and that's why I'm here. I couldn't let Gia die. Not when I'm able to make her better.'

One of the doctors arrives at the bedside of Gia and enquires, 'What is going on here? Gia, may I ask what's happened to you? You don't look sick now. You look positively fine. How did you do that?'

'Let me introduce you to Leila. Leila, this is my doctor. He's not privy to your powers and he's very, shall we say, perplexed. He's trying to figure out what's happened to me. He's never been in the presence of someone with such awesome power but I'm sure he's happy now that I'm better. He doesn't understand what's happened but I'm sure he'll figure it out sometime in the future.'

There is a lot of commotion in the corridor.

At the entrance to the ward are three burly men. They are pushing everyone out of the way. They walk over to Gia's bed and push Leila out of the way. That is a big mistake.

Leila waves her hand the three of them are back against the wall and are motionless to it. She walks over to the three men, looks at them and says. 'If you ever do that to me again I'll make you feel a lot of pain.'

In walks the President. He goes straight over to Gia's bed and asks; 'Are you alright, Gia?' He then looks at Leila, saying. 'I know you! Leila, is it you?'

'Yes sir. It's me I was in your office about one year ago.'

'Gia now first things first, I understood that you were very sick and dying.' He waves his hands about. 'But you look fine to me.'

'I know, sir. Remember when Leila was here the last time I told you about her powers. Well it would appear that she has the power to heal sick people and that's what she has done for me. She has done me proud?'

'Wonderful!' replies the President. 'I was hoping for a miracle. Leila has given us one. I'm so happy I could cry!'

'Please, sir. We've had enough crying for today but don't let me stop you.'

'Well, Leila. How have you been since the last time I saw you how are things back on Earth?'

'Not too bad at the moment but I'm expecting some problems soon.'

'I'm sure you'll be able to resolve them. You're a very well balanced person indeed,' the President replies. 'Now, Leila, may I have my security people back, please?'

'Yes of course you can. Please teach them some manners. I might not be so friendly the next time I meet them! Leila replies. She raises her hand, releases the security people from the wall and they fall to the ground.

They rise up and pretend that nothing happened to them.

One of the security people is not so forgiving. He walks over to Leila and says. 'You try that stunt again and I'll kill you!' He looks down at Leila.

Leila looks up and thinks to herself, 'What an idiot.' I could destroy him in a second.'

The President runs over, faces his security person and says. 'Get out of here! I'll deal with you later!' He then turns to Leila and says: 'I'm so sorry. It will not happen again.'

Leila is quite baffled by the President's intervention. He knows that they are no match against Leila, but is quite happy to let it pass on this occasion. 'Gia, Óisin, Mr President. I must take my leave of you now.' In a flash, Leila is on her way to Earth.

Chapter 48

Leila arrives home late that evening and dad and mum are waiting for her. She arrives in the sitting room and sees mum asleep. Dad is watching television. She goes to dad and gives him a big hug saying. 'I'm sorry, dad. I know that I'm a bit late. It was very important. I went to see Gia for she was very sick and I needed to make her better. Everyone was crying but she's fine now. Óisin was in a terrible way. He thought that Gia was going to die. He was very surprised that I was able to make her better. The President came to see her when I was in the hospital and he was very pleasant and considerate; a very nice person.'

Then Leila's mum wakes up and is startled seeing Leila standing near her. She jumps up, gives Leila a very big hug and a kiss and says. 'I'm glad you're home. I know I shouldn't be worried about you but I can't help it. You're my flesh and blood and I love you dearly.'

Leila asks. 'Could I have something to eat please, mum? I'm very hungry. I've had nothing to eat all day.'

'Of course, let me make you something special,' her mum replies. She gets up and goes to the kitchen.

'Well Leila. You're having a wonderful time going about the Galaxy. Does anything go through your mind?' dad enquires.

'What do you mean, dad?' asks Leila.

'Just wondering how you're going to cope when the time comes for you to make your entrance to the world.'

'I don't think that will be a problem for me. I'm not going to be distracted from carrying out my future with the technology that Gia has given me. You wouldn't want me to stop what I'm doing now, would you dad?'

Dad replies, 'Of course I'm not trying to dissuade you. Your future is already pledged. You are the selected one for this particular vocation. The world will need your intelligence and guidance and who am I to interfere?' All I can do is to be ready if and when you need your family to help you.'

'Thank you, dad, I know the family will not let me down!'

Mum arrives with some food and says, 'There you are, Leila, some nice sandwiches and coffee for you. I hope you like them. They're your favourite food. I'll leave you two together. I'm going to bed. I'll see you in the morning. Good night, Leila, good night, dad!'

'What are you going to do tomorrow?' Leila's dad asks.

'I've some catching up to do in the morning and in the afternoon I'm due to see my tutor at four. I know what he's going to say but I'll pretend to listen to him very carefully and look as if I'm interested.'

'You be careful. We don't want any silly little episodes that you might need to explain at university, especially now. We don't want anyone to see your technological ability yet.'

'Yes I know, dad,' replies Leila. 'I'll be very careful and alert from now on. Anyway, I can remove any indiscretions from people's minds.'

'Yes, I know but, you have to remember, walls have ears and there are lots of places with hidden listening apparatus, especially in universities.'

'I know, dad. I can detect anything out of the ordinary,' Leila replies.

'I'm only trying to make you focus on the future. All you need is one mistake in the wrong place and then the papers and television will be knocking on our door asking questions about you. We don't want that, do we, Leila?'

'No we do not dad. Don't worry. I'll be very careful from now on. I'm very tired now so I'll say good night. I'll see you in the morning.' Leila goes up the stairs into her bedroom, gets ready, falls into her bed and is asleep as soon as her head hits the pillow.

Chapter 49

Morning arrives and Leila is awake. She decides to have a shower and a change of clothes, goes down the stairs to the kitchen. 'What can I have for breakfast today? I know I'll have some crunchy nuts and fruit for a change.'

Upstairs there is a rumbling in mum's bedroom and it is not long before she arrives in the kitchen and says. 'Good morning, Leila. Did you have a good sleep last night?'

'Yes, mum. I was very tired after my journey across the Galaxy. Poor Gia, she looked very sad, very sick and pitiful. She knew she was dying. I think that she thought she was dreaming when I arrived because she was very surprised when she opened her eyes looked at me and started crying. It was very sad but I was able to make her better. She sends her love to you and dad. Poor Óisin, he was in a bad way. I don't think he was in full control of his faculties. He was very quiet, not his usual self. I think he had convinced himself that she did not have long to live. There was nothing he could do to help her until I arrived. He was quite shocked after I'd given her a big hug and made her better. He cried uncontrollably for a while and I gave him a big hug as well. Mum, I must go now or I'll be late for class at the university.' Before you could blink an eye, she is gone. She arrives early, so she decides to materialise in the girls' changing room but unknown to her there is one girl in one of the changing cubicles. She sees a flash of bright light and then Leila is standing in front of her. She panics starts to scream and shout so Leila goes and holds her hand, looks at her and wipes her memory.

She looks up.

Leila says, 'You had a bad turn so I came to help you. Are you all right now?'

'Yes I'm fine. I don't know what happened to me!' replies the girl.

Leila asks. 'Are you sure you're all right?'

'Yes, I'm okay now,' she replies. 'I must go now or I'll be late for my class. Thank you very much.' Off she goes.

'My, that was a close one. I must be more careful in the future!' Leila says to herself as she walks out of the girls' changing room.

Leila joins her class for politics. She is quite bored but she perseveres.

The tutor says, 'That's all for today, thank you, class.'

She has a little time before she goes to lunch, so she sits under a tree and contemplates her future. The problem is she knows her future is going to be very hectic, but will she be able to fulfil her destiny? She says to herself, 'Stop dreaming and go to lunch.' Up she gets, walks to the restaurant, has a light lunch, then goes to the library, picks out a science book and reads it just to keep her mind going until her next class, which is computer science that lasts for one hour. She meets up with some friends and the usual girly talk is about boys. Leila does not need to participate in this conversation so she wanders off.

It is almost time to see her science tutor and to be on time for her four o'clock appointment. She makes her way to the tutor's study, knocks at his door and waits. Half a minute passes and the door opens it is another girl coming out she smiles at Leila and walks away.

Her tutor says. 'Leila, please come in and sit down.'

Leila feels duly obliged to obey and sits down.

Her tutor's name is Ian Mumford. He is a medium size person: plump, going bald and a bit scruffy, not at all attractive. He certainly has no attraction for Leila whatsoever. She senses that all is not as it seems. However, she is here to have a talk about her scientific ability, what she has in mind when she leaves university.

'Now, please call me Ian, Leila. That's more informal.'

'Yes sir. I mean, Ian.'

'Well, I'd like to talk to you about your future in science. Science is a very interesting subject. It would appear that you're doing very well and I think you'll excel when you sit your final exams. You seem be able to learn very quickly.' He looks at her very intently and says. 'I was just wondering; you seem to be able to digest all the science I throw at you. Perhaps you can explain to me how you do that?'

'I don't know. Perhaps it's just a gift I have,' Leila replies.

'I'm not so sure. You're so far ahead of your class that even I'm finding it hard to keep up with you. How do you explain that to me, Leila?'

'As I said, sir, I mean Ian. Maybe, it's a gift.'

'I'm not so sure. I think you're keeping something from me. I don't know what it is but I'll be watching your progress with anticipation to see what the future brings for you. I have to say, I think that you're a very gifted young woman. Anyway, I wish you good luck for your future and I hope you achieve whatever you feel is your future.'

'Thank you, Ian. I hope I can be a credit to this university and its long tradition of excellence.'

'You may go now, Leila. I'll see you tomorrow morning and I still think that you're keeping something from me!'

'Goodbye for now, Ian. I'll see you in the morning.' He just looks at her, wondering what she is going to be when she grows up, picks up his books and places them in his case.

Leila goes out of the door, down the hall, into the quad and breathes a sigh of relief. She says to herself. 'That was very close.

I'll need to keep an eye on him. He's getting a bit too close and too inquisitive.'

Chapter 50

For the next three years, Leila is very happy with her life and her education. She is well versed in all her subjects and her tutors are all of the opinion that she is a very intelligent, gifted young woman. It is May 10th, and all the exams for Leila's year have started. Her exams will start on the eleventh at eight in the morning; three hours for each exam. She proceeds to the examination room and sits down, and she waits for her examination papers to be placed in position on her desk. This time she receives two lots of exam papers: science and computers. She looks at the questions in science; well no problem there. Then she looks at the computer questions. These are very easy questions. She will just bide her time and pretend she is thinking about the answers.

It is nearly two in the afternoon, the exam time is nearly up, so she finishes her answers, walks to the exam desk and hands the exam papers in. 'That was very easy,' she says to herself. 'I've one more this afternoon which starts at three this is a three hour exam.' She communicates with her mum and tells her that the exams were very easy.

'Good for you, Leila. I know you'll excel in all of your exams.'

'I hope so,' replies Leila. 'I'm doing one more this afternoon. When I've finished I'll contact you.'

'I think you'll fly through the exams, no problem whatsoever. Don't forget to let me know when you've finished.'

'Of course I'll be in touch. I don't expect any problems, however, one never knows. I must go now, mum. I'm a bit hungry, incidentally. I'll be home tonight.' She goes to the restaurant, picks up a light meal, then goes and sits down with one of her friends. She asks, 'Did you finish your exam papers this morning?'

Leila replies: 'I think I answered all the questions and I hope that they're all right. How about you? Did you answer all of your questions?'

'Yes. I answered all of them. The question is did I give the right answers? We'll see when I receive my results.'

Now she has about thirty minutes before her next exam that is in politics. She goes back to the restaurant, picks up a coffee and sits down. Now she has to pass the time away and it is irritating her a little bit. Mr Mumford enters the restaurant and sees Leila. He buys a coffee and decides to join her. 'Leila, may I sit with you?'

'Yes of course you can, sir. I mean, Ian.'

'Did you have any problems with your exam papers?'

'I don't think so,' Leila replies. 'I was able to answer all the questions on both papers. I think I've done all right. My last exam is in ten minutes.'

'Which exam paper is that, Leila?'

'The politics paper, Ian. I should be all right with that!'

'I'm sure you will. You've a wonderful mind and I'm sure that you'll pass all the exams with flying colours.'

'Thank you, Ian. That's very nice of you. I need to go now. I've just about ten minutes left to walk to the exam rooms.' Leila rises out of the chair, walks out of the restaurant and proceeds to where she is taking her last exam. She enters the hall, then walks into the exam room, finds a table, sits down waits for her exam papers to be placed on her desk, she glances at them but does not touch them.

On the dot of three one of the tutors stands up and says, 'Class this exam has a time limit of two hours, you can start now and good luck!'

Leila has a good look at her papers, and decides to press on with the answers but does not hurry them. She spreads out the time to ninety minutes, finishes the answers, gets up from the table, walks to the exam desk, hands the exam papers in walks out of the examination room. Outside in the quad, she contacts her mum and says. 'I've finished all the exams and I think I've answered all the questions right, mum.'

'Very good I knew you would be all right. There was no question in my mind that you'd be able to answer the exam paper questions right. I'm over the moon for you. Love you very much. See you in a little while.'

'I must honour my life's mission, mum. I know that it will be very complicated. I'll need to start that part of my life soon. I feel that I'm almost ready to intervene in world politics. We'll talk about that when I return home. See you later, mum.'

At dinner that evening, Leila has a long talk with her mum and dad about her future. She tells her parents that the time is near when she will participate in talks with world leaders but first she asks. 'It might be nice to have a family holiday before my exam results arrive in the ninth month of the Gregorian calendar.'

'Of course, your mum can arrange it all,' replies dad. 'I'll arrange to have time off work as long as I book the time off with my immediate boss.'

'Good. Shall we agree on the dates now?' Leila enquires.

'Yes of course we can,' replies dad.

'Can we go to somewhere hot and sunny, please?' Leila enquires.

'Yes, I think so,' replies mum. 'I'll go to the travel agent in the morning if that's all right with dad and you and book the holiday.'

'That's fine,' replies dad. 'Leila and I will leave it in your hands, mother.'

'Okay. I'll go to the travel agent and book the holiday. I'm looking forward to our holiday already,' replies mum.

'Yes, I'm looking forward to it as well,' replies Leila.

'And me as well,' dad says.

'Alright then I'll need to call Alfie for his dinner then I'm going bed. I'm a bit tired, so I'll have an early night. See you two in the morning.'

'Good night dear!' dad replies.

'Good night, mum,' replies Leila as well.

The next morning, Leila is up early, goes down to the kitchen, has some breakfast and contemplates her future. She knows that she will have a very difficult time soon but is looking forward to the challenge.

Dad walks into the kitchen.

'I didn't hear you come down the stairs, dad.'

'Well, I didn't know you were in the kitchen. Anyway, you're up early. Is there something wrong?'

'No dad. I was just talking to myself about my future and what I might be doing this time next year.'

'I'm sure you'll be fine,' dad replies. 'You're now a very powerful young lady, tall, very good-looking with lovely blonde/Red golden hair. I'm sure that you'll always do the right thing and be a credit to your family.'

'I know that dad, but how do I figure out the good from the bad?'

'I don't think you'll have a problem there. Your technology will see you through any quandary that might come up. You will be the envy and desire by a most of world leaders and they'll try to dissuade you with all kinds of useless information, try to make you look ordinary and stupid. I think you'll be more then able to put them in their places. Anyway, there's no one on this Earth with your technology.'

'You're right dad,' Leila replies. 'Anyway, I think I'll go with mum this morning and help with the holiday booking. I've finished university now, with nothing to do today I'll suggest that I'd like to help with the holiday booking, I'm sure she'll agree.'

'Good idea,' dad replies. 'I must go now. I don't want to be late for work.' He rises up from the table, gets his coat, gives Leila a kiss on the cheek, goes out the front door, into his car and drives to work.

Leila is still in the kitchen when her mum and Alfie arrive in the kitchen. She says. 'Good morning, Leila. You're up early, is there something wrong?

'I was just wondering if I might come with you when you go to book the holiday this morning. Is that all right with you?'

'Yes, we can do a little bit of shopping in town after we've booked the holiday and have lunch as well. I'll need to feed Alfie and get him ready. Then I'll have a bit of breakfast.'

'Good. I'll go and have a shower and get ready,' Leila replies. Shower finished, she gets dressed, walks down the stairs into the kitchen.

Mum asks. 'Are you ready?'

'Yes, I'm ready.' As she looks at Alfie, he puts his hands out for Leila to pick him up. She turns to her mum and asks. 'Is it all right for me to pick him up?'

'Of course you can. You can take him out to the car and put him in his seat. I'll follow you out in a moment.'

'Come on Alfie let's take you out to the car.' She lifts him out of the seat and proceeds out the front door, opens the rear door of the car, places Alfie in the back seat, goes and sits in the car and waits for her mum.

Ciera looks around to make sure that all the windows and back door are secure then checks the gas cooker to make sure that it is safe. She walks to the front door, pulls the front door behind her making sure that it is secure and locked. She goes to the driver's side of the car, sits in, and drives away. In town, she goes to the car park, drives in, takes a ticket from the machine parks the car, goes round to where Alfie is, takes the seat belt off, lifts him out of the seat, places him in the buggy and locks the car. 'Right, Leila. Now we can go and book our holiday.'

'I'm all excited, mum. We're going to have a nice holiday!'

'Not yet. We'll need to phone your dad with the dates while we're in the travel agents to make sure he'll be able to have those dates off.'

In the travel agent's they look at all the brochures.

'Now let's see what the girl can tell us.' Mum looks at the name on her lapel and it reads 'Fiona'.

Fiona says 'May I help you?'

'Yes, please!' mum replies. 'We'd like to have a holiday in Spain if you'd help us, please.'

'Yes, of course I'll help you,' Fiona replies. 'So let me see. A holiday in Spain would be your preferred holiday. Well, there are other places that are just as good nice and hot that is if you would like me to point them out to you.'

'Yes, please! What would have you in mind?' mum asks.

Fiona looks at Ciera and points out holidays in Egypt or perhaps the Crimea. 'That's a very nice place, nice sandy beaches, plus lovely people. Hot and sunny, plus it's very reasonably priced.'

'What do you think, Leila? Which one do you think is the best one?'

'Well I like the sound of Crimea. Could you give us some prices please?' Leila enquires.

'We can do an all in package in the beginning of July to Crimea.' Fiona writes down some dates. 'There are some dates for you to think over. When will you let me know if you would like to make a firm booking?'

'If you can wait a few minutes I'll phone my husband. Is that all right with you?' Ciera replies. Ciera says to Leila. 'You look after Alfie while I go outside to phone your dad to tell him the dates and ask him if it's all right to book the holiday.' Outside she phones her husband.

He answers his phone and says, 'Yes dear? What's wrong?'

'Nothing, John. We're in the travel agents at the moment and I have some dates for the holiday.'

'Okay! First, where are we going on holiday?'

'Well, we'd like to go to the Crimea.'

'Okay. What are the dates?' 'The beginning of July would be a nice time for our holiday.'

'You just book and I'll make sure to get those dates.'

'Fine then I'll go back, and do the booking for the beginning of July.' She goes back inside, and tells Fiona that those dates will be fine. 'Please may we pay now?'

'Yes of course you can. How will you be paying?'

'With a Debit Visa please,'

Fiona takes the card from Ciera places it in the machine and says. 'Please put your pin number in. Can I have your address please, to send you the tickets next week with all the information you will need. Thank you very much. You have a nice holiday. Goodbye Mrs Carney.'

'That was easy,' says Ciera. 'Right, Leila. You take Alfie. I'll open the door for you.'

'Can we go and have some lunch? I'm hungry now. Let's find a snack bar and have something nice to eat.'

'Yes of course,' Ciera replies. 'Alfie must be hungry as well.'

Walking along the street, Leila spots what looks like a nice place so she says to her mum. 'This will do nicely.'

In they go; find a table sit down and look at the menu.

The waiter comes to the table and asks. 'Are you ready to order?'

'Yes we are.' Ciera orders a salad and Leila orders fish and chips. Mum orders chips for Alfie.

The waiter asks. 'Would you like to order your drinks now?'

'I'll have a cup of coffee. Leila, what would you like?'

'I'll have coffee as well and a glass of orange for the little one, please.'

Ten minutes go by and the waiter arrives with the lunch and chips for Alfie. 'Enjoy your meal!'

'Thank you,' Ciera replies. She places Alfie in the chair and places his chips in front of him. 'There you are, Alf. Help yourself!'

Leila has started her lunch so mum starts hers as well.

The waiter arrives back at the table. 'Your coffees and the orange,' he places them on the table.

Mum gives Alfie his orange, takes her coffee pours the milk into her coffee and Leila's then says. 'I'm going to enjoy this lunch.'

Fifteen minutes later, lunch finished, mum goes to pay at the desk and thanks the waiter for the service. She walks back to the table, takes Alfie out of the chair and walks out into the street with Leila following behind. 'What shall we do now, Leila?'

'Can we buy some holiday clothes?'

'Yes of course. Let's have a look in shops and see what we might need,' mum replies.

Two hours pass they arrive back at their car.

Mum places the parking ticket in the machine and waits to see how much needs to be paid. She places the money in the slot and retrieves the ticket, walks to the car and places all the shopping in the boot. She places Alfie in his seat, goes and sits in the driver's seat.

Leila sits in the passenger seat.

Mum starts the car and drives out of the car park, stating, 'I'm shattered. I think we've had a lovely day so far buying nice clothes for the holiday. What more can you ask for?'

'Leila, may I ask you a silly question?'

'The answer's no, mum. I'm not interested in boys at this moment. I don't know why you ask, you know I can read your mind when you're about to ask me one of those silly questions!'

'I'm sorry, Leila. I didn't mean to question you. I'm sure that if it happens, you'll tell me.'

'Yes of course I'll tell you, mum,' Leila replies.

'We're home now. I think dad will be happy with the holiday we've booked,' says mum.

'I'm sure he'll be happy,' Leila replies.

They arrive back home. Leila asks, 'Would you like a coffee mum?'

'Yes, I'd love one please.'

'I'll make two cups,' Leila replies

Five minutes go by and John comes in the front door, walks into the sitting room and looks around and says: 'Good evening everyone. And how is my dear Alfie?'

He picks him up and gives him a big cuddle, then looks at Leila and says. 'Leila come and let me give you a cuddle. I love you as well.

Mum walks into the sitting room and says. 'John, your dinner is on the table in the dining room. Go and eat it before it goes cold, please.'

'Leila what are you and Alfie having for dinner?'

'We had our dinner in town. John, when you've finished your dinner, would you place all the plates and knives and forks in the dishwasher machine. John, will you sort out some holiday clothes for yourself, when you have finished that little task, thank you.'

'I shouldn't need a lot as it's going to be very hot. It's great to be going away for a week. Work's driving me crazy. I'll be glad to get away for a while. Are you excited, Leila?'

'Yes of course I'm excited. We'll have a great time as a family,' Leila replies. 'I'm looking forward to our holiday very much and I know that mum's looking forward to it as well!'

Ciera sits down and says; 'I'm shattered! I'm going to bed. I need a rest. See you in the morning, Leila.' She takes Alfie with her, walks up the stairs. Goes into her bedroom, places Alfie in his bed and gets herself ready for bed

Fifteen minutes later John arrives in the bedroom and says, 'I'll just have a quick shower and come to bed. I could do with an early night as well.'

It is not long before Leila walks up the stairs to bed,

Chapter 51

The next six days go quickly. The day of departure arrives, the luggage is placed in the booth of the car, the travel tickets and insurance cover for the holiday are in Ciera's handbag. The Carney family, including granddad and grandma, are on their way to the airport. They decided to book and to accompany their son and his family. This is the first time this section of the family will be together for this holiday. Dad has a parking space booked; he drives the car to the appropriate parking bay, gets out, opens the boot, removes the entire luggage and places it on a trolley, goes in search of the check-in desk, waits his turn to check in.

Next thing is to go to the passport control. They go through into duty-free area where mum and Leila do a little bit of shopping. Then into the departure lounge to the gate on the boarding pass, wait until the gate to the plane is opened passports and passes checked. They then go into the aircraft, find their seats, place hand luggage in the compartment above their seats and sit down.

'Everybody okay?' dad asks.

'Yes, we're all fine now, dad,' Ciera replies.

'What about Leila? Is everything all right with you?'

'I'm fine just very excited,' Leila replies.

'This is a big plane though not as big as...?'

Leila looks at dad and whispers: 'I know what you're going to say. Please refrain from uttering it.'

'Sorry I got carried away,' dad replies. 'I'll be more careful from now on!'

'I'd hope so,' Leila replies as she looks at him in a very irritating way.

'Right then you two settle down,' says mum. 'We've a four hour journey in front of us and I need to relax, so please be quiet!'

The four hours pass very quickly and the plane is about to land at Simferopol Airport. Mum wakes up and so does Alfie.

Leila is already awake, so is dad. He says 'I'm very excited. We're going to have a fabulous time!'

The plane stops, the door opens and everyone walks down the steps to the bus go inside and wait until it is full. The doors close and off they go. The bus takes them to the entrance of the passport control and there they wait their turn to give their passports to the passport control officer. He scans them and lets them through to the luggage department where they wait for their cases to come through.

Dad says, 'I can see our luggage.' He goes, takes them off the conveyor belt, places them on a trolley and asks. 'Have we got everything?'

'I think so,' replies grandmother. 'We had four cases plus our hand luggage.'

'Let's go out to the front of the terminal and find out which bus is going to take us to our Liana Holiday Hotel in Koktebel.' Dad goes in search of their courier, finds her and asks. 'Which bus are we on please?'

The courier asks. 'Please let me see your paperwork. You're going to The Liana Hotel in Koktebel?'

'That's right which bus takes us there?' asks dad.

'Come with me and I'll show you the one you'll be on,' replies the courier.

The Carney family pick up their luggage and follow the courier to the bus.

'There you are! This is your transport to your hotel,' says the courier. 'Have a nice holiday!'

The driver places their luggage on the bus.

Dad and the family board the bus find a seat and sit down.

The driver gets in the driver's seat and drives away.

'All this travelling is boring me. I could transport us to our hotel now,' says Leila.

'Now, Leila! You must keep your thoughts to yourself,' replies mum.

'I know, mum. I'm sorry but it's so frustrating for me, all this waiting around for things to happen when I can do it instantly.'

'I know but you must be very careful especially in the company of people. They'll not understand. So please, be a little understanding.'

'You're right, mum. I'll try to be careful but it's demanding considerable effort to keep myself from doing anything. However, I'll be careful and subdue my inner thoughts.'

Mum is having a hard time trying to keep Alfie occupied. He can be a little devil and very boisterous at times. 'Alfie, will you please stop running around and sit down!'

Eventually they arrive at their hotel, alight from the bus, pick out their luggage and go into the reception area. They hand their paperwork to the receptionist who allocates them their rooms. A young man takes their luggage and says. 'Please follow me.' The family follow him to their allocated apartment in the complex. He opens the doors, takes the luggage inside and says. 'Please have a nice holiday.' He walks out the door and back to reception.

'Okay. I think we should take all our clothes out of our cases before we do anything else,' says mum. 'And place them in the wardrobe and in the clothes cabinet. So come on.' Everyone, unpacked as fast as they could, and the boring job was completed.

Are all the clothes put away?' dad asks.

'Yes,' mum replies.

'Shall we go and find the restaurant for some food?'

'Good idea,' says Leila. 'I'm hungry!'

'I'm hungry too,' Alfie replies.

'Well that's a first,'

They walk to reception. 'Where is the restaurant?' dad enquires.

'Just turn round. It's behind you, sir and its open,' the receptionist says.

'Thank you.' As he turns around he says, 'Follow me!' He walks into the restaurant, finds a table and the family sit down

A waiter arrives at the table and informs them that it is help yourself. 'So feel free to go and select your food.' He indicates with his hand in the direction of the food.

Food selected they return to their table and sit down.

Dad says. 'This food is excellent. I think we'll enjoy ourselves here!'

'Yes, I agree,' replies Leila. 'The food is plentiful and very good. Mum, what about you?'

'It's lovely, very fresh and nicely cooked!'

'Alfie, do you like your food?' enquires dad.

Alfie looks at dad. He does not say a word, just carries on playing with it.

'Alfie, will you please stop playing with your dinner! Eat it!' says mum.

He does not take a blind bit of notice, just pretends to eat.

Granddad and grandmother arrive in the restaurant together, walk over to John's table and ask, 'May we sit at your table please?'

'The food is very good here,' says Ciera. 'You just go and help yourselves. We'll wait until you've finished your dinner.'

Dinner finished, they arise from the table, have a quick look around the hotel and decide, as it's late, to go to their apartments and go to bed as it has been a long day.

Chapter 52

Next morning Mum is up early as Alfie is already awake. She gives him a quick shower, kits him out in some of his holiday clothes but as usual Alfie is not in a cooperative mood this morning. He just wants to get out and play.

Mum is nearly exasperated when Leila walks into the room, takes Alfie by the hand and looks into his eyes. Then she lets go and a remarkable transformation comes over Alfie.

'What did you do, Leila?' mum asks. 'That's a secret between Alfie and me. Don't worry! He's fine!' She looks at mum and smiles.

'Are you sure you've done nothing to Alfie?' enquires mum as she looks at Leila in a very curious way but does not say a word. She knows that Leila would not do anything that might have an effect on Alfie's brain. 'I'm sure you wouldn't do anything to Alfie, so let's forget it.'

'Mum, don't worry. Alfie's the same now as he was before. I held his hand and he'll do what you ask him to do in the future but he'll still be a naughty boy,' Leila replies.

Dad walks in and asks, 'What's going on here?'

'Nothing,' says mum, 'just Alfie being his usual self!'

'Okay. Are we ready for breakfast?'

'Yes we are,' replies mum. 'John, can you go and see if your mum and dad are ready to come to breakfast please!'

John goes and knocks on his dad's door.

His dad opens it and says. 'We're ready for breakfast. We'll see you in the restaurant in five minutes!' They wait for granddad and grandma to arrive. Then they go and help themselves to breakfast.

Up they get from the table, walk to where all the food is beautifully laid out on hot plates. They pick their preferred food, place it on a plate and go back to their table where dad and Alfie are already eating their breakfast.

Mum and Leila sit down and eat their breakfast. Mum decides to ask dad and Alfie, 'What shall we go to today?'

'Well, we could go into the town and have a look around the historic buildings and enjoy the scenery.'

'Alfie, what do you think?'

Alfie looks at Leila then looks at his mum, shrugs his shoulders but does not say a word.

'Have you lost your tongue, Alfie?' dad asks.

'No,' he replies. 'Look it's still in my mouth!'

Everyone laughs.

'That's a very good answer, son,' says dad. Granddad and grandmother walk in, see the rest of the family at the table, walk over and sit down. 'What's the breakfast like, son?'

'It's very good,' replies John. 'You'll love it. There's a great selection of food. You go and try it out!' Breakfast finished, they go to reception, saying to the receptionist: 'We'd like to go into town. How do we get there?'

'We have our own minibus. It goes every half hour from outside the reception area and it's free to our residents. If you go out to the front of the building one will be along soon. Here are your passes for the minibus. How many of you are there?'

'Six please,' John says.

Chapter 53

Off they go to the front of the building and wait for the minibus. After ten minutes waiting, the minibus arrives back, stops at the front of the building and the returning residents alight from the bus.

John says. 'Come on, everyone. Please get on the bus. Show your passes to the drive of the bus find a seat and sit down.'

The driver looks around and asks, 'Can I drop you in the town centre?'

'Yes, that will be fine,' replies John. He looks at Leila and asks. 'Are you all right? You look a bit sad.'

'I'm fine, dad,' she replies. 'Just thinking and hoping our holiday will be fine.'

'Why? Is there something I should know?' dad asks.

'Nothing to worry about, it's just me. I'll be fine,' she replies.

The bus is just coming into the town centre.

The driver says. 'This is as far as I go. Remember the last return on this bus is five this afternoon. If you miss the hotel bus, you'll need to take a taxi back to the hotel. Have a nice day!' He pushes the button to open the door.

Everyone steps out of the bus, saying, 'Thank you very much!' The family are now standing on the pavement and John says. 'Where do we go from here?'

'We need a tourist information centre,' mum replies.

John looks at Leila and she knows what he is thinking.

'Okay, follow me. I know where there's one.'

They follow her until she locates the tourist information centre.

All the family go inside.

John asks for a brochure of the town and surrounding area. The receptionist hands him a brochure and points out the most interesting places to see and tells him that all the historic buildings are free to enter.

'Thank you very much,' John replies, He turns round and indicates to the family to go out into the street. He follows them out, has a good look in the brochure and says. 'I think we should go and see the old castle first. That's if everyone is in agreement?'

'I'm fine with that,' Ciera replies.

'What about mum and dad? What do you think?' asks John.

'We'll tag along with you if you don't mind?'

'And you, Leila? What do you think?'

'I'm fine with that arrangement. Is there a map on the brochure?'

'Yes,' replies dad.

'May I see it? Leila inquires.

'Of course you can,' dad replies. He hands it over to Leila.

She looks at it and says. 'I'll take us there. I know where to go. Just follow me!'

After walking for about five minutes, they reach the castle entrance, where they go through the front entrance where one of the attendants is taking money from the tourists.

Dad and family walk past the attendant without paying so the attendant runs after them and says to dad, 'You or your family didn't pay the entrance fee you will need to pay me before you can go into the castle grounds.'

'Why?' Dad enquires.

'I'll stop you from entering the castle if you don't give me some money!'

'But we were told that all old historic buildings are free to enter,' replies dad.

The family have gone ahead not realizing dad has entered an argument with the attendant about money.

'Well, I'm not going to give you any money! It's a scam!'

'I'll not allow you to enter until you pay!'

'Look, I've told you I'm not paying you any money for something that's free. I'm going in and you can't stop me!' Dad makes a move to go in when another attendant grabs him around the shoulder. Then the other one runs over and a big struggle breaks out. One of the attendants draws out a knife and tries to stab dad.

He pushes him away and he stabs the other attendant while he is falling to the ground. Dad rushes over to attend the stabbed man to see if he can help but he is dead.

The family rushes back to see what the disturbance is all about and see what has happened.

The first one back is Leila. She asks dad. 'What happened here?'

'That one tried to stab me because I refused to pay! I pushed him away. He stumbled over some rocks and stabbed his friend. It was a pure accident, Leila. Honestly.'

Then the police arrive. The attendant is taken by the police to one side and asked what happened here.'

Whatever was said the police walk over to dad, look at his hands and ask. 'Why are your hands covered in blood?'

Dad tries to explain the situation to the police but they are having none of it, so they handcuff him and send for transport.

Leila is furious.

Dad shouts: 'Don't do anything stupid, Leila! I'm sure when I explain at the police station what happened here they'll let me go.'

Leila goes over to the attendant who started this disturbance and asks what has happened.

He tries to ignore her.

She extends her hand to engage with his hand but he is not reciprocating. He tries not to take her hand. Not a good idea. She makes him place his hand in hers then she sees the whole picture. She gleans all the information she needs from him and tells him to be at work in the morning when she will interrogate him. 'If you decide not to attend, I know where you live. I'll come to find you!'

'What do you want from me?' the attendant inquires. 'At the moment nothing, you just be here in the morning! A lot will depend on what happens to my dad. You do understand?'

'Yes I do. I'll be here in the morning.'

'You'd better be or I'll come and find you.'

The police transport arrives to take dad to the police station. He is bundled into the car.

Leila walks over to one of the police officers and asks. 'May I go with my dad to the police station, please?'

He looks at her and says. 'I'm sorry but you're not allowed in with the prisoner, but you can come to the station in the morning and ask to see him.'

'What about bail?' Leila enquires.

'That's nothing to do with me. You'll need to see the magistrate in the morning. He'll decide whether to grant bail or not. In this particular instance, I don't think that's possible. I'm sorry but that's the situation on this occasion.'

Leila looks at the police officer, asks him to afford her a place in his car and take her to the police station. In the police station dad will try explain to the inspector what happened. While he is trying not to listen to Leila in his mind, she communicates with her mum and tells her not to worry. *'Dad and I will be back at the hotel a little bit later. You, Alfie, granddad and grandmother go back to where the minibus dropped us. I'll guide you back in your mind. Don't worry.'*

Mum communicates back: 'Are you sure you'll return with your dad later?

'Yes of course. Don't worry. We'll be back as soon as I have a word with the magistrate or the commander at the station. I'm sure he'll give dad bail so that we can carry on with our holiday.'

The police officer is looking at Leila in amazement but he is not able to break away from Leila's mind.

'Your car, where is it parked?' asks Leila. 'We need to go to the station now, please. I need to be there when my dad arrives.'

'Yes, just follow me.'

They walk out of the castle. They walk to where the police officer has parked the car.

He unlocks it, they both sit in and he drives away to the police station. He does not say a word to Leila but just looks ahead.

Leila is still in control of his mind; making sure that he understands what is required of him.

They arrive at the station just in time for Leila to see her dad going inside to make his statement. She follows the police officer inside. The two of them walk up to the desk.

Leila asks to see the bailing officer about releasing her dad. The police officer behind the desk looks amused and begins to laugh at Leila.

'Now little girl. You and your dad have no rights in this country. You're a guest here in our country. Do I make myself clear, young woman? We're taking a statement from your dad now. When he's finished we will lock him up in a cell until tomorrow morning. The magistrate will come and he'll be charged with murder!'

Leila has heard enough so she elevates the police officer behind the desk to the front of the desk, raises him even higher, lets him fall to just about two centimetres above the ground.

He panics, places his hands over his face and starts shouting uncontrollably: 'Please don't hurt me!'

She stands him up, still elevated and says. 'You're not in a position to doubt me when I say my dad didn't kill that man. You'd better listen to me.'

Another police officer runs from behind the desk with a gun and says to Leila. 'Put your hands in the air!'

She looks at him and says, 'I can make you turn the gun on yourself!'

He says, 'You're just a little girl. You can't do that!'

Leila does not even look around.

The police officer is trying to stop the gun from turning around to his face. He can't even drop it. It is panic stations.

The police officer is terrified. Two other police officers are trying to turn the gun away from their comrade but to no avail. The gun stays in the same position facing the police officer's face.

Chapter 54

'I'd like to see your commanding officer now because my patience is getting very thin.' She releases her mental hold on the gun, drops the other police officers to the ground and says, 'Go fetch your commander now!'

The people in the police station are mystified.

Leila has locked all the exits so that no one can enter and no one can get out.

The commander emerges from his office, looks around and asks, 'What's going on here?'

Leila looks at him. She is standing half a metre from his face.

He tries to back away from her but he is not able to move.

'Mr Commander. I want my dad now and if you don't concede to my request, I'll raze this building to dust! Do you believe me?'

'No I don't believe you. How can you do that? 'Who do you think you are? That is impossible. You would need incredible powers. Lock this idiot woman up and keep her in a cell until morning, sergeant. Then release her.'

Leila looks at the Commander and beckons him over with her hand.

He is now floating on air and he cannot stop himself.

Leila turns round, walks through the open door into where the cells are with the commander behind her. She walks down past two cells, stops and says to the Commander. 'I'll show you something you've never seen in your life. Just watch! Stand up dad and walk to me through the cell door.'

'Are you sure, Leila? I don't want to frighten the Commander. He might have a heart attack.'

'Just do as I ask, please dad!'

'If you're sure, here I come.'

The Commander cannot believe his eyes. Her dad is standing outside the cell and the door did not open. He faints and dad props him up against the wall.

Leila is in the outer reception area in a flash. Everyone is astonished and backs off against the wall. She points a finger at the sergeant, saying, 'I'd like you to get a cup of water for your Commander because he has fainted.' She is gone again in a flash back to the Commander and her dad. 'How is he?'

'He's fine. He's just woken up a bit delirious and confused.'

In comes the sergeant with the cup of water. He hands it to Leila and asks, 'What happened to him?'

'Nothing happened to him sergeant!' Leila replies. She places the cup of water on the Commander's lips.

He opens his mouth and drinks the water. He looks at Leila with his eyes wide open, stands up and shouts out: 'You're a witch! You have supernatural powers! You stay away from me!' He tries to run away but he is not able to move!

'Commander, please listen to me. I don't want to hurt you. I'm not here to cause trouble. We're here on holiday. Let me explain. What happened at the castle was one of the attendants wanted us to pay to enter the castle. My dad said 'no' he was informed at our hotel that all historic buildings have free entry. One of his colleagues entered the picture with a knife in his hand. My dad pushed him away. He stumbled on some rocks, fell and stabbed his colleague. It was a pure accident. Do you believe me? He'll tell you that it was an accident.'

The Commander throws his hands up in the air and says. 'All right, you bring him before me in the morning and if his account is the same, your dad is free to have the rest of his holiday in peace. May I ask a question? Who are you? Where are you from?'

'Commander, please take hold my hand.' The Commander is standing about two hundred miles above the Earth. He is positively shaking with fright and hangs on to Leila for dear life. 'Now do you believe me when I say I'm not like other people, I'm different!'

'Yes, yes! Please take me back to my office!' Back they go to his office. He looks around and is entirely mesmerised.

'You did ask me to take you back to your office?'

'Yes of course.' He taps the table and stamps his feet. 'I'm dreaming,' as he points up and says.' 'Did I see the Earth from above?'

'Yes you did, sir.'

'It was some experience if I may say so!'

'Did you enjoy it?'

'Well, I don't know. I'll need to think about it,' the Commander says. 'May I have your name, please? I think you're going to be very famous and I want to say I met you on holiday in my country.'

'Yes of course you may have my name. It's Leila, sir. I must go now. My family will need to see me because they might be worried, if that is all right with you?'

'Yes that's fine with me. It's been a privilege knowing you, Leila. Will I see you in the morning?'

'Yes you will. I'll be in your office at nine in the morning with the attendant. Goodbye now.' She walks out into the reception area. Dad is waiting for her; in a blaze of light they are gone and have left the police station in total disarray and confusion. On arriving back at their apartments they appear in their room. Nobody is surprised and questions are being asked by the family.

Ciera is the first to ask, 'Are you and dad all right? What happened to you, Leila?'

'Yes of course we are alright. Did you expect anything else? There's one problem. I had to use my powers to free dad from the police station and everyone at the station has seen how powerful I am. It doesn't matter because I had intended on making myself known to the world sooner than I had anticipated, but it had to happen sometime. I didn't receive all this power for nothing. I have to use it to try to save our planet. Now we can expect all kinds of media attention from now on. I'm so sorry but it was going to happen anyway. Granddad, you've been very quiet. Is something worrying you?' Leila asks.

Chapter 55

'I knew that it would happen someday. However, we have to deal with it now! Granddad replies with a sigh. 'Cool heads are required but I'm sure we'll prevail in the end!'

'I'm going back to the police station in the morning. I promised the Commander I'd take the attendant with me and let him explain what happened. Somehow, I don't think it'll be that easy. I might have to take the whole family back to our home and not use the plane. We'll see. Right then I think it's time for dinner. Shall we go to the restaurant? Alfie, you're very quiet. Is there something wrong? You know that you can tell me.'

'No, I'm fine. Just wondering how you came into our room with me not seeing you,' Alfie replies.

'It's a long story. I'll talk to you soon about it! Leila replies. 'We might as well go to dinner then'

Everyone is very passive, very quiet, very little is said about what happened at the police station.

'Come on, everybody. It's not the end of the world.' Leila is trying to break the ice. She knows that her life will never be the same again; of course the family are aware of the impending changes. 'Mum, dad, granddad, grandmother and of course little Alfie, it's my time to present myself to the world. I know that I'm ready to fulfil my destiny but I'm worried that governments will try to stop me from carrying out my destiny to save this planet. What we need to remember is that the family has this awesome wonderful power. We must be very careful for what purposes we use it. We have this telepathic communication with each other so we'll never be alone. Mum, will you please place your hand in mine?'

Ciera is very reluctant to oblige, however she does trust her own daughter so she does as Leila asks.

'Now you can communicate with me and it doesn't matter where you are in the world. I'm not going to give Alfie this power for a while, that is until he has grown up, then I'll take him into my confidence.'

Ciera gets up from the table and runs out of the restaurant.

Leila looks around at everyone and says, 'Leave this to me please.' She follows her mum out of the restaurant but she knows what the problem is before she catches up to her mum.

Mum is in a terrible state. She is crying uncontrollably.

Leila gives her a cuddle and says, 'Mum, I have to go but I'm not leaving home. I'll be away from time to time.'

'I know,' Ciera says, still sobbing and holding Leila very tightly. 'I don't want you to go. You're my baby.' She is still weeping and tears are flowing down her face. Leila is crying now and is looking very sad. 'It's not fair. It's breaking my heart!'

Leila's dad comes and gives them both a big cuddle saying: 'Come on now! We knew that this would happen someday. It's inevitable and predestined. Leila, you were picked as the saviour of this planet, we can't change that now. It's too late!'

'Look, why don't we go back into the restaurant? The rest of the family will be worried,' says Leila.

'Fine, I think that might be a good idea,' Ciera replies.

'Fine,' says dad. 'Let's do that then.'

The family are back in the restaurant.

'Are we going home tomorrow?' Alfie enquires.

'No we are not!' his dad replies. 'At least I hope not.'

Dinner finished the family go for a walk around the hotel complex.

After a while, Leila says. 'It's getting dark. I think we should return to our apartments and go to bed. I don't know about you lot but I need some sleep!'

Back in their rooms, Ciera looks at Leila and says. 'Good night. See you in the morning my precious baby.' She starts crying again. Grandmother goes and gives Ciera a cuddle and says. 'She's not going away forever. You'll be in contact with her at all times. So what's the problem then?'

'I'm just very sad at the moment but I'll be fine,' Ciera replies.

John says. 'I think we should go to bed and sleep on it. Tomorrow's another day.'

Next morning, Leila is up early. She needs to track down the attendant and take him to the Commander at the police station. She does not say anything to anyone when she leaves. 'She just leaves silently and appears in the old castle grounds a bit early. She has a good look round to see if the attendant has arrived but it would appear that he is not to be seen anywhere.

Leila is not happy. She has a feeling that this attendant will not appear in the castle so she decides to go to his house. She arrives at the front of the house and knocks on the front door.

It is opened by a young woman who is half asleep she is just standing holding the door open, she asks in her own local language. 'What do you want?' What she does not know is that Leila is able to speak the young woman's language, which surprises her immensely.

'I'm looking for the attendant from the castle. Is he in the house?'

'No. He left last night.'

'Where's he gone?' Leila asks.

'I don't know,' she replies. 'He didn't say where he was going, he just left.'

'Thank you. Would you like to shake my hand in friendship, please?' Leila asks.

'Yes why not?' She extends her hand to Leila

This is a big mistake! Leila now knows where he is hiding. She is now in possession of the location where the attendant is staying. In a flash, she is in the sitting room where she finds this attendant asleep on a couch. She taps him on the shoulder to wake him up.

He turns round, opens his eyes, jumps off the couch and shouts out for his brother, 'Help me!'

His brother is holding a shotgun in his hand as runs down the stairs opens the door to the sitting, room looks inside, sees Leila and asks, 'What do you want?'

'I want your brother to come with me to the police station to explain about the tragic circumstances in the castle yesterday. He's not in trouble with the police. It was an accident. Your brother will not be charged,' says Leila.

His brother is standing in the doorway with a shotgun.

Leila looks at him and communicates telepathically with him. He does not understand. She tells him to place the shotgun on the floor.

He duly obliges and places it on the floor. Now she looks at the attendant, tells him to get dressed quickly as he must go to the police station to make a statement.

All this communication is silent and the two brothers are mystified but are too afraid to say anything.

The attendant calls: 'I'm ready!'

Leila puts out her hand and places his hand in hers. In a flash, she is gone. They arrive in the commander's office in the police station.

He gasps in surprise when he sees Leila with the attendant.

'Good morning, sir. I've delivered the attendant as promised so if you'll take his statement now I'll be on my way.'

'Yes, yes. I'll have that done now.' He goes to the door and calls the sergeant. 'Please come into my office and take a statement from this man.'

'Yes sir. I'll just find the statement book and follow you in.'

A few minutes pass the sergeant arrives in the office of the commander and has the statement book with him.

The commander commands him to take a statement from the attendant.

The statement taken down, the sergeant hands it to the commander. He reads it and hands it to the attendant to sign. 'Sign your statement then you are free to go. There are no charges against you. Thank you for your cooperation. Can you see the young man out of here sergeant please! Now, young lady, what do I do with you?'

Leila senses that there is something not quite right so she enquires from the commander: 'Sir, I'd like a letter of apology for my dad please.' She is getting very agitated for some reason she can't define.

'If you'll wait a few minutes I'll have that letter typed up for you.' He calls his secretary on the phone, tells her to write a letter of apology then asks Leila. 'What's your dad's name please? Did you hear that name? Please write the apology and bring it to me as soon as it's ready. I'll sign and hand it over to the young lady.'

'Yes, sir as soon as I have typed it.'

The secretary arrives in the commander's office with the letter of apology. She hands it to the commander who signs it and hands it to Leila. 'There you are, all finished and of course no charges against your dad. Are you happy now?'

'Yes I'm very happy. I must go now. My family will be waiting for me at the hotel.' Then she hears a very loud noise above the police station. She looks at the commander and says, 'What's going on, sir? What's a helicopter doing over the station?'

'We would like you to surrender to us now please. We don't want any bloodshed here.'

'Why do you want me?' Leila replies.

'Well it's not me. It's my government. They'd like to talk to you about your powers.'

'Well, no disrespect to you but they can't have me. I see that there's a small army outside the station. What are they here for?' Leila knows what is going on.

'They're here to take you away for questioning; to try and find out why you're here, and what you want from this country. That is all we would like to know?'

'Commander, why are you so stupid? I'm getting very irritated with you. Have you any idea how powerful I am? Who's in charge out there? Please will you give me his name now?'

'His name is Major Christian Dombrovski.'

'Open the front door! He's waiting outside. He would like to come inside. I need to talk to him,' Leila commands.

'How do you know he's waiting outside?'

'Don't ask stupid questions, sir. I know everything that's going on outside the station. Please let him in before he does something silly!'

He goes to the front door, opens it lets the Major in and directs him to his office where Leila is sitting behind the desk in his chair.

'Come in, Major. Would you like to sit down and talk to me? May I ask you are you familiar with the English language, sir?'

'Yes, but I am not very good.'

'First let me ask you a question: Why do you want me?'

'I'm not sure what you mean.'

'Why are you here in this office?' Leila asks.

'I'm here to take you to see a very high official in the government.'

'What does he want from me?'

'I don't know. I was told to take you into custody and deliver you to this government official's residence, so if you'll come quietly I'll take you there.'

'I don't want to be facetious or jocular but you're not in any position to take me anywhere. I'll decide if I need to go to this official's residence and you or your army aren't capable of taking me there.'

'I can place you under arrest and take you under guard if you don't agree to come with me!'

'You can try if you like.'

The Major stands up and says, 'please place your hands behind your head.' At the same time, he draws his revolver from his holster and points it at Leila!

'What are you going to do with that gun?' Leila asks. She looks at him and says, 'Please place the gun on the desk.'

Without thinking, the Major walks over to the desk and places the gun down on it. He is extremely frightened because he does not know why he placed the gun on the desk. To make it more worrying for him, Leila elevates the gun about sixteen centimetres above the desk and points it in the direction of the Major's head. He raises his hands above his head, waving them in every direction, shouting, 'Please don't shoot me. I'm only doing my job!' The Major is now so terrified and in such a state of denial that he does not know what to do. He is shaking badly, so Leila lets the gun rest back on the desk facing away from the Major.

She walks round to the front of the desk, looks at the Major and says. 'I know how many men under your command are surrounding this station plus the helicopter over us.'

'That would be impossible! You can't see through walls. You're kidding me.'

'Let me tell you that you have thirty special ops men surrounding the station.'

'Who are you?' the Major asks.

'Let's say, just supposing you had twenty thousand troops outside this station and ten helicopters, it wouldn't be enough.'

'I don't believe it! You're telling me that you're more powerful than the whole army and air force in this country.'

'Yes, I'm even more powerful than all the armies, navy and air forces on this planet! Major, do you know where this official has his residence?'

'Yes I do. Why?'

'Good. Give me your hand please,' Leila asks.

The Major puts out his hand, places it in Leila's hand and in an instant the Major and Leila are in the sitting room of this official. He is sitting in his chair dreaming. He jumps up in amazement and is completely confused. He is standing there like a blinded rabbit and he cannot move.

'Please don't be afraid! The Major tells me that you would like to meet me. Well here I am. I'm at your command and behest for the next thirty minutes but first I must make contact with my family. Excuse me. *Mum, it's me, please don't worry. I'm fine. Please tell dad that I've acquired a letter from the police commander relinquishing all charges regarding the dead man yesterday. I'll be back in the hotel soon. I love you very much, must go now.* She looks at the official and says, 'Your name is Vitali Polovinkin. What do you want me for?'

'I don't know. I'm a bit confused,' he replies. 'Who are you?'

'That's not important at the moment. May I call you Vitali just to keep this meeting between us nice and friendly? Will you call for a car for the Major so that he can return to the police station and disband his little army?'

'Yes of course. Do you mind if I make the call now and have a car sent to my front door?'

'Of course not but be very careful. I'll be listening in to your conversation!'

Vitali makes the call. One of his staff takes the call. 'Please bring a car to the front entrance now. Right Major, you can go out to the front door. Your car will be there shortly and thank you!'

'Now Vitali, I need you to tell me who's in charge of this country. Have you a President?'

'Yes we have. He has an office in the government buildings in Simferopol.'

'I'd like to meet him soon. Can you arrange a meeting with him?'

'I'll have to ask. If I'm successful, I'll contact you.'

'No need to do that. When it's convened I'll know,' replies Leila. 'You just think about it and I'll be there. I must go now. I thank you for your courtesy.' Leila puts out her hand. He reciprocates places his hand in hers. Leila has a telepathic encounter with him.

He withdraws his hand from Leila's hand, stands back in amazement and says. 'What did you do to me?'

'Nothing for you to worry about I know your mind now. That's all I need.' In a glint of an eye, she is back in the apartment in the holiday complex and Vitalie is totally confused and perplexed.

He is looking round trying to find Leila saying to himself: 'She must be here somewhere. I didn't see her coming and I didn't see her going.'

The family are at breakfast when Leila arrives at the restaurant. Everyone gives her a big hug.

Mum looks at her and asks. 'Are you all right, Leila?'

'Yes, I'm fine. Dad, here's your letter from the commander so keep it safe. Now I'm hungry.' Off she goes and gets her breakfast

Leila looks at her mum and says, 'I was never going to let dad be charged with something he was not responsible, for that would not be right!'

'Thank you for sorting the mess out. I knew that you would be able to make everything right in the end!'

'I'm truly grateful!' Dad replies, 'it takes a load off my mind. I was worried a little bit, as he lifts his hand showing his thumb and index finger just slightly apart with a smile all over his face.

Alfie looks a bit perplexed and asks, 'Mum, why is dad making a sign with his fingers?'

'It's just a casual expression' replies his mum, just showing he was only a little bit worried!'

'Mum, I was only asking!'

'That's all right then, Alfie,' as she places her index finger to her lips.

Alfie is not happy but decides to keep his mouth closed as he looks at Leila.

Granddad looks at Alfie and smiles, 'You are a very inquisitive boy but we do understand.

There are times when questions are a bit awkward to answer but as you grow older, you'll understand. Alfie are you happy with that answer?'

Alfie answers, 'I think so!'

Granddad replies. 'No more questions for now Alfie.'

Leila looks around the table and says, 'I know that the television and the paparazzi will be coming to the hotel to find me today. I think I'll go to see the hotel manager, have a chat with him, just to make sure that there is no information available on our family, either on the hotel computer or paperwork likely to lead directly to us!'

'That's a very good idea,' replies her mum.

Chapter 56

'Ok then I'll see to that now.' She rises up from the table saying, 'I'll return shortly from the manager's office and let you know the outcome. Is everyone happy with that idea?' Leila asks.

She walks out of the restaurant to the reception area, pushes the glass door open and walks directly to the reception desk. Behind the desk is a plump young girl with short hair jet-black, brown eyes. She is very nicely dressed in a two-piece dark suit with a multi colour scarf tied around her neck. Leila looks at her and says, 'My name is Leila; I would like a meeting with the hotel manager,'

The receptionist looks up at Leila and says, 'The manager is not available to anyone until tomorrow morning!'

'Not good enough,' Leila replies. 'I need to see him as soon as possible please.'

'I don't think you are listening to me,' the receptionist answers. I'll tell you once more, the manager is not available until tomorrow. Now please go away I have a lot to do today!'

'Sorry about that' Leila replies, as she puts out her hand to the receptionist as if to shake hands. She takes Leila's hand and Leila is in her mind before she knows it. Leila now knows that the hotel manager is in residence in his office this morning. She goes outside, has a quick look around and in a flash she is in the manager's office; a nice spacious office with a large teak desk and some chairs placed around the office. It has a water cooler in the corner of the office to the right of his desk and it is nearly full. There are watercolour paintings of boats and sea fronts hanging on the walls with for sale tickets, with the prices on them. There is a large window with the sun's rays flashing and dancing through the glass looking out over the hills.

He is just sitting there in front of the window enjoying this beautiful morning, just relaxing having a quiet drink when he detects that someone has entered his office. He is about five foot nine good looking, going bald, with a little moustache, He is wearing a grey trousers and a white shirt with short sleeves he looks very pleased with himself. All that is about to change now that Leila is in his office.

He turns round, sees Leila and jumps up asking, 'Who are you? What do you want? Leave this office now please. Leave before I call security. How dare you come into this office without having an invitation from me?

'I'm sorry to have startled you, but I need your cooperation if you will hear me out?'

'What kind of cooperation are you talking about?'

'Well, may I show you what I'm talking about?'

'Sure,' replies the manager, enlighten me please?'

Leila vanishes and appears behind him and taps him on the shoulder, He jumps up in amazement and staggers out from behind his desk saying, I'm not impressed. That was a very good trick!'

'Fine,' Leila thinks, what would impress him?' So she takes him by the hand and the two of them appear about two kilometres out to sea. She stands him on the surface of the sea; he panics, starts to fall about. Leila holds him and says, 'Now do you believe?'

'Yes I do believe you, Take me back to my office, please, and we can discuss whatever you want.'

In an instant they are back in his office. Leila says, 'It's very important that I talk to you!'

'Yes, yes, but what do you want from me?' He is not worried because he is not sure whether he might be dreaming, but his eyes are telling him that it would be better to pacify Leila and listen to her.

Leila looks at him and says, 'All I ask is your cooperation in this matter. Will you do that for me please?'

'Alright, I'm listening. What is so important that you need my cooperation?'

'As you now know, I have special powers which I have demonstrated to some people at the police station in the town. The television people and the paparazzi will be coming to this hotel looking for me. The hotel will be swarming with television people and reporters from foreign newspapers. All I need you to do is to go to reception, retrieve all the booking forms that my family names are on, and bring them back in to me I'll do the rest, The name is Carney.'

The manager walks to reception looks at the receptionist and asks, 'May I have all the booking forms for the Carney family as this week's residents, I need them as soon as possible?'

'Yes, sir. I'll go and find them now and bring them to your office, it'll take about fifteen minutes.'

'When you have them, just phone me, I'll come and pick them up from you.'

The receptionist looks at him in a strange way and asks, 'Why do you want those particular bookings? Is there something wrong with the paper work?'

'That is none of your business. You just find them then you must call me as soon as you have found them.' He walks back to his office where Leila is waiting for him she looks at him and enquires, 'Is everything ok?'

'Yes,' the manager replies, 'as soon as the receptionist has found the paper work she will call me. Or I will go and get them for you. Is that all right?'

'Yes that's fine with me,' Leila replies.

Ten minutes pass and he receives a call from the receptionist saying, 'All the paper work you require is at reception, I have it ready for you.'

'I'll come and pick it up now thank you!'

He rises up from his desk, walks out of his office to reception. The receptionist hands him the paper work, he walks back to his office then hands the paperwork to Leila.

She places it on the desk and waves her hand over it saying, 'I have wiped all references to my family from this paperwork. Now you can return the paper work to reception and ask the receptionist to come to your office?'

At reception he hands the paperwork back to the receptionist and he says.

'This paperwork needs to be placed back in its cabinet. Then you can follow me back to my office.' As she enters the office, she looks at Leila and is wondering how she has entered into the manager's office without seeing her passing reception. She refrains from asking any more questions of the manager.

Leila puts out her hand to the receptionist. She reciprocates by holding Leila's hand. Now the receptionist's mind is empty of all communication with Leila and the Carney family. Leila thanks her for all the help she has given her. She looks again at Leila but does not know why she is in the manager's office. She looks at the manager, and he says, 'Please return to your duties thank you.'

Leila says, to the manager as she puts out her hand to him, 'thank you for your cooperation' he takes her hand she wipes all the information about the Carney family from his mind and the computer in reception. She turns round, walks out of his office and goes out through reception back to the family.

Dad enquires, 'Where have you been Leila?'

'I told you, dad. I was going to see the hotel manager. I went to see him to make sure that if the hotel has a deluge of television and newspaper people he is unable to help them and neither will his receptionist be able to give any information about our family. No need to go into detail about this episode, thank you' Leila replies.

Dad says, 'I think that is fine with me,' as he looks at Leila. 'I'm sure you have your reasons.'

Ciera says, 'I think we should go on coach trips then we will not be around when the television and newspaper people frequent the hotel.'

'Good idea,' replies grandmother, 'we can go in search of some historic buildings and sites of archaeological interest. Maybe learn some history about this country, what do you think, Alfie?'

Alfie looks at his grandmother in a questionable way, frowns but does not say a word.

Dad says, 'Alfie, answer your grandmother please!'

Alfie looks at his dad and says, 'I don't know what she is talking about, dad!'

Grandma intercedes saying, 'Do not worry, Alfie, someday you will understand.'

Dad says, 'I'll go to reception and find out about historical buildings and any other listed buildings in this area.' He stands up, 'I'll be back shortly' he says.

At the reception desk he enquires, 'Can you tell me if the hotel might have any knowledge of any historical tours of old buildings in and around the city limits?'

'Yes we do, we have some brochures of interesting places,' as she hands him some of the brochures. We also have our own mini buses they are free to members, plus all the people and family's staying here in the hotel. One leaves the hotel every hour, There is one due very soon now, how many people are in the family, sir?'

'Five people and a little boy' Mr Carney replies.

'Here are your passes for the bus sir' she then hands the passes to Mr Carney and says, 'have a nice day sir I hope you will like our historical and interesting buildings.'

'Thank you' Mr Carney replies. He walks out of the reception looks around sees the family, walks to meet them saying, 'I have the passes shall we find the stop for the minibus again and wait for it to arrive.'

As the bus arrives he gives out the passes and says, 'I hope this historical tour around the country will be very interesting, for the whole family.' The family board the mini bus. Dad makes sure that each family member hands their pass to the driver. The bus is air-conditioned and looks to have very comfortable seating. Dad says, 'We are in your hands now, driver, for the rest of the day.'

The driver looks about twenty-five years old. He has short curly fair hair. Is casually dressed in short trousers a check shirt and sandals on his feet. He checks the passes, He looks around making sure that all the people have their seat belts on then closes the bus door. He picks up the bus intercom microphone and talks into it saying, 'I'm going to take you on a mystery tour today and I hope you'll have a very nice time. Thank you for listening.' He then replaces the microphone back on the amplifier hook.

He drives off and all the family are anticipating what wonders lie ahead for them today.

Alfie is sitting next to Leila, looks at her and asks, 'Leila, what are historical places. I do not understand can you explain them to me?'

'Well, Alfie, they are old buildings of historical significance. They are part of the history of any country and of course they become great tourist attractions.'

'I still don't understand' Alfie replies.

'When you are older you will understand the meaning of historical and past events. You will learn all about this in school but for now let us just see where the driver takes us ok? I'm sure it will be very interesting.'

'I still do not understand but I am happy to wait and learn all about it when I return to school.'

'Good' replies Leila. 'I'm sure that you will be a very good intellectual scholar.'

Chapter 57

Back at the hotel complex all hell has broken out. Television news people, newspaper reporters are pressing the manager for information about Leila.

'Where is she, can we see her?' Everyone is asking the same questions.

The manager is frantic to get away from these unanswerable questions, so he waves his hands in the air and says, 'Please listen to me. I do not know why you are asking me about this Leila. There is no one in this hotel complex with the name Leila!'

All information relating to Leila's and her family has now been deleted from the hotel computers, as if her family had never existed. She also cleared the minds of the manager and staff at the hotel. Now the hotel does not hold any details of Leila or her family.

The manager invites all the reporters and television people into the hotel where he turns the computer screen towards them and says, 'You may help yourselves to any information you can glean from this computer. This covers all residents currently staying in this hotel. There is no person in this hotel with the name Leila. If there was, I would know.' He is looking around, waving his hands in the air at this gathering of people in the reception area. Please gentlemen I must go about my daily rounds now.'

One after another, the television people and the reporters try to glean from the computer any reference to Leila but to no avail. After about half an hour, they decide that maybe this Leila does not exist so they walk away very irritated and disgusted, having wasted all that time and nothing to show for it. One of the reporters is having none of it, so he decides to stay around the hotel for a while hoping that he might make contact with someone that might know something about this gifted and talented person.

News has got out that there was a very gifted young lady in the police station, with very special powers. The press, newspaper people are frantically trying to find Leila. They are inside the police station and all hell has broken out, the word has leaked out about a young woman with special powers. They would like to interview her and ask about her special powers but they must find her first. The silence is deafening from the people in the police station but the story will break soon. It will be up to Leila to let the World know that she is going to make this planet safe from tyrannical governments whether they like it or not. The family are enjoying the last few days of the holiday, going out on bus trips to different places and enjoying all the time they have to themselves for a change, going round the different places of interest. They are tremendously happy but this happiness could be coming to an abrupt end.

Leila does not appear to be worried; in fact she appears to be very calm and is looking very serene. This holiday is doing her good and she is enjoying herself very much. The bus stops outside a restaurant, the driver says, 'I'll be stopping here for about half an hour so if anybody would like to have refreshments please help yourselves.'

Granddad stands up and says, 'anyone for refreshments will you follow me please.'

The family step off the bus and go into the restaurant sit and down.

The waiter arrives and says, 'Good morning, everyone, may I take your orders please?'

'Yes' says granddad. 'May we have five coffees, one glass of orange and a plate of mixed sandwiches please.'

'Thank you' the waiter replies, turns and walks away.

Ten minutes and he is back with the coffee, orange and a plate of sandwiches places the order on the table and walks away, 'Help yourselves' granddad says, as he hands Alfie the glass of orange, 'There you are my boy, you drink it slowly please and help yourself to a sandwich, any one you like.'

Ciera stands up, hands out the cups of coffee, hands the plate with the sandwiches around for everyone to have their choice then sits down again. The conversation around the table is, 'It's good that we are a very special family and we must never forget it.'

Granddad looks around and says, 'I'm sure we are intrinsically entwined with Leila for the rest of our lives whether we like it or not, but I'm sure that we will be involved in many great adventures in the future.'

'Now I wonder where we are going next' says John.

Granddad replies 'Let the driver take us off on a mystery tour I think that might be nice.'

'Yes, that's fine with me,' replies grandma. 'What about you Ciera?'

'I'm fine with that,' replies Ciera.

Leila jumps up and says, 'I do not see Alfie anywhere. Anyone see him?' Somehow he has slipped away without being noticed.

Ciera looks across the road and sees Alfie petting a cat, she shouts over to him, 'Alfie, come away from that cat, get back here immediately!'

Leila looks up, sees Alfie about to cross the road, at the same time she sees a lorry coming very fast down the road. Alfie decides to make a run for it. She knows she has to do something now, this could be a disaster and Alfie could be hurt or even killed. She runs out into the middle of the road, waves her hand, the lorry stands up on its back wheels and comes to a complete stop, and stays in that position until Alfie is safe behind her.

Alfie looks up at Leila and says, 'I'm sorry. Mum called me so I decided to run across the road.'

'That is fine, Alfie, you're safe now,' Leila replies. 'Go to mum please.' Leila waves her hand again to let the lorry down on all of its wheels saying, 'My goodness, that was so easy,' she says to herself.

Chapter 58

The driver alights from his cab and runs over to Leila saying, 'Thank you for saving that little boy's life. I know I was driving too fast, but it has taught me a lesson to be more careful in the future.'

'Good,' she replies, 'because if you had injured him in any way I would have elevated your lorry and placed it in the sea with you in it!'

'You can't do that unless you are God,' replies the driver.

'You just watch.' She does not even look in the direction of the lorry. It has elevated about fifty feet above the road and starts to move towards the sea. The driver is petrified and running around in circles like a headless chicken, shouting, 'Please let me have my lorry back I do believe you now.'

The lorry starts to transport itself in a diagonal line, drops back into its original position on the road, the driver runs over and throws himself down on his knees at Leila's feet, shouting, 'Thank you, thank you, I promise I'll be a very careful driver in future.'

Leila places her hand on his shoulder and says, 'Please stand up you are embarrassing me plus we have a crowd gathering around us, Please stand up, go to your lorry and drive away.'

By now people are taking photos and asking questions like, 'Who are you? Where are you from?'

'I'm sorry but I need to go, my family are waiting for me. I am not able to answer any questions at the moment but watch your televisions next week. There will be an announcement very soon and all will be explained, thank you.'

She walks away to the bus where her family are waiting to board it. Nothing is said about the lorry, just an uneasy silence. As she is getting on the bus she notices that the driver is shaking profusely so she places her hand on his shoulder and says, 'Just drive, you'll be fine now.' She goes and sits down next to Alfie.

Alfie looks up at Leila and asks, 'Leila, did you stop that lorry from hitting me?'

'Yes I did,' she replies.

'Wow that was awesome. Could you do something else?'

'Not now Alfie, but I will do something awesome in the future, I promise.'

Alfie looks up at Leila and gives her a little cuddle saying, 'I cannot believe you are my big sister.'

'Yes of course I'm your sister, why do you ask?

Alfie replies 'Just wondering.'

John jumps up, 'Ok I think it's time to ask the driver where we are going'. He goes to the front of the bus and sits next to the driver and enquires, 'Where are the places of interest in this area, which you advise my family to visit?'

The driver looks very briefly at John and says, 'Just leave this decision to me shall we say, I am taking you on a mystery tour around some of our historic sites.'

'Fantastic that will do nicely. I am sure the family will be excited and thrilled to bits.'

He gets up from the seat goes back to the family and says, 'We are now on a mystery tour. Is that not wonderful a wonderful idea?'

'Yes' replies all the family in unison.

Chapter 59

The driver takes them to their first historic ruins. The first stop Chufut Kale and Mangup Kale they are cave towns. A young woman employee meets the family inside the caves, she greets them and enquires, 'Would you like me to accompany you around the caves and give you some of their history and its importance. After the tour the family say, 'thank you' and they walk to the entrance/exit pick up a brochure, and go and find their driver.

The driver enquires, 'Did you like the tour of the old cave ruins, I hope you enjoyed it with the attendant?'

'Yes it was very informative,' replies John, 'with lots of history, we enjoyed the tour very much thank you.'

'Okay,' says the driver, 'are you ready for lunch? If so I'll take you to a very nice restaurant out in the country side, a very pleasant place with good food.'

'Granddad replies, 'That will be fine with us 'is everybody happy with that?' He looks around at everyone.

Alfie shouts, 'I'm hungry!'

'That's it then' granddad replies, 'If Alfie is hungry we'll do what he wants. That is it. Driver we are in your hands please take us to this restaurant.'

'It will take me about an hour to drive there' the driver replies.

'Fine,' granddad replies.

Chapter 60

An hour later the bus stops outside the restaurant. The driver says, 'Let me go inside and ask the owner if he will accommodate you with lunch.' He leaves the bus, goes inside, has a conversation with the owner comes back out. 'The restaurant owner would love to make you lunch I will stay in the bus as I have my own sandwiches.'

The family alight from the bus and go into the restaurant. It is air-conditioned and that suits the family. The inside of the restaurant is very bright with lovely painted murals of different types of fish on the walls and looks very clean. They are greeted by the owner a fat man going grey, nearly bald but very pleasant who leads them to a table by the front window where he pulls out the chairs for the ladies and makes sure that they are comfortable. Hands all the family a menu each to select their drinks and says, 'I'll return in a few minutes for your drinks order thank you.' Five minutes later, he returns, stands at the side of the table, looks around the table and asks, 'What would you like to drink this afternoon, ladies and gentlemen? We have cold beer soft drinks and cold wine.' John looks around and asks, 'Granddad, grandma, what would you like to drink?' Granddad looks at his wife and says, 'I think my wife and I will have a white wine each if you don't mind thank you.'

'Ciera what would you like to drink?'

'I'll have a soft drink, orange juice please.'

'Leila what would you and Alfie like to drink.'

Leila looks at Alfie. 'I'm going to have an orange drink. What about you, Alfie, what would you like?'

'I'll have the same as you' Alfie replies.

Orders taken the owner hands everyone a menu for the lunch, walks to the bar, pours out the drinks then returns to the table, places them on the table and enquires, 'Have you all decided which food you would like to order?'

Everyone look at each other. Ciera says, 'I'll have fish and chips please. Alfie will have the same as me, a small portion, for Alfie, thank you.'

'Can I have a salad please? Leila asks.

'Can I have your local dish please' John asks. 'Granddad, grandma, have you made up your minds what you want to eat?'

'I think we'll have fish and chips as well' granddad replies.

Chapter 61

The owner walks back to the kitchen with the orders, leaves the orders with the chef. Half an hour later he returns with all the orders places them on the table and says. 'Thank you, enjoy your food.'

'This looks very good' says Ciera,' the fish looks very fresh.'

'The same here says granddad. And so does mine says grandma.'

'My salad looks lovely and fresh,' Leila replies.

Dad enquires what about you Alfie. Is the food to your liking?'

Alfie is his usual self, just looks at the lunch and says nothing just picks at it.

His mum says, 'Alfie, come on, eat up please or the owner will think you don't like his food.' Reluctantly he begins to eat but very slowly.

The owner is watching very carefully, walks over to the table and says to Alfie, 'If you eat all of your lunch I'll give you an ice cream.'

Alfie looks up and his eyes light up he says, 'I'll finish my lunch and you promise to give me an ice cream?'

'Absolutely, I promise hand on my heart,' the owner replies.

Alfie wades through the lunch but it takes a while. When he has finished the owner walks over to Alfie and looks at his plate and says, 'I see you have finished your lunch. Your plate looks clean.'

Alfie lifts up his plate and says, 'Look I have finished all of my lunch. Do I get an ice cream now please?'

'Yes of course you do,' as he walks away and returns with an ice cream and hands it to Alfie. 'There you are for being a good boy.'

Ciera says, 'Thank you for being so kind.'

He says, 'I have a lot of children come to my restaurant. I find if I give them some incentive it works wonders.'

'You're so kind,' replies Ciera.

'May I enquire; would you like a drink on the house?'

Everyone look at each other and John says, 'Thank you, if the drinks are on the house we would love to have the same as before please?'

The owner walks back to the bar pours the drinks and takes them back to the table, places the tray with the drinks on the table and walks away.

Granddad says, 'I think that's nice of the owner to give us free drinks. I will go and pay for lunch as it is on me this time. He walks up to the bar to pay, 'Thank you for the very tasty good food'. Walks back to the table and says, 'I think we are ready to go out and sit in the bus now please.' The family leave the restaurant, waving back at the owner, enter the bus and sit down. Granddad asks, 'Driver where are you going to take us next?'

'I am going to take you to a very special place, I am sure you will appreciate its beauty. It's a bit of a longer journey but I'm sure you'll like it!' replies the driver.

'Yeah,' the family shout in unison.

'Good then,' he replies and off they go.

Leila is thinking about the future not about her but the family's future. In her heart she knows that she can cope with anything but there is always the unknown factor. She is just gazing out of the window, looking at the scenery and thinking in her inner thoughts, 'What a beautiful world. Will she be strong enough to keep it that way and will the world survive?'

She gives Alfie a little nudge to wake him up, He stirs a bit but he does not wake so she decides to let him alone for now.

Alfie has fallen asleep on Leila's shoulder with the momentum of the bus but it keeps him quiet and everyone is happy with that situation.

Leila is wondering in a world of her own about her planet.

The coach driver looks around and says, 'We are nearly at our destination' as the coach rounds the bend and in front of them is a great big waterfall which is very spectacular and very impressive.

Chapter 62

Leila wakes Alfie; he is a little confused as he looks around. The bus stops in the car park and everyone alights from the mini bus. Alfie's eyes are wide open looking at this wonderful spectacle. He is in total surprise at this fantastic visualization in front of him. Water is cascading down from the top of the waterfall, which is about 100mts high. The mist produces a beautiful rainbow as it reflects the glorious sunlight. The water as it falls looks like fairy dust as it cascades down the side of the waterfall. This water cascading down the waterfall has an uncanny look, it looks like diamonds as it hits the bottom and splashes into a foam. All it needs now is some fairies playing around. Leila decides to give the visitors around the waterfall a taste of her powers. She conjures some fairies flying up and down the waterfall. Alfie is totally bemused at this beautiful vision and is shouting to Leila, 'Look at the little fairies flying around the waterfall!' He takes her by the hand and says, 'Come on Leila lets go and see the little fairies.' The mini bus driver walks over to the family, looks at the waterfall sees the fairies flying around and says, 'I have never seen fairies on this waterfall before. That is amazing. Are those fairies real?' he enquires. He looks at Leila and smiles. He now knows that somehow Leila is responsible for this vision.

He proceeds to give them information on this location and says, 'This waterfall is called UCHN-SU Waterfall and it's near Yalta and it's about 100mts high. It is the highest waterfall in Crimea and it's a great tourist attraction and of course the fairies are an added attraction,' as he smiles to himself. 'I see that your little boy is fascinated at what he sees in front of him.'

Leila's mum walks over to her and asks, 'Is that you making those little fairies dancing about the waterfall?' 'Yes of course it is. Do you think that they are real?'

Mum replies, 'It is a beautiful scene. It looks fantastic, just resembling magic, I know that they are not real but Alfie is mesmerised and I am happy about that.'

Leila is watching Alfie very intently, she goes over to him and says, 'Alfie would you like me to take you to the top of the waterfall and if you place your hand out the fairies might land on it?'

Alfie looks at his sister, and replies, 'I think I might like to have the fairies land on my hand but how are we going to get to the top? It's a long way up.'

Leila replies, 'Place your hand in mine.'

Alfie looks bemused at her and enquires, 'I don't see any steps. It's a long way up to the top of the waterfall. How do we get up there?'

'Just give me your hand,' insists Leila. He places his hand in Leila's and in an instant the two of them are standing at the top of the waterfall looking down at the rest of the family. Leila tells Alfie to put out his hand, then two fairies land in his palm. He is totally in shock because he has never had fairies standing in the palm of his hands before. Leila says, 'Be very careful not to harm them.'

One of the fairies a little girl walks up his right sleeve then flies up just in front of his face. She smiles and asks,' Alfie have you been a good boy today?'

'He does not know what to say, he is mesmerized and shocked. 'How is this little fairy able to know my name,' he thinks to himself. He looks at Leila wondering what to say or do, he looks bewildered. Leila can see that he is a little bit in awe of the situation, 'Go on, Alfie talk to the little fairy!'

'I don't know what to say!' Alfie replies.

Leila looks at him, Go on just ask her is it nice being a fairy?' Alfie looks at the little fairy, he is a bit apprehensive but he decides to ask,' Is it nice being a fairy?' 'Yes,' the little fairy replies. 'Would you like to know my name?

'Yes please,' Alfie replies.

The little fairy looks at him and says, 'My name is Imegen!'

'That's a nice name!' Alfie replies.

'Alfie, we must go now, please. Alfie, would you like to wave to mum and dad.'

Alfie is looking around, he does not know what to say, He is looking very confused and starts to cry, and he is totally lost for words. The fairies fly away. Leila bends down, looks at him she knows that he is frightened so she says, 'Shall we go down now, and it is a bit high.' 'Yes please,' Alfie replies, 'I am frightened, we are up very high. I want to go down to mum and dad please.'

'Give me your hand again please.'

Alfie holds out his hand to Leila, as she places her hand in Alfie's hand saying, 'Shall we descend slowly this time.'

Alfie looks at his sister and says, 'We're not going to fall down the waterfall are we?'

'No absolutely not,' replies Leila. She looks at Alfie and asks, 'Are you ready shall we descend then.' Alfie nods his head and decides to take the chance. He knows Leila will not let anything happen to him.

With Alfie's hand in hers, one metre above the ground at the top of the waterfall Leila moves out over the waterfall. By this time, Alfie is holding Leila's hand very tightly and looking up at his sister with just a little bit of worry on his face. The fairies are flying around Alfie's head. Leila says, 'Alfie hold out your hand, then one of the fairies lands in the palm of his hand. He looks at it and smiles, it looks at him and smiles back, it then flies away. Alfie looks at his sister and she says. Hold on tight here we go.' Then the two of them descend slowly down the waterfall. The fairies follow them down to ground level. By the time they reach ground level Alfie is smiling and shouting aloud, 'This is awesome. Can we do this again please?'

'Not now. We will do it sometime in the future.' Leila replies.

Chapter 63

By now, a big crowd has gathered, and they are taking photos of this incredible event. They have video cameras at the ready and they are shaking with anticipation at this wonderful vision. They have never seen fairies flying around this waterfall before and they are quite mystified. The people are very busy taking photographs, 'then the fairies disappear. They walk over to where Leila is standing and ask, 'Who are you? Where are you from? 'What is your name, please tell us?'

The family gather around her and are looking a bit worried. Granddad enquires, 'I see Alfie has been crying. Is he alright Leila?'

'Yes of course, he is fine now I think he was a little bit frightened at the top of the waterfall. I'm alright,' she replies, 'I just wanted Alfie to experience some of my power. Anyway, it is time to let the world know I am here to make changes. I cannot keep this power to myself anymore.'

I know that now, I am ready to do what is necessary to save this world and woe be tide anyone who tries to stop me.'

Leila looks over at her mum goes and stands in front of her and her grandma, takes their hands, and in less than a second they are at the top of the waterfall. They do not realise what has happened, the transfer from ground level only lasted less than one tenth of a second. The three of them start laughing and their emotions are running quite high. Well what do you think' Leila asks.

Her mum looks at her and asks, 'Are we safe up here? I mean it is a long way up.'

'Of course you're safe. Do you think that I would place you in any danger? She holds out her hands again and says, 'Right then shall we descend until we reach the bottom?'

'Yes please,' her mum replies. The three of them have levitated about one metre above the top of the waterfall. Leila asks, 'Are we ready?' They all look at each other and nod. Leila moves out over the edge of the waterfall and they drop down to ground level very slowly. Again, the people with the cameras are taking pictures as quickly as they can. They are looking on in astonishment and wonderment at this truly incredible, hard to believe, occasion of a once in a lifetime event. Leila now walks over to her dad and granddad and smiles at them saying, 'I think it's your turn to levitate to the top of the waterfall. You won't get wet I promise.'

'Yes, please,' they reply together.

'Hold my hands,' Leila asks.

The two of them are willing to oblige Leila by placing their hands in hers. 'Now just relax we will levitate slowly up the side of the waterfall to the top. Are we ready?' Leila asks, 'they both nod, Right then here we go' and in a flash they are inside the waterfall, but surprise they are not getting wet. Leila has placed a shield around the three of them, the water cascades over the top of them. So they rise up to the top of the waterfall out over the top of the waterfall where she holds that position, looks at the two of them and says, 'What do you think granddad/dad. Did that impress you too?'

John looks at his dad and laughs.' Then he replies, 'Well we didn't expect anything else from you. We know how powerful you are. We also agree that it is your time to let the world know that you are here to make changes to governments of the world and we will help whenever we are needed.'

'Shall we return down through the waterfall to ground level? Leila asks.

'Yes please,' they reply, 'you are not going to make us wet are you?'

Leila replies, 'Of course not, are we ready?' She levitates granddad and her dad out over the top of the waterfall. They then descend down through the waterfall very slowly without getting wet until they arrive at the bottom of the waterfall. Leila says, 'Granddad, dad, why don't you two levitate to the top of the waterfall?'

Granddad looks at Leila and says, 'Are you sure we can do that on our own with no help from you?'

'Yes of course you can. Go ahead and try.'

Granddad is not so sure, Leila looks at him and says, 'You just think about it, and you will be fine. It will happen I promise, Go on try.'

Granddad holds out his hand to his son and as if by magic, the two of them levitate to the top of the waterfall and look down.

Chapter 64

'Well, son, what do you think? Do we have the power or what?'

'I don't know dad. Are you sure that we are levitating on our own and that it's not Leila helping us?'

'I don't think so,' granddad replies. 'Anyway shall we descend to the bottom?' They hold hands again and descend slowly to the bottom of the waterfall.

Leila walks over looks at the two of them and says, 'I'm proud of you, you did that on your own. I didn't help you honestly.'

Granddad is still not so sure and neither is John, but if Leila says they did it on their own, they must believe her. At the bottom of the waterfall, they walk out into a barrage of questions. The questions start again. 'Who are you? 'Where do you and your family come from, please tell us who you are and what you're doing here. How do you go from the bottom of the waterfall to the top without some kind of assistance or some kind of invisible aid? Is it some kind of magic trick?'

Out of sight of Leila's vision, she clocks a television crew. So she walks over to them, 'Did you get all my people levitating up and down that waterfall?' She asks, as she points over to it

'Yes we did, they all reply, asking 'was that some kind of trick?'

'Absolutely not,' she retorts. 'What makes you think that it was some kind of stunt?'

The television crews wave their hands in the air and look bemused.

'Now which one of you would like to rise to the top of the waterfall?' Leila enquires.

Not one of the crew steps forward to oblige Leila's request, so she looks at all of them and says, 'Fine, then I'll pick one of you.' She lifts her hand, points it at the nearest to her, levitates him and moves him to the base of the waterfall. In an instant she is next to him. She asks, 'Please place your hand in my hand.'

Now this crew person is looking very worried.

'Please relax,' Leila says, 'don't worry; just enjoy the trip,' as they levitate up the side of the waterfall.

This television crew person has closed his eyes in case he might fall, and is afraid to open them.

'You can look now if you like. We are at the top of the waterfall.'

He opens his eyes very slowly and belatedly, grabs Leila's hand. His whole body is shaking violently. He asks, 'We have levitated from ground level to where we are now at the top of the waterfall? That is just amazing.

Who are you? Could I interview you when you decide to return to the bottom of the waterfall?'

Leila answers. 'I'll have to think about that, we'll see,' as the two of them descend very slowly down the front of the waterfall to ground level where he looks around and is totally confused. He does not know what to say, He just mumbles to himself in some incoherent strange language. The rest of the crew rush over and ask him, 'Did you like your trip to the top of the waterfall? Are you alright?'

'Yes I'm fine now, what an experience.' He looks at his television crew, and enquires, 'I hope you were recording everything that happened, to that family and myself.'

'Yes we did record everything' they reply, laughing in a jocular way. 'How would you like to describe your journey up to the top of the waterfall?'

It was awesome, unreal, but it was fantastic?' he replies. 'He looks at Leila and asks, 'May I interview you now in front of the camera please, so that we can place all the footage on air tonight, That is, if you don't mind?'

'Let me have a word with my family please,' as she walks over to her family. 'She looks at the family and says; this television crew would like to interview me for television tonight is it alright with everyone if I accede to their requests?' Leila asks as she looks around the family.

Her dad looks around and says, 'Sometime soon you are going to show your powers to the world so this must be the day when it happens' The family look at each other and nod.

'I have a better idea,' answers Leila.

Chapter 65

'The United Nations in New York is meeting with world leaders scheduled for next week perhaps that would be a better time to announce to the world how powerful I am. Can we agree on The United Nations then, I don't want to over-rule the family, but I think that is the best solution and there I can be interviewed and show my power to the world?'

The family reply, 'Yes.'

'Good, I'll tell the television crew, that the interview is off. They won't like it but it's my decision'.

Leila walks back to the television crew, looks at them and says, 'I'm sorry but this is not the right place to announce my intentions to the world. My family and I have decided to go to the United Nations Building, New York, to introduce my family and myself to the world next week. I know that I said you could interview me. I hope you will understand that I need a bigger stage and The United Nations is the place to announce myself to the world. I do have good news for you. I will let you use the video footage you have now so that you may use it in your evening news. I hope that you are not too disappointed?'

Then she detects that they are recording, every word she has said. 'Gentlemen, why are you recording my conversation? I said that I was not going to give you an interview.' The camera operator walks in front of her and says, 'We have everything, we need now, of your interview on disk. We need it for our evening news and you can't do anything about it.'

'Have you? Now please play back the interview and let's see what you have recorded?'

The producer goes to the monitor, switches it on and runs the disk back to the beginning of the supposed interview. He can't figure out what has happened. He knows that camera operator did record the interview but he can't find it in the recording that was made!'

'Can you find the interview your camera operator made?' Leila asks.

'I can't find it at the moment' he says, so he beckons the camera operator over looks at him in an angry way and says, 'Please show me the footage you recorded of the interview?'

The camera operator goes backwards and forwards several times then through all of the days recordings, but he cannot find it anywhere.

'I'm so sorry, sir, I know that I did record the interview but I don't know where it has gone.' The camera operator knows in his own mind he did record the interview but he does not know what has happened to it. The producer is waving his hands in the air asking, 'Where is the recording you have done of the interview? It must be somewhere on the disk?'

He is very upset now, losing probably the most important recording of his career for television. He shouts at the camera operator, 'You're an idiot. You haven't heard the last of this. How could you mislay such an important recording? You did record that event?' He walks over to the camera operator and says, 'I'm going to kill you now.'
He places his hands around the camera operator's throat and begins to strangle him.

Leila goes between them saying, 'Mr. Producer, it's your fault, I know you told him to keep recording when we descended from the top of the waterfall so take your hands off his throat please?'

Chapter 66

The producer is in such a rage now that he is not in the mood to listen to Leila asking him to refrain from strangling the camera man. She decides to intervene because the camera operator is going blue. She places her hand on the producer's shoulder. He instantaneously releases the camera operator from his grasp. The camera operator staggers unsteadily backwards, clutching his throat and is having difficulty in breathing.

Leila goes to him looks him in the eyes and says, 'That was a bit hasty of your producer. I can sympathize. I was not going to let him kill you, 'that would not be right. Now do not worry you will be fine, I am sure.'

Leila looks up and says, 'Mr. Producer you can keep all of the levitation video if you like.'

He replies, 'I need the interview. That is probably the most important bit of television news I have ever been involved with. It is without a shadow of doubt world news. I must have it now please!'

'Well you can't have it, it's my decision what happens here, but you have quite a lot of news cover now and that's all you're going to get.'

He runs to the camera, hoping that the rest of the days filming remains intact but before he can rescue it would appear his timing is a little bit slow.

The camera and the tripod, starts to levitate. The crew try and stop it but it is too late, it is at the top of the waterfall.

The crew are in a frenzy running around waving their hands wildly in the air.

'Get up there,' The Producer is shouting, 'bring the camera and the tripod back down, we will need it for our news tonight!'

'Now you see how powerful I am,' Leila says to the producer. 'Would you like your camera and tripod back?'

He looks at Leila. 'Yes, I'd like it back now,' he barks.

Leila looks at him and says, 'You've not said the magic word. I need the magic word before I give you back your camera.

What is the magic word? She asks.

The crew rush over, 'The magic word is please, say it sir.'

The producer answers, 'I'm not going to say it. I don't see why I should.'

'Fine,' replies Leila, 'I will leave.' Then as she walks back to the minibus.

The television crew are discussing the camera and tripod which has now levitated another fifty metres above the top of the waterfall. They are beside themselves with worry, when Leila says,

'Mr. Producer, do you want your camera and tripod back? All you have to say is the magic word.'

'No I'm not going to say it.' His face is twisted in rage.

The camera and tripod jumps another fifty metres it is now one hundred metres above the waterfall. It just hangs there in that position.

'What is the magic word?' Leila asks.

The crew are frantic, 'Please say the magic word, sir.'

'Before you answer that important question, I want you to reflect on your response. You get it wrong and the camera and tripod will levitate another one hundred metres. My family and I will then leave. I can keep the camera and tripod up there forever if I wish. What is the magic word Mr. Producer are you going to say the magic word?'

Chapter 67

He stands there defiant, he wants to say the magic word but his pride will not let him.

'Come on dad, granddad, mum, grandma and Alfie back to the mini bus, we are out of here now. Mr mini bus driver please open the doors on the minibus we would like to leave.'

The driver is very perplexed but he does what Leila asks. He has clocked how powerful she is, and he is not going to upset her in any way whatsoever.

'Mr Driver, what is your name please?' Leila enquires.

He answers, 'My name is David.'

Leila asks. 'David will you drive us to a nice restaurant around here?'

'I know a very nice restaurant not too far away I can drive you there if you wish!'

'Will you take us there, please,' replies Leila.

Just as the minibus is about to go, the Producer runs over and frantically puts his hand up to stop the minibus. The driver looks at Leila, She knows what he is thinking. She communicates with him telepathically. 'David you may stop now please.'

His hands are almost one with the steering wheel. He is holding his hands very tightly onto the wheel but he stops anyway.

'David, I'll deal with the Producer. Please open the door thank you.'

The minibus is stationary now. The Producer runs around to Leila's door, looks at Leila but does not say a word, just throws his hands in the air.

Leila looks at him and asks. 'What do you want Mr Producer? Are you here to give me the magic word?'

'Alright I'm here to give you the magic word. Please, can I have my camera and tripod back.'

'Now that wasn't so hard, was it' Leila replies. Please drive away to the restaurant David. The door closes and the driver resumes his journey taking the family to the restaurant for dinner.

Everyone on the bus look at Leila, she says, 'I've placed the camera and the tripod on the ground already, don't worry.'

Alfie is laughing his head off and shouts out loud, 'That was awesome.'

Leila looks at her mum then enquires, 'Mum you look a bit white, are you alright!'

'Yes of course I'm fine but a bit worried,' mum replies. 'Granddad, you haven't said much all day is there something wrong. Please tell me?'

'I was just wondering how powerful you are? It would seem that you do not need our help anymore!'

'Not so' Leila replies, 'I'll need you all next week in New York at The United Nations Building. The Security Council will be meeting there next week. Then the world will know how powerful this family is.'

Chapter 68

'But how are we going to get there?' Granddad asks.

'Granddad I'll fly the family there it will take less than a minute. We will appear as if by magic. It will be a breathtaking event a scene of utter commotion, furore and panic and of course the television cameras will be there to record the whole event.'

The minibus stops and David points to the restaurant and says, 'We have arrived at our destination, 'Will you please follow me' as he waves his hand in the direction of the restaurant. The minibus doors open. They all follow him into the restaurant. Inside looks very clean and spacious with air conditioning. David goes to find the owner then introduces him to Leila's family. He is a very smartly dressed man and spotlessly clean, about five ten inches in height with a black moustache, a full head of hair going grey at the sides.

He introduces himself to granddad, says, 'Will you please follow me.' He indicates to them to follow him to a large table and says, 'Please will you make yourselves at home and do sit down. What would like to drink? It's all free in my restaurant,' as he hands them a drinks menu.'

Granddad looks at the menu then hands it around so that everyone can order the drinks. The owner arrives back at the table. 'I'm ready to take your orders now please, that's if you are ready to order?'

Granddad looks at the owner and says, 'I'll order for everyone. My wife and I will have a white wine chilled please!'

'Now Ciera what would you like to drink?'

'I think I might try one of the local drinks cold, please.'

'John what is your choice of drink?' 'I'll have one of the local drinks.'

'Alfie I suppose you'll have a litre of beer.'

'Don't be silly Granddad I couldn't drink a litre of beer.'

I'm only kidding Alfie. As he looks at the owner and says, I think he will have an orange thank you.'

'Let me suggest our roast chicken. Everything we cook in this restaurant is delivered fresh every morning. All the chickens are free range. We even make our own butter. You can have lamb or beef if you like. I will leave you to decide what you want. I'll be back in five minutes, to take your orders thank you.'

'Shall we start with Alfie? Granddad enquires. 'What would you like young man?'

'I think I will have the roast chicken please.'

'Ciera what would you like?'

'I'll have the roast chicken.'

'Grandma what will you have?'

'I'll try the roast chicken thank you!'

'John what is your choice son?'

'I'll have the chicken please.'

'Good then I'll go for the chicken as well' replies Granddad, 'and you Leila what do you fancy.'

'I'll have the chicken thank you.'

'So it's all chicken dinners then? He looks up, gives the owner a nod, He arrives at the table and asks, 'Have you decided what you would like for your dinners?'

Granddad looks at him. 'We are going to try five roast chicken dinners but a small dinner for little Alfie please.'

'Good' replies the owner, 'you'll love the chicken it's sumptuous,' as he places his thumb and first finger to his lips,' what about more drinks sir?'

Granddad looks around and says, 'I think we'll have the same drinks again please.' The turns and walks to the kitchen, gets the drinks, walks over and places them on the table saying, 'Enjoy your drinks I'll be back with your dinners in about fifteen minutes.'

'Well, everyone, our holiday ends tomorrow, we need to be out of our rooms by twelve noon,' says granddad, 'but I must say I think that we have had a wonderful holiday. We have been to see lots of very interesting historic places and of course we had the wonderful presence of Leila and I am sure that we all appreciate all the help and protection she afforded us especially Alfie and of course myself. We have a very special granddaughter who will become not just famous in this world she will be without equal in the Universe. We now know we will not be the same family ever again because of her powers but that does not mean we will lose her. She will have to go away from time to time and I assume she will return and we will go on holiday together again. Oh, here comes our dinners.'

The restaurant owner arrives with the chicken dinners, places them on the table and says, 'I'll just go and get hold of the vegetables for you. He turns walks back to the kitchen, picks up the vegetables returns to his customers, places the vegetables on the table saying, enjoy your meals, as he turns and walks back to the kitchen.

'Right, Alfie what vegetables would you like? We have fresh peas, cauliflowers, new potatoes onions and lots of gravy.'

'Ah, I think I'll have new potatoes, peas and a small bit of cauliflower and gravy please,' he replies.

Granddad places all the vegetables on his plate and the gravy over the vegetables saying, 'there you are, you eat up all the vegetables and the chicken it looks lovely to me. Come on everyone help yourselves this dinner looks wonderful.'

'This is a fantastic dinner' says Ciera, 'it tastes wonderful. 'What about your dinner grandma.'

'Oh yes, I could have this dinner every day, it is indeed wonderful' she replies.

'Leila what is your opinion, 'I think that it is amazing, 'It tastes fantastic. I would like to come here again, sometime in the future, 'So she carries on eating.'

'What do you think John. 'Is it up to your mother's, standard?'

'Now dad, 'I wouldn't want to offend mother, but I'm sure that she would agree with me, on that subject. I must say that it's probably the best dinner I've had in this country!'

'And you Alfie, 'Do you like your dinner granddad asks?'

'I like it as he looks at his mum and says, 'I do like the chicken it's lovely.'

'Well as long as you liked something Alfie that's fine with me. Isn't it amazing this restaurant is way out in the sticks and the food is so fantastic it doesn't make sense, how does he make a living here?'

'With this kind of food he can't fail to make a good living, Even if it's way out in the sticks and good luck to him,' says John.

John asks. 'What about our driver? I'll go and pay the owner and ask about the driver.'

John has finished his dinner, so up he gets up walks over to the owner, he enquires, 'Has our driver had something to eat?'

'Yes of course, we give him lunch when he brings us customers that is if he needs a meal.'

'That's fine. We wouldn't want him driving us around all day, and not having anything to eat.'

'No, no sir, we always allows him food we look after him very well.'

John takes his credit card from his wallet, places it in the machine, puts his pin number in, then he removes his card and says, 'Thank you for the lovely food.' John goes back to the table and informs the family that, the driver does also have a lunch here every time he arrives at the restaurant with customers.'

Grandma says, 'That is ok then, 'Now if we are all finished lunch I'll go and thank the owner for this amazing lunch, and the friendly atmosphere.'

She gets up, walks over to the owner, congratulates him on his fantastic restaurant, and the wonderful food the family had. Thank you very much and goodbye.'

The family walk out to the minibus. The driver is waiting for them.

Granddad looks at the driver, and gives the thumbs up and says, 'David we thank you very much for driving us to this restaurant, that food was fantastic.' 'Our next port of call is an old monastery about ten kilometres from here. Would you like to visit it?'

Granddad looks around and enquires, 'Shall we go and see this old monastery and we have plenty of time?'

'Yes' is the answer from everyone.

'That's it then David, 'It's the monastery, everyone into the minibus!'

All the family are in the minibus, the driver closes all the doors starts up the engine and drives off.

Chapter 69

Ten minutes later the minibus arrives at the monastery, everyone alights and David says, 'Will you follow me, please. Let me take you to reception then you'll be taken on a tour of the monastery.'
The family follow him into reception and one of the monks (he is a small person with a long brown habit going bald and a little grey but he speaks perfect English) greets all the family with a little bow saying, 'Will you follow me please. I am your tour guide for today.' As he is walking around he informs the family, 'This monastery was built in the eight century and it was taken over by the Russians later in the eighteen century and they put all the monks to the sword, 'all the monks were killed. After the fall of the Soviet Union, the Monastery reversed back to the monks again. We have been here ever since. We make, and grow everything we need here. Now we can walk to our wine making facility. We make two kinds of wine here, red and white wines. Please follow me, I will show you to where we make all the wines. Right please, gather round me. As you see those large containers in front of you carry about two thousand litres of wine each and there are six containers; three for white wine and three for red wine. Now if you will follow me into the tasting area you may wet your palate with all of our wines. You may buy any of the wines to take back to your country. We also do an internet service if you need to purchase some extra when you are back in your country.'

In the tasting area, the monk invites them to pick up a glass and try any of the wines on the table. 'There is a pail at the side of the table if you wish to discharge the wine from your mouth or you can sip and swallow if you like.' Granddad and his wife decide that the wines are delicious but can't make up their minds about the dry and the medium. They both like the reds. John and Ciera are not so keen on the red wine. But they are very keen on the white medium wines. After about twenty minutes, the tasting is finished. Everyone likes the taste of the two wines, the monk again says, 'Follow me please to the next area on our tour around the factory.'

The family walk behind him and follow him into the sales department where he indicates with his hand saying, 'All our wines are for sale if you decide to purchase. Now I must take my leave of you. Thank you very much for your time. I now hand you over to our sales person.'
    She introduces herself, 'My name is Anna' as she looks around and says, 'In this room you will see there are thousands and thousands of

bottles of wines on racks. This is a very old part of the monastery, it has no sunlight and it is very cool with just artificial lighting.'

Granddad picks up one of the leaflets has a quick look at the prices and says, 'John these prices are very fair. I think I'll buy a few bottles to take home.'

Ciera looks at the leaflets and says, 'We'll have a few bottles as well, the prices are very reasonable and cheap.' Ciera looks at Leila and says, 'Leila come on let's go and have a look at the wines. We could get slightly intoxicated.'

The two of them walk over to where the wines are stacked. Some bottles are already on the table in buckets of ice, with the white wine, 'Let's have another glass and see what it tastes like.'

Leila is not sure, but to keep her mum happy, she picks up a glass of white wine, followed by her mum. She picks up a glass as well.

'Oh that is lovely and sumptuous,' Says her mum. 'I could drink this all day.'

'I agree, but I'm not so sure, if I could drink it all day. It's very palatable and pleasant' Leila replies. 'Come on let us find dad and Alfie,' Leila shouts over to granddad and grandma asking, 'Have you seen dad and Alfie.' 'We cannot see them anywhere.'

'No we haven't seen them for a while.' they reply. Leila says, 'I'll communicate with John and find out where they are.'

It takes less than a tenth of a second to find out where dad and Alfie are.

'Come on mum follow me. I know where they are.' Ciera walks after Leila out through a side door and would you believe it, there they are by a little stream of water, 'Alfie is throwing little sticks into the stream. 'Dad is watching him.

Ciera shouts at John. 'Please take Alfie away from that stream he might fall in. 'He is fine, the stream is only about twenty centimetres deep,' as he looks around at Ciera.'

'I do not care, I want him away from that stream now, please!'

'Ok, come on, Alfie, mum wants you away from the stream.'

'Oh, but I like it here,' replies Alfie, 'I am just playing.'

'I know son, but your mum has spoken. You and I must obey her. Come on let's go back inside please.'

'It's boring in there, I don't want to go,' Alfie replies.

'Fine then, let us go and have a drink, shall we?'

'Yes please,' replies Alfie, as he runs inside.

'Alfie please sit down in that chair,' he points to a chair.

'I'll go and buy you a drink, 'He walks over to one the sales people and asks, 'May I buy a drink for my son please?'

'Yes, of course sir. What would he like?'

'May I have an orange juice for him please?'

'Yes, of course sir. You go and sit with him. I'll bring it to him shortly.'

'Thank you,' replies John, and returns to Alfie saying, 'Your drink will be here in a minute.'

Alfie looks around then looks at his dad and asks, 'Can I have some wine please; I might like it!'

His dad looks at him in amazement, and says, 'Alfie you are not allowed alcoholic drinks and your mum would go mad if I let you have one.'

The sales person arrives with Alfie's drink and places it on the table next to him.

'There you are, your very own orange juice,' says the sales person.

Alfie says, 'Thank you,' and sips the orange. 'This is nice, dad.'

'I'm glad you like it,' dad replies.

Ciera and Leila arrive at the table and ask, 'Alfie, what are you drinking.

'I am having an orange and it is very nice.'

John, says, 'I have bought a bottle of white wine and a bottle of red I hope you do not mind. What about you, Leila have you bought anything yet?'

'I think I'll buy a couple of bottles of red wine.'

'Good for you,' replies Ciera, 'What about granddad and grandma. Have they bought anything?'

'I don't know, but they are just coming over, 'so you can ask them yourself.' Leila replies.

Ciera turns as granddad and his wife arrive at the table.

'Granddad, have you acquired any of the wines here?'

'Yes we have two bottles of white, two bottles of red. 'I think that is all we need, what about you? Have you invested in anything?' 'Yes Ciera replies.

'Then it would appear we are well stocked up with drinks for a while. If we are finished buying I think we should go and find the minibus driver.

'Outside in the car park David the minibus driver is sitting on a little fold up chair. He sees them and stands up asking, 'Have you had a nice time in the monastery, did you buy anything?'

Granddad replies. 'Yes we did, we bought white and red wines.'

'Good,' replies David. 'This place makes a very good wine, and it's exported all around the world. Now if you are all ready please board the minibus. It is going to take me about one hour to return to the hotel. I think we should go now. That is if you don't mind.'

John looks around and asks, 'Is everyone ready to go back to the hotel?'

'Yes please,' everyone shouts at the same time.

'Please fasten your seat belts we are about to have lift off, says David, the driver, in a jovial way.

Alfie sits next to Leila, looks at her in a strange way and enquires, 'Leila, can I ask, are you more powerful than Superman?'

'Yes I am more powerful than Superman. I'm even more powerful than anyone on this planet or the Universe.'

'Awesome. And you are my sister, Wow!'

'Yes, Alfie I'm your sister forever.'

Alfie is like a Cheshire cat with a mischievous grin on his face and asks, 'Could I be as powerful you?'

'Well not at the moment. However when you grow up into a man I will give you some powers, but you can never be as powerful as me, I am a one off. When I was about three months in my mum's tummy, the Aliens gave me this amazing technology. Mum, dad, granddad and grandma all have some of the powers I have. I can make them more powerful as and when I need them. I know that you don't understand yet but in time you will appreciate the wait.'

'Why can't I have some powers now.' he asks.

'Because you're not ready and they would get you into trouble very quickly and we can't have that, can we Alfie.'

'I suppose not. When I grow up, you promise to give me some powers?'

'Yes, I promise I will give you some powers when you grow up.'

'Cool!' replies Alfie.

Ten minutes go by and Alfie is asleep on Leila's shoulder.

Ciera looks around and asks: 'Is he alright Leila.'

'He's fine now. I think he is away in the land of the fairies,' Leila answers.

'Good' Ciera replies, 'that should keep him quiet for a while.'

Chapter 70

Leila is wondering about next week and what she might need to do, so she decides now that she is going to wing it when the time comes because the questions will come quick and fast and she will need to be on her guard at all times in the United Nations Building. She is not contemplating missing any questions that might be relevant, or any of the wiles or trickery in her address to the populace in the debating room. Leila will consider what the World Leaders intentions are but only if they are in favour of Leila's wish for a better World. They will not take precedence over her agenda. The rule of law will be suspended in all countries until all governments come to heel, and understand that her recommendations will be indubitably be adhered to.

The minibus is just about to arrive back at the hotel. Leila gives Alfie a little shake to wake him up, Poor Alfie he is not sure where he is. He looks up and asks, 'Leila where are we?'

'We're back at the hotel, 'Be careful when you step off of the minibus.'

The driver opens the doors and the family evacuate the minibus.

Alfie is a bit unsteady so Leila holds his hand, making sure that he does not fall.

John goes and gives Fifty Euros to David and says, 'Thank you for your diligent service which we greatly appreciate and looking after the family in your meticulous way. He goes back to the family and says, 'Shall we go and get ready for a late meal?

'We'll all meet in the dining room at 7pm. Is everyone happy with that time?' 'Everyone nods in unison. 'Ok we'll meet at 7pm then.'

The family return to their respective apartments. They have a quick shower and put on clean clothes for their last night in the resort.

Ciera and Leila are the first into the dining room and wait for the rest of the family to arrive. Ciera looks at Leila and asks, 'Did you have a nice time today?'

'Yes' Leila replies, 'I had a very good time today with the family, it's been a marvellous holiday, I've enjoyed myself tremendously and yes we will do this again mum.'

I'm not so sure' Ciera replies.

'Mum let me tell you something I'm not going to abandon my family. I will make time to be with you for a long time into the future. I have no intention of leaving my own family of flesh and blood. What I have to do will not take long I can tell you that for sure and the same applies to the

Universe. Just you think if I had a job, I would be away from home a lot of the time and have no control over my own destiny. This way I own all my time so I can do what I please with it. Now do you understand?'

'I think so, but it's a bit above me However, I do believe you.'

'Mum there is something else you need to know before the rest of the family arrive for our late meal.'

Ciera looks at Leila in a very perplexing way says, 'You are alright? Do you want to tell me something that I don't already know?'

'Give me your hands, please, I must tell you something very important about myself.'

Leila takes her mum's hands in hers, looks at her very intently and says, 'I'm never going to grow old. My Bio/Dna technology is such that it rejuvenates my body every second I'm alive, do you understand mum?'

'No I don't understand. Are you telling me that you will never, never grow old?'

'Yes, mum, I'll always look the same as I am now, eighteen years old. I will never look older.'

'Will you never die?' Mum asks.

'I don't know. At the moment that will depend on the technology in the future. Anyway I wanted to tell you first. I should tell the rest of the family but I think it might be too much for them, they might not understand. I know it's very confusing and mystifying. What do you think mum?'

'I think you will have to decide, 'When and if you feel the time is right to inform them that will be your decision.'

'Look, Alfie, John, granddad and grandma just arrived for the late meal.'

They walk over to Ciera and Leila, 'Shall we go and help ourselves to late tea Alfie you come with us please' his mum says.

'Ok mum I'll come with you.'

Now the family are sitting in position at the table with their late meals. The talk is about going home tomorrow.

Alfie looks around the table and asks, 'Why are we going home tomorrow Leila?'

'Well, we paid the hotel for the holiday and now we need to leave because our holiday time is up in this hotel. There are other people waiting to take our rooms tomorrow. We will have another holiday soon is that all right with you Alfie?'

Alfie looks at Leila and says, 'You promise that we will have another holiday soon.'

She answers, 'Alfie I promise we will have another holiday soon.'

'Good, I'm happy with that,' Alfie replies, and carries on eating his late meal.

Granddad looks at Leila and says, 'We are very fortunate in having you as our granddaughter we have such a wonderful time with you we don't want it to end but if you say that we will have another holiday soon, we think that is going to be even a better holiday.

I will make time for another holiday with the family. I am not going to abandon my own family.'

Granddad says, 'Leila, we do not want to put you under any pressure, are you sure you will be able to make the time to have another holiday with the family?' 'Granddad when I say we will have another holiday together, I mean it, you are not to worry I will make time to be with my family!'

Granddad asks, 'May I ask about next week, Leila?'

Chapter 71

'Of course you can. I don't have any secrets from my family what's the question granddad?'

'Well, I, we, are wondering why you need us to be with you next week at The United Nations?'

'Now that is a strange question from you, granddad. I will tell you why I want my family with me next week. To prove to the world that we will not tolerate any interference from any World governments no matter how important they might think they are. I also need to make sure that if they try and overpower any one of us, there will be repercussions. I need to show the world my family, so that there are no excuses whatsoever that you come under my umbrella of safety and I will deal with anyone who tries to stop us from delivering our message to the world!'

'But will they listen?' asks her dad.

'They will listen, they might not like it but they will listen. Now I would like everyone to be at our house Tuesday afternoon from where we will transport to the United Nations Building in New York. It will take about one minute, any questions?'

'This sounds as if it's going to be very exciting. I can't wait,' replies granddad.

'What about Alfie?' Ciera asks.

'Leila looks at her mum. Do you think we will leave Alfie behind?' No, he comes with us. Do not worry I will look after him; He will be under my protection all the time we are in New York. What about grandma? Do you have any questions.'

'I don't need to ask you anything, I know whatever you need to do will be for the benefit of the world so I'm quite happy with whatever decision you make regarding our world.'

'So we are all going to New York next week ok. I'll inform JK about our decision and I'm sure he'll accommodate whatever is needed to help make this World a better place in which to live.'

'Leila, if you look over your right shoulder, there is a man watching us very intently' says her dad.

'I know I have clocked him already, dad. Do not worry. I will have a word with him.' In an instant, Leila is sitting next to this very inquisitive person before he knows it. He is totally bemused and looks very frightened as he leans backwards away from Leila asking, 'How did you get from there to here,' as he points his finger first to where Leila was and then to where she is sitting now.

'Hello, my name is Leila. May I have your name please? On second thoughts let me tell you; am I correct in saying that your name is Edik?' He nods his head but does not say a word. 'Now Edik don't be afraid of me I'm not going to hurt you.'

Edik is absolutely and completely flabbergasted. He is looking at Leila with his eyes wide open. He does not know what to say. It would appear that maybe he has lost the use of his tongue, He is talking in a garbled unknown language and even Leila does not understand. She places her hand on his right shoulder and says, 'Would you like to ask me something? What is your pleasure? Can you talk to me in a coherent manner?'

He rises up from the table and runs away as fast as his legs can carry him.

Leila returns to the family table and says, 'What a strange man. I wonder why he ran away.

Ciera jumps up from the table and runs out of the restaurant. Leila looks around and says, 'Leave this to me, please. I think I know what the matter is with mum.'

Leila follows her mum out of the restaurant and finds her at the side of the restaurant. She is crying hysterically. She looks very distressed so she walks over to her, puts her arms around her and says, 'This is the second time you have cried since we came on holiday. Come on mum tell me what is the matter, why are you crying. I don't like to see you in such a state!'

'It's not fair, you're going away, I'm going to miss you very much when you go, I know that you will have to go soon!'

'Mum, I am not leaving forever, 'I do not need to be away for long periods. I will always be in telepathic communication with you when you need to talk to me. Come on, mum, dry your eyes so we can return to the family!'

Back the two of them go into the restaurant. The family do not say anything although everyone knows that Ciera is very upset.

The late meal finished, the family vacates the dining room and walk to the swimming pool area where they find a table and sit down.

'Would anyone like to go for a swim?' Ciera asks.

Alfie replies, 'I'll come for a swim, mum.'

'I'll have one as well, replies Leila.

'Ok, then I'll go and get some swimming costumes. 'She gets up saying, 'I'll be back in ten minutes. 'Do you want to come and get the swimming costumes with me, Alfie?'

'No mum I'll stay with Leila thank you.' Ciera returns with the swimming costumes. Leila, Alfie and Ciera go for their last swim. After about ten minutes Alfie says. I'm cold now can I get out? 'Yes of course you can. Come on mum lets go back to the rest of the family.'

The rest of the evening goes very pleasantly and John calls for the last drink of the holiday, before they retire for the night. 'We'll meet at eight in the morning at the restaurant.'

Then all the family retire to their respective rooms for the night.

The next morning everyone is up early, all the cases are packed and ready when the bus arrives.

John and granddad are the first to arrive at the restaurant, walk in and sit down, and wait for the rest of the family. Ten minutes later the rest of the family arrive and the family are very self conscious and uneasy so the talk is about the weather.

'Are we going to have breakfast, or just talk about the weather?' Ciera asks.

'Come on, Alfie, you and I will get our breakfast and the others can follow us.'

'Yes, mum, I'll come with you,' as he places his hand in his mum's hand and off they go to the breakfast bar.

It does not take long for the rest of the family to arrive at the breakfast bar. They all pick their preferred meals and return to their table to start their breakfast. They leave the restaurant when they have finished their breakfasts, they go outside. Then decide to sit by one of the swimming pools to pass the time away before their bus arrives to take them to the airport. Leila stands up and says, 'I must go now but I will not be away too long, I have business to attend to.'

She stands up. In a second she is gone. Seconds later she is in the President's office.

Chapter 72

When she arrives in the office of Mr. Sokulsky, the soldiers surround her, with their guns pointing at Leila.

The President Mr Nicolaus Sokulsky is standing up behind his desk, looks at Leila, says, 'Welcome to my office young lady.'

Leila looks mystified and asks, 'Why are your men pointing their weapons at me? Is there a problem?'

'To make sure we can place you under arrest is his answer.'

'Why would you want to place me under arrest? 'What have I done wrong?'

'It would seem that you have very special powers and we would like to know where you received them from?'

'Mr President, that is none of your business, 'What, are you going to do about it?' Leila asks.

'Well, I'm going to place you under arrest and send you to Moscow by plane this morning to see the President of Russia, Mr Pavel Bragin.'

'Mr President, I don't want any trouble with you, I know that you have instructions from Russia to arrest me. I dare say that you are a very principled person and I would not hurt you, but if you have to send me to Moscow fair enough. Shall we shake hands before I leave here, 'that is if you want to!'

'Of course I'll take your hand.'

Leila places her hand in his and in a flash they materialize in the office of the President of Russia Mr Pavel Bragin. He is dressed in a light grey suit and white shirt with black shoes and black socks. He is about six foot three high and has a good head of hair. He is very uneasy, frightened and he looks worried, he is shaking violently. He does not know what to do or say, He is rubbing his eyes and looking around in a very worried way.

Leila walks over to him and says, 'Mr. President you wanted to see me. My name is Leila,' as she looks at him, 'well I am here, what do you want from me sir?'

The President is moving his right hand towards his panic button, but Leila has clocked him, so she levitates him to the front of his desk. 'Mr. President, I'll ask you once more. What do you want from me? Can I help you in anyway?'

The Crimean President Mr Nicolaus Sokulsky decides to try and help the Russian President by putting a gun at Leila's head, saying, 'I have you now, please place your hands over your head. You are under arrest?'

Leila looks at him asking, 'Are you some kind of idiot? Are you trying to kill the President of Russia?' As his hand turns and points his gun in the direction of the Russian President's head.

The Russian President places his hands over his head, thinks to himself. 'I am going to die. This idiot is out of his mind why is he pointing his gun at me?'

Leila intervenes and then she looks at the Crimean President and says, 'That is not the way to address the Russian President, Place your gun on the desk, please?'

He duly obeys and places his gun on the desk, takes a step back and shudders violently. His mouth is wide open and he gasps at the thought of pointing his gun at the Russian President, thinking to himself, 'I am going to prison for the rest of my life, 'How am I going to redeem myself?'

There is heavy knocking on the President's office door, he shouts out, 'who is it, what do you want?'

'It's your security guards sir, may we come in?'

'I don't need you at this moment. Go away thank you.'

The security guards ask, 'Are you sure sir.'

'Yes I am sure. Now go away, I will call you if I need your assistance.'

Leila looks at the Russian President and says, 'Thank you sir no harm will come to you while I'm in your office, I promise. Now may I talk to you freely and tell you why I am in your office. The first thing you need to know, there is no army, navy or air force in the world able to capture me. Sir, you might laugh, I will give you a demonstration of my powers. That red phone on your desk connects you to all of your silo underground missiles?'

'Why do you ask? The President enquires.

Leila does not say anything; she does nothing, just smiles to herself.

The red phone rings. The President picks it up. 'Yes what's the problem?'

A voice at the other end says, in a very excited way, 'Sir, the missile silos have opened, the missiles have armed themselves. What do you want me to do sir!'

'I don't know who authorized the count down?'

'We don't know sir.'

'How far are they into the countdown?'

'All the missiles are ready to go, sir and we can't override the computers, We are helpless to stop them, We don't know what to do!'

'Where are they pointing to?'

'Sir, I don't want to frighten you but they are scheduled by our computers to hit Moscow if we can't stop them!'

'Oh, my God, we are going to be annihilated. What am I going to do?' He looks at Leila and now he knows she has the power to arm and send them to wherever she decides. He points his finger at the other President and says to him, 'You get out of here now. All this is your fault I'll deal with you at a later date. Mr Nicolaus Sokulsky goes to the door. It opens as if by magic. He walks through to the other side.

Two of the President's security guards try to run into the President's office only to find their way blocked by an invisible shield. They just bounce off it but do not understand what happened. The door closes and the Russian President and Leila are now alone in his office. He looks very anxious and a bit scared.

'Mr Bragin, you don't mind if I call you by your last name.' What would you like me to do?' Leila asks.

He is shaking all over and he is having a difficult time talking. He knows what he wants to say but he can't get the speech out.'

Leila sees that he is in great difficulty, so she takes him by the hand.' Look at me Pavel; you are wasting valuable time you need to make a decision. What do you want me to do?'

'What can you do? You can't be that powerful that you can arm our missiles and let them go where you want to send them, 'That's impossible. No one is that powerful!'

'Pavel, I'm the most powerful person on this Planet and in the Universe. I'm not kidding you. Sir, the missiles will fly very soon if we do not stop them. Pavel, your stubbornness and implacability will get you killed and a vast number of your people will die as well. Now we don't want that, do we, you don't want to destroy your own people do you?'

He looks at Leila but he does not want to give in as it is not in his nature and asks, 'Can you stop them from flying now?'

'Yes, sir, I can, replies Leila.

'Do it then. You and I have a lot to talk about after you have stopped the count down on the missiles, I don't want to be responsible for killing my own people do I?'

Chapter 73

'Pavel, you will have a call any second now to tell you that the countdown to fire the missiles has stopped.' His red phone rings, the voice at the other end says, 'Mr. President the missiles countdown has stopped and the silos have closed. We are safe, sir, thank God!'

'Incidentally what's the time on the countdown clock?'

'Ten seconds sir.'

'Thank you very much' the President replies, then he replaces the phone.

'Now young lady what can I do for you. I nearly had a heart attack. Please sit down and let us talk in a meaningful way.' The President is perplexed, but what can he do? It would appear that this young lady seems to have some very advanced technology on her, or she is an Alien. Either way, I think that it may be better for me, to find out how advanced she is. *Little does he know, 'That Leila is listening in on his thoughts, but she is in no hurry to tell him.'*

Leila now knows that she has the attention of the President and she is going to make the best use of her friendship with him and she will need him as an ally and supporter in the future.

Leila looks at him asking, 'Sir is there anything that you have never done but maybe you would like to do it now.'

The President pauses for a minute and then he looks at Leila. 'Yes, there is, I would have loved to have been an astronaut but it's too late for me to do that now!'

'Sir, it may not be too late.'

The President looks at Leila and thinks to himself, I think that I would rather be on her side than against her. *Little does he know that Leila has scanned his mind and she knows everything he is thinking about but that does not worry her, if it keeps him happy, that's fine no worries there, so she decides to humour him.*

'Pavel, may I have your hand please?'

He is reluctant but he decides to take her hand and instantaneously they are one hundred miles above the Earth. He is totally lost for words, very unsteady as he looks down on the World. He is hanging on to Leila with grim determination.

'How did we get up here and how are we breathing up here?' he asks.

'Sir, we are cocooned in a shield with all the air we need' Leila replies. She looks at him and says, 'What do you think of your World sir?'

'It's amazing, so beautiful but am I safe up here?'

'Yes, of course you are. Now would you like to keep your World like that for a long time? Because the way you're going, this World this Earth will be a wilderness in less than one hundred years. Is that what you want for your people and grandchildren?'

'Definitely not but what can I do about it?'

'Not you Pavel, I'll decide the future of this planet with your help, Shall we return back in your office now?'

He nods his head, and in the blink of an eye, they have returned to his office.

'You now know that I'm all powerful, I can tell you that I'm able to stop any missiles anywhere in the world even from here, from being launched.'

'You are that powerful?'

'Yes, I'm that powerful' Leila replies.

'What can I do for you that you can't do yourself?'

'I would like your support at the United Nations General Assembly on Tuesday afternoon next week. Do you think you can be there, and if I need your support you will back me, but only if I need it!'

'Yes, of course. I wouldn't have the courage to go against you, not after you kindly let me see how powerful you are.'

'Thank you, Pavel: I'm sure that we'll be good friends for long time. I need to return to my family now. Goodbye sir. See you next week.'

She finds the Crimean President Mr Sokulsky takes him by the hand and in seconds he is back in his office, she looks at him and says, 'Goodbye, sir, thank you for everything.'

In a flash Leila is back, next to her family at the swimming pool. 'So sorry I had to go I was summoned by the Russian President Mr Bragin to his office in the Kremlin. Do not worry I think I've won him over to our cause.'

Her mum enquires, 'Is this Mr Bragin a friendly person?'

'Very nice and friendly, at least he is now,' Leila replies, with a little smile.

'Did you have any trouble in the Kremlin?' 'Granddad asks.

'Nothing to worry about, I do not think I will have any problems there' Leila replies.

John says, 'Alfie, look, here is the bus that will take us to the airport. Everyone make sure that our luggage is on the bus before we leave the hotel.' Dad looks at Alfie and says, 'Alfie, wave to the people in the hotel as the bus drives away.'

Alfie looks at his dad, does not say a word, just waves.

Chapter 74

Some forty-five minutes later the bus arrives at the airport, the doors open and everyone alights from the bus onto the ground, finds their respective pieces of luggage and file into the departing area inside the airport. There they wait to join the queue and wait their turn to show their departing tickets and receive their boarding passes.

Alfie by this time is very fidgety. Leila is a bit worried so she goes and gives him a cuddle and asks, 'what's the matter, Alfie, don't you want to go back home?'

He looks at her and enquires, 'Are you going away soon?'

'Only for a while but you are coming with me. Does that make you a bit happier.'

'Yes I think that will be alright,' Alfie replies.

'Off you go then have a look in the shops you might like to buy a souvenir from Crimea to take home with you.' Alfie is a bit apprehensive about going on his own. Leila senses he is a little bit afraid to look around on his own!'

'Go on Alfie, I'll be watching you, don't worry, nothing will happen to you,'

Leila now has a minute to herself so she decides to send a telepathic message to Gia and Óisin asking, 'Can you be in orbit above Earth on next Tuesday morning. I'll explain when I see you. I would appreciate an early response please. I need your advice. It's important we have a reunion. When you arrive in orbit above my planet, I will know. Then I will transport up to your craft and give you all the necessary information. I do not want to worry you. It is in both of our interests regarding my world and yours.'

After about fifteen minutes, Gia and Óisin's answer to Leila is, 'We will be in orbit Tuesday morning and await your presence in our craft. It will be marvellous to see you again; it has been a while since we last met regards, Gia and Óisin.'

Chapter 75

On arriving back in their country they embark from the plane. They then go to luggage pick up area and retrieve their luggage. Ciera is hoping that there will be no trouble going through customs because the family have wine and they would like to keep it. The family walk out through the custom green area without a hitch. That is until one of the custom officers stands in front of Leila and indicates to her to place her case on the table for inspection. Leila looks at him, 'Then she places her case on the table.

He asks, 'Is this your case young lady?'

Leila answers. 'Yes it is. Why?

'No particular reason, 'We, just randomly pick any person coming through the Green Security Lane with nothing to declare. Please open your case. I need to check the contents inside.'

Leila doesn't look at the suit case just looks at the Custom Officer and says, 'It is open sir!'

He looks at her then looks at the lock on the suit case and says, 'The lock is still attached to the suit case!'

'Look again, sir. The lock opens itself very slowly then drops onto the table. He backs off from the case with his hands in front of his face looks at Leila and asks, 'Is there a bomb inside your suit case miss?'

'No sir, there is not a bomb inside my suit case. Then the zip starts to undo all the way around, the cover lifts up and falls backwards, Leila is standing about two feet from her suit case. Now the suit case is open so that Custom Officer can see inside.

He is in panic mode so he phones for help. In the meantime Ciera arrives at Leila's side and asks, 'Is everything all right here Leila?'

'Yes, mum, everything is fine, just waiting for the Custom Officer to check my suit case, he seems to think that it might have a bomb inside!'

'What would give him that idea?'

'I don't know mum, I don't look like a terrorist do I?'

'Of course not, as she looks at the Custom Officer.

By now assistance has arrived in the persons of two extra Officers. They walk to the side of the Officer then one of them asks, 'What is going on here?'

He takes the two of them to one side, has a conversation with them, then all three of them look at Leila, then they all approach Leila's suit case with a little bit of worry regarding this suit case. The tall officer looks at Leila's case and enquires, as he points to the suit case, 'This is your suit case, miss?'

'Yes it is.' Leila replies, 'Why do you ask?'

'My colleague is under the impression that you might have a bomb concealed in your suit case, 'Is there anything in this suit case that we should worry about?'

'Not to my knowledge, sir. Why don't you look inside and see for yourself!'

He throws his hands up in the air shouting, 'Clear this area of all personnel then inform SAS, the bomb squad, security people and the police response team. 'We have a person with a suspected bomb in a case in the Custom Green area in the Airport, lock down all this area.'

By now Custom Officers are running around in circles, they don't seem to know what they are doing, it seems to be follow the leader.

Leila's dad and Alfie have passed through the Green Lane area without any problems, so have granddad and grandma. It sounds as if all hell has broken out, in the green area, 'Everyone is running for the exit to vacate the airport, shouting, 'There is a bomb in the airport. Run for you lives. Run for your lives.'

Leila walks over to the tall Custom Officer then she says, 'Your name is William. Can you and I have a private conversation with you please, before someone might get hurt?'

He looks at her in astonishment and asks, 'How do you know my name? Who are you?'

'William, I'm not going to hurt you, please believe me. First, there is not a bomb in my case, I'm not a terrorist. I don't know why your Custom Officer has perceived that I am carrying a bomb in my suit case, but in any case he is wrong!'

'I'm sorry miss, but I have to do my duty by this airport. My Officer is under the impression that there is a bomb in your suit case. I have to believe him until the bomb squad arrive and check out your case. I can't take that chance he might be right, I don't know you. Who would you believe, if you were in my shoes?'

The police response team have arrived with a SAS squad and surround Leila. The Custom officer walks away from the side of Leila.' The police response team stand back and let the SAS squad take over.

The SAS commander has a Browning FN GP35 strapped to his right waist, he shouts, 'Young lady get down on your knees and place your hands behind you head or I will give the order to shoot, do you understand!'

Leila's mum starts to walk towards her daughter. Leila stops her from moving in case she might find herself in line of fire from the SAS squad.

Leila looks at him and nods but she stands quite still. The first thing she does is place all the SAS squad and the response team in a semi conscious state then she puts out her arm, beckons the Commander to her, he levitates about twenty centimetres above the floor, He tries to stop himself from moving but to no avail. He knows that he is moving towards Leila but he doesn't know why or how. He looks very nervous and beads of sweat are forming on his forehead. As he arrives in front of Leila, she asks, 'What are you doing in this airport? Then she asks would you really shoot me?'

'Yes, I would. My job is to protect this airport against all terrorists. We will shoot first and ask questions afterwards!'

Leila smiles to herself, and then she looks at the commander, 'Please turn around and face your squad!' The Commander asks. 'Why?

'I'll show you something spectacular, you just watch and see what happens.' She points to one of the squad and says, 'Robert that is your, name.' He nods his head doesn't know why but he nods anyway, 'Please remove the safety catch on your M4A1 Colt,' he looks at his M4A1 Colt, and does what he is told, 'Now point your gun in my direction and squeeze the trigger.

Robert tries not to squeeze the trigger but he can't help himself. He does not seem to have control of his hand. His index finger wraps around the trigger then he squeezes the trigger. The M4A1Colt jumps into life, the M4A1 releases all 700 projectiles in the magazine the bullets fly at 2.900 ft/sec. They fly towards the commander and Leila and stop twelve centimetres in front of the commander and Leila. He faints. Robert looks around at his fellow officers, throws his M4A1 on the floor shouting, 'I could not help myself! The gun went off on its own!'

All the Custom Officers are flat on the floor, hands outstretched and shaking badly hoping that they are still alive, some have wet their trousers. Leila bends down on one knee, taps the commander on the shoulder, he wakes up, places his hands on his chest feeling for blood and if he has been shot but to his amazement no blood, no bullets in his chest. He looks up, sees the bullets hanging in midair, he faints again. Leila again taps him on the shoulder. He opens his eyes. She says, 'You are safe now. I have no intention of letting you die. I just wanted to show you how powerful I am. There is no way you would be able to kill me. Now stand up, I'm going to show you something that is even more bizarre.' The commander stands up but he is still very nervous and he is shaking very badly. Leila places her hand on his shoulder and asks, 'How many bullets do you think are facing you and me?'

He looks at Leila and says, 'About 700 why?'

'How many men did you bring with you into the airport?'

He looks at her wondering what the hell is she going to do, he is very nervous of this young lady. Then he answers, 'Ten men, why?'

'I would like you to count out ten projectiles/bullets?'

He looks at her, he knows that he is not in a position to reject her request, so he points his index finger towards the projectiles and counts out ten, the rest of them fall to the floor.

'Thank you commander, now please ask your squad to stand in a single line including Robert.'

'The commander looks at his squad and shouts, 'Attention squad!' Form a single line and you Robert, you stand in line as well.'

'Now commander I want you to watch very carefully to what happens next. The ten projectiles turn with the points facing the SAS squad. Leila looks at the commander, 'Are you ready for this?' She has a very big smile on her face.'

'I don't know what you are talking about!'

'You just watch.'

'The projectiles seem to have a life of their own. Off they go as if fired by a M4A1 and stop twelve centimetres in front of each of his squad members. Then a very unusual thing happens. The projectiles go round each of the squad members in a circle and stop at the forehead of each one of them. Their hands are up in the air. They are shouting, 'Please don't shoot us, 'We are only obeying orders.'

The squad are freaked out. They cower back in amazement then they cover their faces hoping that they are not going to die!

'Now, commander, have you ever seen anything so special in your life? I could have killed all of your squad if I wished and I don't have an M4A1. Come with me, commander,' as she walks over to where the projectiles are suspended in space. As he arrives at her side she says, 'Commander, please tap those projectiles one by one, and they will drop to the floor. Go on, 'Don't be afraid they will not hurt you!'

He puts out his hand but he is not sure if he can believe her, so he just touches the first one. It falls to the floor. He is now smiling to himself so he carries on touching each projectile and they in turn all fall to the floor.

'Now, commander, do you think I need to have a bomb in my suit case. If I wanted to damage this airport, could you or your elite squad stop me?'

The commander is speechless, he scratches his head, looks at Leila, laughs out loud and says, 'Who are you? Where are you from?'

'I was born in this country (England) as were all my family. Commander would you do me a very big favour?'

He looks at her and says, 'Just ask me?'

'Tomorrow afternoon in New York I'll be addressing all the world leaders in The United Nations Building including your Prime Minister at 3pm. Be sure and make time to watch, then you will see how powerful I am and all your friends will envy you, 'Then you can say, 'I was in her presence yesterday at the airport.'

'You are kidding me.'

'Of course I'm not kidding you. Why would I want to do that? Anyway I must go now, that is if you are finished with me!'

'I wouldn't even try to stop you!' The commander replies.

Leila looks at her suit case. The cover lifts up from the back over the top of the suit case, then the zips start to zip up the suit case and then the lock jumps up, and locks the zips together. She puts out her hand and the suit case flies to her, she looks at the commander and sends him a telecommunication to his mind which says, *'Thank you James!'*

He looks astonished and just stands there in wonderment at this amazing person.

Leila doesn't look around, just walks away with her mum and she is smiling. The two of them walk out into the reception area, see the rest of the family then they walk towards them.

Leila tells the family what happened in the Green Nothing to Declare area. They smile to themselves knowing full well that the people inside the Green custom area were politely and positively given a lesson in diplomacy. Alfie wants to know all the details of what happened, so Leila bends down, takes him by his hand, looks him in the eye, then she says to him, 'Now you know what happened.'

He looks at her and says, 'I could hear you in my mind but you didn't talk.'

This is the first time Leila has transmitted to Alfie's mind without actually talking to him. He is mystified but excited as he looks at her. Then he says, 'Could I do that trick?'

'Not just yet but, in the future I will teach you how to do it? Are you happy with that, Alfie?'

'Not really, but I suppose it will have to do for now.'

'That's it then. Let's proceed to the bus terminal.

They walk out of the airport to the pickup area. There they wait for the next bus that will take them back to where they have parked their cars. Ten minutes pass, the bus arrives, the doors open, they go inside with their luggage, the driver drives back to the reception area, where they have parked their cars. They pick up their car keys, and go to the pickup point for their bus. After a five minutes wait the bus arrives. It takes them back to where they parked their cars. The bus drives to the car park where they can retrieve their cars and then drive home. Everyone is very tired so John's family go straight home, and decide to go straight to bed. Granddad and grandma find their car. Then they drive home and they too go straight to bed.

Chapter 76

The next morning Ciera is up early, as she has a lot of washing to do, before the rest of the family arrive down for their breakfast. She walks out to the car, retrieves the luggage from the boot, carries it back into the house and places it by the washing machine. She sorts out the whites from the rest of the colour garments. She places the whites in the washing machine first. Then she starts the machine.

Alfie arrives down from his bedroom into the kitchen, 'asking can I have my breakfast please, mum?'

'Yes of course, what would you like?'

'I'll have a boiled egg and a slice of toast please?'

'Did you like your holiday Alfie?' 'Yes mum it was very good I liked it when Leila did all those magic things especially when she stopped the lorry that was awesome. I wish I could do something like that it would be fantastic!'

'In time, Alfie, in time you will be able to do some of those magic things but not yet. Now here is your boiled egg and toast. Would you like coffee or tea with your breakfast?'

'May I have tea please,' he replies.

Chapter 77

Leila walks down the stairs, enters the kitchen sits down and says, 'Good morning everybody, she looks at Alfie then she says to her mum, 'May I have some coffee please?'

'Yes, of course you may, let me make some, 'Would you like a slice of toast with your coffee?'

'Yes, please,' Leila replies. 'Now, Alfie, did you like your holiday?'

'Yes it was awesome, but when am I going to have some magic tricks of my own?'

'Well let me see, at the moment you are too young to have magic tricks but when you grow up, I'll give you some.'

'Why can't I have some magic tricks now?' Alfie enquires.

'Because if something were to go wrong you might not be able to correct it, you might hurt some people and that would not be right. Now you wouldn't want that to happen, would you, Alfie?'

'I would be very careful not to hurt anyone.'

'I know but we can't take that chance not just yet. Tell you what, 'When you grow up a little bit more into a big boy, then we will see if we can give you some of the magic tricks. Is that alright with you?'

'Alright then as long as you promise that I'll have some magic tricks when I'm a big boy that's fine with me,' Alfie replies.

'Shall I take the top of the egg off for you?' Leila enquires.

'Yes please' Alfie answers.

'Are you ready for your coffee and toast, Leila?'

'Yes mum, thank you,' she replies.

Mum places her coffee and toast on the table and says, 'I'll just sit down for a little while and have a cup of coffee with you two.'

Alfie looks at his mum then at Leila and asks, 'When are we going on holiday again?'

'We're going to New York in America on Tuesday for a short holiday. I have told you already.'

'I have never been there, have I, mum?'

'No, Alfie, you have never been to America but I'm sure you will find it fascinating.' Ciera looks at Leila, 'You tell him again. I know that you told us but you know Alfie, it goes in one ear and out the other with nothing in between.'

'I know, mum. Just like all little boys he is in his own little world. Now, Alfie we will be taking a trip to New York in America, Tuesday and that includes you. Do you think you will enjoy that?' she asks.

'Yes I think so; Can I meet the President of America?' enquires Alfie.

'Well that is a big request, Alfie. You must know that very few people meet the President. It would require a very special person to get an audience but we'll see, you never know what might happen.'

Chapter 78

Ciera looks at Leila and says, 'I must go and call your dad.' She shouts up the stairs,' John, I'm going to make your breakfast. 'What would you like?'

John comes to the top of the stairs and says, 'I'll have my usual Sunday breakfast please, I'm going to have a shower first then I'll get dressed and come down for my breakfast. Is that alright dear.'

'Yes, John, I'll give you fifteen minutes then I'll start making the breakfast for you.'

John replies, 'That's fine with me.'

'I think it was a pity Delia didn't come on holiday with us, such a pity,' Ciera says. Delia is Ciera's sister in law.

'I know,' replies Leila, 'I think she lost out on this occasion. Maybe I should give her a call and ask her if she would like to come to America with us Tuesday.'

'Do you think that is a good idea?' enquires mum.

'Well she will need to know sometime about my powers and now is a good time to tell her. What do you think mum? The rest of the family know and it's not fair to keep her in the dark any longer.'

'I'll phone her now and ask her over to dinner this afternoon and see what she says.'

'Fine then.' Leila replies, 'You go and phone her, I'll attend to dads breakfast when he comes down to the kitchen.'

Ciera goes into the sitting room, dials Delia's number, waits until the phone is picked up and a voice says, 'Who's calling me at this hour of the morning?'

'Delia, its Ciera, 'So sorry to trouble you this early. I hope I didn't wake you.'

'Well I'm awake now, what can I do for you this early in the morning?'

'We were wondering that is Leila and I, are wondering if you would like to come to dinner this afternoon to our house. We haven't seen you for such a long time.' Leila has never seen Deila in the flesh. She has seen lots of photos of the wedding as she was growing up.

'That is very sweet of you. Let me get up have a shower and think about it, then I'll phone you and let you know in about half an hour. Is that alright with you.'

'Yes that's fine with me. Hope to hear from you soon,' Ciera replies. 'Good bye for now,' as she replaces the phone.

Ciera goes back to the kitchen and John is sitting at the table eating his breakfast. He looks up and asks, 'Who were you talking to on the phone?'

Chapter 79

'Leila and I thought that it's time to ask Delia over to dinner this afternoon.'

'Why?' asks John.

'Because Leila and I think that, it's time to tell her about Leila's powers. John, what do you think?'

'Well I don't know. Why you want to tell her now?'

'Because she is the only one of the family that doesn't know about Leila and that is not fair on her.' Ciera replies.

'That is fine by me I only hope she understands after all this time why we didn't keep her in the circle about Leila's power. She might not believe you.'

'Don't you worry; I'll talk to her and explain the situation. I'm sure she will understand why we didn't inform her!' Leila says. 'We have not seen her since the wedding and she does live a long way from here, but we do need to tell her today.'

'Right then, Leila, this is your responsibility. We'll just wait and see how she reacts,' replies dad.

'Good.' Leila replies, 'I am looking forward to seeing her. I am sure she is a very interesting person.' Leila looks at her mum and says, 'the phone is about to ring!'

'Leila, please don't do that to me, it makes me jump.'

'Sorry, mum, I didn't mean to make you jump!'

The phone rings. Ciera picks it up and asks, 'Is that you Delia?'

'Yes it is.' she replies.

'You are coming to dinner this afternoon? Please say yes.'

'Yes, of course I'd love to come to dinner this afternoon, 'It's been so long since we last met. I'll see you later. Goodbye for now Ciera.'

John asks, 'What did she say.

'She will be here for dinner then we'll have a quiet chat and Leila can tell her everything. I'm sure she will be fascinated with Leila and Alfie.'

'Mum can we go into town tomorrow I would like to buy a white long dress for my trip to New York on Tuesday. That's if you don't mind and we can take Alfie with us as well.'

'Why do you want a white dress?' asks her mum.

'I'll need it at the United Nations Building on Tuesday.'

'Why?' enquires her mum.

'I'm going to surprise you and all in the Great Hall. I can't tell you now but you will be very surprised.'

Her mum looks at her and smiles but does not say a word.

Leila looks at Alfie and enquires, 'What would you like to do today, Alfie?'

'I don't know, sis. What do you think we should do?'

'We could go for a walk to the play ground. There you can have a go on the swings, 'Would you like that Alfie!'

'Yes, can we go to the playground now please?

'Ask mum if you can come with me to the play ground.'

'Please, Mum, can I go with Leila to the playground?'

'Yes but be very careful. I don't want you to hurt yourself on the swings!'

Alfie can't get out the front door quick enough, shouting, 'Come on, Leila, I'm ready!'

'I'll see you soon; I'd better go now mum. Look at him, he's all excited. Bye dad, see you later!' Off she goes with Alfie. Down the road they go together, and into the playground.

Inside Alfie goes straight to the swings and jumps on one of them, 'Come on, Leila, push me!'

'Leila pushes him very gently but Alfie is not satisfied, he wants to go higher.

'Push me a bit higher? Please, Leila.'

She is a bit apprehensive at this request from Alfie but she complies anyway.

Alfie is squealing his head off at being pushed higher and he is enjoying himself enormously. After a while he jumps off the swings and runs to the slide, he climbs to the top and slides down to the bottom. He does this several times and like all children he gets fed up so he goes back to the swings.

Leila sits down on one of the benches and contemplates her visit to the United Nations Buildings on Tuesday and how she might be received. This is going to be a very big occasion for her but she is very confident she will win the World leaders over to her way of thinking, about the world's future and the future of all the people on this planet. Out of the corner of her eye she sees two boys about nineteen years old watching her. They are standing about twenty yards from her trying to decide what to do. In the end they pick up the courage to walk over. They have decided they would like to talk to Leila so they sit down one on either side of her. The taller one asks, 'Do you have a name please?'

Leila looks at them and says. 'What do you want my name for?'

He looks at her and smiles, 'We would like to know your name please. That is, if you don't mind?'

'Well, I do mind. Now please go away and leave me alone!'

The tall one is being very insistent and asks again, 'May I have your name please?'

That is not a very good idea as far as Leila is concerned. 'I'll ask you once more; please go away or you'll be sorry,' Leila retorts.

The tall one makes a grab for her but in an instant she is not there. The tall one looks very confused as he looks around sees Leila about ten feet away from where she was sitting. Now she has a large bear on his four legs by her side. She looks at the two boys, has a word in the bears ear. He walks slowly towards the two teenagers. They run for their lives with the bear running after them.'

Leila calls the bear telepathically. He stops, turns round and returns to Leila's side and sits down. The two teenagers have run for their lives and have made up their minds that they are not going to stop for anything or anyone. The bear was only an illusion. Only the boys can see him but they don't know that so they keep on running.

Who were those boys and why did they run away from you? Did you hurt them?' enquires Alfie.

'I think that they had a prior engagement. Perhaps they were late. Whatever, they are gone now!' Leila replies.

'I'm hungry,' says Alfie. 'Can I have some crisps please?'

'I think not.' replies Leila.

'Why?' Alfie asks.

'Well dad, mum and I will be having dinner with your dad's sister, Auntie Delia, when we return home. Anyway mum would not be pleased, if I let you have crisps, she would not be happy.'

Alfie replies. 'Surely not.'

'It's just an expression!' she replies.

'What is an expression?' Alfie asks.

'It's just a way saying we must not do something that is not right!'

But Alfie is about to ask another question.

'Alfie, please, that's enough!' replies Leila.

'I'm bored now!' Alfie says.

'Ok what shall we do now?' Leila asks.

'I'm hungry!' replies Alfie.

'Shall we go home then?' Leila enquires.

Leila looks across the playground she sees the two teenagers coming towards her. It looks as though they have company, so she stands where she is. 'Alfie you stand behind me and don't worry about anything!'

'Why, what is going to happen to me?' Alfie asks.

'Nothing is going to happen to you while I'm here!'

Chapter 80

The teenagers walk over to where Leila is standing. Then they announce to Leila, 'These are our dads and we want to talk to you about the bear we saw in the playground!'

'Are you kidding me? What would a bear be doing in a children's playground?' She looks up at the dads and asks, 'Do you think that there is a bear running around this playground where children are playing. What do you think?'

'Well our boys have told us that they did see a bear running around. They said, they were followed by a bear, and that they had to run for their lives!'

'Come on, where is the bear now then?' Look around. Can you see a bear anywhere in this playground?'

However the dads look around, they can't see a bear anywhere.

Leila enquires. 'Look, if there was a bear in this playground, don't you think that the police would be here?'

One of the dads walks over to his son the tall boy, looks him in the eye and says, 'Are you on those drugs again?' He slaps him on the side of the head saying, 'I have told you to give up taking those drugs!'

'I'm not on them, dad!' he says.

'How do you account for seeing a large bear in this play ground? You must be on something which is playing on your mind. Go home. I'll talk to you later. Sorry, miss, I'm so sorry if they gave you any trouble,' as he turns around and walks back the way he came. The other dad follows his son and pushes his son in the back telling him, 'you're grounded for a week I'll teach you to see a bear. You're a bloody idiot. You must be on something, what is it?'

'I'm on nothing, honest, dad!'

'I've heard that one before. Go on go home, before I lose my temper. You're grounded as well for a week. Don't tell your mother. She'll laugh her head off. A bear running wild, can you believe it?'

Leila has a little smile to herself. 'Come on, Alfie, let's go home. Dinner will be ready soon. She takes him by the hand and asks. You did have a nice time?'

'Yes it was alright, I thought we were going to have some fun with the two big boys!'

She looks at him has a smile and says, 'Right then, I'll race you to the gate!' She lets Alfie win the race and says, 'Alfie, you are so quick, I couldn't catch you up!'

It takes about ten minutes to walk to their house. When they arrive at their house there is a car in the drive which makes Alfie very curious.

He looks at his sister and asks, 'Who owns that car?'

'Shall we go inside and see?' Leila replies.

Inside Alfie tells his mum that two big boys tried to chat up Leila and then they ran away.

'Alfie, where are your manners? We have a visitor,' as she looks over to Delia. 'Alfie, this is your Auntie Delia. Give her a big hug!'

Alfie looks at her, he is a bit reluctant but Leila takes him by the hand and walks him over to Delia.

Leila says, 'He is a bit shy. Give your Auntie Delia a big hug and a kiss.'

Alfie plucks up the courage, he gives Delia a big hug and a kiss saying, 'Are my auntie?'

'Yes I'm your auntie Delia. How do you do Alfie?' She looks at Leila saying, 'He's very cute. You are Leila, I presume?'

'I'm Leila, and yes I'm very pleased to meet you, as she gives her a hug and a kiss on the side of the face!'

Delia looks at her and says, 'You are quite tall, lovely complexion and beautiful hair. I think I'm going to like you a lot!'

'Alfie, what do you think of your Auntie Delia?' Dad enquires.

Alfie looks at her, smiles and says, 'I think she is nice!'

'John, the dinner will be ready in about ten minutes, Will you go and set the table in the dining room please!'

'Let me help you?' Delia asks.

'No I'm fine! John replies.

'Come on, John please let me help you set the table?'

'Alright if you must, you place the knives and forks on the table.'

Ciera walks back into the dining room,' asks Delia, 'what would you like to drink?'

'May I have a dry white wine please?'

Off she goes, pours out the drinks, then she returns to the dining room, 'There you are your drink. I'll leave it on the table for you!'

Alfie is very inquisitive and curious. He walks over to Delia and asks, 'Where do you live?'

'I live a long way from here. Why?'

'Just wondering!' replies Alfie.

'Why would you need to know where I live?' She asks.

That's a very strange question indeed!' 'Alfie looks at her and asks, 'Why didn't you materialize from your house to my house?'

Leila looks at Delia and says, 'He has a vivid mind. Don't listen to him. He's into Spider man, Batman, Superman and all kinds of other rubbish!'

But Delia is fascinated by Alfies statement and enquires,' Well, young sir, what do you mean?'

Before Alfie answers Delia's question, Leila says, 'Alfie, go and help mum please,' as she pushes him towards the kitchen. Mum has already received a message from Leila telepathically to take Alfie out of the dining room because Delia is asking awkward questions.

Mum comes into the dining room, walks over to Alfie and says, 'Come on Alfie, you come help me in the kitchen and help with the dinner!'

'Can I mum? Good, what do want me to do? Alfie asks.

'Well you can count out all the plates but be careful not to drop them!'

'I can do that mum. How many plates do we need?'

'Alfie, count how many people for dinner?'

'Well there are you, dad, Leila, Delia and me?'

'Good how many people for dinner. Count on your fingers?'

'Alfie puts out his hand and counts out loud.' I think its five people mum!'

'Well done, son, that's right. You are a clever boy. You go and call your dad tell him that the meat needs carving up?'

'Yes mum?' Off he goes into the sitting room and shouts, 'Dad, mum wants you in the kitchen to cut up the meat!'

'Alright son, go and tell her I'm on my way!'

Alfie turns around, runs back into the kitchen and says, 'Dad said he is coming now to cut the meat!'

'Thank you, Alfie,' Mum replies.

Dad arrives into the kitchen, finds a carving knife cuts up the meat nicely, slowly places it on a large plate, takes it into the dining room places it on the table.

He goes back into the kitchen, picks up the vegetables, walks to the dining room places them on the table saying, 'Come on, everyone, take you places now please!'

Mum takes the plates from the oven, walks into the dining room. She places them on the table saying.' The plates are a little hot!'

Delia is still agonizing over Alfie's statement about materializing. I wonder what Alfie means about that. She decides to say nothing, waits until after dinner is finished.

John sits down and says. 'Come on everyone join me for our dinner!'

'Alfie, you sit next to me please?' Leila says.

'Why?' asks Alfie.

'But I want to sit next to my auntie, please let me sit next to my auntie?'

Ciera interrupts, 'Go on then sit next to your auntie, but no talking, just you eat your dinner please!'

'Thanks mum,' replies Alfie.

Ciera looks at Delia and enquires, 'What kind of work do you do now, what are you doing these days?'

'Not a lot. Just the usual chores working, cleaning the house, doing the washing and whatever else needs doing!'

'What exactly do you do for a living?' Ciera asks.

'Well, I have a small sandwich shop where I sell drinks and of course sandwiches, split rolls with different kinds of fillings, tea, coffee, cakes and a little cafe at the back of the bar for people to sit down and have a chat. Nothing big, it's just the right size shop for me. I have two other girls helping in the shop. It's quite profitable little business, I don't make a fortune, but I make a very good living!'

'Very nice,' Ciera replies. 'It's nice to know that you are doing quite well. I'm pleased for you! It's hard work these days to make any kind of a living!'

'I know but I get by.' Delia replies.

'Have you any children yet?' Ciera enquires.

'No children at the moment, I'm quite happy.' Delia replies.

'Would you, like another drink, Delia?'

'Yes please, she replies, 'white wine if you don't mind!'

'John what about you what would you like to drink?'

'I'll have a red wine please?'

'Leila, what would you like to drink?'

'May I have an orange please?'

'What would you like to drink, Alfie?'

'I'll have an orange as well please.'

'Fine then I'll go and get more drinks. She returns to the dining room places them on the table and says, 'Please help yourselves!'

'I'll go and place all the dirty dinner plates in the dish washer while I'm waiting,' says John.

'Ciera asks, 'Have you been to see your mum and dad lately Delia?'

'Not for a while now, it must be about three years I think,' she replies. 'You know what it's like when you are running a business, its seven days a week. It wears you out,' she replies. But, I hope to go and see them soon!'

'What about JK, have you had any contact with him?'

'No I've not seen or spoken to him for awhile but I must find time to make contact with all the family soon. I do worry that I've not made the effort but I'm glad you invited me to dinner today. What about your family. Tell me what you have been doing these past eighteen years?'

'You know, having babies, looking after them and I can tell you it's a night mare worrying about their futures and running the house. Sometimes

I could run away from it all, but I'm a mum and I have responsibilities so I just get on with it and tell myself it can only get better!'

'Can I ask how John is getting on?'

'Nothing fazes him he just plods along without a care in the world. He's a good husband and I wouldn't change him. As they say, its better the devil you know, then the devil you don't know. If you know what I mean!

'What about you. Do you have a boy friend?' Ciera enquires.

'Not at the moment I don't. To be honest I don't have the time to worry about boys or men. I have enough to worry about with the shop. I'm quite happy looking after myself. We'll see what the future brings!'

Ciera thinks to herself, 'She is in for a big surprise when she has a discussion with Leila later today. Her future will change big time from today forever.'

Chapter 81

Leila is just listening to this conversation and decides to invite Delia out into the garden. 'Come on, Auntie let's go for a walk down the garden. We can have a talk about the future. Alfie, you stay with mum!'

'Why must I stay with mum?'

'Because you will make tea for your Auntie and me, then bring it down the garden to us. Will you do that for me please?'

'Yes, I can do that. Mum will you help me?' Alfie replies.

'Good, off you go then!'

Leila and Delia walk out the back door and down the garden and sit on the bench. Leila looks at Delia and says, 'I have something very important to tell you but I needed to talk to you on your own!'

Delia looks at Leila and enquires, 'You're not pregnant are you?'

'Absolutely not, it's more important than that. May I take your hand please? In an instant the two of them are back in Delia's house, 'She looks around and faints. Leila places her hand on Delia's shoulder and she wakes up asking, 'Where am I?'

'We are in your house. Don't worry I will explain everything to you!'

Delia looks perplexed as she gazes around her house and asks. 'What are you? Who are you? Are you my niece? 'How did I get back to my house?'

I must apologise for looking into your mind; that is how I know where you live. Incidentally you have had a bad time with one of your boyfriends, Peter Gooding. He gave you a very hard time?'

Delia is very worried now. How does Leila know Peter? 'He was a right bastard and obnoxious to me. Nobody knows that.'

'I'm sorry I frightened you. Where do I begin? I know that you are confused about what has happened. But it's necessary that you know. I'm not like other people. My intellectual capacity is far greater that anyone on this planet. I'm human and I'm your niece. I can do anything I put my mind to and I mean anything. Is there anything you would like to do but never had the time?' enquires Leila.

Delia is totally bemused and mystified and she is laughing her head off. She has a hundred questions but she doesn't know which one to ask. 'I know I would like to go and see mum and dad.'

She is thinking that this could never happen, this is all an illusion. It must be the wine. It's gone to my head!'

In an instant they are in her mum and dad's sitting room.

They don't look surprised. Dad stands up and says, 'Hello, Delia lovely to see you and Leila. Please sit down. I see Leila has shown you her wonderful powers.' He has a smile at the two of them. 'I was wondering when she would contact you. She is just amazing.' He looks at Delia and says, 'Did she tell you how she gained this wonderful gift?'

She looks at Leila and thinks to herself, 'So that was what Alfie was trying to tell me, I can't take all this in. What is she, is she a robot. Is she a human being like me, I hope that she is?'

Leila decides to communicate telepathically with Delia; 'I don't want you to worry about anything it's all true!'

Delia looks at Leila and says. 'I can hear you in my mind how do you do that?'

Leila looks at granddad and says. 'Granddad would you like to tell her the full story, it might be better coming from you!'

'Delia, my dear, when Leila was conceived and in her mum's womb she, that is Leila and her mum, were removed from their house by Aliens to a space craft in orbit around our planet. I know this is hard to understand but if you will listen to me, I'll try to explain, and bring you up to date. Are you ready to hear the most wonderful news that has happened to your niece and our family?'

Delia looks at her dad. She is now totally confused, perplexed, puzzled and bewildered.

'Are you sure I'm the right person to give this very important information to?'

'Yes, we think so!' replies dad; 'you are one of our family so why shouldn't you know? The Aliens came and removed Ciera to a spacecraft the first time when Leila was in the womb. They came back later to give her upgrades of that special technology and have it placed into her brain. Let me start from the time she was in her mum's womb. Babies in the womb do not have intelligence. Their minds are shall we say are empty of all information except instinct, nothing else. The Aliens needed a clear brain to take this technology. They decided that in the interest of humanity she should be a one off, of her kind. Because there was nothing in her mind the Aliens programmed her with a little bit of knowledge called Bio/Dna technology. Apparently its technology from the future, 'don't ask me about it. It's way above my intellectual capacity. It was necessary that she needed to return back to the craft at different times as she was growing up to have her update of this new technology from time to time. As a baby she wasn't subjected any kind of pain or anything that might have distressed the baby in the womb. I only found out when Ciera told me when I went to pick her up from the hospital to take her home and I can tell you that I was quite worried. When she was born we went to the hospital to see her. Now she was only a day old when she communicated with me telepathically. I was totally flabbergasted. I thought I was going funny in the head. Your brain or mind if you like, only works at about twenty, maybe twenty five percent of its capacity. Leila's mind, brain, works in excess of one hundred percent. I know that this is a lot of information to take in but in time you'll be able to digest it and understand the implications of its potential for this planet. The family have a certain amount of Leila's power, just enough to help if she needs us, but up to now everything has been just amazing. I'm sure that you'll agree with me from what you have seen today that, Leila is a very special person to us. You have seen something extraordinary today. It is going to be very hard for you to appreciate and understand!'

'I don't know what to say, this is way above my head.' She looks at her dad, waves her hands in the air, and then drops them to her sides!

Dad looks at her and says, 'Give me your hand please?'

She looks very apprehensive, a bit reluctant to hold her dad's hand; 'But what the hell, I can only die once!' She holds out her hand, dad takes it and instantly the two of them levitate about two foot above the sitting room floor. She looks down and laughs out loud and asks, 'Are we levitating?'

'Yes,' dad says, 'we are. Now do you believe me when I tell you we are a very special family?' Dad decides to descend to the floor. 'Only Leila has full power to do what she likes. Ask, Leila where JK is?'

'Why?' she asks.

'Ask me please?'

She looks at Leila and enquires, 'Where is my brother JK at this very moment?'

'He is standing behind you if you would like to turn around!'

'Oh, my God, is it really you, JK?'

'Yes it is me in person. It's lovely to see you after all this time. How are you? I know we had a bit of tiff some time ago. I hope that is all behind us. So you have met our little niece. What do you think of her?'

'She is amazing. I'm totally bemused and puzzled. How powerful is she?' She looks at Leila.

'There is nothing on this planet or the Universe more powerful than her, 'She can do anything you think of she can do it without thinking about it and she has given the family some of her powers!'

It's time, Leila decides, to give Delia some powers like the rest of the family so she walks over to her and says, 'I don't want you to worry. Something strange will happen. Place your hands in my hands, don't be afraid?'

Delia looks a little worried but she knows in her heart that Leila will not put her in any kind of danger. She places her hands in Leila's hands. Then a surge of power emanates from Leila's body into Delia's body.

Delia is astonished at this surge of power but she doesn't feel any different. She is wondering what this power is all about. She looks at Leila and asks. 'What can I do with this power now?'

Leila stands back and looks at Delia and says, 'Just think about levitation!'

She levitates off the room floor but she is a bit chary and asks, 'How am I going to descend?'

'Just think about it!' Leila replies.

'Delia descends rather slowly until she reaches the floor. She looks around to make sure she is on the floor.

'Well, what do you think of your new powers?' Leila enquires.

'Fascinating and mesmerizing, but why would I need this wonderful gift. What would I do with it?'

'You'll be called on to help the family from time to time. That time will be next Tuesday afternoon in New York at the United Nations Building!'

'Why? How am I going to get there? I'm working Tuesday. I can't afford to fly to New York at such short notice. I would like to help but on this occasion I'll have to give it a miss I'm really sorry!'

'Can you allow your two girls to run the shop for a few days? I'll keep an eye on it for you. Here is the best bit. You need not book a flight, I'll do all that for you so what do you say to that?' Leila enquires.

'Well then I suppose if it can be done I'll inform the girl's tomorrow morning that I'm going away for a few days. I'm sure they will look after the shop while I'm away. That's it then, I'm going to New York.' She goes to Leila and gives her a very big hug and a kiss saying, 'Thank you very much I will not let you down.'

'I know you will keep your word!' Leila replies 'Now, JK you're expected to be with us Tuesday afternoon. Is that alright with you?'

'Yes that is fine with me. Can you send me home now?'

'Yes, of course,' and in a blink of an eye JK is gone! 'We must return to Ciera's house now, granddad and grandma, hope to see you soon in New York. I'll be in touch Tuesday late morning, good bye for now and in a flash Delia and Leila are back sitting on the garden bench.

Alfie runs down the garden path saying, 'your tea is ready now can you come back into our house? Please.

Leila and Delia stand up from the bench walk up the path into the sitting room and sit down laughing to themselves. 'Delia, how did you get on with your new powers?' Ciera asks.

Ciera smiles to herself, knowing Leila has enlightened Delia about her amazing powers.

'Amazing that is all I need to say. It was out of this world, it was truly incredible!'

'Did you have a good time with Leila?' Alfie asks.

'Yes I did. It was incredible!'

'How about tea, John asks, would you like some tea Delia before you go home?'

'Yes, that would be wonderful, thank you very much!'

'Alfie, what would you like for your tea?' His mum asks.

'Can I have an orange instead, please?'

'And you Leila, what would you like?'

'I'll have orange please!'

'John what would you like?'

'I'm fine.' He replies.

Ciera goes to the kitchen, makes the tea, returns places it on the table and says help yourselves.' She returns to the kitchen and makes Leila and Alfie an orange drink returns saying, 'Come on Alfie, and you, Leila, your orange drinks are on the table, please come and drink it!'

Tea finished, Delia says, 'I must go now. I have an early start in the morning, but I've had a great adventure. It's been a very informative day for me. Leila, I know that you'll do wonderful things for our world. I'm very pleased and I'm so glad you're my niece. I wouldn't change it for the world. Hopefully we will meet on Tuesday I can't wait, it's going to be very educational for me!'

'I'll see you out to your car, that is, if you don't mind!'

Chapter 82

Delia gives a hug to Ciera then Alfie. She looks at him and says, 'Alfie you are a lovely boy,' then she gives a big hug to her brother, goes to the front door, waves, then goes and sits in her car. Leila sits in the passenger seat, in a flash they are at the front of Delia's house in the car space which gives Delia a fright.

'My goodness, you are extremely powerful. I'm so happy for you, Leila,' and she starts to cry.' I'm so sorry I don't know what came over me, please forgive me!'

Leila holds her in her arms and says, 'don't cry now, it's natural it's a human thing and I understand' Leila decides it's time to leave; 'Until Tuesday then!' Without blinking she has gone.

Delia says to herself,' What an extraordinary day,' as she gets out of her car steadies herself, walks to the front door, opens it and goes inside locks the door behind her. She decides to get ready for bed as she will have a busy day tomorrow. She is having a hard time going to sleep, her mind is running wild. She is twisting and turning but eventually she does fall asleep.'

Leila doesn't return home just yet, she decides to go and see Mr Peter Gooding. This information she has gleaned from Delia's mind. She arrives in his living room. He is asleep on the couch unaware of Leila's presence. She walks up the stairs and has a look in all the bedrooms. In one of the bedrooms there is a young lady in the bed asleep so she retreats to the bathroom, looks in, and then she goes down the stairs to the kitchen then back into the living room. She sits down in the chair in front of him and waits very patiently until he awakes. She sends a communication to Peter's mind. 'I would like to have a talk with you now?'

He opens his eyes, sees Leila in front of him, jumps up shouting, 'Who are you?' How did you get into my house?' He then takes his mobile out of his pocket and dials 999.

It's answered by a policeman, 'Yes, sir, can I help you?' 'Now this conversation is going to be very funny. Peter starts to talk gibberish, gobbledygook down the phone.

The policeman at the other end asks, 'Sir what are you talking about? Please will you talk in English? I don't understand you, please talk slowly. Now tell me your name first and your address, please?'

Peter is very frustrated so he takes a deep breath and starts again. He cannot utter an intelligible sentence. He can't stop himself talking this silly garbage.

The police constable is getting exasperated with this idiot on the other end of the phone. He tries again. 'Sir, what is your problem?'

Again Peter starts this unintelligible language and meaningless gibberish. Even he doesn't know what he is talking about. Consequently he doesn't even understand himself.

Now the policeman on the other end of the telephone is losing his patience very quickly. He says, 'OK, shall we try again sir? Now sir, will you please talk slowly so that I can understand you. Please sir will you tell me your problem?'

Peter slams down the phone, looks at Leila and says, in perfect English, 'Ok, what do you want and who are you?'

He is looking around to see if there is anything to hand which he can use to protect himself, from what he doesn't know. Before he even moves she elevates him to the ceiling. He is petrified, looks at Leila, 'Please tell me what you want?'

'Are you familiar with a young lady called Delia?'

'Yes, I used to go out with her, why?'

'I know that, she is a very timid nervous person. Well you are a very big bully and very unsympathetic to this young lady. She is my auntie. Now I'm going to make you suffer but I'll make you an offer and I want you to listen very intently. You will phone your work place first thing in the morning and say that you have to go to your bank about some mistake in your bank statement. You will draw out all the money she advanced you for the purchase of this house. You will take the money to her shop and tell her that you are very sorry for all the trouble you have caused her. Do I make myself clear, Peter?'

'Yes I understand I'll not let you down!'

'I understand that Delia bought this house but you threw her out. When you have finished your little transaction at the bank you can return to work. I'll know if that money has been withdrawn. If it has, I'll let you talk normally, and then you will go to work, talk to your boss and tell him why you are late. That is, if you have carried out my wishes. If not you'll talk gobbledygook. When he asks you what you are talking about you will answer in gibberish. He will say I'll fire you, if you don't talk in English. You will not be able to communicate with him in any language other than mumbo jumbo. You do understand?'

'Yes I do understand. Please let me down I'm getting dizzy up here.'

'If you do as promised I'll allow you to talk English to your boss. Now that is not very hard to do is it? I'll know if you have delivered the money to Delia and if you don't deliver. I can promise you'll lose your job. Don't make me come and see you again!'

In an instant she vanished. He is totally perplexed but decides to carry out her wishes just in case he was not dreaming as he descends from the ceiling.

Leila is in her sitting room. Her dad looks up and asks, 'You were a long time. Is everything alright then?'

'Yes everything is alright now!' Leila replies. 'Dad, I'm off to bed I'll see you in the morning!'

Monday morning arrives. Leila decides to get up out of bed. She goes for a shower, gets dressed and goes down to the kitchen. There she makes herself some breakfast of cornflakes and a cup of coffee.

Her mum arrives in the kitchen and says, 'Good morning,' she looks at Leila. 'You were a bit late last night,' as she makes herself a cup of coffee.

'Yes, mum, I had a bit of business to do for Delia. Yesterday when she was here I found out her last boy friend gave her a very bad time!'

'What do you mean?' Mum asks.

'Well it would appear that she bought a house with her own money, allowed this boy friend to move in with her. He then had the cheek to throw her out of her own house. Can you believe that mum?'

'Well why did he throw her out of her own house?'

'Mum, she is a very timid person and I suppose she didn't want the family to know. I think she had a big crush on this boy friend. He decided that she was a push over. He then took advantage of her!'

'What did you do to him?'

'Nothing, mum. I persuaded, convinced him it would be better if he returned all the money with which she bought that house!'

'You didn't harm him, did you,' as she looks at her, intently.

'Mum, I didn't harm him. I didn't lay a finger on him. She places her hand over her mouth and smiles!

'You must have done something to him. Is he returning the money to Delia?'

'Oh yes, I don't think he has any option!'

'Come on, Leila. I know you did something to make him return the money. 'What was it?'

'When I arrived at his house he was asleep on his couch. I kind of woke him up. He was very surprised he picked took his phone out of his pocket, dialled 999. Then he tried to have a conversation with the policeman at the other end. Now here is the funny bit. He started to talk gobbledygook, gibberish and all kinds of rubbish. The policeman at the other end was very patient but he could not understand him. This went on for about ten minutes then suddenly he slapped down his phone. Then we talked about how and when he would return the money to Delia, so you see mum I didn't touch him I kind of persuaded him to give it back. He is going to his bank this morning to withdraw the money, and then goes to Delia's shop to give her the money. If he doesn't do that I'll know. Then when he goes to work his boss will call him into his office. Peter, yes his name is Peter Gooding, he will talk gobbledygook and gibberish. He will not be able to stop himself. All I have to do is just bide my time and when nine o'clock arrives I'll know if that money has been returned to Delia. If he doesn't return it, he will suffer the indignity of losing his job. Did I do the right thing mum?'

'Well as long as you believe you done the right thing, that is all that matters Leila!'

'I think I'll have a cup of coffee please, mum!'

'So will I. Mum replies. 'First, I'll go to the bottom of the stairs.' There she shouts up, John, I'm getting your breakfast ready it will take about in ten minutes.' She walks back into the kitchen, picks up her cup has a sip of coffee then asks, 'What shall we do today Leila?'

'I think we should go into town and do a bit of shopping as intended!'

'What about Alfie?' she asks. What will we do with him?'

'I think we should take him along with us. I know that he can be a devil sometimes but he is only a little boy. I'm sure we can keep him occupied. What do you think?'

'Ok then he comes with us,' replies her mum. 'I think I had better make your dad's breakfast and have it ready and under the grill when he comes down the stairs because he'll be ready for work!'

Ten minutes go by. Dad comes rushing down the stairs and into the kitchen and sits down at the table. His wife places his breakfast in front of him. He says, 'Thank you, I'm late this morning but I'll finish my breakfast, I don't want to waste it. So sorry I forgot to say good morning, dear wife, Leila, Alfie. What are you three going to do today, might I ask?'

'We're going to do some shopping today,' replies Alfie.

Chapter 83

'Well, I hope that you have a nice day and be careful not to spend too much money. He looks at his wife and says, 'I'm only kidding, dear, you buy what you need!'

Leila is completely at ease with her life now. She is at the height of her ability. There is nothing she can't deal with. The Bio/DNA technology she has now is in all probability one of a kind in the Universe, and most certainly one of a kind in the Earth. Only time will tell if this is true or not. She is looking forward to going to New York on Tuesday and she knows that it will be a good test of her knowledge of world politics. It does not worry her, it's just going to be the first time she will be facing an audience of such a high calibre and quality. She should be able to handle that situation with confidence and conviction. She will need to scan all the people in the Great Hall and pick out any awkward or discomfited statements that might frustrate her. She doesn't have to answer any questions. She can just pre-empt all questions levied at her. She also knows that there will be dissenters. They will ask stupid questions, to try and unsettle her but she is ready for any question.

Dad finishes his breakfast, rushes out the front door into his car and drives away to work.

'Right then, let's get ready to go to town,' Ciera says. 'Alfie you have ten minutes then we leave, so you'd better get ready please and you, Leila, I presume you'd better be going and get dressed thank you!'

'Yes, mum, I won't be long, I promise!' Leila replies. Ten minutes later Alfie runs into the kitchen shouting, 'I can't tie my shoe laces, mum, please   help.'
'Stop shouting, Alfie, come here and I'll tie the laces for you!'

Leila walks into the kitchen saying,' I'm ready mum.'

'Good let's go then!'

The three of them walk to the car. Alfie sits in the back seat, Leila and her mum sit in the front seat mum in the driving seats. Off they go to town. In town finding a place to park is difficult, but they are lucky a car is just coming out of a space and as he drives away another car drives into that vacant space without looking. This makes Leila furious. The driver gets out, looks at Leila, gives the hated one finger sign and that further infuriates Leila even more. Across from his car there is a little space with a wall and another car. It's just wide enough to slide a car inside it. She places his car in that space with no room to get in or out of any of the doors. He looks at his car and is wondering how it got into that space and how he is going to get into his car when he finishes shopping. He scratches his head. While he is wondering what to do about his car, Leila's mum drives her car into the vacant space his car has vacated.

He runs over to Leila and says. 'You're in my car space!'

'No I'm not. You don't own this car space. Your car is parked over there, next to that car,' as she points to his car in the little space!

He is very agitated so he decides to punch Leila but to no avail, she is not where he thinks she is. He tries several more times but to no avail. Every time he tries she is somewhere else.'

Then as if by magic, Leila conjures up a tiger. He sees the tiger approaching him so he runs as quickly as his feet will carry him.

'That will teach him manners. He'll keep his fingers to himself in future!' Alfie is laughing his head off and shouting out, 'Awesome!'

Leila's mum says, 'How is he going to retrieve his car from that space? It is very small.'

'That's his problem,' Leila replies. 'He'll be very careful in future!'

'Come on then, let's go to the shops and if you are good, Alfie, we'll have lunch a bit later!'

'Yes please,' Alfie replies. 'I'll be good!'

'Have you something special you would like to buy, Leila?'

'Yes, mum, but first let us just browse around in the shops and see what's available.' After about half an hour Leila spots a fashion shop. 'Come on, mum, let's go inside and see what they have. You never know I might find something!' (She knows what she wants and this shop might have that special something.)

Her mum and Alfie follow her in to the shop. An assistant comes towards them, and asks, 'Can I help you?'

'No,' Leila replies, 'we're just looking. That's if it's alright with you!'

'You just look around. If you find anything I can help you with please don't hesitate to ask me. We are here to help!'

Ciera looks at Leila and asks, 'Have you seen anything that takes your fancy yet?'

'Not really, 'She replies, 'Let's try another shop!'

Off they go again, and then Leila spots a beautiful white dress just inside the department store entrance in the window. 'This is just what I'm looking for mum. What do you think? Doesn't it look fantastic, magnificent and gorgeous?'

Mum looks at her, then at the dress and says, 'Well, it does look marvellous. Are you contemplating getting married, Leila?'

'What makes you ask that kind of question?'

'I don't know of any other occasion you would need a white dress!'

'We are going to New York tomorrow. I need to look stunning, spectacular and gorgeous. I think I'll try it on!'

'Come on, mum, you hold Alfie by the hand. Let's go in and see what happens.' Leila goes straight into the department store, over to one of the sales persons and asks 'May I try on that white dress in the window please?'

The sales person looks Leila up and down then she says, 'I'll need to ask the manager if you would like to wait!'

'That will be fine!' Leila replies. 'We'll wait here!'

A few minutes pass when the manager approaches and asks, 'Are you the young lady waiting to try on the white dress in the window?'

'Yes I'm the one. Is it possible to try it on?'

The manager goes to the window where the dress is on show he removes it from the mannequin, 'You go and sit in the changing room. I'll bring it to you as soon as possible!'

So off they go to the changing room and wait for the manager to arrive with the dress. It doesn't take long before the manager arrives back to the changing room with the dress, looks inside, then hands it to Leila saying, 'There you are young lady, if there are any alterations to be made we can do that today. We have our own dress maker on the premises if the need to make any alterations arises!'

Chapter 84

Ciera tells Alfie to wait outside the changing room while she goes inside to help Leila. After about ten minutes Ciera comes out and looks around. She sees the manager and asks him to come to the changing room. She tells him that there are some alterations to be made to the dress!

'Fine, let's go and see what needs to be done!'

As the two of them arrive inside the changing room, Leila is standing on the bench waiting patiently.

He looks at the dress and says, 'Let's see now what alterations need to be done.' He goes over to Leila, runs his hands over the dress and down the sides goes round the back, has another look at the back and decides that there are some alterations to be made. The question now is, 'Are you happy with the butterfly sleeves. Are you happy with them the way they are?'

'Mum what do you think. They look fine to me?'

'It does look fantastic on you. If you are happy with the sleeves on the dress that's fine with me!'

'Ok sir, if you can do the alterations this afternoon, I'll take it!'

'Good, I'll have the alterations done straight away. The dress will be ready for you about four this afternoon I hope that will suit you!'

'Yes that's fine with me. I would like to know if you have any boy's white clothes to fit Alfie, my little brother?'

'Yes, we have quite an extensive range of boys' clothing!'

'Mum, will you please go and find Alfie and bring him in here?'

Off she goes to find Alfie. In the mean time Leila removes the dress and puts on her own clothes. The manager goes to find the clothes for Alfie. He returns with a trolley full of boy's white clothes. He takes them out of the trolley and hangs them on the hooks on the wall. He takes the dress from Leila and says, 'I'll just take it to my dress maker and she can start on the alterations!'

Mum arrives back with Alfie and takes him into the changing room. Leila asks, 'Where did you find him, mum, he wasn't doing anything bad was he?'

'He was talking to one of the sales people. You know what Alfie is like, he'll talk to anyone!' Ten minutes pass when the manager arrives back, looks at Alfie and says, 'Are you the little boy having a fitting for some new clothes?'

Alfie doesn't say a word; he just stands there, and looks at his mum.

'Mum what's this about, why am I having new clothes?'

'I don't know, son, ask your sister.'

'You do want to go to New York tomorrow, Alfie?' Leila Inquires.

'Yes I do! He replies

'Well, then, I would like you to have new clothes. So if you don't mind, the manager would like to measure you!'

'Ok, I'm happy with that.' he replies.

The manager takes his measuring tape from his pocket goes to Alfie and measures him then looks at Leila and asks, 'What kind of clothes would you like him to have?'

'I think, white shirt, white trousers, pastel blue socks. White shoes, a light pastel blue waistcoat, and a light pastel blue bow tie?'

The manager goes to the boy's clothes department.

There he takes two pairs of the trousers from off the rack hooks. He has a quick measure to see if they might fit Alfie. He then he goes back and hands them to Alfie's mum saying. 'Please, you help him to try them on while I go and find a white shirt, a light pastel blue waistcoat. White shoes, light pastel blue socks and a light pastel blue bow tie!'

'Come on, Alfie; try these trousers on please, so that if there are any alterations to be made we can tell the manager. Now let's look at you. I think the trouser legs are a bit long, let me turn them up to the right length. That looks better, Alfie. Leila what do you think?'

'That looks fine now, mum. Let him keep the trousers on until the manager comes back. Then he can see what needs to be done to them!'

The manager arrives back with three white shirts, pastel blue waist coat white shoes, socks, and a pastel blue bow tie. He looks at Alfie and says. 'These trousers you have on look fine, just a little long but we can fix that for you. Now if you would like to try on these shirts to see which one fits you the best. The manager opens up the boxes Alfie tries on the shirts, one by one, and decides the last one fits him very well. His mum and his sister look at him and they agree that the shirt looks well and fits him.

'Alfie, can you please fit the pastel blue waistcoat on to see if that fits you?' It looks lovely. Now try the shoes please?'

He tries them on. Mum asks him, 'Are they alright? They're not too tight are they?'

'No, mum. I like them. They're not too tight!'

'Ok, that's it then, you are all done, just to have the trousers taken up a little. Off with the trousers Alfie and give them to the manager. He'll take it to his dress maker for alteration!'

'Mum, now it's your turn, I insist you have some new clothes as well!'

'I don't need new clothes, Leila, I've plenty of clothes in my wardrobe!'

'Mum you'll be in front of a large audience tomorrow of World leaders and I need you to be dressed immaculately and looking very serene and calm. Now you go and look at all of the clothes in the ladies department. Better still I'll come with you and help you to find what you like then come back into the changing room and we'll look at them on you. Come on, then let's go and see what we can find, come on Alfie!'

'What about dad? Mum, do you think he will need a new suit?'

'I don't think so; he has about five suits in his wardrobe. They are new and they are tailored made to measure suits so he'll be fine. Anyway he's not here!'

'If you think that he will be alright that's fine with me, mum!

'OK how many dresses have you picked, mum?'

'Just four that I like,' she replies.

'Come on then you can try them on in the changing room.' In the two of them go, she tries them on one by one and says, 'I think I like this one best,' as she stands in front on the mirror on the wall!'

'I like the colour,' says Leila, 'It's a lovely light green it hugs the body quite well. It has elbow length sleeves and its knee length. It looks very sexy, I do like it!'

'So do I,' her mum replies, 'I like it a lot!

Chapter 85

'That's it then. We have everything we need so let's go and find a restaurant and have something to eat!' Leila looks outside and sees Alfie sitting patiently in the window of the department store. She goes to see the manager and inquires, 'What time shall we return to pick up our clothes?'

'If you can be here about four this afternoon that will be fine!' the manager replies.

'Thank you for being so kind. Good bye for now!' Leila replies. 'What's the time now mum?'

'It's just coming up to half past two!'

'Good then we have enough time to go to a restaurant. Come on, Alfie, we are going to get something to eat!'

Alfie replies, 'I'm a bit hungry!'

Off the three of them go, walking down the high street in search of a restaurant.

Alfie spots a burger bar and says, 'Can I have some burgers please, mum?'

Mum looks at Leila, they both nod so they proceed into the burger bar. They walk up to the front of the ordering bar, discuss between themselves what they like and order from the menu above the bar, and a child's meal for Alfie.

The assistant says, I will bring your meal to you, you go and find a table.' Five minutes later she arrives at their table places the meal on the table and says, 'Enjoy your meal and walks away!'

Mum places Alfie's meal in front of him and says, 'There you are, son, your very own burger and chips. Do you want anything on them?'

'Can I have some red sauce please, mum?'

'Of course you can,' as she pours out the sauce from the bottle onto his plate. 'Do you need anything else, son?'

'No, mum, I'm fine now, thank you! He replies. Ciera then looks at Leila and says, 'Are you alright?'

'Yes, mum, I'm fine!' Leila replies.

'Good, let us begin our meal, shall we?'

Meal finished, the three of them walk out into the street. Mum looks at Leila and says, 'Where shall we go next?'

Leila looks at her watch and replies, 'The time is almost four o'clock. We may as well go and retrieve our new clothes from the shop!'

'That's fine with me,' she replies.

'Come on, Alfie, let's go and fetch our new clothes.'

Off they go along the high street. It takes about five minutes to arrive at the shop. Mum opens the door and the three of them go inside and look for the manager. He appears from behind one of the tills, walks up to them and says. 'Your clothes are ready. Would you like to try them on, I'm sure that all the alterations have been done,' as he opens the changing room doors saying, 'Please just go in and try them on, thank you!'

The three of them go inside, close the door behind them and change into the new clothes to make sure that the alterations have been done.

'Alfie let me see you in your new clothes. You look fantastic. Ok you can take them off now and put on your own clothes.' She looks at Leila and says, 'Well that dress looks absolutely fabulous on you. Are you happy that all the alterations are complete?'

'Yes, mum, everything feels fine. Now it's your turn to fit your new clothes on. So please change, that is, if you don't mind!'

Mum changes into her new clothes. Leila looks at her then at Alfie and says, 'Alfie what do you think, doesn't she look lovely and pretty?'

Alfie looks bemused and his mouth is wide open.

Leila looks at him and asks, 'Are you alright Alfie?'

'Yes, I'm fine,' as he looks at his mum, and replies, 'you look awesome!'

Mum looks at him and smiles, saying, 'Thank you Alfie that is very nice of you to pay me such a nice compliment.' She removes the new clothes and puts on her own clothes. 'Now let us place all the clothes into the carrier bags then go and pay the manager for them!'

Mum looks around the changing room to make sure that they have not left anything behind. She opens the changing room door, walks out into the shop, up to the pay desk.

The manager walks over and tells the assistant that he'll take over now. He looks at Leila and asks, 'Are your instructions for the alterations to the dress carried out to your satisfaction miss?'

'Everything is to our satisfaction thank you!'

'What about you, little boy, are you happy with your new clothes?'

'Yes I think so,' Alfie replies.

His mum looks at the manager and says. 'Can you tell me what we owe you?'

He places all the tag prices into the till hands Ciera the bill. She hands him her credit card, he places it the machine and says. 'Will you put your pin number in the machine please?'

She duly obliges, he says. Thank you for your custom.' Then he hands her credit card back and says, 'Please come again!'

Outside Leila asks, 'Did I spend too much money on our new clothes, mum? 'What will dad say?'

She looks at Leila and replies, 'I don't want you to worry, your dad will be fine. It's not as if we go out every day spending money on new clothes, is it? He did say buy what you like! Now I think it's time to go back to the car park for our car!'

Chapter 86

At the car park Ciera places her ticket into the slot on the pay machine, places the money in the next slot and retrieves her ticket, walks to the car. When they arrive at the car, there are two policemen and the owner of the car in the little space waiting for them, Leila looks at her mum and says. 'Leave this to me, please, I'll talk to the policemen I know what they want!'

Ciera looks at Leila and asks, 'Are you sure you can resolve what they want?'

'Yes of course I can. You just wait and see I won't hurt them. I'll just have a conversation with them. Don't worry!'

She walks over to the two policemen and asks. 'Can I help you? Is something wrong here?'

'Well, we are wondering how this car,' as he points to it, ended up in such a small space. How did it get in there?'

'Why ask me, officers how would I know? I'm not the owner of that car.' She points to the driver of the car in the small space and says, 'He is the owner of that car. My car is over there,' as she points to her car!

'Don't be smart with me, young lady we don't like people who are too smart for their own good. Now we would like to talk to you about that car in that space,' as he points to it. 'What can you tell me about it, 'How did it get in there?'

'How would I know? Why don't you ask the owner, maybe he knows?'

'Look, miss, the owner of this car has made a complaint about you and we are obliged to investigate. So please don't make our job hard!'

'I see the owner, I don't see or hear him making a complaint against me!'

'Well he has made a complaint against you and we are obliged to arrest you!'

The owner of the car is just standing with his hands folded and smiling to himself.

The officers look at each other and one of them says, 'If you would like to stand where you are for the moment.' He walks away and takes a call from the police station. He walks back to where Leila is standing and says, 'I'm obliged to arrest you for infringement of the peace in a public place. Please put out your hands in front of you?'

Leila looks at her mum and says, 'Mum you carry on home,' as she winks at her. I'll be home shortly don't worry, I'll be fine, go on home now please!'

One of the police officers places the handcuffs on Leila's wrists and they just fall off. The officers look at each other, 'Then they examine the cuffs again. They try again, this time one the policemen has the hand cuffs on his wrists.

Leila's mum sees what is happening, so she drives off home smiling to herself.

Alfie asks, 'Why are we leaving Leila behind, mum?'

'Nothing to worry about Alfie. The police officers are just being silly. Leila will be home soon ok!'

The police officers try again. This time the two officers are handcuffed together so they start to blame each other and start to fight.

'Gentlemen please, what's the matter? Is there something wrong with the handcuffs?'

They both look at each other then at Leila and say, 'Well, we don't know!'

'Look, officers if you want to take me to the police station,' can we go now please, I would like to return to my family as soon as possible thank you!'

'Please follow us to our car if you don't mind,' replies one of the police officers.

'Fine,' Leila replies.

The police officers and Leila walk out of the car park to the police car, keeping in mind that the two of them are still handcuffed together.

One of the police men looks at his colleague and says 'How are we going to drive to the police station with these handcuffs on our wrists? This is stupid. Which one of us is going to drive?'

Now a miracle happens. The handcuffs fall from the police officers' wrists and they are mystified baffled and bewildered as to what has happened.

They look on the ground; one of them bends down, picks the handcuffs up and examines them.

He hands them to his colleague and asks. 'Can you find anything wrong with them?'

'No,' his colleague, answers. 'They look fine to me!'

One of the police officers asks, 'Please, young lady, will you sit in the back seat of the car thank you! He then looks at his colleague and says. 'Please drive to the station as quick as possible.'

It takes ten minutes to travel to the station. The police officers alight from the car, open the back door of the car to let Leila out.

As she gets out she thanks the police officers for their courtesy and enquires. 'Where do I go from here?'

'We will need to place the handcuffs on your wrists again please!'

'That's fine!' Leila replies. She puts out her hands and one of the police officers places them on her wrists.

Chapter 87

'Follow us please,' says one of the police officers. Into the police station the three of them go. Inside they walk up to the desk, look at the booking sergeant and say. 'This young lady is to be booked for an infringement of the peace!'

The sergeant looks at Leila and asks. 'Why is this person not handcuffed?'

They both look at each other; lift their hands, then it dawns on them. They are handcuffed together again.

The sergeant looks at his two colleagues and asks. 'Why are the handcuffs on your wrists? Are you two playing silly devils?'

They answer, 'No sir, we are not playing silly devils.'

'Then why is you handcuffed together? Please answer the question. I would love to know, is it some new kind of game? Please give me some explanation, why you two have come in here handcuffed together. Come on I'm waiting to hear, this is going to be very interesting, let's hear the answer!' He is laughing at these two imbeciles.

By now there are quite a number of officers in the charge room. They are very interested in this strange phenomenon in view before them. They too are waiting for an explanation from the two officers.

Leila doesn't say a word, she just smiles.

However, the sergeant is not impressed seeing Leila smiling and takes the course of stupidly slapping Leila on the face and saying, 'Why are you smiling, young lady, I would like to know? Would you like another slap on the other side of your smiling face to match the one on the other side?'

Leila is furious. She knows that she should not lose her temper but this different. Violence for violence sake she will not tolerate. She takes him from behind the desk. She slams him against the wall. Then she walks over to him looks him in the eye and says, 'Sergeant Williams, why did you slap me on the face?' she enquires.

He looks at her and asks, 'How do you know my name?'

'I know every one's name in this station.' Now she slams him against the back wall of the station but she doesn't move a muscle, she doesn't even blink.'

All the officers in the charge room make a move to come to their sergeant's assistance. They are frozen in their tracks. They can't move, not even to blink, but they are quite lucid and know that there is something holding them back but what is it? What could be so strong as to hold about

251

ten police officers back from helping their sergeant? There is something uncanny going on here.

Leila walks over to the sergeant and says, 'I could demolish and flatten this building to the ground if I wish!'

'I don't believe you. Who do think you are? Super woman?'

'No I'm not super woman, I'm more powerful than her!'

'That's impossible, nobody is that powerful!' the sergeant replies.

It takes about one second for Leila to reduce all the furniture in the charge room to dust. 'Now, Mr Williams, do you want this building razed to the ground? Yes, I can do that as well. How dare you slap me in the face, why did you do that, are you some kind of bully. Do you think you could intimidate or frighten me?'

The two policemen that put her under arrest are standing with their mouths wide open. There is nothing coming out so Leila releases them from their statue dead stance and beckons them to her.

They reluctantly walk to her and she asks, 'Why have you arrested me? I will not ask you again.'

They look at each other and one of them says, 'We were told to arrest you by the Chief Constable. Apparently you did something to his son's car. That is all we know please, don't hurt us!'

'Where is this Chief Constable now?'

'We don't know!' they reply.

'Is there anyone here that knows where this Chief Constable lives?'

The sergeant answers, 'Yes I do.'

Leila looks at him. He arrives at her side without flexing a muscle. She places her hand on his shoulder and says. 'Thank you very much!'

In a flash the Chief Constable is standing next to Leila.

Chapter 88

He is totally bewildered, confused and disorientated. He asks, 'Where am I?' as he looks at the carnage in the police station asking, 'Is this, my police station and who is to blame for all this damage? Someone please tell me as he looks around. 'Alright who is to blame for all this?' He waves his hands about in the air.

Everyone in the room looks at Leila and the sergeant points his finger at her saying, 'She is the one that made this mess, sir!'

He looks quite stunned at this litany of words and enquires, 'How could she make this,' as he points his hand at all the damage. 'With half the station officers here it's not possible. Why didn't someone arrest her before she did this damage!'

'We tried, sir, but we were unable to stop her!'

'Ok why did she do this damage to the station? Surely someone could have stopped her!'

'One of the arresting officers replies, 'May I speak, sir, I think I know why all this happened.'

'Good, I'm glad someone knows what happened here. Please tell me, I'm dying to know?' The Chief Constable is still bewildered and confused and he is losing his temper!

'Sir, I was one of the officers that placed her under arrest. When we arrived at the station the sergeant said something, this young lady was smiling. Then the sergeant decided to slap her face, then all hell broke loose sir!'

'Why was she arrested?' The Chief Constable asks.

'Someone please tell me!'

'She was arrested on your orders sir. Apparently it has something to do with your son!'

The Chief Constable looks at Leila and enquires, 'What do you know about this, did you do something to my son?'

'No, sir, I. didn't touch him. I, my mother and my brother went into the car park in the town. We found a space to park our car. It was going to be available when the car there had vacated that parking bay. We were just about to enter that space when your son decided to push his way into that parking space, giving us the obnoxious one finger sign that is not a sign of good spirit. He ended up in a smaller parking space that didn't please him. He must have phoned you for help and you foolishly decided without any evidence whatsoever, to have me arrested? I didn't break any laws so why did you want me arrested? I would love to know, sir?'

'My son told me that you were giving him verbal and causing a scene in the car park so he phoned me for help. I dispatched a car with two policemen to attend the disturbance!'

'That was a bit premature of you. Would you have done the same thing for me?' I think not sir.'

'Now will someone please arrest this person before I lose my temper?' The Chief Constable replies.

Not one person moves in Leila's direction in the station.

The Chief Constable points at the sergeant, 'You are the cause of this damage, you arrest her?'

'You are the senior officer in this station. It's now your responsibility sir. I'm certainly not going to arrest her. You have no idea how powerful she is. She turned this station into dust in less than a minute. We don't even know her name. We don't know where she lives. We didn't have the time to ask!' If you want to arrest her please be my guest, sir!' 'I'll do that then,' so he walks over to Leila and says, 'Young lady you are under arrest for the damage you have done to this station. Please put out your hands while I handcuff you!'

Leila puts out her hands. The Chief Constable tries to place the handcuffs on her wrists. They just fall to the ground as if nothing was there.

The Chief Constable is blinking and wiping his eyes. He looks down at the handcuffs on the ground makes a grab for Leila but his hands go right through her body as if she is not there. He tries to hold her arms but to no avail it's as if she is invisible, no substance, as if she is a hologram. He is perplexed so he says, 'Stay where you are while I make a phone call.' He walks to his office but Leila is in there before him. He looks at her and says, 'I told you to stay where you are in the charge room. What are you doing in my office? 'I told you to stay in the charge room

'I'm waiting for you. I have come to help you because you will not be able to make a phone call unless I do it for you!' replies Leila.

He doesn't listen to her, he has his own agenda. He picks up the phone, tries to dial a number but nothing happens. He tries again with the same result so he slams the phone down. He is looking very worried now and he is trying to decide what to do about this situation. He knows that there is no alternative, so he throws his hands up in the air saying, 'OK, you win, what would you like me to do for you?' Please tell me!'

'Your call is just coming through.' The phone rings, he looks at it, then at Leila she says, 'Pick it up it's for you.'

Reluctantly and with hesitation, he picks it up and asks, 'Who am I speaking to?'

Then a voice at the other end of the phone says, 'This is Colonel Phillip Amery of the SAS. What can I do for you?'

'Phillip, this is Chief Constable Tim Ronan I need your help?'

'Hello, Tim, it's a long time since we had a talk. Tim, you know that we don't get involved in police work unless it has to do with the security of the country. How can I help you Tim?'

'We have a problem at one of my stations. It could be a very big problem for you!'

Leila decides to communicate telepathically with the Colonel. He is hearing this voice in his mind saying, 'I'm coming to see you in a minute, sir!'

He jumps up from his desk drops the phone, falls backwards against the wall, and says to him-self, 'My God, I'm hearing things.'

Leila is now in possession of the exact place in the world where the Colonel is staying. 'We must talk, Colonel,' then she places her hand in Tim's hand. He looks at her she says, 'Don't be afraid I'm not going to hurt you.' In an instant the two of them are in the Colonel's office.

He is flabbergasted and very much taken by surprise. He pulls out one of the drawers in his desk and retrieves a gun. Then he points it at Leila and tries to pull the trigger. Nothing happens. He looks at it, tries again, nothing works, so he throws the gun at Leila and shouts out, 'Sergeant, please come into my office immediately.'

Chapter 89

The sergeant rushes into the office, with a revolver in his hand. He goes around to the front of Leila, shouting, 'Place your hands on your head and get down on your knees.'

Then something strange happens. The sergeant turns and faces his superior officer, points his revolver at the Colonel's head and just stands there as if transfixed.

Leila tells him to shoot the Colonel. He pulls the trigger and the bullet flies out of the barrel of the revolver and stops one inch in front on the Colonel's head.

'Now, gentlemen, I have just demonstrated how powerful I am and I could kill all three of you with that one bullet, but I'm here to talk to you!' Then the bullet just falls to the floor.

The Colonel looks at the sergeant, says, 'That's all, sergeant, you may go back to your desk now, thank you!'

He looks at the Colonel asking, 'Will you be alright? I mean do you trust this person, sir, she is very dangerous. She could kill you!'

He is looking at Leila, then at the sergeant. 'Yes I'll be fine, sergeant. That is all for now, you may return to your office!'

Leila looks at Mr Ronan and says. 'This problem has been instigated by your son. Now let me explain, your son has you wrapped around his little finger. He will get you into very big trouble if you don't talk to him about his attitude. One of two things will happen. One, he will kill someone. Two, he will get himself killed. He needs to grow up sooner rather than later. Do I make myself clear, sir!'

'Yes I do, but what can I do to make him understand he is obstinate, unruly and wilful. I know he needs help!'

'I think you should consider retiring from the police force. I know that is a very drastic move but maybe some kind of therapy, psychotherapy or psychoanalysis would help. I'm not saying he will be better but it should help. I could cure him but I'm not allowed to interfere.'

'I'll have a discussion with my wife and then make a decision.'

Outside in the sergeant's office he is on the phone to the captain of the SAS. He is informing him that the Colonel is a prisoner in his office and he needs help now. 'Please come and rescue him as soon as possible sir?'

'I'll be there in about five minutes. Don't tell the Colonel anything. Wait for me I'll bring some of my men to rescue the Colonel!'

'Thank you sir, I await your presence here!'

Leila knows what is happening out in the sergeant's office but doesn't say anything. She knows that she is not in any danger.

The Colonel looks at Leila and asks. 'Who are you, do you have a name, where are you from?'

'My name is Leila, that is all you need to know for the present!'

By now she knows that there are twenty SAS men in the sergeant's office. They are ready to storm the Colonel's office. She waits for their entrance into the Colonel's office. She decides to make herself invisible and moves to a different part of the office.

Colonel Amery and Mr Ronan have noticed that Leila has suddenly disappeared. They are looking everywhere but she is nowhere to be seen in the office. They look at each other, shrug their shoulders, but this game is not over yet.

The twenty SAS men burst into the office with their Colt M4A1's at the ready, look around the office, then the captain walks in, salutes the Colonel saying, 'We have come to rescue you, sir.'

'Well you are too late she has gone. I don't know where, perhaps it's all an illusion. Thank you, captain. It looks like a bit of hoax, a deception. Wherever she is gone now, I don't know where!'

Leila turns her attention to the SAS men. She tells them through telepathy to surround the captain, the Colonel, and the Chief Constable. They are traitors to their country!

Then the sergeant rushes into the office shouting. 'What are you doing? Are all of you crazy? What's the matter with you, I told you that the Colonel was being held captive in his office!'

The SAS men take no notice of the sergeant.

Now Leila makes herself visible. She walks around the room over to the sergeant, looks him in the eye and says, 'There are fools, idiots, and stupid people, and you are all three!'

The sergeant starts to shout, 'Captain, please let me shoot her, she is a terrorist!'

'Sergeant, please, look at me. Do I look as if I'm going to kill anyone here? I don't have a gun, a rifle. Do I have any explosives on me? Please feel free to search me.'

The Colonel walks out from the back of his desk, walks over to the sergeant, puts his arm around the sergeant's shoulder and says, 'Sergeant, please return to your post, I don't think you can do anything here. If I'm in need of help I'll call you!'

Leila looks at the SAS men. They look a bit fidgety they are looking for a fight. However, that is not going to happen. It's too dangerous someone would die from gunshot wounds. She needs to defuse this situation quickly or it might get out of hand. She walks around the SAS men very slowly saying, 'Gentlemen, do you want to confront or challenge me. If not please leave the room.'

One SAS man breaks rank, walks up to Leila, 'We are not leaving until you are dead!'

'That's not a very nice thing to say. What makes you think that I'm a threat to your Colonel or anyone else? I'm sure that the Colonel would agree with me that I'm asking you very nicely to leave this room please. If you do not there are consequences to pay.'

Now the SAS man is getting very agitated, he points his gun at Leila's head takes the safety catch off saying, 'I going to kill you, I don't like you. I think you are a terrorist!'

It doesn't faze Leila in any way. She walks back about four paces, looks at this idiot pointing his gun at her and says, 'Pull the trigger please, young man, go on. Don't be afraid you want to kill me, now is your chance. Go on, I dare you to pull the trigger.'

The Colonel jumps up from his desk and shouts, 'Soldier put down your weapon now!'

He looks at the Colonel and says, 'Sir, please, she has to die now, I'm sure my colleagues will back me up. I know that I'm going the right thing, sir!'

Leila has had enough of this idiot threatening her, so she pulls the trigger herself through her mind, everyone in the room fall to the ground except the idiot and Leila. This rifle is automatic. It shoots all the projectiles/bullets in the magazine in one burst. Now this is just amazing all the bullets stop about two inches from Leila's body. They just hang there, no movement what-so-ever. Everyone is amazed and looks horrified. The Colonel is hiding behind his desk with the Chief Constable and the captain. They look up over the top of the desk thinking that he has shot Leila and wondering what might happen next.

Leila just walks to one side and leaves the bullets in mid air. She is not angry, just baffled at this idiot and why he is convinced that she is a terrorist.'

The idiot is running around shouting, 'Colonel I didn't pull the trigger,' then he throws his rifle across the office floor and shouts, 'It just went off, sir!'

However, it's time to disarm the rest of the SAS soldiers before someone is at the end of a bullet. The rifles jump out of the soldier's hands and dismantle themselves in front of the Colonel. They then fall in a mangled group of metal on the ground to everyone's surprise.

Chapter 90

The Colonel is beside himself with wonder at what he has witnessed.

'Now that is something I'm glad I witnessed. It's beyond logical imagination. It can't be analyzed in the true logic of a scientific awareness. However, I've seen it happen with my own eyes so it must be true. No question what so ever. I believe that this young lady is not of this world!'

'Colonel, please, I insist that you make your men leave the room. They are no match for me or is anyone else on this planet. Now you might think that I'm conjuring up some kind of magic. Far from it, I could raze this building to the ground if I wanted to. Ask your friend, Mr Ronan.' The bullets are still hanging in the air so she takes them one by one and drops each one on top of the mangled rifle metal on the ground.

The Colonel looks at his captain saying, 'Captain I'm giving you an order; place the idiot that caused all this trouble under close guard, arrest him, then take him back to the barracks where he will have a trial by court martial. Now remove your detachment of soldiers from this room. Return them to their barracks now please. I'll talk with you later!'

Leila looks at the Colonel. 'Now, sir, I'm able to make my position clear. I'm human like you, my parents are human, and my DNA is human. My technology is from another world. That is all I need to tell you for the moment. However, there will be an announcement tomorrow afternoon from the United Nations Building in New York so be sure and watch your televisions. Mr Ronan, I think it's time to return you to your office,' and in a flash the two of them are back in Mr Ronan's office.

'Now, sir, you must rein in your son before he does something he will regret. Thank you for your time!' She has vanished in the blink of an eye.

The Colonel calls the sergeant into his office and enquires from the sergeant, 'Can I have your honest opinion? Did we see something special in my office five minutes ago something I can't explain?'

The sergeant looks bewildered and confused. He really doesn't understand what he has witnessed. He is trying to form an opinion but his brain doesn't seem to be able to decipher what has happened. So he just throws up his hands in the air shouting,' I don't know sir; I can't get my head around this. I have never seen anything like that young lady before. Is she for real?'

'I don't know sergeant. All I know is that we had no control of the situation and I was petrified. I think that we should make a report in writing to the Minister for the Armed forces and let them decide what action they would like to take, but in all honesty I don't think that there is anything anyone can do. She is very powerful but not vindictive. She didn't hurt anyone she just demonstrated her powers. I must admit I was petrified but amazed. When that young soldier pulled the trigger on his rifle and the bullets were flying everywhere, not one of them damaged anything or anyone in my office, and then they just stopped about two inches in front of the young lady. She just walked away and they just hung in the air. You didn't see that, did you, sergeant?'

'No, sir, I didn't see that but it must have been amazing and astonishing to witness!'

'It was, sergeant. I was hiding behind my desk wondering how many people were dead. When I dared to raise my head above the top of the desk I couldn't believe what had happened. She was just standing there with the bullets hanging just in front of her, not one person had been hit. A miracle was the first thing to enter my head. It wasn't a miracle, it was that young lady. Somehow she defied all scientific logic of our world. I felt quite humbled to be in her presence. I knew then that we were witnessing something way above our intellectual capability and the ability of understanding in this young lady. I'll tell you something else. She is stunningly very beautiful and her presence is all inspiring!'

Chapter 91

The Chief Constable calls the sergeant into his office, 'Sergeant, you have a cleaning job to carry out!'

The sergeant walks to the door, opens it, looks out and can't believe his eyes. He turns around and faces the Chief Constable, 'Sir, I think you had better come and look at this!'

The Chief leaves his desk, goes to the door and looks out into the charge room and it looks as if nothing has happened. All the furniture is back in its rightful place. No one can believe what they are seeing. The charge room furniture was in dust, now everything is as it was before the young lady was arrested!

'Yes, sergeant, she is all powerful,' he has a big smile to himself, 'now get on with your job!'

In a flash she is in her own home. Mum looks at Leila and asks, 'Did everything work out ok?

'Yes, everything is fine. I'm glad to be home. May I have some tea please?'

'What would you like?'

'I'll leave that to you, mum. She looks at Alfie and asks, 'Alfie what have you been up to?'

He looks at his sister and says, 'I've been a good boy all day!'

'Good for you, Alfie!' Leila replies.

'Mum, I think it would be a good idea to have a change of clothes with us when we go to America tomorrow. You never know we might need to stay there for a while?'

Mum looks at Leila and asks, 'I don't know, what you mean. Can you be more specific please?'

'Well, what happens if all the business I need to finish can't be concluded in the time we are in New York?'

'In that case, how are you going to resolve that problem?' Mum asks.

'Easy, we have a small case of clothes each. We leave them in the sitting room. I'll teleport them from here to New York tomorrow at the same time when we leave!'

'Are you sure you can do that?' her mum asks.

'Yes, of course I can, I'll contact granddad, grandma, JK, Delia and ask them each to have a change of clothes packed in a small case and leave it in their sitting room, and if we have to stay, I'll teleport all the cases to New York if needed. How does that sound!'

'If you think we might need to stay I'm happy with that arrangement,' she replies.

'Good, then I'll contact the rest of the family now to make sure I keep them up to date with what we might need to do.'

Leila communicates with the rest of the family, gives them all the information about the change of clothes and asks, 'Are we all in agreement on my strategy? If so, I'll arrange everything including making sure that if a change of clothes is needed I'll transport all we need to New York.'

Leila contacts granddad, tells him that it might be a good idea to have extra clothes in case he needs them in New York.

'I have no problem,' says JK,' I'm fine with that arrangement!'

Delia is not so sure and asks, 'may I ask if I might be staying in New York for an extra day, will the shop be looked after in the hands of the girls?'

'Of course the shop will be fine. You can tell your girls that you might need to stay there for an extra day. I'll make sure of everything else. Don't you worry one little bit!'

'Ok then I'll pack a little case and leave it in my sitting room. Are sure you can have it in New York if I need it?'

'Yes of course I'm sure and promise if your case is needed it will be in New York before you can blink an eye! Are you happy with that?' Leila responds. 'You make sure that your girls are up to speed on your trip to New York and one last thing, Did you have a visitor to your shop this morning?'

'Yes, I did, how did you know that?'

'I know everything. Did he give you anything?'

'Yes he did, he gave me a lot of money. He said that he was sorry for the entire heart break he gave me, which was very strange perhaps he had a change of heart how he treated me but I'm not taking another chance on him. I'm happy the way I am now!'

'Good for you, Delia. Actually you might consider giving your staff an extra bonus at the end of the week if they perform well in the shop. You must tell them what you intend for them, I'm sure they will be very pleased at what you have planned, regarding extra money. I think you should go to the bank now and deposit that money!'

'Incidentally, what are the arrangements for tomorrow regarding New York? I don't have my tickets yet. Do I go to work in the morning as usual?'

'Yes you do,' Leila replies.

'That's it, mum; everyone is up to speed now. I know everything will be alright. We will have a very good time in New York!'

Ciera looks at Leila and says, 'you're up to something I know you,' as she has a little smile and a quite laugh to herself. 'I don't know what but I'm sure that everything will be fine!'

'Why are you suspicious, mum? Do you think I'm up to something devious?'

Ciera says, 'You're hatching something up but I'm sure you mean well!'

Leila on this occasion doesn't confide in her mum. She knows that there will be a problem in New York with the American President. He is a very devious person but she'll keep an eye on him and monitor his brain and behavioural patterns.

'Mum, I think that Alfie should pack whatever clothing changes he might need for tomorrow afternoon. Do you want to call him down from his room!'

'Yes, alright, I'll call him down. She goes to the bottom of the stairs and shouts out. 'Alfie can you come down as quick as you can to the sitting room I need to talk to you!'

'Alfie comes to the top of the stairs and says. I'll be down in a minute mum!'

'Fine then as long as you promise to be down soon! Mum replies.

'Mum, I'm going to go to the United Nations Building as soon as I have finished my tea!'

'Why do you need to go there today?' Mum asks.

'Because I need to make sure that there will be no problems tomorrow when we arrive in the Great Hall. I'm sure that I'll not have any problems but it's better to make sure. Then there are no worries or any last hitches. I need to make sure that our time in New York is used to the best of my ability.'

Alfie runs down the stairs and into the sitting room and says, 'I'm here now, mum. Can I help you in any way?'

'Would you help me to pack a little suit case for you. In case we decide to stay in New York tomorrow?'

Alfie looks at his mum and smiles to himself and says, I'm looking forward to New York I might like it there.'

'It's just one or two days in New York you might need a change of clothes there!'

Leila smiles at Alfie's curiosity. He is always asking questions but like all children, curiosity is the name of the game.

'Come on, Alfie, let's go and see what you would like to take to America tomorrow.' he looks at Leila and smiles.

Leila has now turned eighteen years old. She looks stunning. She looks every inch a goddess and she knows it. She has a beautiful complexion, piercing blue eyes with long Golden/Red hair and she is quite slim. She is about 183 centimetres from head to toe, or about six foot one. She can feel the power of the Bio/Dna technology. It's building up inside her brain and mind. She knows that this technology can and will change her life forever.

Leila's time is fast approaching when she will declare her amazing powers to the world. How and when this is going to happen depends on Leila herself. She knows that the technology she has been given is way above anything on Earth. She is not seeking power for power's sake, her remit is to make governments understand that she will not allow or tolerate any more wars of any kind. If they do not comply with her vision, she will remove all or any who are belligerent and replace them with a more cooperative people. She will make laws in conjunction with World leaders. She need not force her ideology on others but she will insist that it is for the good for all the people of this World. Leila's technology is now so advanced, that she is able to prevent any Army, Air force, Navy from any country instigating any reprisals, attempting to initiate or incite war.

That will be made clear to all governments including Caliphate (Islamic State) and if necessary she will give a demonstration of her powers so that there is no question in any one's mind what is required from them. Of course, there will be dissenters, but she will win them over in the end but hopefully in a friendly way. She will present a favourable agreement, which will be pleasing to everyone. Governments will try and discredit her. They will try to sidetrack her. They will place all kind of obstacles in her way, hoping to trip her up. What they don't know is that she is far superior and intellectually way above their intelligence, able to converse in all languages, so any underhand discussions behind her back will make no difference. Leila will play along with their silly games. They will try to have her assassinated, not once, it will happen many times but without success. This is not a worry for her. She is on a mission to stabilize World governments whether it is in their interests or not. The power will be dictated by the people. They will understand in the end the only way to save Earth is if Leila's makes her powers available to stop this war mongering elite, whose only interest is greed and power. Now the ordinary people of Earth have a champion and she will prevail in the end.

Leila knows that her Bio/Dna technology powers are advancing at an extraordinary pace. Fortunately, for her, she is in total control of this situation, but she does have a slight worry. Will she be able to keep this Bio/Dna technology in check in the future, Leila is very confident that no matter what happens, she will be able to keep control of her body, and her mind. Time will have no meaning in her life, she will come and go and do whatever she feels will make a better World, and keep her family safe.

Mum asks, 'Do you need to go to the United Nations Building today?

'Yes I do because I need to make sure that there will be no problems tomorrow when we arrive in the Great Hall. I am sure that I will not have any problems but it is better to make sure then there are no worries or any last hitches. I need to make sure that our time in New York is used to the best of my ability.'

'Not exactly just one or two days in New York you might need a change of clothes there!'

Ciera looks at Leila and says, 'don't be away to long please, we do worry when you are away from home.'

In a flash she is in the United Nations General Assembly Building in New York, where she materializes in one of the ground floor toilets, walks out into the reception area, then over to the receptionists desk waits her turn then asks, 'Who do I ask about looking at the Great Hall where the world leaders will be meeting tomorrow?'

The receptionist looks a bit bewildered and asks, 'Why would you want to see where the world leaders are in session tomorrow?' The receptionist hits a button by her knees and that triggers an alarm in the security office of the building.

Leila knows that the receptionist has pushed the security button, but she is not worried one little bit. It does not take long for the security office to organise an armed party to go to reception to determine the problem. He then needs to secure the building against any security risk, not knowing what hostility he might be walking into in reception. When they arrive at the reception desk the sergeant goes to the receptionist and asks, 'What is the matter? Do we have some kind of security problem, 'If so where is it?'

'Yes we have this lady,' she points to Leila; 'She would like to know if she could have a look into the Great Hall where the world leaders will be in session tomorrow.'

He looks at Leila and thinks to himself, 'She does not look like a terrorist, but I cannot take chances,' He tells his security team, 'lock down the area now.' He walks over to Leila and asks, 'If you don't mind, it's just that I'm obliged under the rules of this building if I think there is a security problem I'm obliged to take action. You do understand. Now may I have your name please?'

'Of course, my name is Leila Carney.'

He looks at her with his gun pointed at her and asks, 'What are you doing in this building, 'do you have business here, are you an employee in this building, do you have a job or do you work in this building?'

'No I'm not an employee here but I would like to talk to the President of the United Nations Security Council. Would you be so kind and take me to him please?'

He looks at her intently, laughs at her and asks, 'You are joking, is this some kind of wind up?'

'Absolutely not, sir, I would not insult your intelligence, I am not here to damage anything.'

'Ok, you are under arrest. Please come with me. He looks at the receptionist and says, 'Thank you very much for your diligence.' He walks away with Leila surrounded by his men.

They take her to a holding room. The security officer tells Leila to sit down at the table in the room. He leaves two of his men at the entrance of the room and tells them, 'No one in or out.'

He goes to find the Chief of Security. When he arrives at the door he knocks.

'Please come in, the door is open.'

The sergeant opens the door, goes inside, looks at the Chief and says. 'Sir we have a young lady in the holding room who is asking questions about the World leaders in tomorrow's session in the Great Hall. What do we do with her.'

'Sergeant, did you search her for explosives?'

'No, sir we did not. She doesn't look like a terrorist.'

'Well I suggest you go back and search her just in case she might blow the buildings up!'

Chapter 92

'Yes sir.' He turns around, walks out of the Chief's office back to where Leila is confined. He indicates to his two men to open the door and says, 'Come with me please. I have been told to search that girl. Would one of you go and find a female officer and bring her to me. Now young woman I have sent for a female officer. When she comes she will search you. Do not make my job any harder than it is please. Would you oblige me and open your coat so that I may see if you're carrying any kind of time piece for explosives on your person. Thank you?'

Leila opens her coat just to keep him happy and shows him that she does not have any kind of explosives on her body.

He looks at her and says, 'I don't see anything that might trigger an explosion but I must be sure,' then the door opens and a female officer walks in asking, 'Is this the lady I'm to frisk for explosives?' She walks over to Leila she says, 'I hope you don't mind I'm only doing my job.' 'That's fine with me. You carry on,' Leila replies.

While the female officer frisks her, Leila has looked into her mind to find out which part of the building the Chief has his office. When the female has finished frisking Leila, she stands up and says, 'I'm finished now. I have nothing to report sergeant. Then he looks at Leila and says, 'Thank you for that cooperation young lady, may I ask would you like a cup of coffee?'

'No thank you very much,' she replies.

'You will be held here for further questioning until such time as we are satisfied that you are no danger to this building or the world leaders tomorrow, but don't be offended it's my job and I must carry it out without exception. Thank you again for your cooperation in this matter. I will leave you now for a short time but I'll have two of my officers outside the door in case you might need something. All you have to do is just knock on the door.'

The sergeant, his two officers and the female officer leave the room, the two officer's stand outside the door. The female officer goes back to her office and makes her report about the young lady in the holding room.

The sergeant goes directly to the Chief's office but unbeknown to him, Leila is there before him. The Chief looks like he is transfixed in the lights of a car. His eyes are wide open. He is leaning back in his chair his hands are waving about in the air. Now he is wondering how this woman has entered his office without him seeing her come in. 'Who are you, how did you get in to my office. What do you want?' Are you some kind of nut?'

'First thing first, my name is Leila, secondly I'm able to transport, teleportation whatever you might like to call it, and thirdly I'm as sane and normal as you are. Please don't be afraid, I'll not hurt you, I'm not a terrorist. I'm not anything like that but just to show you what I'm able to do,' she levitates his desk about two foot off the office floor and lets it descend back to its original place. 'Now that might surprise you but do not let it worry you. I also know what you are thinking. Your mind is abuzz with lots of questions and you are hoping that someone will come through your office door in a minute. Sir I am here to ask you a question or a favour if you like.'

'What would that question be,' I'll try and facilitate you as best I can.'

'Tomorrow there is a meeting of world leaders here in this building and I would like to address them about our planet?' Leila replies.

Chapter 93

'I don't think I can accommodate you for this meeting. It has been scheduled for a while now and it can't be changed, only on an emergency and then only with the express authorisation by the Secretary General of the United Nations

'Sir, you're about to get a knock on your door.'

'How do you know that?' he replies.

'It's the sergeant of security sir.'

Then there is a knock made on the door.

'Come in, sergeant!' the Chief shouts.

The sergeant opens the office door, walks into the office, he sees Leila standing next to the Chief. He looks dumfounded, and astonishment he points at Leila asking, 'how did she get in to your office, sir?' I left her in the holding room with the door locked.'

'Do not worry, sergeant I will not hurt your Chief or you, so please be calm and composed' Leila replies.

The sergeant looks at the Chief and asks, 'What is she doing here sir?'

'That is a very good question, he says. She tells me she would like to address the world leaders tomorrow afternoon. What are your thoughts on that, sergeant?'

'Sir, I think she should be locked up now before anything happens!'

'Fine then you arrest her and lock her in our security facility and let the police decide what to do with her,' the Chief replies.

'Ok young lady, 'Please place your hands over your head while I call for help. He takes out his internal communication phone from his jacket has a conversation with his understudy telling him to come as quickly as possible to the Chief's office we have an intruder!'

Now all hell has broken loose. Security people are running in all directions but mainly to the Chief's office. When they arrive at the office door, they draw their guns take the safety catches off burst into the office, shouting. 'Hands in the air and don't move. You're under arrest.'

'Gentlemen, please, what is all this commotion?' It's all about nothing. I am not armed I do not have any explosives or knives on me. As you know I have been searched outside in the reception area so why am I under arrest?'

The sergeant walks over to Leila saying, 'You think you are very clever don't you?'

'Why does that worry you, sergeant?' Leila enquires.

'How did you get out of our holding room, 'Please tell me I would love to know?

'I transported out and into this office!'

'Impossible!' shouts the sergeant.' Do you think you are Houdini, I don't think so,' he adds.

She decides to make herself invisible. The sergeant looks bemused, puzzled and baffled and asks, 'Where is she, find her!' he shouts. Everyone is scrambling about looking in cupboards under the chief's desk but she is nowhere visible in the office.

Chapter 94

The Chief looks bewildered and confused, 'Sergeant she must be somewhere in this office the door hasn't opened so she must be here somewhere find her he shouts.

Leila is now invisible, so she decides to play a little game with the security men saying, 'I'm still in the room, open your eyes, and I'm over here.' Then she moves to the other side of the office saying, 'I'm over here, gentlemen, are you all blind.'

She decides that this could become very dangerous if they were to start shooting one of their own down. She cannot have that so she decides to become visible again to the astonishment of all the people in the office. Now she can demand to see the Secretary General of the United Nations General Assembly. She looks at the Chief and says, 'May I call you Gerald? Sir, I could walk into this building anytime I might care to, and be in the Great Hall tomorrow and you wouldn't know I am there, so please let me see the President of the United Nations now!'

He picks up his phone, dials the number. It is picked up at the other end by a woman. He says, 'Gerald here, is the Secretary General free I would like to speak to him please it's extremely important.'

'Hold the line sir. 'Twenty seconds later she is back. You're through to the   Secretary General now sir.'

'Yes, Gerald what is so important? I'm in a meeting, can't it wait until tomorrow?'

'No sir that's what it's all about.'

'What do you mean, Gerald, why do you need to see me now? Why can't it wait until tomorrow?'

'Sir in my office I have a young lady who insists she needs to address the world leaders tomorrow and I think you should see her now!'

'Are you mad, Gerald, I don't have the time now, people can't just turn up and ask for an appointment. My secretary will make an appointment for next week for her to see me. I must return to my meeting good bye Gerald'.

Leila puts out her hand to Gerald and says, 'Thank you very much you have been a great help.'

Now she knows in which office the Secretary General of the United Nations is located.

In a flash, she is in the office of the Secretary General of the United Nations Mr Michael Hester. He jumps up as do all the people around the table in his office, 'He is shouting, 'Who are you? Where did you come from? Someone please call security now!'

It is pandemonium, everyone is trying to make the call to security but none of the phones are working.

Leila decides to take control of the situation and looks around the table. She can see that everyone is petrified and the colour has drained from their faces.

'Sir, I am not here to hurt anyone in this office. She looks around, everyone please be quiet.' There is stunned silence at this sudden request from someone that no one knows, or that the people in the office have never seen before, but they comply anyway, thinking that she might have a gun.

'Sir, may I suggest we have a discussion in another room please.'

'About what?' the Secretary General asks.

'Sir, please, it's very important we talk privately about tomorrow. I can take you and me somewhere private where no one will be privy to our discussion and I promise that nothing will happen to you. The two of them leave the room, 'you have a house in Florida why don't we go there?'

He looks at Leila and say, 'I don't have the time now to leave here and fly to my home in Florida. Are you kidding me!'

'Sir, may I call you Michael?'

'Yes, if you must, but I'm not going to leave here to accommodate your foolish request. The security people will be here any minute now.'

Leila holds out her hand saying, 'Thank you sir,' He reciprocates, puts out his hand and in an instant the two of them are in his house in Florida.

Chapter 95

The Secretary General is totally lost, he looks around his home to make sure that he is in his house but he cannot quite make out what has happened. He does not know what to say, or what to do. He looks at Leila and enquires, 'You are going to kill me, are you not?'

'No, sir, I'm not going to kill you, I'm on a mission to save the world.'

The SG asks. 'What is going on here? What exactly do you want?'

Leila is way ahead of him.

'Please, sir, I don't want you to try and analyse what I'm telling you. Without being facetious or underhanded in any way, I do need your help but if you don't cooperate I'll be there tomorrow anyway but it is better that we agree. You phone your office and tell your secretary to reschedule the speakers for tomorrow. If she asks for the names, just tell her not to worry. It will all fall into place tomorrow, which is all she needs to know.

Please, sir, will you make the call now I would very much appreciate your cooperation at this time.'

He picks up the phone, dials his office. His secretary picks her phone up and before she can say a word, he says, 'This is Michael here, I need you to reschedule the speakers for tomorrow's meeting.'

'Why, sir, all the arrangements are made.'

'I know that,' replies the SG, 'hold the line please; I'll have a think about it.' He looks at Leila and says, 'I think that it would be better to leave the schedule alone. You just come and do what you need to do. You're not going to kill anyone, tomorrow, are you?' I have no intention of killing anyone? Leila replies 'Are you happy with that? He asks.

'Yes, I am happy with that, sir. What do you want me to do?'

'Leave everything as it is, I couldn't stop you anyway!' The SG replies.

'I'm happy with that arrangement. Sir, I truly need you to have trust in me. I will help you beyond your wildest dreams. Now I want to show you something.' In an instant she has changed into an exact copy of the SG.

He is just amazed and perplexed; he is looking at himself as if in a mirror. He throws his hands up in the air saying, 'I'm glad you're on my side.'

'Sir, I can do anything I want. You will witness something special tomorrow that will amaze you. Now I must change back to myself. Before you can blink she has returned to herself.

The SG looks at Leila and says, 'You are for real? You are not an illusion, are you?' he enquires.

Chapter 96

'No, sir, I'm not an illusion I'm a real human being. I was born on this planet. My parents are human as are all my family, we are all human. Is there anything else you would like to know about me?'

'I don't think so. Just one question?'

'Ask me and I'll try to give you a truthful answer,' She replies.

'How powerful are you?' He looks very intently at Leila.

'I'm all powerful, in fact I'm the most powerful person on this planet!'

'Did I hear you say, that on this planet you're the most powerful human, even more powerful than the President of America? I can't believe that.'

'Yes, sir, you did,' she replies. 'Let me show you how powerful I am.'

She looks at Mr Hester and enquires, 'When did you last have a rainfall here in Florida?'

He looks at her wondering what she is going to do and enquires, 'Are you going to make it rain?' He has a little laugh to himself.

'Look out the window, sir, what do you see?'

He looks out his window and sure enough it's raining. He says, 'Now I'm finding this hard to believe.' As he has a little laugh out loud, he opens the window puts out his hand to make sure it's not an illusion; sure enough it's real rain. He draws his hand back in from the rain and starts to laugh quite loudly saying, 'This is hard for me to believe. It has not rained here for six months, 'He looks at Leila and enquires, and can you stop it raining now?' He looks out the window sure enough it has stopped. 'Amazing, this has been an education and a lesson in diplomacy for me. The way you have managed to communicate and converse with me is amazing. You did not need to ask me for anything. All this was an exercise in diplomacy. I do appreciate you being candid with me. You could use your power to do anything and there is nothing to stop you, is there?'

'No, sir, if I wanted to be a bad person, no one on this planet could stop me. I could create havoc in this world but that is not why I am here talking to you. I just need you to have trust in what I am going to do tomorrow. I can assure you that the world will benefit from my power. Now, sir, I think we should return to your office and please don't say anything about my powers or our diplomatic exchange of ideas. I need to make a good entrance tomorrow, and I'm sure that you will be well pleased.'

Chapter 97

Leila places her hand in the SG's hand and he is back into a room in his office. The two of them walk back into his office where the other people are waiting patiently. He pretends as if nothing happened. He looks at Leila, is about to shake her hand and says, 'Nothing is going to happen to me is it?'

She looks at him and smiles, 'No, sir, you're quite safe now. I'll see you tomorrow and thank you for being so cooperative.' She turns and walks to the office door, opens it, walks out into the reception area.

He turns and says, 'Now let's get down to the rest of the business for today.' He smiles to him-self, wondering what kind of amazing powers will she going to present to the world tomorrow.

She finds a quiet place, then decides to return home and in a flash she has left the United Nations Building and she is in the sitting room of her own house. Her mum is asleep on the couch so Leila goes over and taps her on the shoulder. She opens her eyes sits up and asks, 'Did everything go according to plan?'

'Yes of course it did. I needed to make sure everything would be in place when we arrive in New York tomorrow. I had a long talk with the Secretary General of the Assembly at the United Nations, I coerced him into giving us all the time we need there tomorrow.'

'What kind of person is he? Mum asks.

'Quite pleasant, a very nice man, very articulate, tall man, slim with a lovely head of hair but I talked him around to my way of thinking but with diplomacy if you know what I mean? She has a little smile. 'Now mum I'm a bit hungry, could you make me a sandwich and a cup of tea please?'

'No problem,' her mum says. She goes to the kitchen to make a sandwich and tea. She returns with the sandwich and the tea, 'There you are, help yourself.'

'Where is dad, mum?'

'You missed him, he went to bed about thirty minutes ago but he said he will see you in the morning. I am going to bed as well,' she gives Leila a little kiss on the cheek saying, 'Good night I'll see you in the morning.'

When she has finished her sandwich and tea she gets up, takes the plate and the cup and saucer into the kitchen, turns and walks up the stairs to her bedroom, falls down on her bed and falls asleep.

Chapter 98

Early the next morning she is aroused from sleep by Alfie at about 2am, he is standing at the end of her bed. She sits up and asks, 'What's the matter Alfie?'

'I cannot sleep, can I come into your bed please?'

'Yes, of course, you can, come on get in,' Leila pulls the covers back and he slides in beside her. 'Did you have a bad dream Alfie?'

'I do not know. I thought I felt a presence of something in my room. It was very strange.'

Leila is a bit suspicious and decides to investigate. 'Now I'll just go and have a look in your bedroom.'

She walks out into the corridor, opens the door to Alfie's bedroom, goes inside and sits on his bed and sure enough she feels a presence in the room. So she places a shield around his bedroom and waits to see what happens. She walks back out of the bedroom through the shield, closes the door and waits there for about two minutes. Now she makes herself invisible, walks back through the shield into the bedroom and now she can see that there is a visitor present in Alfie's room but it cannot see her. She decides to make it visible. Her technology is far greater than the Alien,' It materialises, it looks at itself and wonders, how did that happen, I didn't make myself visible, it thinks, not realising that it is being watched by Leila. It is about five foot nine high, kind of grey in colour. It looks like a species kind of human. Its features look human, its arms are similar to human arms, and the body is thin, with long legs. Again similar to human legs, but it does have some kind of clothing on its body. It is probably very intelligent, 'What does it want in Alfie's room? Leila senses it is not of her world. She walks around it to see if there is anything else, that might give her a clue about its origin. She decides to look into its brain/mind to see if she might be able to ascertain and discover its origin. She is not familiar with this kind of Alien but she does know that this Alien is no match for her so she sits on the bed and just watches it for five minutes. It is trying to beam out but does not understand that Leila it has a shield around the room.

Chapter 99

She decides to go into orbit and have a look to see if there is a spacecraft anywhere above the planet. Sure enough, she detects one. It has cloaked. She decides to enter the craft through the cloaking device and into the control deck, has a look around the inside of the craft, and then decides to go back to the control deck again. In the control deck there are six Aliens all buzzing among themselves, not realising that they have company on their craft. She detects that they are an advanced species but nowhere near as advanced as her. She decides to materialise in the control deck in front of the Aliens, then she decides to place a shield around them. They look amazed, but how did she materialise in their craft? They try to intimidate her through mind manipulation but she throws them back against the side of the craft. This is a worry for them, not being able to have control of the human being. Now the panic and worry sets in. The Aliens know there is nothing they can do about it. They are now prisoners in their own craft, so she walks around them, she looks at each one in turn then she detects one who is more intelligent than the other five. She decides that she will communicate with him. She walks through the shield, places her hand on his shoulder. Now the two of them are in Alfie's room. The other five she leaves in the craft with the shield around them to make sure that the craft is unable to leave orbit until she decides what they want. Leila needs to interrogate the two of them so she places the shield around them, then she walks to her room to make sure that Alfie is asleep, and sure enough, he is out to the world. She walks back to Alfie's room and communicates telepathically with the two Aliens. 'Language is no problem, so if you don't mind, what do you want here on my planet? I need to know, I don't want to hurt you. I just need to know what you want and why you are here. Please tell me, I know that you can talk in my language, that's how we'll communicate?'

They look at each other and decide that it would be better to answer Leila's questions.

'Firstly I would like to know your names please?'

They look at each other then the intelligent one says, 'My name is Zaid and my colleague's name is Cutri.'

'That's a start,' Leila answers. 'Now if you tell me what you are doing on my planet, I would be very thankful and pleased?'

They answer. 'We came to see you.'

She says, 'Why would you want to see me?'

'Gia and Óisin are friends of ours, and we know that you're probably the most powerful person in the Universe/Galaxy. At least we were told so by your friends Gia and Óisin. We are very good friends of theirs. We asked for their help and they told me about you. Incidentally, we would not have done anything untoward or objectionably, which might cause problems for us with the little boy. I presume he is of your family?'

Chapter 100

'Yes, he is.' He is my brother and if anything had happened to him you would not be standing here talking to me. The consequences would be dire and ominous for you. However as Gia and Óisin vouch for you I think we should transport up to your craft. Are we ready?'

'Yes.' they reply. In an instant they are inside the space craft that is in orbit above the Earth.

'I didn't want to talk while we were in my house in case we might have woken my family and I didn't want them disturbed. Now tell me your problem. It must be very important otherwise Gia and Óisin wouldn't have given you my name and address here in this planet?'

'We know that the little greys tried to abduct you when you were a baby, but they were not successful, then they tried again some years later without success. From an advanced technical set-up, they are a more advanced species than my own nation. We are having a problem with them. They want to take over our planet, to make slaves of us, and we are not able to stop them. Gia suggested we make contact you for help, so here we are. We don't want to be at the mercy of the greys. We know what they are like. So please help or we are a dead species.'

'I'll help you, but you must tell me the situation regarding the greys. I'll need to know, how many space craft's they have in orbit above your planet?'

'They have about twenty craft above our planet and we are very worried. The situation is quite serious and it could be quite critical. They have given us an ultimatum of one month in your time and language. Then they will invade my planet. Please help us,' as he goes down on his knees. Leila realises that they have a very big problem. The other five Aliens rush over and start hugging her and saying, thank you, thank you. This lot are friendly Aliens.

Zaid looks at Leila and asks, 'When can you come and help to save us?'

'Gia and Óisin will be in orbit above my planet tomorrow so if you will stay in orbit until tomorrow I should be able to give you an answer as to when I'll be able to help your planet. May I place my hand on your head please?'

'Why?' asks, Zaid

'I need your planet position from your star chart.'

'Ok, that is fine with me,' Zaid replies.

Leila places her hand on his head and she is inside his mind. She now has the position of his planet in her mind.

'Is that it then?' enquires Zaid, 'That's all you need to know as to where my planet is in the Universe!'

Chapter 101

'Yes I know exactly where your planet is situated. I must leave you now but we will meet tomorrow. Do not worry I will stop the greys from taking over your planet. Good bye.' She is gone back to her own bedroom. Alfie is away with the fairies, sound asleep, so she slides in next to him and in minutes she is sound asleep as well.

Next morning she is woken by her mum asking, 'Where were you last night? I heard Alfie talking to you so I looked into your bedroom but Alfie was on his own.'

'We had visitors last night mum; a different species, this time very friendly but they have a problem.'

Mum looks at Leila and asks, 'What do you mean? What kind of problem are they having?'

'Do you remember when I was born we had visitors from another planet and they came to abduct me? Well, they are going to take over the planet of the visitors I talked to last night. They came to ask for my help, I said I would help them.'

'How do they know about you?' mum asks.

'You remember Gia and Óisin? Well it would appear that they advised the visitors to see me, so last night they came into Alfie's room by mistake. He came into me and told me that he thought there was someone in his bedroom. I went to Alfie's room to investigate. I was able to see the Alien. After communicating with him, we transported up to his craft. There I was able to extrapolate why they needed me, to help them. I was able to find out what they wanted. They are very friendly so I was glad to say I would help them to save their planet. Where is Alfie now mum?'

'He's down stairs having his breakfast. Why?'

'Just wondered, I didn't hear him get up from my bed,' Leila replies. 'I'll have a shower, get changed mum, then I'll be down for breakfast.'

'Ok,' her mum replies, 'see you down in the kitchen for breakfast'. She walks out of Leila's bedroom and down the stairs into the kitchen.

Alfie asks, 'Is Leila coming down for breakfast?'

'Yes; his mum replies, 'she'll be down as soon as she has a shower. Alfie you go and call your dad tell him that I'm getting his breakfast ready!'

'Yes mum.' Off he goes up the stairs, knocks on his dad's bedroom door shouting, 'Dad, mum said she is making your breakfast now.'

'Yes, son, please don't shout again. I'll be down as soon as I can get into the bathroom; Leila is in there at the moment.'

Ten minutes later Leila walks into the kitchen and sits down, looks at Alfie and enquires, 'Did you have a good sleep last night?'

'Yes I did, why?' he answers.

'I just wondered why you came into my bed last night.'

He looks at Leila and says, 'I didn't feel right.'

Chapter 102

Leila decides not to question him any more about last night. She thinks if he does not remember, why keep asking him questions.

Mum places her breakfast on the table saying, 'Eat your breakfast. You have a very big day ahead of you young lady.

Leila looks at Alfie and asks, 'Did you enjoy your breakfast?'

'Yes' he replies, 'I had scrambled eggs on toast they were delicious.'

'I'm having egg and bacon and it's delicious as well. What did you have for your breakfast mum?'

'I had a boiled egg and that was very nice!' she replies.

Dad walks down the stairs and into the kitchen sits next to Alfie and asks, 'Did you have a good sleep last night son?'

'Yes I did, dad, I climbed into Leila's bed because I didn't feel well!'

'Oh why was that then?' his dad enquires, as he looks at Leila and smiles, 'Did you feel sick?'

'I don't know dad, I just didn't feel well.'

Leila looks at her mum and says, 'I think he had a bad dream. You know what Alfie is like; he is in dream land most of the time.'

'Yes' her mum replies, 'I think you are right, Leila.'

Mum goes to the oven and retrieves dad's breakfast, 'Eat up, we have a big day in front of us.'

Leila looks at Alfie and asks. 'Alfie, have you packed your bag for our visit to New York today?'

'Yes, I have, it's all ready in my bedroom.'

'Good,' replies Leila, 'my bag is packed as well, What about you,' as she looks her dad and mum, 'are your bags ready?'

'We are ready. I think we should bring them down to the sitting room. Alfie, why don't you help me carry them down.'

'Yes mum I'll help you.' Off he goes up the stairs with his mum behind him. After about ten minutes they arrive back in the sitting room with four bags, they place them on the floor, 'That's it then we have everything we might need.'

Her mum says. 'I hope that is all we will need in New York.'

Chapter 103

Leila decides to go and see Delia in her shop to make sure everything is all right. She looks at her mum and her dad and says. 'I must leave you for a little while. I'm just going to see Delia. I think I'll bring her back here with me, that is if it's alright with you and dad.'

'I don't see a problem with that,' replies her dad, 'off you go then.'

Leila is in Delia's shop before you can blink. She materialises in the back storeroom of the shop and walks out into the shop. Delia is not surprised. She looks at Leila and says, 'It's lovely to see you,' goes over and gives her a big hug saying, 'I have had a word with the two girls and they are quite happy to run the shop until I return.'

'Good' Leila replies, 'I knew you would do the right thing. Incidentally have you been to your bank and deposited the money?'

'Yes I have. That was a very big surprise when Peter came into the shop yesterday. I was quite surprised when he handed me the money for the house. Did you have something to do with that, Leila?'

'Come on, Delia, let me ask you a question; did you tell me anything about Peter, for instance where he lives or his bank?'

'No, but I have a feeling you know something about it, but I am glad I had my money returned to me.'

'Right, would you be so kind and make a cup of coffee for me?' Leila asks.

'No problem. You sit by the window and I will bring it to you. I will not be long.'

'I can wait,' Leila replies, as she sits down on the chair by the window looking out the window and contemplating about New York this afternoon. It's not a worry for her she knows that whatever happens she will be in control.

Delia walks over with the coffee, places it on the table, enquiring. 'May I sit with you for a while? I am a little bit worried about this afternoon and our trip to New York. 'She looks at Leila and asks, 'which Airport, are we flying from, what time do we need to be at the Airport to check in our bags?'

'I have all that sorted out, nothing for you to worry about. We will transport to my house when you are ready but not yet, I have not finished my coffee, and it's a bit hot, 'You have your bag ready and where is your car?'

'I came by bus, it's much quicker and anyway there is no parking anywhere around here.'

'Leila looks t Delia and says. I can hear a lot of noise coming from next door. I'll go and have a look. I'll be back in a few minutes,' she rises up from her chair, walks out into the street up to the door of the shop next to Delia's shop. She looks inside, sees three men smashing up everything, trying to take all the jewellery they can get their hands on, and they are wearing masks over their faces.

Leila walks into the shop and asks, 'What are you boys doing? You are not committing a robbery are you?'

Chapter 104

They look at her and say, 'It's none of your business. Go away before you get hurt.'

'Now, boys, it's not very nice taking all that jewellery and not paying for it. That's not right is it? So please stop smashing the shop up.'

The three men look at each other and decide to make an example of Leila, shouting, 'We're going to kill you if you don't mind your own business.' Then the three of them lunge at her with the hammers and the crow bars they have been using in the robbery.

Very big mistake; she looks at them, levitates them to about one foot from the ceiling leaves them hanging there, goes to the shop owner and says, 'You phone the police now please.'

They look at her in amazement, mouths wide open, totally lost in a world of astonishment and wonderment. How did she levitate the three robbers from the shop floor up to the ceiling and stop there. She never touched them. They do not say a word, just nod their heads and just stand frozen in time. It takes about one minute for them to return to sanity. The first thing they do is phone the police, giving them all the information and the location of their shop, where the robbery has taken place, then replace the phone on its base.

'I will be next door in the little cafe when the police arrive. You explain everything that happened and tell them where I am. Then I will release the idiots from the ceiling for the police. Then they can take them into custody. Do not worry about them they will not fall down to the floor until the police arrive into your premises. I am sorry I did not stop them from smashing up your shop. I am sure that your insurance company will reimburse you so that you are not out of pocket. If you have any trouble with them tell Delia next door. I'll back up your story.'

She'll know where to contact me.' She turns around and walks out the shop door. The three robbers are still shouting,' let us down.

Delia is standing at her shop front door when Leila comes out and asks, 'What was all that noise going on in the jewellers next door, Leila? Is there some kind of robbery going on? Are the police coming?'

'Yes, there are three idiots trying to remove something that doesn't belong to them like jewellery. Don't worry I've sorted them out. Now let's go inside I suppose my coffee is cold, now. Be a dear and make me another one please, Delia.'

'No problem; Delia replies, 'you just go and sit in your chair I'll bring it to you.' A few minutes pass. She arrives back with Leila's coffee places it on the table, sits next to her, looks her full in the face and asks, 'Tell me what you did to the robbers in the shop next door, Leila?'

'I didn't lay a finger on them. I didn't touch them'. As she looks out the window the police arrive in two cars and run into the jewellers next door walk up to the proprietors and asks, 'Where are the robbers have they gone?'

Chapter 105

The shop owners look up to the ceiling and say, 'There they are, as they point up to the ceiling.'

The police look up and cannot believe their eyes, then enquire, 'How did they get up to the ceiling, are they stuck up there?'

The owners just shrug their shoulders saying, 'It has nothing to do with us we don't know how they got up there. All we know is if you need any more information, you need to go next door to the cafe. There is a girl there; she'll tell you all you need to know.'

'Thank you very much. We'll be back for those three.' Off they go, out the front door and into the cafe next door asking, 'Does anyone here know anything about the robbery next door? If there is please put your hand up, we would like to talk to that person.'

Leila puts her hand up the police walk over; they sit down next to her. 'Now, young lady, can you tell me what you saw next door regarding the robbery.'

His phone starts to ring. He looks at it and says, 'Please excuse me, I need to take this call. He stands up walks out to the front of the shop places the phone to his ear and asks, 'Who am I speaking to?'

'This is the Chief Constable, I want you to listen very carefully to what I'm going to tell you.' (He is the same Chief Constable Leila had a confrontation about a week ago. Leila has been in touch with him by telecommunication. She has relayed all the information about the robbery. Saying 'I don't need to be interviewed thank you.')

'Yes, sir, I'm listening.'

You are in a cafe by a jewellery shop. There is a young woman in that shop. She has witnessed a robbery in the jewellers next door. Whatever information she volunteers to you, you had better believe her. Do I make myself clear?'

'Yes, sir, that is perfectly clear.'

'Now go back into the cafe, take a statement from that lady, then leave her alone, do you understand.'

'Yes, sir, I'll do what you ask.' Back in the cafe he takes his note book out and sits next to Leila.

Leila knows everything that the Chief Constable has said to the police man, but he does not know that she knows.

'Now, young lady, I'll need your first name please?'

'My name is Leila.

And your surname is what?'

'I don't need to give you my surname. You have my first name, which is all you are going to get.'

The policeman's phone rings again. He places it to his ear, it's the Chief Constable. 'If this lady says, her name is Leila. That is all she is going to give you. Don't pursue it any further. Now I hope you understand me, constable. You just take her statement and leave her alone otherwise you'll be very sorry. Carry on constable!'

'Yes sir,' then turns the phone off.

His colleague asks, 'Who was that on the phone? He sounded a bit angry what did he want?'

That was the Chief Constable again he told me to take a statement from this young lady and just use her first name.'

Chapter 106

'That's very strange,' his colleague says, as he looks at his partner, 'What will we do about this situation?'

'We'll do as we are told or suffer the consequences.'

'Now young woman, I do not know who you are, and I do not care so let us begin. You tell me what you observed and I will write it on my pad.'

Leila gives an account of what happened in the jeweller's shop next door.

After she has finished her statement the police officer looks at her and says, 'That is quite some story. Are you having me on, young lady.'

'No, sir, that is what happened, the statement I have given you is true, 'why would I lie to you? I have no reason to make a false statement.'

'Fine, I have to believe you. I do not like your statement, it is far too silly. I don't want to be in trouble with the Chief Constable so thank you very much for you cooperation.'

Delia walks over and places two cups of coffee on the table and says, 'There you are constables, a cup of coffee each with milk and sugar.'

'That is very nice of you, thank you very much.'

'No problem,' replies Delia. 'She looks at Leila and walks away.

The constable looks at Leila asking. 'Are you're sure you don't want to add anything else to your statement?' as he drinks his coffee.

'I don't think so,' answers Leila.

They finish their coffee stand up. 'I think that is it for now. We will go next door and arrest the three robbers. How are we going to get them down from the ceiling?'

'I would not worry about the robbers, I am sure they will descend from the ceiling as you walk into the shop. Then you can arrest them and take them to the police station and have them charged.'

Both the police officers look at Leila and laugh, turn and walk out the front door still laughing, then go into the jeweller's next door. They enter the jeweller's shop, and then the three robbers start to descend from the ceiling, very slowly, to the amazement of the two officers.

When they reach the floor in the shop, the two officers examine them, to see if there are any strings, or anything that was holding them to the ceiling. There is nothing; no strings no ropes or anything that might have been holding them to the ceiling. They both shake their heads. Even the proprietors of the jewellery shop are mystified. They do not have a clue what has happened, but are very pleased that their jewellery in their shop is safe.

Chapter 107

One of the police officers says, 'You are under arrest.'

The three robbers are told to place their hands behind their backs. The handcuffs are placed on the wrists by the two police officers. They walk out of the jeweller's to the police van and are placed inside. Then they are taken to the police station and charged with committing a robbery in a jeweller's shop. The two police officers are none the wiser about what happened.

Everyone is curious about the robbery next door and asks Delia, 'What is going on?'

'I don't know but I'm sure that the police have it in hand!' she replies.

Leila looks at Delia and says, 'I think it's time to leave here and go to my house. Come on, Delia let us go. Follow me please, now where is your travel bag?'

'It's in the back room.' Delia replies.

'Fine, let's go, I don't want to be here when the newspaper media swarm outside the jewellers shop!'

Into the back room they go, Delia picks up the travel bag and in an instant they are standing in Leila's sitting room.

Her mum comes in from the kitchen and sees Leila and Delia standing there. She looks at both of them and says, 'Good afternoon, Delia, nice to see you again so soon. 'You are ready for your trip to New York a bit later?'

'Yes, I'm looking forward to the trip it should be an experience. I have never been to America!' she replies.

'Neither have I,' Ciera replies, 'but it should be an education to see how the other half lives. Have you left your girls to look after the shop?'

'Yes I had a word with them this morning. They are quite looking forward to being in charge. I think that they will be fine. They should be well able to run the business while I'm away without any problems. I live in hope.'

'I'm sure they will be fine. You trust them and they will reciprocate by making sure everything goes without a hitch.' Ciera replies.

'Where is Alfie?' Delia asks.

'He is down the garden with his dad, tidying up some grass cuttings before we go to America.'

'I think I'll go down and see how they are getting on.' Delia replies.

'Don't be too long I'm just about to make afternoon tea. It should ready in about ten minutes'.

Delia looks at Leila and says, 'Come on, Leila, let us go and see what they are up to down in the garden shall we.'

'Ok, I'm fine with that,' Leila replies. The two of them walk out the door down the path to where they see dad and Alfie.

Alfie sees them and runs to meet them shouting, 'We're going to America today,' as he runs into Leila's arms.

'Please do not shout, Alfie, I know you are very excited, just calm down.'

He looks at Delia and enquires, 'Are you coming to America with us as well?'

'Yes I'm coming to America with you as well; she replies.

'Cool,' Alfie replies. He looks at Delia and enquires, 'How big a country is America, is it as big as England?'

'It is a very big country, Alfie. Yes it's a lot bigger than England. Why do you ask?'

'Just wondering,' he replies.

Chapter 108

John walks up to Delia. 'He gives her a hug and a kiss on the cheek and says, 'It's lovely to see you again so soon. So you have left your shop in the hands of your two girls. I am sure that they will be fine while you are away. You trust them and that is all that matters. I see mum at the back door waving her hand which means that our afternoon tea is ready. Shall we go and have it? What about you, Alfie, are you hungry?'

'Yes, dad I am a bit hungry!' he replies.

'Ok I will race you to the door. Alfie are you ready 1-2-3 go.'

Alfie is off, runs as if he is a bat out of hell arrives at the back door before his dad and says, 'I'm faster than you, dad.'

'Yes, of course you are, son,' he replies, 'you are faster than me,' as he smiles to himself. The three of them follow Alfie into the kitchen and sit down at the table, Mum says, 'Alfie you sit next to Delia and behave yourself please.'

Dad asks, 'Anything happen today, Leila?'

She looks at him and says, 'There was a robbery at the jeweller's next to Delia's shop and I went to help the owners.'

'Oh, and what happened?' Dad enquires. Leila filled her dad in on the incident in the jeweller's shop.

'I didn't lay a finger on them.'

'Good girl, that was very nice of you to go to their assistance I'm sure that they are very appreciative of your help.'

He looks at Delia and asks, 'You are coming with us to America. At least I hope you are?'

'Yes I'm coming with you to America. I think we are going to have a fabulous time there.'

Ciera looks at Leila and asks, 'You're alright, Leila, aren't you, and you look a bit worried?'

'Yes, I'm fine; I think I'll just go down the garden. I've a few calls to make if it's alright with everyone here.'

'Whatever you want to do, is fine with us,' replies mum.

Chapter 109

Leila walks out the back door and down the garden path. She sends a telepathic communication to Mr Michael Hester: 'Sir, I know it's very early in the morning in your country. Can I ask would, you be so kind and let me have your private office for the rest of the day. It's very important that no one knows we are coming to New York.'

Mr Michael Hester is dumfounded. He is receiving a communication from Leila asking for the use of his private office for this afternoon.

He looks around the boardroom office and says, 'Ladies and gentlemen, I have something very important to do. I must take my leave of you for awhile. We will resume this meeting in about ten minutes, thank you!'

He rises up from his chair, walks to his office, and goes inside, closes the door behind him.

Leila is still in communication with him so he goes to his desk and sits down.

Leila says, 'Michael may I call you by your first name please? You can talk out loud or you can just think what you want to say to me is that alright with you!'

He thinks, 'Am I able to communicate with this person and she is not even in this country or is it some kind of illusion?'

'Michael you are communicating telepathically with me. I'm not going to hurt you. All I need is to have the use of your office this afternoon. Can we agree on that request please?'

He thinks, 'Why not, I am not using it. Yes of course you may use my private office this afternoon.'

Leila says, 'Thank you, Michael I knew you would agree to my request!'

He is utterly confused as he says to himself, 'I was only thinking about it and she is able to hear me and I her. I cannot get my head around this but it must be true. Leila may I ask a question.'

'Yes, of course, you can ask me anything you want!'

'Where exactly are you now?'

'I'm sitting in my garden in England, admiring the garden.'

'That's amazing, this is unbelievable, you are thousands of miles away from me and I'm able to communicate with you in my mind. How do you do that?'

'That is how powerful I am. I can communicate with anyone on this planet wherever they are situated. It is just as if they are in my front sitting room.'

'I'm lost for words. I just can't begin to understand, but I'll tell you what I'm glad you're on my side.'

'Of course I'm on your side, your aspirations are almost the same as mine, the only difference is, I will make it work. There are a few things I would like you to organize for me?'

'Anything I can help with please just ask me!'

'At the back of the Great Hall behind the podium I would like nine comfortable chairs placed against the wall for my family. Will you arrange that for me, Michael?'

'Yes I'll arrange that for you it will be my pleasure!'

'When you stand at the podium in the Great Hall, it will be up to you to introduce my granddad. His name is Mr Richard Carney; he will give the opening speech of the afternoon. That is all I ask you to do for me. Please do not mention to anyone about our communicating, as I need this occasion to be a very big surprise for the World leaders. You do understand, Michael, I'm counting on you.'

'Yes, I understand,' Michael replies, 'the need to be very discreet. I will not mention our communication to anyone. Incidentally what time can I expect you to arrive in America?'

'The family and I will be in the United Nations Building at 2 pm in the afternoon. Don't let me down, Michael, I'm depending on you to do what I have requested of you.'

'Don't worry, I'll make sure that everything is in place before you arrive in the United Nations Building.'

'Good bye, Michael, I'll see you this afternoon.'

'Just a minute,' he says to himself,' did I hear her say she will be in The United Nations Building at 2pm this afternoon? How is she going to do that? She just told me that she is in England. If she says that she will be in The United Nations Building about 2pm, who am I to think any different?'

Leila is quite happy now. She has made all the arrangements for the family when they arrive in the United Nations Building. Now she needs to contact Gia and Óisin to make sure that they are in orbit over the planet. She sends a communication to Gia, asking if they are in orbit around earth yet.

She receives one back.

'We are about one hour away from your planet. How is everything going with you?'

'Fine,' Leila replies, 'I have just finished finalising my requirements with Secretary General of the United Nations, a Mr Michael Hester, a very nice man, very pleasant person and everything is ready for me in the Great Hall in the United Nations Building in New York. Incidentally we had some visitors last night. They said that they are friends of yours. Apparently they're having trouble with another race of beings from a different planet. We will need to talk about this situation when we meet this afternoon. When you arrive in orbit, I will know. I will transport up to you and tell you what we will do in the United Nations Building. That's if it is alright with you, Gia?'

'Yes, I'm fine with that. We'll see you when we arrive in orbit.'

'Good bye for now,' replies Leila. She walks back up the garden path and into the kitchen. Her dad looks at her and asks, 'You've done everything you needed to do and everything is fine for this afternoon no problems?'

'Yes, everything is fine now, no problems Gia and Óisin will be in orbit very soon then I'll transport up to see them. Then I'll put our agenda into operation.'

Delia, who is also in the kitchen, is looking confused. So she looks at Leila, saying.'

'Just a minute, Leila, did I hear you say that you will transport up to a space ship when it arrives in orbit? What's that all about? This is getting weirder by the minute. What are you talking about Leila, is this space craft in orbit above our planet, and who are Gia and Óisin?'

Leila looks at Delia and says, 'It's a long story, but all will be explained this afternoon.'

Alfie grabs Delia by the hand and says, 'Do you want to see my toys in my bedroom? Come on, then, I'll take you up to my bedroom.'

'When will you transport granddad, grandma and JK?' Mum enquires,

'I'll transport them here as soon as I communicate with them.' She is now in communication with granddad asking, 'When you and grandma are ready to come to our house, please let me know.'

Alfie runs down the stairs with Delia behind him and into the kitchen.

Dad looks at Delia and enquires, 'I suppose Alfie showed you all his toys and bored you stiff with them.'

'No, actually, I quite liked the attention he gave me. He is quite a young lad, so full of energy. I wish I was his age again.'

Leila receives a communication from granddad saying, 'We are ready now to transport to your house. What about our travel bags?'

'Just place them next to the two of you?

In an instant, they are in Leila's house and their travel bags are with them as well.

'Hello, everyone here. That was quick' says granddad. Leila is now in communication with JK. 'Are you ready to transport to my house, JK?'

'Yes, I'm ready. I have my travel bag with me?'

'If you're ready, then I'll transport you now.'

As quick as a flash he is in his brother's kitchen enquiring, 'Can I have a cup of coffee please, Ciera?

'Yes of course you can, anything else what about a sandwich?'

'No thanks, just coffee, thank you,' replies JK.

Leila receives a telecommunication from Gia. 'We are in orbit now we have arrived sooner than we anticipated.'

Chapter 110

'I'll be there shortly,' replies Leila. She looks at the family saying, 'Gia and Óisin are in orbit now. I'll go and see them to finalise all the arrangements for this afternoon. She looks at Delia, 'Would you like to come with me? Let's just say to some place different.'

'I have nothing to lose, why not? In for a penny in for a pound,' replies Delia.

'Give me your hand.' In less than one tenth of a second the two of them materialise on the control deck in Gia's craft, which is a surprise to Gia and Óisin. They look surprised and ask, 'Who is this lady with you in our space craft?'

'Let me explain. This is my Auntie Delia. I hope you don't mind me bringing her on board your craft.'

Gia looks at Delia and says, 'You are very welcome in our craft. So you are Leila's Auntie that's a nice surprise, we were only expecting Leila,' replies Gia.

Leila goes and gives both of them a kiss and a hug saying, 'I am so pleased to have you here again. I do miss you both. Now, first things first, 'Your friends are in orbit above my planet at the moment so if you don't mind I'll beam them aboard your craft. In an instant the seven Aliens are aboard Gia's craft. Gia and Óisin welcome them aboard and greet them accordingly, Gia asks, 'We don't see your craft anywhere in orbit?' As she looks to see if there is anything on her computer screen.

'That is because Leila has placed a special cloak around it. We don't have her technology. However, she might let us have it if we need it. At least I hope so,' Zaid says, looking at Leila. Who is this lovely lady standing next to you?'

'She is my Auntie, her name is Delia.'

Delia is looking on, totally lost, and doesn't know what to say. Leila looks at Delia and feels that she is about to faint so she places her arm around her waist. Then she places her on top of a table that she has materialized on the deck of the craft saying, 'Are you alright Delia?'

'Hold me tight, Leila, I'm very frightened. This is all above me. I hope nothing is going to happen to me?'

'Not while I'm by your side. Just relax,' she places her hand on Delia's head. 'You'll be fine now.'

She sits up, and says, 'I'm very sorry,' and asks, 'Is this real, me being in a space craft? I'm not dreaming am I?'

'What you see is real. I'm sorry, I should have left you at home.'

'No I'm glad I came. It just overwhelmed me but I'm alright now. Are you sure you're my niece?'

'Yes, of course I'm your niece!' she answers

Leila looks Gia and asks, 'I need to finalise our agenda now. Will you be alright, Delia?'

'Yes, you carry on with your business, I'll be fine!'

Leila looks at Zaid and just shrugs her shoulders saying, 'I'm not promising anything. We'll see how things go in the future. That is not making your problem any less important than mine. I have some important things to worry about now; you let your people know that I will protect your planet as soon as I have convinced the idiots on my planet the way things are going to be in the future. I am optimistic that this will be arranged in the next two days. I will not need your presence on my planet. You can stay in orbit in your craft until I'm ready to go to your planet and help your people. Are you happy with that?'

'Yes as long you promise to help; we, that is my other colleagues and I, are happy,' replies Zaid, as he looks around at his friends and they nod in unison.

'Now, Gia and Óisin, I'll give you the agenda for this afternoon. The first speaker will be the Secretary General of the General Assembly at the United Nations Buildings in New York. He will do the opening speech. When he has finished his speech, he will announce my granddad as the next speaker. When granddad has finished his, he will announce you and Óisin. Then the two of you will materialise at the podium in the Great Hall to give your speeches. Will that be a problem for you, Gia.'

'I don't think so but I would like to know what the content of my speech might be, Can you give me some idea?'

'You can talk about your planet, give a few bits of information, but not too much just keep the audience interested in something way above their heads. Right Óisin will take the podium before you, now Óisin you can tell when you arrived on my planet, why you came and of course that you are humanoid the same as earth people and anything else you might think will be helpful to win over the people in the Great Hall. Gia, it will your privilege to announce me. I will communicate with you when I am ready to enter the Great Hall. My entrance will be from the ceiling in the Great Hall and I am sure that you will make a wonderful speech as will Óisin. I am going to be very proud of you two and your continued support with this wonderful technology you have given me. I will make sure it will used for the right reasons. It will be of great benefit to all species of life, wherever they might be in this Universe. I know that I am going to have a hard time convincing the world leaders that I am not going let them destroy my planet because of their stupidity. I just will not let it happen. My vision for the future is very clear. However, I will listen to any valid argument but I will not be side tracked from my vision of a healthy planet. It will happen in spite of the dissenters. They have had their chances. Now it's my time to take up the baton to guide this planet forward and have a better world in which we can live peacefully. That is my vision.'

'Zaid, can you tell me how much time you think your planet has before an invasion becomes imminent?'

'I think maybe a week, with a little luck maybe two weeks.'

'I think you should contact your superiors on your planet Suhrien and convey to them that I'll be coming to help in one or two weeks and just keep negotiating with the aggressors. Tell them whatever is needed to keep them at bay until I can persuade them that their invasion of your planet will not happen. It is imperative they must not know that I am coming to rescue your planet. That is extremely important. I can't emphasize and stress the importance of keeping me secret from the aggressors, you do understand?'

'Yes we do,' Zaid replies.

'Good; then you can contact them from Gia's craft here if you wish. It's up to you or you can return to your craft and make the communication there. Whatever you decide will be fine with Gia, Óisin and me, so what is it going to be?'

Zaid looks at his colleagues and asks, 'I think I should make the communication from here in Gia's craft and then if any additional information is needed Leila is on hand to talk to our superiors. I think that is the right way forward, are we agreed?' Zaid asks.

'Yes, we think that is the best way,' his colleagues reply.

Zaid asks, 'Gia, how are we going to make contact with our planet from here?'

'Ask, Leila, I'm sure she'll make that communication with your planet.'

'Yes, I'll do that for you but I need to place my hand on your head again, please.'

Zaid looks at Leila, and then walks over to where she is standing. She places her hand on his head. 'I will not hurt you,' then as if by magic a picture of his Galaxy is in 3D above him in colour and everyone in the craft is totally bewildered and puzzled. Zaid looks at Leila and asks, 'How did you do that? It is just surreal, unbelievable.'

Leila goes into the middle of the vision of Zaid's Universe, has a look then looks at Zaid and points to his planet, 'Is that your planet?' she asks.

'How did you do that? Yes that is my home planet. Why?'

Leila backs out of the 3D picture of Zaid's planet then something very extraordinary and astonishing happens. Zaid's planet starts to leave his Universe and comes within visual distance of Gia's craft

Gia and Óisin are totally and completely amazed. Gia looks at Leila and enquires, 'Is this real?'

'Yes it is real. I am sorry if I frightened you. I will talk to you and Óisin later.' Leila looks at Zaid and asks, 'That is your planet is it not?'

'Yes, it's my planet that is just amazing. Did you do that?'

'Yes I did. Now will you please tell me your senior person's name, I'll need to communicate with him thank you.'

Chapter 111

'His name is Pacyo, he is one of the most senior people on my planet he is the one I need to communicate with.'

'That is done. You are in communication with him now. Just tell him what I intend to do when I arrive at your planet.'

Zaid looks perplexed and confused. He did not think that communication by mind at this distance was possible. He gives all the information to his senior representative and explains the situation to him. When he has finished he asks to talk to Leila. What he does not know is she has been privy to that conversation, so she says, 'Good afternoon, Pacyo, what is your question please?'

'Will you be able to save our planet from these evil species? We will be at their mercy; we will be slaves if you are unable to stop them.'

'You just keep negotiating with them until I arrive above your planet.'

'What do I say?' Pacyo replies.

'You just tell them that there are a few things to negotiate and as soon as a decision is made you'll return to them and give them an answer. Then say that there is no point in destroying the planet for the sake of a week or two. If they are unwilling to wait for the time already agreed, communicate to me and give me their answers as soon as you can so that I can make arrangements and come to you.'

How will you travel to my planet in that time frame?' It will take too long, we could be slaves by then.'

'I'll be above your planet before you know I'm there. Don't you worry one little bit? My travelling through space is not a problem. I have a very special way of travelling.'

'Well, as long as we know that you will be coming to save us, I'm quite happy. I will inform the rest of my colleagues and I am sure that you will keep your word.'

'Of course I'll keep my word. That's a promise and I'm sure you know what a promise means.'

'Yes I do,' Pacyo replies. 'Thank you immensely. I am very happy now that I know you are coming to help us!'

'Pacyo you are not to tell the Aliens above your planet about me. The less they know the better. Thank you and good bye.'

Zaid's planet begins to fade in the distance right before their eyes. Gia looks at Leila and enquires, 'Just how powerful are you now?' Gia has a very worried look on her face, and she asks, 'I would like to know please?'

'We'll talk about this soon, if that's all right with you and Óisin.'

Gia looks perplexed and a bit worried but if Leila says she will talk to her about her powers soon, she is happy with that, and that is good enough for her.

'Are we all ready to do our bit for the good of humanity?' Leila asks.

Everyone is quite happy with this situation, and nod in unison to Leila's question.

'Zaid, if I need your presence on my world and if I were to make a call on you, will you be willing to come to the Great Hall for me?'

'Yes of course I'll come, that's the least I can do for you.'

'Good, then I think we are up to speed with our agenda that we will need when we arrive in the Great Hall. Are there any other questions before I leave you, because I need to return to my family and finalise the rest of this afternoon's agenda with them. That is it then. Come on, Delia, we are away,' and in an instant the two of them have gone and materialise in her dad's sitting room. She looks around the sitting room and asks, 'Mum will you look after Delia I think she had a culture shock.'

Chapter 112

Ciera goes to Delia, looks at her and says, 'Come with me?' As she guides her into the kitchen finds a glass and pours her a glass of brandy. 'There now you drink this and you'll be fine.'

Delia looks at Ciera in a curious way and says, 'Your daughter, my niece, how powerful is she?'

'You have seen it. I do not think she is at full power yet, but she is amazing. Delia, do you not think so?'

'It is beyond me, she frightened the life out of me.' Delia replies.

'She is your daughter? I mean she is the child that you gave birth to in hospital?'

'Yes,' Ciera answers. 'I was there when she was born. I sometimes wonder if she is my daughter, but she is amazing and I love her dearly.'

'That's good enough for me. Boy these government bodies are going to get a shock today.'

Back the two of them go into the sitting room.

'I presume we are nearly all ready to make our presence felt in the Great Hall of the United Nations Building in New York. I am looking forward to this challenge with the world leaders. I am sure that there will be some very stupid questions regarding their powers, what they want in return for giving up all their claims to power in their respective countries. They can jump up and down as much as they like but their power is going to be reduced. I will allow them to keep some of their power. If they do not agree, I will replace them with a more convivial welcoming people. I am sure that there are people willing to help bring around a peaceful solution to this madness of trying to make this planet uninhabitable for humans and all kinds of life. Do our present world leaders have the right to decimate and lay waste to this planet of ours? It has to stop, and stop soon, before it is too late. I will not let it happen under any circumstances whatsoever. Right then let's hold hands.'

Everyone of the family puts their hands together and in a split second, they are in the President's office in the United Nations Building in New York. No one is more surprised than Delia. She is flabbergasted and astounded and asks, 'What's going on here Leila, 'How did I get in here? This is a very strange place.'

Leila answers, 'I told you we were going to New York to the United Nations Building.'

'I know you told me that, but I was under the impression we were going from an Airport in a plane!' Delia replies.

'Delia, I told you that I've special powers to do anything I want. I thought you understood me, I did show you my powers. Did you think I was kidding you?'

'No I just thought I was dreaming. It's very difficult for me to understand this quite extraordinary gift you have. I have great difficulty in separating reality from fiction. In your circumstances, it is even more daunting because you are my niece. However, I think I am beginning to understand its implications and I must say it's extraordinary, to say the least, that my niece is more than likely the most powerful being on this planet. I find it amazing, puzzling and baffling but I'm so proud of you!'

'I'm glad you are beginning to grasp this situation because it's imperative that the world leaders understand what I'm here to do,' Leila replies.

Chapter 113

It is nearly 3pm in the United Nations building and the Great Hall is buzzing, government officials are taking their places and wondering what is going to happen this afternoon. The word is out that there is someone very special going to make a very important speech, but no one knows what it is going to be about or who he or she is.

All Leila's family except Leila and Alfie are sitting on the chairs provided by the Secretary General (Mr Michael Hester,) behind the podium but in front of the six foot high, twelve foot long, Green Marble at the back of the podium. Everything is in place for granddad to make his opening speech to the world leaders.

The Secretary General walks in from a side door up to the podium, touches the microphone to make sure that it's turned on and just stands there waiting for silence in the Great Hall. He is determined and resolved to wait until all the chattering stops before he makes his first announcement to a packed audience of leaders and thinks to himself, 'Boy, are they in for a surprise this afternoon.' After the people in the Great Hall settle down and silence has been re-established, he looks around this bastion, this citadel of Jacksonian democracy and decides the time has come for him to make the first announcement.

'Ladies and Gentlemen this meeting is going to be a very historic time in our lives and our world. I know you are wondering what I am talking about, but I assure you that the wait will be worth it. We will have five different speakers this afternoon plus some of the world leaders here today and I ask you to pay particular attention to our special guests when they arrive.'

There are quite a lot of murmurings in the Great Hall so the Secretary General calls, 'Can I have silence please.

We need your attention so that we can start this meeting. I know that there will be questions to some of the speakers this afternoon, to which I hope you will keep an open mind. This is not a scheduled meeting for this afternoon but the circumstances dictate that I made a decision as to its importance regarding our world as it stands today. Ladies and gentlemen, please put your hands together and give a very warm welcome to Mr. Richard Carney as it's his first visit to New York and to his first visit to this Great Hall, thank you!'

Chapter 114

Mr. Richard Carney walks up to the podium, looks at the SG and thanks him; he then has a good look at the audience. He is very worried but he must keep his mind focused on the immediate situation regarding his visit to this Great Hall. He takes a minute to steady his nerves; he is not here to satisfy his ego regarding his presence in this Great Hall. This afternoon will be Leila's introduction to the world leaders so he is required to make a low profile speech but it must be authoritative and convincing. These world leaders are not fools but he has something in his mind. 'Ladies and Gentlemen, I know that you have never heard of me but I'll try and explain the circumstances why I'm here. Just to start off the afternoon may I ask two of the audience if they would like to help me. Don't be shy, please come up to the podium. What about you Mr President of France? He points to him, and then he points to the Prime Minister of Sweden. 'Please sir I won't eat you. I have had my lunch. Please come up to this podium.' Reluctantly they decide to humour Mr Carney so the two of them walk up to the podium, he indicates to them to stand on either side of him. This is a very unusual start to any sessions in the Great Hall. However, on this occasion a bit of light entertainment will not go amiss. They are going to need it when Leila enters the Great Hall. That will be something very special to behold.

Mr Carney looks at the President of France, and asks, 'Would you place your left hand on my right shoulder, and you, Mr Prime Minister of Sweden, please place your right hand on my left shoulder. Bear in mind, he has not done this before with two people. 'Right, gentlemen, we are going to levitate about three foot above the floor so please don't let go of me because you might fall to the floor. You do understand.'

'Yes we do' they reply.

'Good here we go,' and as if by magic the three of them levitate to the desired height above the floor. 'Now we are going to move forward about ten foot, and away the three of them go, floating out to the front of the audience. 'Gentlemen you can let go of my shoulder and descend to the floor, if you wish. Do not worry you will not fall.'

Back down on the floor they look mesmerised and look up at Mr Carney.

'Now, gentlemen, I would like you to look all around me to see if there are any wires or a harness inside my clothes. Please, gentlemen, do search me!'

The two Prime Ministers do a thorough examination of Mr Carney; they look inside his coat, frisk him down his legs; shake their heads throw up their hands and say, 'We can't find any apparatus of any kind holding him aloft.'

He says, 'Thank you, gentlemen, please return to your seats, thank you.' He turns and floats back to the podium and descends to the floor, seemingly without any help whatsoever.

The audience gives him a standing ovation. He responds by saying, 'Thank you very much, I'm not here to do magic tricks. I'm here to tell you that you will see an amazing woman this afternoon, and she will tell you some home truths about our planet which you will not like but I'm hopeful you will listen to her and digest what she is trying to tell you.'

Chapter 115

'There are all kinds of problems in today's world and most of it is caused by world leaders past and present but that subject will be discussed later and in depth, but not by me. I know that you are wondering about that fascinating trick I performed, but the strangest thing about it is it is not a trick. All my family have the same gift, except Alfie, my grandson, he does not have that power yet, when he is older he will be introduced to this awesome power. The world leaders have for many years, fooled the ordinary people. They keep giving us the same old rhetoric year in year out but still the wars go on.' He has another look around the audience and decides that is all the information he needs to let them know at this time. 'Ladies and gentlemen, I think that you will have a very fascinating and informative time this afternoon and I wish you all well.' He steps back from the podium.

Granddad has made his opening speech to the World leaders, telling them that they will meet someone very extraordinary later today. He has a telepathic communication from Gia and Óisin, telling him that they are ready to make their appearance in the Great Hall.

'Ladies and gentlemen, please put your hands together for our first visitors.' There is total silence then Gia and Óisin materialise in the Great Hall on the platform next to the podium. Everyone is startled and recoil in amazement at this sudden appearance of Gia and Óisin. The two of them are dressed in one-piece suits, each in a very light green material. They look awesome and have an air of grace and importance about them, which is hard to analyze. You could cut the air, it is so tense, and you could hear a pin drop.

The audience is asking, 'Where did they come from? What do they want? Why are they here?' Now there is total silence in the Great Hall, everyone is completely mystified by this sudden appearance of two strange people who look exactly like humans; very tall, and very good looking.

Óisin looks at granddad and says, 'It's great to see you again,' then he asks. 'How do I speak to all these people what kind of electronic vocal system does this building have?'

Granddad walks over to him, leads him to the podium, points to the microphone and says, 'Just talk into that round gold piece of equipment in front of you.'

Óisin looks around and is feeling a little bit worried because this is the first time he is standing in front of an audience of Earth people. So he beckons Gia to him saying to her, 'Please stand next to me, I might need assistance.'

He looks out over the audience with trepidation, nervousness and his heart is pounding inside his chest. 'Ladies, and gentlemen, please don't be afraid. We are not here to hurt anyone in this building. That is Gia and I. Let me start by saying that Gia and I are not from this Planet,' as he waves his hands in a circular movement. We arrived on what you call a UFO. It is in orbit above your Planet today.' The audience are getting fidgety and a bit uneasy. They have never been in the presence of a being from a faraway planet. They are a bit sceptical and doubtful. 'This is not the first time we have been to your Planet. We have been many times before. In fact my people have been coming to your Planet for some thousands of years. We, that is, Gia and I, arrived on this planet some eighteen years ago after deciding that it was time to help make a better World of your Planet. We were sure that it would be in the best interests of your world that we should give certain very advanced knowledge to a new baby of your World.' He looks around at Ciera and points to her saying, 'We abducted Ciera, the baby's mother from her bedroom to our craft which was in orbit around your planet. We installed very special technical knowledge into the mind of the foetus in Ciera's womb called Bio/Dna technology. We implanted this technology very carefully before the baby was born and returned Ciera to her bedroom when we finished. We did not hurt her or the baby in any way whatsoever. When her baby was born, she could telepathically talk to her granddad and the rest of her family. She also gave them certain powers to help her while she was growing up.'

'The first night when the baby was in Mr Carney's home, they had visitors from another Alien planet. They arrived with the intention of abducting the baby but she thwarted their plans and placed one of the Aliens in a very safe place on this planet. They were no match for her technology, and she was only a baby. These Aliens are not friendly they are very vicious and sadistic. They wanted to abduct the baby for that knowledge and use it for unscrupulous and unprincipled advancement to the detriment of your Planet and very probably my Planet as well. She was more than able to thwart their plans. We returned at later intervals to install the rest of the technical knowledge into her mind. I am sure that you will be suitably impressed when you meet her later this afternoon. Now Gia will try to explain this wonderful technology without giving away any secrets. It is not that we do not want to give you a technological advancement, we are not allowed, because it would be used to the detriment of your planet, you

310

are not ready to use it in a peaceful way for the benefit of this planet. Ladies and gentlemen, please give a very big welcome to Gia.'

Gia goes to the podium looks around and says, 'Good afternoon to all.' Gia knows that she is more advanced than all the people in this building, she does know that. Whatever she decides to tell them she hopes will be enough just enough to keep them interested and hope that it will not just ride over the top of their heads.

'We are here to help all the people of your world that is Óisin and I. We cannot interfere in the every-day running of your planet. We can give assistance but not give you advanced technology. Our remit is to stop this war mongering among the differing nations and establish peace, and stability in this world of yours. Why are your governments hell bent on destroying the ecology of this planet? Is it just stupidity or is it fawning to the rich people of your planet. All the money in the world is no good if you destroy it. Why are people of Earth so violent? You seem to be at war for the last two thousand years. It does not make sense all this killing. What is the life span/expectancy of people on this planet? We think you have about eighty maybe ninety years-it is not a very long life expectancy. We live to well beyond two hundred years or more on my world. I am sure that a longer life span is achievable on your world if you can establish long-term peace. Can you imagine if people like Marie Curie, physicist, Alan Turing, mathematician, Niles Bohr, physicist, Max Planck, physicist, Charles Darwin, biologist, Leonardo de Vinci, mathematician, Galileo Galilee, physicist, Albert Einstein, physicist, just to name a few, had they lived to be over two hundred years, the advancement your world could have made in technology would have been tremendous. Everyone could have benefited from that technology. We decided to look for a way to help your world out of your war mongering ways but it is going to take time and a lot of cooperation from your world leaders. We have made tremendous strides in my world with technology focused on the needs of our people, and that is all the people. The first thing we focused on was peace, the environment, ecology, food for all. Making sure that everyone played their part in the environment, and making sure that everyone understood the consequences. Not like your world where everyone has a different slant on their agenda, but you had better wake up, because you are heading for a cataclysmic change in your world weather, which will destroy your planet and have grave consequences on the Universe, which would have an effect on my home planet and we will not let that happen.

This planet has a great chance of moving forward into the next hundred years. You are beginning to understand computing, and the significance of it. Cognitive computing, smart phones, multi-core processers, optical computers and many more great ideas for your scientists to work on. That is what you should be looking into, instead of wars and constantly wasting your time killing each other. All that time and money should be diverted into computing. Then, you will make much more progress for the benefit for the human race, on your planet.'

Chapter 116

'It has nothing to do with the ordinary people, let me explain.' She pauses for a minute looking out over the audience. It has to do with your leaders. The most important issue for you now is the war mongering nations, this has to stop. Then the environment, you get that right and you might have a chance. After your Second World War your governments decided to make atomic bombs then it was hydrogen bombs of which there were more than one hundred, which they tested. Now where did all the generated heat from these bombs go? It went into the sea, into the atmosphere and created problems for the environment. Which in the future will not help your planet, we cannot let that happen and it must stop. The ice caps north and south started to melt but we think that they have stabilised now. And who paid for all this destruction to your world? The ordinary people of your planet are paying the price for that destruction. This problem was initiated by your world leaders past and now in the present, not by the ordinary people. It has to stop that is why we are here to assist you but not for us to change things, that will be done by someone else. Not one person is able to own any part of our world or the land, the world it belongs to all the people. You can own your own house and everything in it. We have shops, commercial buildings and all other kinds of technological buildings but the land/world belongs to future generations of our world. That is all I need to say for the present. I will now tell you all about our technology, but I will not give you any information on how to use it, that is not authorized. We decided in my world that your planet is getting out of control we needed to do something about it. It was decided that we could give some of our technology to one human being in this world of yours, so it was decided that a baby in the womb of a woman would be the best way to make your governments pay attention to what this baby would say when she would grow up.

We did choose someone of your world to have that baby and we hope that we have made the right decision giving this technology of ours to her.

This technology is more than two thousand years old. My eminent great, great, great grandfathers developed the science and it carried on down to my father. I carried on and finished developing this technological science and that is why Óisin and I are here today to introduce you to a very special person, she is not a baby anymore,' as she points to the roof of the building in the Great Hall. 'Ladies and gentlemen I give you **Leila.**' Leila has selected the music from The 2001 Space Odyssey Theme Music and it has started playing.

Chapter 117

In Australia the time is 7am.

The ABC Corporation is about to relay a very special meeting of world leaders in the United Nations Building in New York. They have received a communication from one of their news reporters in New York that something very special is going to be announced at the meeting today. All the television companies in America are in attendance. What they have seen so far has given them some food for thought. Two Aliens from another planet are in attendance, and they are at the podium giving a report on the Earth. On what is going to happen, if the world leaders are not willing to listen to their warning. They are in for a very big surprise, as is everyone in this Great Hall. At the moment everyone is speculating as to what, and why this meeting is so special. What they don't know is Leila is ready to announce her plans to save the world, and how powerful she has become. She is about to break her silence, regarding her powers to the world leaders and they are not going to be happy.

In Sydney, Australia, Mrs Julia Halshram is sitting in the kitchen having breakfast watching television, not really interested. However her eyes nearly pop out of her head. She has just spotted her daughter Ciera sitting at the back of the podium with Mrs and Mr Carney, JK and Delia. This is happening in the United Nations Building in New York. She runs out of the kitchen up the stairs shouting, 'Steven you're not going to believe what's on the television, I think you had better come down and see what's happening in America!'

Steven is fast asleep. He jumps up in surprise, shouting, 'What are you talking about Julia?'

'Please, Steven, come down and see for yourself, Ciera is on the television.'

'There must be some mistake,' he replies. 'What would Ciera be doing on American television? She lives in England.'

'Please, please, as she tries to pull him out of his bed.'

'Ok I'm coming.'

Julia runs down the stairs with Steven behind her and into the kitchen. They both sit down at the table and he is mesmerized at what he is seeing. He looks at his wife and says, 'You are right, it is Ciera, but what is she doing in America? 'Look, the rest of the family are sitting with her.'

Julia is shaking quiet badly, so he goes over and sits by her side saying, 'I'm sure that there is a very good explanation, maybe it's not Ciera, maybe it's someone like her.'

'Come on, Steven, don't you think I know my own daughter. I know we have not seen her since the wedding,' she stands up, points to the television saying, 'I know that is our daughter.' She starts to cry uncontrollably. He goes and takes her in his arms saying, 'Let's just watch and see what happens, I'm sure that there is a perfectly good explanation for all of this.'

They sit back down trying to analyze what they are seeing. His wife is still shaking and she looks perplexed.

Leila materialises just inside the roof of the building. With the fantastic lighting in the inside of the roof, she is silhouetted in a beautiful white dress that cascades down to her ankles and two butterfly sleeves. She has white socks and white shoes. She has two male lions one on either of her. Alfie is holding her right hand. He is dressed quite gentlemanly in trousers that are white, light pastel blue waist coat, white shirt and a light pastel blue bow tie. He has white shoes and pastel blue socks. He looks very cute and well mannered. He is totally mesmerized and amazed at what his sister is able to do. He is in awe of everything that is happening around him but not able to make sense of it all. Alfie is living the dream and loving all the attention he is receiving. The lions look magnificent with their beautiful long golden manes, a very proud animal; they are standing there with regal splendour. White is for peace which is badly needed on this Planet and Leila is going to have it, whether the world governments want it or not.

Alfie is there for all the little children that suffer under tyrannical rule in whatever country they live. Representing all the other animals on this Planet are the lions, being slain for the sake of pleasure and trophies, they are being indiscriminately slaughtered!

'Look Steven, that's our Leila. I don't understand. What she is doing ascending from the ceiling of the building. How is she doing that, there doesn't appear to be anything visible holding her up? She starts to have palpitations and she is getting very distresses, and she is beginning to feel faint. Her husband sees that she is looking very unsteady. He rushes to her side asking; are you all right dear, as he places his arms around her waist, to stop her from falling to the ground, where she might hurt herself?

She looks at him asking, 'am I just dreaming, I mean, what we are seeing now, is it real?

'Well.' he replies 'I think that, what we are seeing is real, at least I think so. It must be real; it is being broadcast from the United Nations Building in New York. Look why don't we just watch and see what this is all about. It must be very important otherwise it would not be broadcast live from America. But what is our family doing in New York?'

315

Leila looks very serene and beautiful with her long Golden/Red hair flowing down her back. It appears a physical force against the law of gravity is suspending her. That is not so, she is able to levitate as high or descend as low as she wants. Levitation is not a problem to her as she descends slowly down to floor level. The audience are spell bound, totally in awe of this wonderful spectacular vision. Gia and Óisin are absolutely amazed. The tears are flowing freely down their cheeks, with their hands waving in the air. The expression on their faces says, 'Behold beauty is among us.'

Gia looks at Óisin and says, 'This is the most beautiful scene I have ever witnessed in my life. She looks amazingly fantastic I am so proud of her. We certainly picked the right baby.'

Óisin looks extremely happy.

Gia asks, 'Are you alright? You look overwhelmed.'

'Yes, I'm fine, just a bit overwhelmed by this beautiful, stunning, gorgeous human being. I'm very pleased for her. We certainly did select the right baby. She is something else and she will make the world sit up and take notice, I'm sure of that.'

Leila looks at her mum and she is crying quite openly, her dad is smiling, as are JK, Delia, granddad and grandma; all of them have their thumbs up. Delia is in a different world, her mind is running wild. 'Is this really my niece? I know that it is not a dream. Three days past I had a nice settled life, not a worry in the world and now I am witnessing my niece performing miracles. Well, that is how I see it. It cannot be real but it is and I have to accept it. There is no getting away from it, I am so welled up inside with pride. My life has changed forever. Do I want that change? I do not think I have any choice in the matter but I must make the best of it.'

Leila at this stage is looking fantastic. Her presence is just awesome, amazing and all inspiring. You could hear a pin drop, 'the atmosphere feels electric and there is total silence in the Great Hall.

Gia looks at Óisin and says. 'This is the most beautiful scene I have ever witnessed in my life!'

'Look, Steven, that is Leila, Ciera sent photos of the family. I'm sure now that is Leila.'

'Well it looks as if you are right. Look at Leila, what is she going to do now, it would seem that she is the centre of attention in that building.' He asks, 'How did she float down from inside of the roof.'

'I don't know,' his wife replies. 'All I want to know is, is that my granddaughter? 'Is this really real, I mean this is not a dream, at least I hope not.' She gets up from the table saying, 'I'm having a hard time believing this, who is this young lady?'

'You know that is Ciera, so that must be Leila and Alfie. I mean seeing them on the television is true, that must it is real. We have no other alternative until we make contact with her.'

'Anyway, why don't we just watch the rest of this amazing program? Perhaps we will learn exactly what is happening.'

By now Leila has locked all the doors in the building so that no one can leave without her express consent. She looks at the lions, has a word in their ears they duly oblige and lie down, surveying all around them. She takes Alfie by the hand walks over to Gia, gives her a big kiss and says, 'This is my little brother Alfie!'

Gia bends down to Alfie's height and says, 'Good afternoon, Alfie? What do you think of your big sister?'

'She is awesome!' replies Alfie.

Gia looks at Alfie and smiles, then looks at Leila and says, 'I would love to take Alfie with me back to my planet for a little holiday?'

'Well I don't know about that. We'll see, I'll ask mum and dad.' Leila then introduces Alfie to Óisin. He says; 'How do you do young Alfie. You're a fine looking boy,' as he taps him on the head. 'Are you very proud of your sister?'

'Yes, sir, she is something else!'

'Now, Alfie, you go to mum and dad but you must sit very quiet, Will you do that for me,' Leila enquires.

He replies, 'Yes,' off he goes and sits with mum and dad.

Leila goes over to Óisin, gives him a big kiss then walks to the pedestal, looks at the audience and says, 'Good afternoon to one and all here today!'

Chapter 118

Leila goes for the jugular straight away. 'This meeting in this Great Hall here this afternoon, is not a question and answer scenario I'll tell you what I need to save this world and you'll agree. There is no other option on the table. Your interference in the ecology of this planet will not be allowed or tolerated anymore; neither will you be allowed to wage wars against each other, under any circumstances. All querulous or argumentative views will not overrule any of the decisions I make for the good of this world. No government will overrule any of my decisions. I'm your doorway to saving this planet and I will save it whether I have your help or not.' There is total silence in the Great Hall. 'Now that I've have your attention there are a few home truths which I must inform you about. The first feature highlight you will see this evening will astound you.' She switches all the television monitors in the Great Hall on. 'Television is being broadcast throughout the world so that everyone can understand why I'm standing here today Now I would like you to see how powerful l am. This is a view from one of the television studios in New York looking out to sea. You will notice that there is a very big wave coming towards the city it's about two hundred metres high. I can stop it but I have a request to make,' as she looks around her very frightened audience. Suddenly she has one dissenter who decides to challenge her and he is shouting,

'I don't believe you are as powerful as you think you are. You are manipulating everyone in this Great Hall. I for one think you are a charlatan, mountebank, imposter and a fraud!'

Leila looks furious at being called a charlatan; she levitates him from his chair up to the top of the Great Hall close to the roof. Then she looks at the lions, they rise up off their haunches, walk to the centre of the Great Hall. They look up to where Leila has this dissenter levitated to the roof. He is looking down at the lions hoping that he will not fall to the ground and very probably be eaten or killed by the lions, which is very frightening for him. He looks at the lions then he looks at Leila in a very worried and disquieted way, hoping he is not about to be the lion's dinner. The lions are an illusion conjured up by Leila. Fortunately Leila is not going to feed him to the lions. She just wants him to understand that she is not a charlatan or an imposter. She sends him a telepathic message before she allows him to descend to the ground, that he will behave himself for the rest of the evening. He looks down at Leila and nods his head profusely. She knows that he is petrified and scared stiff!

Then something happens that makes everyone in the Great Hall including Gia and Óisin gasp in horror. Leila lets him drop very quickly to within five metres above the lions. The lions just look up at him and lick their lips in anticipation of a good meal. He is screaming his head off; 'Please I don't want to die.'

He is looking down at Leila hoping she will have compassion on him his hands are together as if he is going to pray. 'Please, I do believe that you are not a charlatan. I don't want the lions to eat me!'

'Your name is Peter, is that true?'

'Yes that is true.'

He looks at Leila and asks; 'How do you know my name?'

'I know everyone's name in this Great Hall!'

Leila looks at the two lions they walk back to her side, 'where they lie down as if nothing happened.'

She lets Peter place his feet on the ground and says, 'You can return to 'your' chair now and keep your mouth closed unless I speak to you.' She has another look around her captive audience making sure that everyone's eyes are now on her. 'Why are governments so blind on this world? I'm talking to all of you in this Great Hall, yes, every one of you, 'as she points at everyone in the Great Hall. 'People have put their trust in you, and governments present and past have ignored the wishes of the people. You have betrayed them, fortunately for you nothing could be done about it. That is why I'm here today. Over the past two thousand millennia, your world has been waging wars with one nation or another. We, my family, Gia and Óisin will not tolerate it any longer. All the Nations representing their respective governments in this Great Hall will vote this afternoon and cooperate with me. All laws in every country are to be taken out of all statutes of legislation from today, except domestic laws and there will be only one overriding law. It will be called Leila's Law or I'll let the wave advance and destroy New York. Just to prove how powerful I am I'm going to move the wave two hundred metres closer to the shore!' The wave moves closer to the shore and there is pandemonium. Everyone is trying to go through the doors but to no avail because they will not open.

'Ladies and gentlemen, please sit down. There is no way out. If you don't accede to this request you'll all drown.' Leila is not about to let that happen, she knows that. But, the people in the Great Hall are not privy to that information. Ladies and gentlemen in spite of the cynics, the doubters and the sceptical I will save this world from this war mongering power crazy lot, stopping them from inflicting misery on ordinary people, whether you or they like it or not. Make no mistake I will stop them but I would rather negotiate in a peaceful way. I'm sure that will happen anyway!'

Everyone is cowering with their backs to the walls shouting; Please, don't drown us!'

'Sit down then and vote?' Leila replies.

Reluctantly everyone sits at their respective places and as if by magic every place has a voting paper.

'On the voting paper in front of you there is only one option and that is Leila's Law. You will vote for it and sign your name on the voting paper now please. If anyone thinks that I'm not able to detect any forged signature, just try me!' Leila has made eye contact with the Russian President so she makes him invisible and takes him from his chair. She stands him next to her on the pedestal and asks; 'Mr. President are you ready to give your speech?'

'Yes, he replies, 'I'm ready but I'm invisible!'

'Don't worry, sir, as I announce you, I'll make you visible providing that is alright with you!'

'Yes, that is fine with me,' he replies.

'Good then sir,' she replies. 'Shall we begin?' As she looks out over the podium at all the world leaders?

'Ladies and Gentlemen, I would like you to put your hands together for the President of Russia!'

The President appears at the side of Leila as if by magic.

Leila turns to face the President she gives him a big smile, a big hug, and says; 'Thank you for coming, sir!'

'No problem!' replies the President. 'I'm very happy you have considered me above all the rest of the government heads here today!'

'Thank you, sir, the podium is yours!'

The Russian President has a very good look around, then looks at Leila. She knows that he is worried about assassination so she telecommunicates with him.

'Don't worry, sir, I've placed a shield around you. It's not visible to anyone in the Great Hall. You just carry on as if nothing is happening!'

'Ladies and gentlemen if you think you have seen something this evening let me tell you that this very gorgeous young lady is more powerful than anyone in this world can imagine. I for one would not go against her in anyway whatsoever. I'm sure that the American President was well informed, of what was going on in Russia. All our silos were open and the missiles were ready to fly. Now I must be very honest and say this had nothing to do with my government and I'm sure that you, Mr President, must have been very worried about what was going on in Russia. Let me explain to everyone in this Great Hall. We did not open our silos, it was done by Leila. Don't ask me how. I don't know. It was a very frightening time for me because I had no control of my own missiles. Then

I realized that it was Leila controlling the missiles. Then I understood what was happening. You have no idea how I felt. It was very humiliating for me as a World leader that I was not in control of my own missiles. Once she explained to me what was needed, regarding our Planet and the damage we were doing to it, I began to understand the necessity to put a stop to it before it will be too late. I'm not easily frightened but after seeing the power displayed by Leila, I had second thoughts about my own safety and the safety of my people. I can tell you now that all the computers in the World linked together are no match for this young woman by my side. The most wonderful news is that she will bring to our Planet peace at no cost. I'm on her side and I think all governments will make the same call in the end. This young woman at my side is not here today to harm anybody or anything on this planet. She is here to save our planet and we would be fools not to listen to her. I know that I'll have to give up most of the power I have, but if that will help save our planet, I'm all for it! That is all I need to tell you now.'

Leila looks at the Russian President and says, 'Thank you, Mr President, that was a very good speech and I loved it. Now you can introduce The American President please.'

'Are you sure?'

'Yes, sir, I'm sure.'

He smiles, goes back to the microphone and looks out over the audience. 'Ladies and gentlemen, the President of America, Mr John Shields Adams would like to reply to my statement. I don't think he believes me,' as he waves the President up to the pedestal. The Russian President looks at Leila. He whispers in her ear, he is in for a surprise and has a little smile, himself, knowing that Mr Adams will probably try to discredit Leila. He sits down on the chair just behind Leila.

The American President, Mr John Adams a tall man going grey on the sides of his head, immaculately dressed in a dark blue suit, starts to walk up to the pedestal when four of his bodyguards follow him. They get as far as the lions, the lions rise off their haunches the bodyguards stand very still. Leila walks over to them and asks, 'What are you following Mr. Adams for? Where do you think you are you going, gentlemen?'

'We are the President's bodyguards, we need to be next to him!'

'Why?' Leila asks.

The four bodyguards look at each other then draw their pistols and decide to barge through to the side of the President.

Leila has anticipated this rash move, the pistols have left their hands, they have turned round facing the four bodyguards and start to move towards their heads, they stand very still as if transfixed. The bodyguards are now in a very dangerous position. Their pistols are touching their foreheads. Their hands are up in the air. They don't know what to do in this situation.

'Gentlemen, there is no need for you to be on this podium. Please return to your seats now!'

One of the bodyguards looks at Leila he says, 'The safety catches are still on. How do you think you're going to release the safety catches from where you are standing? It's not possible!'

'Please look at your individual pistols,' Leila tells them.

The four are very much amazed as the safety catches are slowly releasing themselves, which makes the pistols very dangerous.

Leila decides to test their fortitude. One of the pistols turns down to the floor and fires itself. The four bodyguards run in all directions. Leila says to the Russian President. 'Such brave men wouldn't you love to have them as your bodyguards!'

'I don't think so!' Mr Bragin replies.

Chapter 119

The American President is not very amused at this charade and is visibly shaken so he pulls himself together and stands up straight looks around and decides to have his say about Leila. Mr John Adams looks around at Leila and her family then looks at the audience of World leaders. He decides to try and denigrate and malign Leila, her family and Óisin and Gia. Leila already knows what Mr Adams is going to say. She sits very quietly and has a little smile to herself; she is going to let him hang himself slowly but will later in the afternoon cut him down to size.

Mr John Adams starts to wave his hands around in a classic gesture of a World leader to get the attention of his audience and then he starts, 'We have seen some wonderful tricks in this Great Hall this afternoon. I must say I was nearly taken in by this wonderful display of shall we say sleight of hand, illusion of mysterious trickery which I must say is the best I have ever seen. He starts to laugh out loud. 'But can we believe our eyes? Come on ladies and gentlemen, please don't be fooled by all this powerful special effects it's not real.'

There are special companies out there that can do all this astonishing magical tricks. I must admit I don't know how she has presented all this illusion and artifice but it is very creative and stunningly awe inspiring. Now this alliance, pact, deal, whatever you might like to call it is just to try and make us think that the Government of Russia is trying to tempt us into believing that they are the good people here, not so. We have tried for years to placate them but to no avail. They have this in built fear that Western powers are trying to overpower the Russian people. They just don't trust us; maybe it was something in the past. We have worked with them on the space stations in orbit around the world. We, the USA and the rest of the world have tried to keep the peace. We don't need people like Leila or her family trying to interfere in world politics. We are quite able to manage world affairs without any outside interference or so called people from other planets. We don't need them. We don't want their help. We certainly didn't need their help!'

Leila is now extremely agitated,' however she refrains from interfering, while Mr John Adams is making his speech at the podium.

Mr Bragin looks at her and takes her hand, she looks at him. She knows that Mr John Adams is trying to make her look a fool so she decides to be quiet and wait her turn at the podium. She looks around at her family and tells them telepathically that everything will be fine, not to worry. She has a look at Óisin and Gia and says the same to them with the added words.

'I'm in total command of this situation. Please don't worry; my time will come when I'll put this Mr John Adams in his place!'

'Aliens from another World on this Planet. She is kidding me. There are no Aliens in this world because I would know about it. Come on, would I the President of the USA lie about something like that? Of course I wouldn't. It's not in my nature to lie. Maybe she would like to reply but I don't think she has the answers to my questions.' He turns to Leila and says, 'Please young lady,' the President puts out his hand to Leila, please do come to the podium my dear. It's your turn, as he smiles in a surly impolite way.

Leila stands up walks to the podium and says, 'Thank you, Mr. Adams, for allowing me to make my statement. Please may I ask you to stand next to me, sir, I might need your assistance and clarification on some issues you have just told some 'untruths' about. Or if you like very economical with the truth Good afternoon, again, ladies and gentlemen, just to let you know that I'm human the same as you, however, Óisin and Gia are not of this world, contrary to what Mr Adams has stated. However, you will believe what you see from now on.' In a flash, in front of all in the Great Hall a little figure appears just to the front of the podium, it's about four foot high, large eyes, long arms, large head, small legs with feet to match. He is grey all over and his name is Commander Gruber. 'Any questions you would like to ask him, Mr Adams, please feel free. He will talk to you in the English language.' Leila beckons him to the podium. She has a few words in his ear. She communicates telepathically. *'Commander Gruber, can you remember the human baby you came to abduct from this world this Earth some eighteen years ago. Well, I'm that baby now I'm grown up and I'm going to realise you very soon from you incarceration on this planet. I'll need you to help me in the future, 'that is if you are happy to help me?'* He looks at her nods his head and smiles. She ushers him to the front of the podium and then stands him on a chair so that he can speak into the microphone.

'Mr Adams would you like to stand next to him, he will not bite you. Who would like to question this being from another world? She looks around and asks, 'Is there anyone in this Great Hall willing to ask questions of this little being. He will answer any question you might like to ask. Perhaps you would like to know what he is doing on this planet of ours, please ask him?

Leila looks around sees one person standing up she says; 'You are the Prime Minister of England?'

'Yes, I am!' he replies.

'Would you like to question this little Alien person standing next to me on this podium?'

'Yes I would!' the Prime Minister replies.

Leila responds, 'Just ask him what you like!'

'Commander Gruber, where are you from?'

Gruber looks at Leila she nods her head.

'I'm from another Galaxy many light years from this planet!'

'What are you doing on this Planet?' the Prime Minister asks.

'I arrived on this Planet about eighteen years ago to abduct Leila. She was only a baby then but we were not successful. She was too powerful even as a baby. She destroyed all six of my spacecrafts and all of my staff. We arrived to abduct her because we knew that she had the power and we wanted it at any cost. Fortunately, for your Planet she was able to stop us. Now she is the most powerful being in the Universe and I mean very powerful. There is nothing on this planet or any other Planet in the Universe powerful enough to stop her. I know because even as a baby she was too powerful for all the technology of my Planet. I wouldn't stand up against her now at any cost. She is not a vindictive person, she treated me reasonably well and I thank her for that. This is the first time I have seen her since my capture. We have been coming to this Planet for over two thousand of your years. We have abducted many of your people down through the years. All that stopped when Leila was born!'

'Where have you been hiding all these years?'

'I think you should pose that question to Mr Adams. He should know!' Commander Gruber turns to Mr Adams. Sir, 'that question is for you to answer!'

'Why should I know where you have been incarcerated?'

'Because, I'm in one of your hidden underground facilities, where I've been tortured, tormented, distressed, but could I expect anything else from earthlings? You are nearly as sadistic and dangerous as the beings on my planet. This was the first time I had been captured by anyone from any Planet!'

'I have no idea what you are talking about!'Mr Adams replies.

The Commander looks at Leila and nods.

Leila doesn't say a word but in an instant in front of the podium stands another ten grey Aliens.

'Well, Mr Adams, how do you account for this lot of Aliens?'

He points his finger at them. 'They have been incarcerated some fifty years in your underground facilities in your country working for your intelligence people. Why are you lying? I know that all Presidents of this country are fully informed when they take office about Aliens and UFO's. Mr Adams, I would like you to shake hands with the ten Aliens to prove that this is not an illusion.'

The Commander beckons the ten Aliens up to the podium and one by one, they take Mr Adam's hand look at him and smile. 'Well, Mr Adams, they are real, I mean they are solid beings?'

'Yes, they are!' he replies.

'Sir, you are very lucky you have Leila. She is the best thing that has happened to this Planet in over two thousand years. You should be very proud and honoured by her presence. If we had her technology, we would capture this Planet. Then make you our slaves and that is why we tried to abduct her in the first place. This Planet is no match for this young lady and you'll never be able to match her technology. She can do things you can only imagine!'

Leila makes a telepathic communication with Óisin and Gia. *'Please return to your craft now I'll see you there shortly. Don't worry about me I'll be fine, there is nothing on this Planet that might worry me!'*

Gia and Óisin transport up to their craft in orbit. There they wait for Leila's arrival.

Leila looks at Mr Brett Harrison, Prime Minister, nice looking man going bald, age about fifty years old, wearing a light grey suit and black shoes. 'Sir, please proceed to the podium, that is if you would like to learn some more about me and my powers!'

On his arrival at the podium, Leila indicates to him to stand at her right side then she indicates to Mr Adams to stand at her left side. She looks out at the audience. 'Will you please stay in your seats until we return thank you.' Now she lets the two hundred foot wave recede back into the Atlantic Ocean.

In the blink of an eye, the three of them disappear and are in Óisin and Gia's craft. That leaves all the rest the World leaders and people in the Great Hall completely astonished.

Chapter 120

The security people for Mr Adams and Mr Harrison are in total shock. Their leaders are nowhere to be found.

Leila leaves a message with her family. *'I don't want you to worry I'm going to teach Mr Adams and Mr Harrison a lesson that they will never forget and please make friends with Mr Bragin. Granddad, you can now converse in Russian, please keep him happy. I may need him, so don't worry if he disappears. He will be in Gia's space craft with me but I will return. I'll have a talk with you when I return.'* Leila communicates her thoughts to Commander Guber's mind, saying. *'I'm sending all of you back to your place of residence for now. Have a word with the other Alien visitors for me. Maybe I'll discuss with them their release them from this Planet. I will need you to help me very soon on a matter of diplomacy. Thank you, Commander Gruber!'*

Leila, Mr Adams and Mr Harrison materialise in Óisin and Gia's craft. The technology on this craft is way ahead of their intellectual capacity. They look around, but don't know where they are.

Óisin walks over to welcome them to their space craft, introduces them to Gia again she says; welcome aboard!'

'Right, Mr Adams and Mr Harrison, we need you to go into that cabinet,' he points to it. 'Do not be afraid, it will not hurt you, it will only cleanse you. We need to do that to make sure that you do not bring anything that might contaminate our craft with bugs, bacteria or viruses so please go inside.' The two of them reluctantly enter the cabinet.

The door closes behind them. They then hear a low buzzing noise, and then a blue light arrives at the top of the cabinet they are in and encapsulates them. Then it moves slowly down around them until it reaches the bottom of the cabinet and rises back up again.

The door opens and Óisin beckons them out and says, 'everything alright? I hope that you were not too inconvenienced. You are all debugged and cleaned. Apologies for any discomfort you may have had in the cabinet but it was necessary in the circumstances. We are now going to take a little trip to the Moon!'

'That's impossible,' replies Mr Adams. 'It would take too long to get there and back!'

Leila looks at both of them and enquires. 'Is it possible to be somewhere at a particular moment in time, any idea where that place might be?'

'Both the World leaders look at each other. Mr. Harrison replies. 'I don't know but I'm sure that we are nowhere near the moon!'

Leila says, I did ask the question, is it possible to be somewhere at a particular moment in time, and the answer is yes!' Gentlemen I'm trying to give you a little glimpse into the future. Please, don't ask me to give you some of my technology because you would abuse it. From a scientific point of view the world is not ready to embrace this technology.'

'What do you mean, 'surely we are not orbiting the Moon!' Mr. Adams replies.

Leila looks at Óisin and Gia and they all smile.

'Gentlemen, please observe in front of you a vision of your Moon and it's real. We are in orbit at this moment!'

'That's impossible,' says Mr. Harrison as he goes over to the side of the craft looks around, nods his head and says,' Is that real?'

'Yes it is!' Leila replies. 'Would you like to walk on the Moon's surface?'

The two men laugh out loud. Mr. Harrison says, 'Are you kidding us, how will we survive without space suits on the Moon!'

'Perhaps we should try. Are you ready?'

'Are you trying to make us believe all this nonsense is real?' Mr Adams enquires.

Leila walks over. She stands between the two of them. In a blink of an eye the three of them are standing on the surface of the moon, not a space suit in sight.

'Gentlemen what do you think now? I hope all this scepticism, cynicism, and disbelief, has now left your little stupid minds!'

'How are we breathing with no air on the Moon?' Mr Adams asks.

'I have placed a shield around us otherwise you two would die. We have as much air inside this shield as we need. Are we ready to transport back to the space craft?'

'Yes,' they reply.

'Fine here we go again!'

In an instant they are back inside the craft. They are very badly dazed and shaken from this experience.

Gia looks at them and says; 'Did you like standing on the Moon?'

They look at each other. 'Yes it was different, we find it hard to believe we have actually been standing on the Moon without space suits, unbelievable!'

'Shall we return to your Planet now? Óisin asks.

Leila nods her head at Gia and in seconds the craft is in orbit above the World.

'Gentlemen, I will now show you the World from about two hundred miles away, and again the panoramic views from the craft are stunning and astounding!'

The two World leaders are totally in awe of what they are viewing. 'Is that our World? Mr Adams asks, as he points to it, 'It's so beautiful!'

Leila replies, 'good because that world will cease to exist in less than one hundred and fifty years. That is if you carry on in the same old destructive way. I hope that is not the legacy you are going to leave for future generations. Your stupidly is just amazing. I hope that is not what you want for your grand children?' This is not prolific or creative, to sustain the people of your world. That's not a nice legacy to leave. You can change it for the better, for all the people on your planet. I'll help you achieve your wish!'

They both look at each other, baffled and perplexed.

'The question is how can it be done?' The two leaders ask.

'You can leave that to me. If you don't mind I'll make the necessary arrangements when we return to the Great Hall!'

Gia walks over to Leila, looks her straight in the eye and asks, 'How did our craft travel so quickly to the Moon then return back to their World in less than ten seconds? This craft should not be able to travel at that speed or any craft I have ever been in before we must have travelled twice as fast as the speed of light, how do you account for that Leila?'

'Yes, it was me. I'm able to traverse any distance at any speed I care to achieve. Don't worry I placed a shield around your craft. I haven't done any damage to your craft but I can update the technology on this craft if you wish!'

Gia looks at Óisin and asks, 'What do you think, Óisin? He is totally bemused and asks, 'Leila how powerful are you?'

'I'm all powerful now and that power will be made to help mankind or beings anywhere in the Universe. I hope that you and Óisin are not dissatisfied or upset with me now!'

'Absolutely not,' replies Gia. 'After all, my technology is what has made you so powerful.' She runs over to Leila, gives her a great big hug and says. 'I'm so proud of you, I'm sure that Óisin feels the same!'

Óisin goes over and the three of them hug each other. Óisin looks at Leila and says; 'When we picked you for this experiment all those years ago we were a bit apprehensive. It was a very big decision but now we are sure we picked the right person!'

Óisin starts to cry, then Gia starts as well, they are so overwhelmed with their godchild, they are so proud of her.

Leila looks at both of them and says, 'You'll always be my godparents, I love you dearly. I will always protect you and your Planet from all tyranny of any kind. I'm sure that you know that anyway. Two other things you need to know,' as she looks at both of them and says, 'I will never grow old and your Bio/Dna technology has now advanced by at least another two thousand years. The Bio/Dna technology I have now is ten thousand years far ahead of anything in the Universe and getting stronger every second, but I can slow it down when I need to!'

Gia is astounded at this statement and asks, 'Leila, you are sure because my technology is not made to do that!'

'I know,' replies Leila but it upgrades itself all the time, but I can override it if the need to slow it down is necessary. We will have discussions on this subject at a later date!'

Leila walks over to the two World leaders. She looks at Mr Adams says, 'Sir about your missile silos, I don't suppose you will tell me where they are situated in your country?'

'I don't think so!' The President replies.

'Fine, you have a chief of staff at the White house a Mr William Knight?'

'Yes I have. 'How do you know that?'

Leila replies, 'He would like to talk to you now!'

'How do I talk to him from up here?'

'You're through to the White House now, I don't want you to be afraid there is nothing to worry about. You can talk to Mr William Knight now, sir!'

Mr Adams is very amused by this statement by Leila. He looks around as if searching for some kind of apparatus, a phone or something to talk into. He shrugs his shoulders and says, 'Can you hear me Bill?'

'Yes, sir, I hear you loud and clear. What do you want Bill?'

'Well, sir, we have a big problem!'

'What kind of problem, Bill?'

'Sir I know that you are at a very important meeting at The United Nations Building in New York. You know that I wouldn't phone you unless there was something very important to tell you!'

'Bill, for goodness sake, what are you talking about. Please tell me?'

'Well, sir, you already know we have missile silos in Iowa!'

'Yes, yes, Bill. What's the problem?'

'Well, sir, the silo doors are open, the computers are on count down!'

'Who gave the authority to fire those missiles?'

'We don't know sir. They started the count down by themselves!'

'Why don't you put in the code to stop them?'

'We have, sir, but the computers don't respond. We can't stop the count down!'

Leila decides to transport Mr Bragin up to the space craft. He materializes next to Mr Adams who jumps back in amazement saying. 'Has this something to do with you?'

Mr Bragin can now speak in English which surprises him immensely. He can't stop himself saying, this has nothing to do with me!'

'Mr Bragin looks at Leila and asks, 'Where am I?'

Leila answers, 'You are in orbit above Earth, aboard Gia's space craft. Mr Adams is having trouble with some missiles in Iowa. It would seem that they have started their count down. His chief of staff is unable to stop them. What do you think Mr Bragin?' Leila looks at him and winks. He knows the problem he had the same problem with his missiles in Russia.

'Mr Adams, may I have a word in your ear!'

'Not now Mr Bragin. You can see I have a very big problem at the moment.' He shouts out, 'Bill can you still hear me?'

'Yes, sir, I can. May I ask you a question?'

'Yes but be quick please!'

'Where exactly are you? We now know that you are not in the United Nations Building!'

'I can't explain now. We have more important things to worry about. Please tell me the missile countdown has stopped?'

'No it has not. What do we do, sir? The countdown hasn't stopped!'

'There must be somebody down there able to stop the countdown!'

'What do you mean sir? You said down there, where are you?'

'Never mind that! The President replies.

'We do have a direct line to the missile silo.'

'That's no good sir, as you know once the countdown starts there is no way to stop the missiles flying!'

'There must be something we can do to stop them?'

Leila looks over at Mr Bragin. She places her finger to her lips, smiles then turns away.

The President says, 'How about sending a squadron of F/16 to bomb the silos?'

'Sorry, sir, they would not arrive there in time. The countdown has gone below five minutes and that is not enough time to get the F/16 into the air and to the silos!'

Mr. Adams has decided to ask Leila what to do.'

He turns around faces her and asks, 'Do you know anything about the missile silos in Iowa? I have a feeling that you know something?'

'Mr. Adams, you think that this is all an illusion but I've been telling you all afternoon that everything I have done is real'

'What do you mean everything is real?'

'Sir, there is nothing I can't do, I can place all of your missiles on countdown now if I please. I've taken all the information from all of your military satellite stations in orbit and I know exactly where all of your missiles silos are. I can see you don't believe me sir. Ask Bill what's going on?'

'Bill you are still listening, please give me some good news about the missiles.'

'Sir, all I can give you is that all of our missile sites have started to countdown and we can't stop them!'

'That's impossible,' as he looks at Leila, 'what's the countdown number now?' 'We have less than two minutes left to stop the launch sir!'

'Where are they pointing?' Mr Adams asks.

'We think, at all of the big cities in our country sir!'

He starts to run around, hands waving in the air.' What am I going to do; it's going to be a massacre we are all going to be wiped out by our own missiles.' He turns to Mr Bragin, 'This is nothing to do with you?'

'It has nothing to do with me. Listen to Leila, she can stop them from flying!'

'Bill what is the update on the countdown?'

'Sir, it's still counting down. Sixty seconds left!'

Leila looks at Mr Adams. 'Sir, please swallow your pride and ask me for help?'

Óisin and Gia are looking very amused at the stubbornness of Mr Adams but they do not interfere.' 'Sir, you're at the edge of a precipice, you must make a decision. You have twenty seconds left before the missiles fire!'

'Alright Leila, please stop the countdown?'

'Thank you sir. 'You can now ask Bill what is happening!'

'Bill, you are still there?'

'Yes, sir, I'm still here but I've good news for you. The countdown has stopped on all the missile and the doors are closed on the silos!'

'I'll see you soon. Thank you Bill!'

He walks over to Leila, looks her in the eye, puts his arms around her and says, 'Thank you and yes, I do now believe you are a very special person!'

The three World leaders shake each other's hands. The only one to know what was happening was Mr Bragin. He walks over to Leila and says, 'You would make a wonderful poker player!'

She looks at him and smiles. She says, 'He had no option but to give in. Will you excuse me for a minute, I must contact my family!'

Granddad receives a telecommunication from Leila saying, *Granddad go to the podium, call the attention of the rest of the world leaders, tell them that this meeting will resume tomorrow at three in the afternoon. We would like everyone to be in the Great Hall at that time. We have a very important announcement to make. The doors are open. 'I'll see you very soon. Bye now!'*

Chapter 121

Granddad walks up to the podium, taps the microphone and says, 'Ladies and gentlemen, may I have your attention please.' He waits for a minute until everyone is sitting down when complete silence has descended in the Great Hall. Mr Carney stands up at the podium, has a look around the Great Hall and says, 'I wish to inform you, that this meeting will be reconvened tomorrow at 3pm sharp. Leila has something very important to tell you and she wishes that everyone will make them-selves available. That is all I'm permitted to say about this announcement, the doors are open now and you may leave if you want. Thank you and good bye for now!'

Leila looks at Mr Adams and says, 'I would like you to make a reservation, six VIP apartments at the Ritz Carlton Hotel for one night with breakfast in the morning plus dinner this evening. I'll phone the reception desk for you, will you book the rooms for me please?'

'Yes of course I will!' he replies

At the Ritz Carlton hotel the phone rings. It's answered by one of the receptionist, 'This is the Ritz Carlton Hotel. How may I help you?'

'Listen, young man this is the President of the United States of America. Who am I speaking to?'

'My name is Ryan sir, 'How may I help you Mr. President?'

'Well, Ryan, I would like to book six VIP rooms for tonight for some special friends of mine, with dinner this evening, and breakfast in the morning. I'm waiting your answer!'

'Yes, just a minute sir.' Ryan looks at his computer and says, 'Sir we have only three VIP rooms left in the hotel out of six!'

The President replies, 'Ryan, I want six VIP rooms tonight. Do I make myself clear?'

'I'll see what I can do for you; give me ten minutes, sir!'

Leila goes to Óisin and Gia and says; 'I know that what I'm going to ask you might be a little strange. But I would like you to stay on my Planet at the hotel with me until tomorrow please?'

Gia looks at Óisin and asks, 'What do you think?'

'Well we have never stayed in a hotel on your Planet but will it be alright? I mean will we look out of place?'

'I think not,' Leila replies. 'No one will take any notice of you. There are stranger things around New York.

Anyway you will stay for another day?'

'Yes, we will, what about our craft?'

'Don't worry I'll take care of that!' She goes back to Mr Adams. 'You can talk to Ryan now please!'

Ryan picks up the phone in reception, 'May I ask who am I talking too?'

'Ryan, this is your President, I hope you have good news for me?'

'Yes, sir, we have six VIP rooms ready for you now!'

'Thank you Ryan. One more thing; will you send a minibus to the United Nations Building as soon as you can please. I would my like friends picked up from the United Nations Building, they are the Carney family. Oh and make sure that there is plenty of food laid out for them when they arrive at the hotel. Thank you. Tell your manager to send the bill to the White House, for the attention of the President. Good bye Ryan!'

Leila communicates with granddad. *I'll be back in the Great Hall in a few minutes!'*

'Right, gentlemen, I think it is time to return to the Great Hall. I have convened another meeting for tomorrow at three in the afternoon. I hope that's alright with everyone here!'

The three leaders just nod in unison, 'Yes that is fine with us Leila!'

Leila goes to Gia and Óisin, 'You will follow us down to the Great Hall?'

'We promise!' Gia replies.

'Good, see you in the Great Hall then!'

In an instant the three leaders and Leila are back in the Great Hall. The security guards have been frantic, not knowing where their leaders have been. Mr Adam's security guard runs over to Mr Adams asking, 'Where have you been, Mr President, we looked everywhere. 'Where have you been sir?' We have searched the whole building!'

'I'm not able to answer any questions at this time. I'm fine now no harm was contemplated against me. Take me to the Waldorf Astoria Hotel as fast as you can please!'

Leila has detected a worrying thought from Mr Adams. She makes a mental note to keep an eye on him for the next twelve hours.

'Leila goes to her mum and says, 'I'm so sorry mum but I had to get agreement with the three strongest leaders today. It did take more time that I wanted but I'm here now!'

Leila goes to her lions, says something in their ears and they disappear. She walks to her Granddad, takes him by the hand and says; 'You were marvellous and awe inspiring. Thank you granddad, Thank you for taking my place and addressing all the Leaders about tomorrow's meeting!'

'It's getting late. What are we going to do? John asks.

'We are guests of the President and he has booked us into the Ritz Carlton Hotel VIP rooms with breakfast in the morning plus dinner this evening. What do you think of that as a present?' Leila replies. 'What do you want to do, will we accept his invitation or will I take you home?' JK looks around and says, 'Well if the President of the United States of America has booked us into the Ritz Carlton Hotel I would like to stay.'

I would like to stay shouts Alfie, and me, replies Delia.

'What about you granddad and grandma, would you like to be a guest of the President? 'Granddad looks at grandma and says, 'What do you think dear, shall we stay?'

'Yes, of course we will stay!' she replies.

Leila looks at her mum and dad walks over to them gives them, gives them a big hug each and they say, 'Of course we'll stay. We've never stayed in such a prestigious hotel in our lives we're looking forward to it, aren't we, John!' He nods in anticipation.

Gia and Óisin arrive down from their spacecraft and they are dressed like natives.

Leila looks bemused and says, 'Well you just look like us.' She looks at Gia and asks, 'Everything alright with the craft?' Leila enquires.

'Yes of course why do you ask?'

'Fine I'll just make sure that it is cloaked until tomorrow!'

Gia enquires; 'Can you do that from here?'

'Yes, of course I can, no problem!' Leila replies.

'Everyone out to the front of the building, we have a minibus waiting for us. Please follow me. Come on, Alfie, give me your hand. We don't want you to get lost, do we?'

Alfie looks at his sister and says, 'Why would I want to be lost?'

'Never mind. I was just joking, Alfie!'

Outside Leila looks around, sees the minibus with 'The Ritz' painted on the sides and tailgate, 'Come on, everyone, follow me.'

They follow Leila to the mini bus she walks to the front of the bus. She asks the driver. 'Is this our transport to the hotel?'

'Yes, replies the driver. She walks back to the family and says, 'This is our mini bus. She opens the side door and says; 'Everyone into the mini bus please!' Gia and Óisin come on.'

Gia and Óisin have never been in a minibus before. They are looking forward to this adventure.

As the mini bus is driving to the hotel Gia and Óisin are consumed with laughter. They are very amused and say;

It's manic out there. How do you go about your daily work without having an accident?'

'We're used to that kind of havoc, confusion, chaos, whatever you might like to call it. You could say it's a way of living but we arrive where-ever we set out to go but not always in one piece. Sometimes there are accidents. It causes a little bit of a hold up, but generally we get by!' Leila replies.

'This is a crazy world of yours. We are not surprised that you have accidents but we are enjoying the tour!' Gia replies. Fifteen minutes later they arrive at the Ritz Carlton Hotel. The driver gets out and opens all the doors on the minibus.

'Everyone out,' says Leila, follow me please. Don't forget your luggage bags.' She walks into the hotel foyer and up to reception desk. 'You're Ryan, I presume!'

'Yes, I'm Ryan, how may I help you?'

'We are the Carney family and we have a booking made by the President of America, Ryan can I ask for our electronic keys please. May I also ask, what time will dinner be served this evening?'

Ryan looks at Leila and says, 'The dining room will be open from eight till eleven tonight, casual dress please!' He hands the electronic keys to Leila and points to the lifts. 'They are behind you or you can walk up to the top floor if you wish but I would advise the lifts. The family turn around, then they proceed to the lifts, the lift doors open and the family go inside, Gia and Óisin follow them into the lift and are quite amused at this confined space.'

Leila presses the button with VIP and off they go to the top of the building. The lift slows down and stops, then the doors open and Leila says, 'Come on everyone, let's see these VIP rooms. I'm sure that we will be quite surprised at the elegance and sumptuousness of each suite. I think mum and dad should have the first choice.' Leila puts out her hand with the electronic keys and says; 'Mum, the choice is yours. Pick one please!'

Mum looks at Leila then at the electronic pass keys, she picks one that corresponds with the suite number on the door, places the electronic key in the slot on the door. It opens. All the family walk inside the suite and are astonished at the enormity of the suite and the sheer size of the rooms. This VIP apartment has all the usual refinements attached to it

Alfie is running around, asking, 'Is this my room?'

'No, Alfie, this is mum and dad's suite but you can come into it anytime you like, but you have your own suite with me!' Leila replies.

'JK, here is your key; you know what to do, go and settle in. When you have had your shower and changed, you'll return here so that we all go to dinner together.'

'Delia, now it's your turn' as she hands her the key. Take your bag and I'll see you a little bit later. Have a shower if you need one. Don't forget we will need to meet here and go to dinner together! Granddad and grandma you stay here with mum until I return. Help yourselves to drinks from the fridge if you wish!' 'Gia, you and Óisin, can you stay here with mum. I'll take Alfie to my suite give him a shower. When he is finished in the shower, I'll have mine. Then I'll return here. Don't worry I won't be long!

'Now, Alfie, you're going to stay with me in my suite are you happy with that?'

Alfie looks at Leila and enquires, 'Can I have my own bedroom?'

'Yes you can, there are two bedrooms, you have one and I'll have the other one. Will that be all right with you!'

'Yes I think that will be fine with me!'

'Right, Alfie, let's go and see our rooms.' Off they go out into the corridor Leila looks at the key, goes to the door, inserts the electronic key, and opens the door walks inside. Leila says, 'Alfie you go and pick which ever room you like best.'

Off he goes looking into all the rooms, comes back, takes Leila by the hand and leads her to one of the bedrooms and says, 'I like this one. May I have it please?'

'Of course you can, if that is the one you want, it's yours. Now Alfie you go and get yourself ready for a shower. I'll set the temperature of the water for you. When you have finished I'll come and dry you. Don't take too long in the shower room; I need to have one as well!'

Ten minutes later Alfie is still playing in the shower. Leila goes into the shower room and asks; 'Alfie, have you finished? I need the shower now?'

'Yes, I'm ready now to come out!'

Leila lifts him out of the shower, dries him off, puts clean clothes on him and tells him to go and watch television in the sitting room while she takes a shower. She removes her clothes, places them on a chair outside the bathroom door, goes inside, and has a quick shower, which takes about ten minutes. She gets out of the shower, dries herself, puts on clean clothes then walks into the sitting room. The television is on and Alfie is watching it. She goes out the door into the corridor to her mum's suite, knocks on the door.

Dad opens the door and says; 'Please come in Leila, Gia and Óisin are waiting for you!'

'Right then, Gia and Óisin, shall we go and see your suite.' The three of them walk out the door, down the corridor Leila looks at the electronic key. It matches up to the suite number. She pushes it into the receptacle on the door. In they go. It's exactly like mum's suite.' Sitting room, two bed rooms, bath and shower room, kitchen and loads of beautiful furniture.

'What do you think Gia?' Leila enquires.

'I like it! Gia replies. What about you Óisin what do you think?'

'It's very different to our living quarters. However, I think that it's very elegant I like it very much!'

'Good,' replies Leila. 'I was a bit worried in case it might not be to your liking.' Now you have two bedrooms. You can have one each or sleep wherever you please,' as she looks at Gia and Óisin. She has a little smile to herself. 'Now I'll show you how to use the shower if you will come with me.' She opens the bathroom door beckons Gia and Óisin inside saying, 'This is the shower room. If you need to have a shower all you have to do is remove your clothes. Leave them outside the shower room, Go inside adjust these two chrome taps as she point to the two taps. 'One has cold water; the other one has hot water. All you need to do is balance the temperature to your liking but don't let it get too hot or it will burn you. Let me give you a demonstration on how to achieve the right temperature. All you need to do is turn on the cold tap. Then turn on the hot tap like this,' as she turns that tap on. 'Now you adjust it to your temperature. There are lots of towels in here. When you have finished in the shower you dry yourselves with the towels. So if I were you I would try the shower and see if you would like it. I'll go and see to the rest of the family, I'll then return to see how you are getting on. Ok!'

Off she goes out the door, down the corridor, back to mum's suite. She knocks on the door. Dad comes and opens it. He sees Leila and says; 'Come in, Leila, what do for you want?'

She walks into the sitting room sees granddad and grandma, hands the key to granddad and says 'Right off you go to your suite, you have a drink from the fridge have a shower!'

Off they go to their suite with their bags.' Leila walks back to her suite opens the door and walks in. Alfie is watching television. Leila picks up the phone, dials reception; it's picked up by Ryan.

'Ryan. I need to have all the clothes we were wearing today dry cleaned, is it possible to have that done tonight, and ready for tomorrow?'

'Ryan answers, I don't think so!'

'Ok, I'll phone the President at the Waldorf Hotel. He will not be very happy with the service here in the hotel,' Leila replies.

'No, please don't phone the President. I'll be in very serious trouble and probably lose my job!'

'Fine, then you will phone me back in ten minutes with the right answer? Will you do that for me please?'

'Yes leave that with me I promise I'll phone you as soon I have the right information!' he replies.

Fifteen minutes later the phone rings. Leila picks it up and it's Ryan, he says, 'Your clothes will picked up in fifteen minutes to be dry cleaned so please have them ready. Thank you?'

'That's fine,' Leila replies. 'I'll have them ready when your colleague arrives at my dad's apartment!'

Leila sends a telepathic message to the rest of the family including Gia and Óisin to have all their clothes that were used today ready to be picked up for dry cleaning in dad's apartment in ten minutes.

'Come on, Alfie let's gather our clothes up so that we can take them into dad's apartment!

'Why?' asks Alfie.

'Because we need to have them dry cleaned for tomorrow afternoon when we address the world leaders. We need to be nice and clean. Now you wouldn't like to put on dirty clothes would you?'

Alfie answers, 'Of course not, I don't want to look grubby!'

'Come on Alfie lets go to dad's apartment!'

The rest of the family plus Gia and Óisin bring their clothes to dad's apartment.' Then a few minutes pass, there's a knock on the door, dad goes and opens it. Standing in the corridor is a young man, with a trolley. He says, 'I'm here to collect your clothes for dry cleaning sir,

'Please come in,' dad points to the clothes on the table. 'They are ready for you to take away for cleaning!'

'Can I ask when may we expect our clothes back?'

'You'll have your clothes back at eight in the morning sir, is that alright with you?'

'Yes, that's fine with us, thank you very much!'

The young man picks up all the clothes for dry cleaning, places them in his trolley, then he opens the door and walks away.

'Now, if we are all ready, shall we all go to the restaurant?' Dad asks.

'Gia and Óisin would you like to come down to the restaurant and have a look at what's available in food that might suit you. There might be something you might like to sample?' enquires Leila.

Gia looks at Óisin and Gia answers, 'We think that we would like to see what's available in the restaurant first. Then decide if we might like to try your Earth food!'

'Good,' Leila replies. 'Let's go down to the restaurant and see what's on the menu!'

Down in the lift they go and into the restaurant where one of the waiters takes them to a table, including Gia and Óisin, and they all sit down. Over comes another waiter and informs them that the menu tonight is a carvery dinner, 'But first may I take your drink orders please?'

Dad looks at Leila and says, 'I think that we should have Champagne in honour of Gia and Óisin. It is through their technology that we are here tonight. Is everyone in agreement if so please put your hands in the air!

Alfie looks at his dad and says, 'Can I have Champagne as well, dad, please?'

'We'll see, son. You might be too young for Champagne!' dad replies.

'Oh please, dad, let me have some. I just want to try it. I might like it?'

'Alfie, I said we'll see. Please don't ask again!' dad replies.

Dad looks at the waiter and says, 'We are guests of your President and we are allowed to have whatever we want, so we will start with two bottles of Moët & Chandon Champagne chilled, please?'

Leila looks at dad and enquires, 'Two bottles of Champagne, are you sure, dad? That will make us quite merry.' well, we are here tonight to enjoy ourselves with my godparents and my family as well. Dad, you order the Champagne, I'm sure we'll enjoy ourselves anyway!'

Dad looks at the waiter and says, 'That is it then, waiter. Two bottles of Champagne!'

'Thank you sir,' replies the waiter. He turns goes to the bar and orders two bottles of Moët & Chandon Champagne. The barman looks at his colleague and asks him, 'Are you sure about this?'

'Yes, they are guests of the President if you are not sure, ask the manager!' Down he goes to the cellar. He returns five minutes later with two bottles of Moët & Chandon Champagne, places them on a tray with nine glasses. He picks up the tray and walks back to the table, places the tray on the table. He then places one glass in front of each person. He opens one bottle, pours a taster into dad's glass. He picks up his glass, puts it to his lips, has a taste then nods his head saying, 'that's fine, waiter.'

The waiter walks around the table filling each glass with Champagne, gives Alfie a half glass and the waiter says, 'This is Champagne, Alfie, just a sip at a time!'

He looks at the waiter and says, 'Must I just sip the Champagne? I think I might like it?'

Dad looks at Alfie and says, 'But you might not like Champagne.'

'Right, everyone, shall we give a toast to Leila, Gia and Óisin. Go on, Alfie, you have a sip as well. Gia what do you think of our Champagne?'

'Well it's different from what we have on my planet but it tastes lovely, lots of bubbles.'

'Óisin what's your impression of our most famous drink?'

'It is very nice I like the bubbles. It's certainly different to anything we have on our planet. I like this drink very much!'

'You can have some more if you want it!' replies dad.

The waiter arrives at the table and says; 'Please go and help yourselves, have whatever you like on the menu?'

'Yes,' replies Dad. 'I think we are ready, to choose our individual meals!'

Gia looks perplexed. Leila senses she is having a problem with the menu, so she goes to her saying; 'Let me help you decide which meal you might like, would you like meat as in beef, chicken, pork.' Gia answers, 'we just have what you call supplements. We do have vegetarian meals some times. If that could be arranged I would be very grateful.'

'Waiter, does the restaurant cater for vegetarian meals as well!'

'Yes, we cater for all kinds of food, in this establishment!'

They pick up the hot plates and stand in front of the chef.' He takes the plate from Leila, she looks at him and says; I think I'll have some chicken please?'

He places three slices of chicken on her plate, and then he points at the vegetables as he hands the plate to Leila. Please help yourselves!'

'Alfie what do you want for your dinner?'

'I'll have chicken please!' he replies. 'Mum you look after Alfie, Dad, granddad, grandma, JK, and Delia know what to do, I will see what I can do for Gia and Óisin. She goes over to Gia and Óisin and says; 'Come on let us look at the vegetarian meals. Leila takes a spoon places it in the vessel where the vegetarian meals are. She lifts a little piece and hands the spoon to Gia saying, 'Have a taste you might like it.' Gia takes the spoon from Leila and places it in her mouth, takes a minute to sample the food. She smiles and nods to Leila saying, 'Oh yes I think I like the food it's very tasty it's very nice.'

'What about you. Óisin would you like to try it? Oisin replies, 'If Gia likes it I'm sure it will be fine for me thank you!'

Leila places the vegetables meals on plates, hands one to Gia and the other one to Óisin saying; 'try the other vegetable in the dishes!'

Gia asks; what are those white things? She points to the roast potatoes.

'Try them and see; 'they are very nice!' Leila replies.

Gia places two roast potatoes on her plate and two on Óisin's plate.

Leila places a selection of vegetables on her plate and the three on them walk back to the table. They sit down and wait for the rest of the family. Leila rises up from her chair, goes to Gia, picks up her fork in her left hand, shows Gia what to do and invites her to sample the food.

Leila goes back to her chair. She sits down and starts to eat her meal, keeping an eye, on Gia and Óisin. She is making sure that they are enjoying their first earth meal.

Granddad looks around and says; 'I must say that this meal is sumptuous.

'Good for you replies Ciera, 'it's like being on holiday again. I'm going to enjoying myself in this great city of New York while I'm here!' Dinner finished the waiter removes the dinner plates.

Granddad looks at Leila and enquires, 'If you need anyone of us tomorrow to fill in for you before you take the podium, it would be nice to know. We are prepared to help.'

'Well, that will depend on the President of America. I feel that he is trying to keep something from me. I'll pay him a visit tonight and see what's in his mind I don't trust him. I know where he is staying. He will be with his chief of staff and all his experts who will give him advice. 'Don't worry, I'll be invisible all the time I'm in the Presidential suite!'

'Mum, will you have Alfie tonight please?'

'Yes of course I will!'

'Gia, you look worried, please tell me if I'm doing something wrong?'

'No, I'm just fascinated how stupid earth people are, they are so gullible and susceptible to world leaders telling them lies and taking advantage of them. It's amazing how they get away with it!'

'Well ordinary people of this world are not as educated as world leaders so whatever they say, the people believe them. I know that is hard to understand and believe. That is why you gave me this wonderful gift. I will ultimately infuse some kind of sense into world leaders minds!'

Óisin looks at JK very intently and asks, 'Have you finished the project you were given some years ago. I know it was very advanced for a human?'

'Yes I've finished it, sometime ago, It was indeed a very mind blowing examination project I'm sorry that it has taken so long but I was determined to solve it however long it would take me!'

'Good,' replies Óisin. I was not sure if you were talented and gifted enough. Now I think maybe if my superiors will allow you to visit my planet as a reward,

'I think I would be eternally grateful, if that would be granted for me. I would love to visit your planet. I would be immensely proud and privileged, 'It would be a great honour. The only problem I might have is my job. That could prove a bit tricky, and complicated, but if my superiors grant this request first!'

'I'm sure they will be glad, to grant you this prestigious opportunity.

But you are not allowed to tell anyone, outside of your family, or your immediate boss. That has to be a pre-requisite condition of your visit. Will you agree to that?'

JK replies, 'Yes of course I will!'

'Good, we'll be in touch in the next two to three weeks of your time,' Óisin replies. 'Are you happy with that, JK?'

'I'm fine with that,' JK replies. 'I hope I can visit your world soon!'

'Anyone for more Champagne?' asks dad. He picks up the bottle of Champagne, goes around the table again pouring into the glasses. He looks at Alfie and says, 'I think you have had enough Champagne for now, son. What about a nice coke!'

Alfie replies, 'Yes, dad, I'd like a coke please!'

'Good, when the waiter returns I'll ask him for a coke for you, are you happy with that?'

'Yes, dad, I'm happy with that!' he replies.

He walks over to Gia and Óisin and asks, 'Will I pour you more Champagne?'

'Yes please!' replies Óisin.

'What about you Gia,' enquires dad.

'I think I'll try another glass please!

'Everyone topped up then,' says dad, as he sits down!'

The waiter returns with Alfie's coke in a glass, places it in front of Alfie, and says, 'Your coke, sir.' he smiles and walks away.

After about fifteen minutes, granddad jumps up, and asks; 'Shall we finish this Champagne, before we retire to our suites?'

'Good idea!' replies Ciera. 'I'll have another glass please!'

Granddad walks around the table and pours Champagne into all the glasses walks back to his chair sits down and fills his glass and says good health to everyone!

Alfie looks around the table and asks, 'May I have another half glass of Champagne please, I do like it?' 'Now he is smiling like a Cheshire cat hoping his mum will concede to his request.

'Absolutely not, replies his mum, 'you have had enough alcohol for one night but you drink your coke if you wish but no alcohol, am I making myself clear Alfie!'

'Yes, I'm sorry,' as he looks at his mum, with not a too happy expression.

She looks at him and says, 'Don't you look at me that way my son you are not going to get your own way tonight.'

Dad jumps up and says, 'We have had a wonderful day here in New York. I'm glad I came. It has been a very interesting time for the family and of course for Gia and Óisin. I'm sure that everyone will agree it's been fabulous especially in the Great Hall. The world leaders were totally flabbergasted and bemused with Leila and they are beginning to understand how powerful she is. She is a very special person to us and we know that she will need to go out there in the Universe from time to time to help other planets. We know that she will be well looked after with Gia and Óisin, her godparents as she calls them.' He is now welling up with tears in his eyes so he decides to stop talking and sits down. His wife hands him a tissue which he accepts rather reluctantly.

Leila stands up and says, 'I know it's going to be very hard for the family when I'm away, don't worry. I'm only going to be in the next Universe and I'll be in touch all the time. I'm just going to see Mr Adams. I don't expect any problems. I'll be home faster than a peregrine falcon out of his cage. Gia and Óisin perhaps you would like to come with me to the Waldorf Hotel. Don't worry, no one will see us, the three of us will be invisible. I think it will be an education for you and a chance to see the other side of this President, Mr Adams. I don't trust him and I think he might try to find a way to negate my powers but you and I know that's not possible. Now, mum, would you be so kind to look after Alfie while I'm away in the Waldorf Hotel. If you can have Alfie in your suite, I will be very grateful. I don't want him on his own tonight. Any problems just send me a message otherwise I'll see you in the morning!'

Chapter 122

In a flash Gia, Óisin, and Leila have transported to the Waldorf Hotel into the President's suite.

JK stands up and says, 'Well I'm off to bed,' so the whole family stand up. They walk to the lifts wait for it to arrive. JK presses the button for the VIP suites they go inside, wait, until the lift stops at the VIP corridor. They alight from the lift walk to their suites, place their electronic keys in the slots and walk into their respective suites.

Mum looks at Alfie and says, 'Alfie you're sleeping in our suite tonight, so in you go and get ready for bed.'

Alfie doesn't say a word just walks into the sitting room,' I'm sleeping in here tonight mum?'

She takes him by the hand, leads him into the bedroom and says, 'Yes you'll be sleeping in that bedroom tonight, you get ready for bed then I'll come and tuck you in. 'Is that alright with you?'

'Yes, mum, that's fine with me!'

Leila, Gia and Óisin arrive into the President's suite without anyone noticing their entrance. It would appear that all his advisers including his Chief of Staff have arrived from the White House by special White House Jet. The top General of the Army, the Admiral Chief of Naval OPS, and the General of the Air Force are present in his suite. The head of the CIA and the FBI are present. Leila indicates to Gia and Óisin to sit down at the back of the room next to her with a telepathic message, *'be very careful don't make a noise of any kind please. We will just listen and learn what could be useful for me tomorrow!'*

Then there is a knock on the door. The President nods to his head, the Chief of Staff goes and opens it and ushers the person into the room. It's a young woman. The President stands up, walks around to the front of desk, puts out his hand to the young woman and she reciprocates by placing her hand into his hand. He indicates to her to sit down. He returns to his chair behind the desk and sits down.

'Now young woman, may I have your first name please?'

'Yes, sir, it's Maria!'

'Right, Maria, I've been told that you have very special powers, is that true?'

'Yes, sir, I do have special powers. Why do you want to know!'

'Well we would like you to help us!' he replies.

'What do you want from me, sir?'

'We would like you to give us a demonstration of those powers, that's if it's not too much trouble, Maria?'

She looks at the President very intently. She then decides to make the lights go on and off without touching the switches.

'Very good,' says the President,' but we would like something a little more exciting. Can you do something more spectacular for me?'

She looks at his desk then she levitates everything on the desk up to about six inches. She holds them in that position.

The President looks quite amused. It doesn't fill him with inspiration that she is as powerful as Leila.

Leila decides to help her so Leila levitates the desk up to the ceiling.

Now he takes notice and asks; 'Is that you doing the levitation Maria?'

'Yes, sir, that's one of my powers I hope you like it!'

'Yes that's quite interesting. Can you return the desk back to the floor please, It worries me when something is floating above my head and I'm not in control of it, so if you don't mind, please place it back on the floor!'

'Yes, sir, she looks at the desk. She is wondering what to do when the desk starts to descend slowly to the floor. She doesn't know how she achieved this wonderful levitation vision before the President. She thinks to herself, 'It must be me perhaps I'm getting better with my powers.'

The President looks at her and asks, 'I would like something more spectacular please?'

She is now in a dilemma as to how she is going to please the President.

She looks around hoping that something will happen to please him. Leila intervenes on her behalf. She levitates all the people in the room including the President. Then she lets them rotate around the room three times, stops them, and lets them descend to the floor. Leila looks at Gia and Óisin and smiles they know that Leila is doing all this levitation but why?

The President looks very interested now and says, 'Maria, I think you are the one I'm looking for, that is something I can relate to.' He looks at his Chief of Staff and says; 'I think it's time to take Maria into the next room, close the door behind her and return back here!'

The Chief of staff does as he was asked. He rises up from his chair walks over to Maria smiles, and leads her to the door of the next room. He tells her to go inside. He closes the door behind her and walks back to his chair and sits.

'Well, what do you think of that, gentlemen? She is quite powerful but is she as powerful as Leila?'

'All we know is she is very powerful!' replies the Chief of Staff, 'But she is the best we have, even the Russians don't have the powers that

Maria is equipped with. We could ask her if she has anything else she might like to show us!' replies the Chief of Staff.

Leila looks at Gia, sends her message saying, *'I'm going into the room where Maria is, so don't worry. Whatever happens, do not interfere because I'll be in Maria's body when she returns!'* In a flash she is in the room with Maria, but she is still invisible. She walks up to her and materialises just in front of her. Leila places her hand over Maria's mouth and says; 'I'm not going to hurt you, please don't cry out, I need to talk to you.' Leila looks at Maria quite intently and says; 'I'm hoping I can count on you not to shout out because nobody knows I'm in here in this room with you!'

Maria nods her head quite quickly. 'Most of the levitation you performed in front of the President, was done by me, you did do some of it. I need your help. The President will send his Chief of Staff to fetch you very soon. I'm now going to enter your body. Please don't worry I will not hurt you but I'll show you things you will not believe. Will you help me?'

Maria looks at Leila and asks; 'Who are you, why should I trust you? I have never seen you before, please don't hurt me?'

'I'm not here to hurt you, but I must ask you again will you help me?'

'Yes I'll help you.'

'Maria, you'll not regret what I'm about to do. Are you ready for our two bodies to combine together? Just one other thing I'll do all the talking through you.' She is in Maria's body before she knows it. She asks, 'Are you alright?'

'Yes I'm fine. I don't know how you do this but I'm very impressed!'

'The Chief of Staff is about to arrive to open the door for you. You must be calm I'll do the rest!'

The President looks at his Chief of Staff and says, 'Ok go and bring Maria back into this room. I'll ask her if she can do something even more spectacular.'

Back goes the Chief of staff and opens the door. He invites Maria back into the room and stands her in front of the President again.

'Ok young lady, I need you to perform something very spectacular for me can you do that?'

'Yes, sir, I will do something quite extraordinary. Please come out to the front of the desk (this is Leila speaking now not Maria.) Can I ask your Chief of Staff to stand on my right side and you, Mr President, please stand on my left side?'

In an instant the three of them, (actually there are four of them but only Leila and Maria know the truth) are two hundred miles above the earth.' Mr President what you see now is your planet down below you. I know that I have been up here earlier today. The President blurts out.

Yes, I know that sir.' Maria answers,

'How do you know that, Maria? The President is bit suspicious.

Leila has to think quickly, otherwise the game is up.

'I'm able to read your mind sir that is how I know. You have been up here earlier today. What do you think of the view of your planet at night?'

The Chief of Staff is not very happy he is about to panic asking, 'Please tell me I'm not dreaming, I hope I'm not going to die up here looking down at the world. How are we breathing up here with no atmosphere I would like to know?'

'Don't worry sir,' says Maria, 'you have a shield around you with enough air. Now Mr President is this enough power to satisfy you?'

'Yes,' he replies. 'You are super human. Can we return to my suite in the hotel now please!'

'Yes of course sir!' Before you could blink an eye, they are back in the President's suite. All of his other advisers, including the Army Five Star General, the General of the Navy, and the General of the Air Force, the CIA and the FBI are amazed.'

They look astonished and ask; 'Where did you go, sir. We were very worried for you, where have you been. One minute you were here, the next minute you vanished. Now you are back again?'

'Mr Dankin, you're the head of the CIA. Do you know anything about Leila and her family?'

'No sir, we've not had the time to investigate her or her family but we are on it now and hopefully by tomorrow I will have some information about her for you!'

'Thank you, Mr Dankin, I look forward to hearing from you tomorrow then!'

'Mr. Luddie, as head of the FBI, how did she and her family enter this country without you knowing?'

'I don't know, sir. She and her family didn't arrive by plane or ship because I would know!'

'Fine, Mr Luddie, but it would appear that all is not well with your organization I would advise you to put your house in order or you might be removed. Now you wouldn't like that would you!'

He looks at the President a bit sheepish and answers, 'No sir, I'm on it now,' he replies!'

Mr Luddie is furious at being told off by the President. Heads will roll at the FBI Head Office in the morning

'Now I must ask all of you except the Chief of Staff and this young lady to leave us please. Go into the next room and close the door behind you, thank you.' He waves his hand saying, 'Off you go!' He looks at Maria and says, 'Tomorrow afternoon I have a very important meeting at the United Nations Building in the Great Hall. I would like you to be present because I'll need you to do something for me?'

'And what would that be sir?'

'There will be another young lady in the Great Hall. I want you to negate her powers for me so that we can take her into custody. I'll make sure that you will be well paid for your valuable time. Can I rely on your cooperation?'

Maria replies, 'Yes sir. I think I can do that for you!'

The President looks at the chief and says, 'Will you organise a car for the young lady? Make sure that she will be available when I give you the signal to bring her into the Great Hall tomorrow. Is that alright with you Maria?'

'Yes, sir, that's fine with me!'

'You can go now. Thank you very much, Maria, see you tomorrow. Good bye!'

The chief goes to the door, opens it and ushers Maria out saying, 'A car will be at your disposal when you go to reception to take you home.

Tomorrow at two in the afternoon a car will arrive for you at your apartment to escort you to the United Nations Building. I will meet you at reception. Please be ready when the car arrives, I don't want you to be late.' He closes the door to the President's suite and walks back to the President saying, 'I think we will be alright, sir, with Maria!'

'Chief, let the other guests back in, please, I just want to make sure that they know what is expected of them tomorrow afternoon!'

The chief goes to the room door opens it and invites all the guests back in. The President looks up from his desk.

'Now men will you please sit down. Just a few words before you leave here tonight. Now you have seen some very wonderful and special super human things happen in here, but was it an illusion, a trick? I'm not sure. What does worry me is, are there more super human beings out there somewhere. I need you to find out sooner rather than later. I'll want the most up to date information on Leila and her family. I don't want excuses. Do I make myself clear Mr Dankin? 'I don't want to be humiliated again tomorrow afternoon. Good night, gentlemen, see you this afternoon and don't be late!'

Leila exits Maria's body and says, 'I want you to understand whatever might happen tomorrow afternoon I don't want you to worry, I'll protect you. I'll let you keep your own powers you have now, but I must tell you I could remove the powers you have. You pretend you are in control and I'll do the rest. Have I made myself clear, Maria? I'll be in touch with you tomorrow afternoon!'

'Yes I understand,' she replies, as she walks down the corridor to the lift.

The chief goes to the door, opens it and ushers the guests out into the corridor. He closes the door behind them, walks back to the President.'

Leila is back in the President's VIP suite, sitting next to Gia and Óisin she looks at Gia and smiles. The President is very happy now. His conversation with his Chief of Staff has been very good as far as he is concerned. 'Now we have someone who is probably as powerful as Leila, tomorrow we will see who is the most powerful person on this world. Here is the plan for tomorrow afternoon, Chief. I want you to organise with the General of the Army for a squad of SAS to be close to the Great Hall and when Maria negates Leila's powers you make sure that the SAS take her into custody then I'll deal with her. This little upstart thinking she can overrule me is ridiculous. How dare she think she is more powerful than the President of America?' And he has a chuckle to himself. 'Chief, I know that we don't have a lot of time to put this together, but I'm counting on you to make it work, 'Are you happy with that!'

'Yes, sir, don't worry. I'll make sure it works perfectly!'

'I'm sure the plan will work very well,' the President replies,' and I don't want any excuses!

'Chief, I just wanted to make clear to you the importance of tomorrow's plan it must work, I don't want to look foolish in front of the world leaders. It would look bad for me plus our foreign relations with the other world leaders might not go down good for us. We don't want that, do we, chief? We are the best nation to rule the world and you have to keep that in mind!' The President looks at the chief and asks, 'Would you like a drink Chief. I need one anyway?'

'Yes, please, sir. May I say that Maria impressed me; my instinct tells me that she might just be the one to save us, I think she might be the answer to our prayers!'

'We'll see. What are you drinking tonight chief?'

'I'll have a brandy, please sir!'

'The President pours a brandy for the chief then hands it to him, pours himself a whisky, walks back to his chair behind his desk, sits down and says; 'Sit down Chief and enjoy your drink. He looks at him-. 'This Leila is something else, but if she thinks she can overrule me, she must be mentally deficient. I know that she is powerful but not as powerful as the President of America!'

'What happens when we capture her sir?'

'We will interrogate her to find out who she is working for. Now that should not be hard. We have very special drugs to make her talk. I'm sure that we can glean from her all the information we need. Right chief!'

'Yes, sir, we have the means to extract whatever information we need from her, she will not even know she is helping us!'

'Well, chief, I think that is all until tomorrow, so I bid you good night. Please see yourself out!'

'Good night, sir, see you tomorrow,' as he walks to the door, goes out into the corridor and proceeds to his room goes inside, removes his clothes. Has a shower. The President is pondering about tomorrow, hoping that everything will go as he has planned, so he decides to have a shower, and not worry too much about tomorrow.'

Chapter 123

Leila has heard enough so she decides to return to her hotel with Gia and Óisin and materialize in her suite. She looks at Gia and says, 'what a carry on, quite unbelievable. What a charlatan, do you think we can do business with him or what? This President is a bit of a flyboy. We know now where we stand regarding his agenda in the Great Hall at the United Nations Building. I'll be ready for him when he stands at the podium. I knew I was going to have trouble with this President but I'm much wiser now. What do you think, Gia?'

'I think he will try anything to hang on to power at any cost!' replies Gia.

'What do you think Óisin?

'I don't think he understands how powerful you are; that is to your advantage. He doesn't know you were in his suite tonight. You have outwitted him already this evening in his VIP suite in the hotel. The beauty of it all is he doesn't know we were listening to his rhetoric or speechifying. He had a very attentive subordinate minion people at his behest. If that is a sample of democracy, people of your planet have a problem!'

'I agree with the two of you. Isn't it amazing the audacity of this supposedly people's President. If he is not careful he could be removed but in the end I hope common sense will prevail!'

'Gia and I are not allowed to interfere as you well know but we can advise you if you need help!'

'I do appreciate your advice. However, I'm not going to waste all this technology that you have given me. The world will change no matter what happens in the Great Hall tomorrow. I don't have the time to analyze all the stupid questions plus the delaying tactics. That will be part of the agenda tomorrow afternoon especially by Mr Adams. He will try every trick in the book to try to derail this very special meeting. I think I'll play this by ear then see what happens.

'Óisin, Gia, do you know what a nightclub is?'

'No,' replies Gia,' please explain!'

'Well, it's kind of lively place, Lots of music and lots of people dancing and jumping about!'

Gia looks at Óisin, then looks at Leila, and says; 'I don't see any harm in going to a nightclub. Yes I think we would like to try it!'

'Good!' replies Leila. 'I think I'll go and see Delia, maybe she might like to come with us.' Leila materializes in Delia's room where she is watching television. She looks up, she is a bit startled and asks; 'Leila, what can I do for you?'

'Well, I was wondering if you would like to come with Gia, Óisin and myself to a night club. You don't have to. I'll understand. What do you think?'

'I don't know. I haven't been to a night club for a long time. Ok, what the hell, I might enjoy myself. Yes I'll come with you!'

'Good. When you are ready come to my suite then we shall go down to reception and ask about night clubs at the desk.'

Leila returns to her suite and relates to Gia that Delia is coming with them to the night club!

'That's nice,' answers Gia. 'We will have a very good time. Are you happy to come with us Óisin?'

'Yes,' replies Óisin. 'We won't get into trouble by going out to a nightclub?' 'Absolutely not,' replies Leila.

Gia enquires. 'What about Alfie?'

'My mum will keep an eye on him you know what I mean!'

Delia knocks on Leila's door she looks at Gia and says, 'That will be Delia I'll let her in.'

She goes to the door, opens it, Delia walks in and enquires,' I presume you are ready to go out to a night club!'

'Yes I'm ready to shimmy. I hope you are ready as well!'

'Yes we are, answers Leila, 'so let's go!'

Off they go out into the corridor to the lift. Leila presses the button and they wait for the lift to arrive. The door closes and they descend in the lift to the reception area, exit the lift, walk to reception, ring the bell and wait.

The receptionist arrives at the desk and apologizes. She looks at Leila and asks, 'Can I help you do you need something?'

Leila looks at her and says, 'We would like to hire a taxi please!'

'Certainly, miss, I'll phone for one, where would you like to go this evening?'

'We would like to go to a nightclub somewhere nice please!'

'If you could go and sit down over there,' as she points to some seating by the window, 'I will phone for a taxi for you!'

'Thank you,' replies Leila. She indicates to Delia, Gia and Óisin to follow her.

Gia quizzes Leila about this nightclub enquiring, 'Will we be safe there, will the people like us?'

'Don't you worry, we will be fine. Now let me ask you a question. Who is going to worry us, we'll have a great time!'

'Yes but we are Aliens on this planet and there could be trouble!'

'Listen, no one is going to bother us, if that were to happen I'll take care of it, you are happy with that information!'

'Yes,' replies Gia. 'If you say so I hope we are going the right thing!'

'We'll be fine!' Leila replies.

Gia asks, 'Can't we just teleport to wherever we want to go. Why are we going by taxi?'

Leila looks at Gia a little bemused and answers, 'I need to be normal now and again. It makes me feel good!'

The receptionist walks over to Leila. She informs her that their taxi is waiting at the front of the hotel. The four of them stand up and follow Leila out to the front of the hotel. The taxi driver gets out of his taxi, opens the back doors. The four of them are sitting comfortable inside. The driver sits in the driver's seat and asks, 'where would you like to go?'

'We, that is we four,' as she points to Delia, Gia and Oisin. We would like to go to a good night club in the city is that possible?'

'Yes, of course, let me take you to one of our best nightclubs!'

Leila looks at Gia, smiles and says; 'I can't wait to enjoy myself.'

Off the driver goes, Ten minutes later he stops outside The Emperor Nightclub.

Leila asks, 'How much do we owe you from the hotel to here?'

He looks around and says, 'Ten dollars please!'

Leila opens her purse, takes out ten dollars and hands it to the driver. 'Can we book you and your taxi for 3am please?'

'Yes, of course you can. I'll be here at 3am waiting for you!'

'Thank you very much.' She looks at him as he points to the nightclub. This is one of the best in New York?'

'Yes ma'am I think you will be very happy in there. It's very groovy, hip and posh!'

Leila alights from the cab and lets Delia, Gia and Óisin step out onto the footpath. They wave to the driver and walk to the entrance of the nightclub. Leila walks up to one of the bouncers and enquires. 'Can we go into this club? We are only here for one night?'

The bouncer looks at Leila and asks, 'Are you a member of this club?'

'No,' she replies.

'Well, you can't go in. Go away please.' He looks at her again with a smirk on his face. 'You can't go inside this club unless you are a member!'

'May I speak to the manager of the night club please?'

'Yes, of course you can, but it will make no difference unless you're a member you can't go in. However, I'll go and fetch the manager. You wait here!'

Ten minutes pass, the bouncer arrives back and the manager is with him. They walk over to Leila; the manager looks at Leila in a strange way, 'I watched you on television to day in the United Nations Building,' and starts laughing out loud. 'Well now what can I do for you four people?'

'Well we would like to go inside your nightclub. It was recommended by a taxi driver!'

'Are you a member here, young lady?'

'No, sir, I'm not a member here!'

'I'm not at liberty to allow you inside my club unless you're a member. I'm so sorry!'

Leila enquires, 'May I use your mobile phone please?

'No you may not,' he retorts!'

'His mobile rings he takes it from his pocket and asks,

Whom am I talking to? He looks around at Leila!

'You're talking to the President of the USA. Please hand the phone to Leila.'

The manager looks perplexed and worried but he hands the phone to Leila and says, 'The President of the USA would like to talk to you!'

Leila takes the phone from him and says, 'Good evening we speak again, Mr President. I wonder if you might be able to help me?'

'What can I do for the most powerful person on this planet?'

'Well, Mr President, I don't want to prove anything to the manager of this nightclub. I could, but I just want a quiet evening. Can you help please?'

'Hand the phone back to the manager I'll have a word with him!'

'Thank you, Mr President, good bye for now. See you tomorrow!'

Leila hands the phone back to the manager. He is just standing there with the phone up to his ear, eyes wide open saying, 'Yes sir, yes sir, right away sir, I'll do that right now, sir.

He takes the phone from his ear, looks at Leila, 'Please come with me!'

The bouncer places his hand on Leila's shoulder as if to stop her from entering the club. In less than a second, he is pinned against the front of the club as if something or someone is holding him there and he can't release himself. He is a very big man about six four, eighteen stone and looks very menacing. He has an attitude problem and is quite rude. Leila doesn't need to get involved. However, a little lesson would not go amiss with this bully.

Leila goes over to him, looks at him says, 'Don't you ever again try and stop me from entering this club I'm only here to enjoy myself. Consider yourself very fortunate,' and she walks away with the manager into the night club. Inside the manager beckons the four of them to follow him. He finds a special table and indicates to them to sit down.'

'Now I've been told that whatever is your pleasure I'm to give it to you and it's all on the house!'

'In that case, we'll have a couple of bottles of your best Champagne. Don't try and fob us off with cheap rubbish because I'll know,' answers Leila.

Outside the club the club bouncer drops to the ground and feels quite embarrassed which is not nice in front of the people outside the club waiting to go inside and of course everyone is tittering and giggling at him. He stands up, brushes himself down and says to one of the other security people, 'I'll be back in a few minutes look after the door.' He proceeds to walk inside the club, has a good look around until his eyes get accustomed to the lights, then focuses his eyes until he finds Leila and her three friends sitting at a table and thinks to himself. Now, young lady we'll see what you're made of. He walks past some dancing people brushing them aside until he arrives at Leila's table. He stops in front of her and says; 'Who do you think you are? The Queen of England, we have an issue to settle?'

She looks up and says hello, 'Nice to see you again, Mr Bouncer. You don't have to apologize to me because you looked like an idiot. That was your own fault, you shouldn't be so aggressive. What can I do to keep you happy?'

'I want satisfaction, you are going to apologize to me now!'

'I don't think so,' Leila answers. However, you could do a strip dance for us?'

He looks at her and says, 'you must be joking I'm not a strip artist. I think you should get on the floor and you do a strip dance for me right now!'

Suddenly he walks out on to the dance floor where he starts to dance to the music. He then starts to strip, he tries to stop himself but he is unable. He is swinging his coat above his head moving in gyrating circles around the dance floor. He is keeping time to the music with the lower part of his body. The people leave the dance floor and watch in amazement thinking, this must be a new kind entertainment supplied by the club. Off comes his shirt, he throws it across the floor, then drops his trousers. The dancers are going wild shouting, 'Get them off, off, off.' He is lost in a pool of fantasy, he can't stop himself. He is just about to drop his boxer shorts when the manager and two of the bouncers rush over to try and stop him but he is having none of it. He is determined to keep stripping his clothes off.'

Leila decides to stop him, 'Suddenly he stops stripping, looks around and everyone is shouting, 'Get them off, off, off!' 'He is beside himself with embarrassment; he looks around the dance floor. He can't quite figure out why he has removed most of his clothes. He doesn't know why he has made a fool of himself, so he gathers up his clothes and runs off the dancing floor, totally confused and embarrassed.

Gia looks at Óisin, then at Leila and Delia. She enquires, 'what was all that about? Is that man crazy, I don't understand him, what was he doing?'

'No, he is not crazy. I made him do that dancing. I wanted to embarrass him and cut him down to size!' replies Leila.

'Yes but what was he doing?' Gia asks.

'Well he was going to take all his clothes off!' Leila replies.

'Why would he want to take all his clothes off?' enquires Óisin.

'Well, usually it's a very provocative dance by young ladies that make a living out of that kind of dancing.' Leila replies. 'On your planet there must be places where young men go to see young ladies stripping all their clothes off!'

'Well I have never been to any clubs on my planet that cater for that kind of dancing. Have you been to any clubs on our planet like that Óisin?'

He looks a bit embarrassed, 'Well there are clubs like that on our planet but I have never been to one. Some of my friends have been and they did try and entice me to go there, but I declined the invitation. It's not my kind of club or entertainment!'

The manager and the two bouncers follow the dancing bouncer. The manager guides him into his office asking, 'what were you doing on the dance floor, have you gone mad?'

'I don't know sir; I just had this urge to strip. I don't know why, I just wanted to do it!'

'Well you're suspended until further notice. We can't have bouncers strip dancing in this club. This is not a strip club. This is a very up market club. You are supposed to be watching the door, not strip dancing in the club. I'm disgusted and appalled at your wayward behaviour. You haven't heard the last of this,' replies the manager. 'I think that you might as well go home until tomorrow I'll see you in my office at 2pm in the afternoon. You can go now!'

He is disgusted with the manager he is very agitated and he thinks I'm not going home just yet. I'll wait until the troublemaker comes out of the club whenever she decides to leave. He goes around to the side of the club and stands there. Each minute he stands there, he is getting wilder and wilder. He is working himself into a fury but he doesn't care. He is so fired up for a fight and she is going to apologize, one way or another.

Inside the club Leila has coerced Delia, Gia and Óisin on to the floor where she gives them a quick lesson about dancing and jumping about. The four of them are enjoying this mad dancing. After the music stops Gia asks, 'Is that it,' then? What do we do next?'

Leila looks at her and answers. There will be more dancing a bit later. 'They decide to return to their table and placed on their table, there are two bottles of Champagne and four glasses. Leila decides to pour the Champagne into the glasses saying, 'this is for the four of us I hope we have long lives and lots of fun in-between!'

'Yes I'll drink to that!' answers Gia.

The four of them raise their glasses together and touch in the middle shouting, 'Here's to us.' They replace the glasses back on the table and sit down. Leila enquires,

Gia and Óisin, are you enjoying yourselves what do you think of this night club?'

'Well it's very different from our home planet but we are enjoying ourselves tremendously, very enjoyable!'

Delia stands up and says, 'I'm going to the ladies room I'll be back shortly,' and off she goes.

The music starts up again, Gia jumps up saying, 'Come on then let's do this dancing again,' as she pulls Leila and Óisin onto the floor again! Leila senses Delia is in trouble. She looks at Gia and Óisin and says, 'Delia is in some kind of trouble I need to go to her and help her I'll be back shortly. You carry on dancing, please, don't worry I'll be fine.' In an instant she arrives in the women's toilets, where she finds Delia surrounded by five young women shouting at her asking, 'Are you here from England? We don't like the British we're going to make an example of you.'

Leila places Delia in a shield unbeknown to the young ladies and sends a telepathic message to Delia, *I'm here don't worry you are safe. I've placed you in a shield leave the rest to me!'*

'Now ladies what are you going to do to my friend?' enquires Leila.

'We are going to beat her up, and if you interfere you'll get the same, so clear off!' Leila locks the door, takes each girl one by one, she places their heads into hand basins, 'Turns the taps on with the ladies heads under them. She doesn't touch them. They are now very wet and screaming their heads off but they can't get out from under the taps. Delia is laughing her head off at these stupid ladies because they don't understand what is happening to them. Leila decides to leave. She unlocks the door and says, 'I think we should go back to Gia and Óisin and carry on dancing. Come on Delia!'

Delia asks, 'What about these ladies under the taps?

What are you going to do with them?'

'Well, I think that they need cooling down. They are a bit hot under the collar. I think I'll leave them to cool down for a while!'

Back inside the club Delia and Leila walk over to Gia and Óisin and join them on the dance floor. Gia looks at Leila and she asks, 'Is everything alright with Delia?'

'Yes everything is fine,' then Delia bursts out laughing. Óisin looks at her and asks; 'What's the matter with her. What is so funny Delia?' She can't stop laughing. Then Leila has a fit of laughing as well.

Gia looks perplexed and says; 'I think we should sit down at our table. Then the two of you can tell me why you are laughing, what is so funny?' She takes Delia by the hand, leads her off the dance floor to their table and Leila follows her.

'Alright tell me what happened in the ladies room. I'm intrigued?'

Delia looks at Gia and answers, 'Well I was touching up my make up when some young ladies walked into the ladies room and started to give me verbal. Gia asks, 'What is verbal?'

'They were looking for a fight.' Delia answers.

Then they surrounded me and asked me if I came from England. I thought that they were just being friendly. I said, yes I'm from England, and then they said they were going to beat me up. That was when Leila arrived inside the woman's toilets and everything else is a blur. The last thing I remember was the five, at least I think it was five, women, started to place their heads under the taps. Then the taps turned themselves on. The water was flowing over their heads in the sinks, it was amazing!'

'Leila, you didn't hurt them did you?' enquires Gia.

'No, I didn't hurt them, but I left them cooling down.

However, I have released them now from under the taps!'

Delia starts laughing again saying, 'It was ever so funny!' she looks at Leila.

Leila doesn't say a word just looks up to the ceiling and has a little giggle under her breath. She looks at Gia,

Come on we're enjoying ourselves!'

The four of them are having a whale of a time drinking and dancing. Óisin and Gia are getting very merry on the Champagne.

Leila is a bit worried, so she looks at her watch. The time is three in the morning. She looks at Gia and says; 'I think we should vacate this night club, when this dance is finished!'

Gia looks at Leila and answers, 'But we're having such a good time. This is the first time I've been clubbing on this world or any Planet!'

'We do have a very big day in about twelve hours from now. We will need sleep and to keep our wits about us and anyway the taxi will be waiting for us outside the club. Right, then let's gather our things and walk out to the front of the club!'

'Ok,' Gia answers. I'm sorry I know today is going to be a very big day in all of our lives. We came to stabilize your world. That has to be our first priority!'

The four of them leave their table Gia and Óisin are falling all over the place they are very tipsy from the Champagne. Leila and Delia are trying to hold them up. They walk to the front of the club. One of the bouncers opens the door and says, 'Good night, ladies, please come again!'

Leila and Gia look at him and have a little giggle as they walk out into the street.

Leila senses that something is about to happen, so instinctively she places a shield around the four of them. Out of the side of her vision she notices the bouncer with the dancing feet and thinks. I hope that he is not going to make a fool of himself again. The bouncer rushes out from the side of the club shouting. 'I'll have my revenge now and you will apologize to me for all the trouble you caused me inside the club or you will be sorry!'

Leila stops him in his tracks, levitates him five feet into the air then draws him very slowly towards her. She drops him to the ground and enquires, 'Have you a problem with me, why are you so angry, and riled up?'

He looks amazed, baffled and bewildered. He is shaking all over. He is sweating   profusely.
Leila looks at him and enquires, 'Have you some kind of death wish, or are you just a stupid person? I would like to know, I don't want to hurt you.'

He is unable to speak, not a sound emanates from his mouth. His eyes are wide open, he doesn't even blink.

Leila looks at him and says, 'I'm going to walk away now and if you pursue me in any way again I will hurt you, do you understand, sir?'

He nods his head, still looking at Leila, not understanding what she has done to him! By now a crowd has formed in a circle around Leila and the bouncer.

A girl of about eighteen breaks the circle, walks to Leila and says, 'Good for you, he is a right bastard. It's time he had his bullying cut down to size. He is always pushing his weight around. I like you, you're special I can see that,' as she looks Leila in the eye.

Leila looks at her and telecommunicates with her.

'Yes, I'm special, it's been nice talking to you, 'Watch your television this afternoon at three, you'll see something very special good bye!' The girl looks confused as she looks at Leila. 'You were talking to me in my mind, how are to do that? I don't understand.'

The crowd are clapping profusely and shouting. 'Down with the bullying, down with the bullying!'

The manager arrives at the front of the club and sees the bouncer who he presumes has started being abusive again. He walks over to him and says, 'I told you to go home hours ago. Why are you still outside the club you have no business here. I think it's better for this club and for you to find alternative employment away from this club. You've been nothing but trouble since you arrived here. If you do not leave the front of the club now I'll call the police!'

The bouncer throws his hands up in the air saying, 'Ok I'm gone from here now,' as he turns and he reluctantly walks away.

'Come on, Gia, Óisin and Delia, we're out of here now!' Across the road Leila's taxi driver is watching the fracas outside the club but doesn't really understand what has happened but he is quite amused when he sees it's the four people he is picking up.

Leila looks up and sees the taxi driver standing up against his taxi.

'Come on, Gia, Óisin and Delia our taxi driver is waiting for us shall we go please!' The four of them walk across the street, the taxi driver opens the back door of the taxi and enquires, 'What was that fracas going on outside the club?'

'That was nothing; replies Leila. 'One of the bouncers was pushing his luck. The four of them enter the taxi. The driver sits in the driver's seat, and heads for the hotel.

The driver looks in his mirror and enquires; 'I hope you had a nice time in that club? It's one of the better clubs in New York.'

'Yes, we had a great time it's a very nice club thank you for taking us there!' replies Leila.

Gia looks at Óisin then at Leila and Delia enquires, 'Will that bouncer be alright, I mean he looked very distressed?'

Leila replies, 'He'll be fine. He was over the top and I wasn't going to let him stop us from enjoying ourselves, come hell or high water. What about you, Gia, did you enjoy yourself?'

'Yes I did enjoy myself very much. That was the most enjoyable time I've ever had!'

'What about you, Óisin, did you have a good time?'

'Yes of course I did, it was an experience I'll never forget. What a crazy world you live in. We will have to do it again sometime in the future!'

'Delia, did you enjoy yourself?'

'Yes I had a great time, the best I've had for a long time!'

The taxi arrives at the hotel Leila asks, 'Driver how much do we owe you?'

'Fifteen dollars please, it's fifty percent after twelve at night!'

'That's fine,' replies Leila. She hands him twenty dollars and says. 'Keep the change. Thank you very much for looking after us!'

The four of them alight from the taxi. They walk into the hotel past reception carry on to the lifts. Leila presses the button. The doors open, they walk inside press the button for the VIP suites. When the doors open they alight from the lift. 'Good night, Delia I'll see you in the morning!'

'Now, Gia, you and Óisin, you are familiar with our sleeping arrangements? I mean you do know what to do, so good night then I'll see you in the morning?'

'Yes we know what to do,' as they smile at Leila. 'Ok then we'll go to our room and get ready for bed. We'll see you in the morning. Good night to you as they walk down the corridor to their suite.

Leila places her electronic key in the door. It opens, she goes into her suite, flops down on her bed, says to herself. What a night, and falls asleep.

Chapter 124

Leila receives a telecommunication from her mum, *'Come quickly Alfie is dead!'* She wakes up and sits up in the bed, gathers her thoughts. She thinks to herself, 'What is mum talking about? In one tenth of a second, she is in her mum's suite asking, what is wrong. Ciera is distraught; she is crying uncontrollably she is unable to talk. Dad is holding her in case she faints. Then she notices that there are soldiers with AK47's in the room. She looks around trying to focus her mind on what is going on. 'Where is Alfie?'

Her dad points to the bedroom, she walks into Alfie's bedroom. He is laid on the bed. She walks over to him, his eyes are closed and not a movement of his body is apparent. The bullet-ridden body of Alfie is lifeless, and his blood is everywhere. For the first time in Leila's life, she starts to cry out hysterically, shouting, who did this? Someone is going to pay.'

Her dad arrives into the room, takes her into his arms and says, 'The soldiers burst into the suite about ten minutes past, shouting and screaming. Everyone get down on the floor now. Alfie must have been woken by the noise. He came running into the sitting room, the soldiers started to fire their AK47's. Bullets were flying everywhere. Unfortunately Alfie was mowed down. He must have died instantly. He was already dead when I picked him up off the floor, so I placed him on his bed. He looked so peaceful with a lovely smile on his face. It brought tears to my eyes! I couldn't believe my eyes, Alfie was dead, and I didn't know why. What are we going to do, Leila?'

Ciera rushes into the bedroom shouting, 'Leila, this is your entire fault, we should never have left England, we should have stayed at home.' Ciera is beside herself with grief and she is having great difficulty in breathing. Leila walks over to her, places her hand on her shoulder and says, 'Mum I will fix this, please listen to me. I will bring Alfie back from the dead'

Ciera looks at Leila and says, 'That's impossible, I do not believe you, you are not God.'

Leila looks at her dad and says, 'I have something very important to do, dad will you please look after mum. She walks out into the sitting room. By now Gia and Óisin have entered the room asking, 'What has happened here?' Leila looks at Gia, 'They as she points at the Spec/Ops, 'they have killed Alfie.'

'Oisin asks, 'Who are these people as he points to the captain and his soldiers. 'This lot of idiots with AK47's burst into this suite and shot Alfie,' replies Leila.

Gia is dismayed and recoils in horror at what Leila has said, as does Óisin. Leila places a shield around the suite.

What are you soldiers doing here in this room, I need to know?'

Their captain steps forward, a tall man about six feet tall, with short dark hair. 'We are Spec/Ops under strict orders to capture you and take you into custody, so please do not make my job any harder than it is. I am so sorry that the little boy is dead. He came running into this room. What were we to do? We are trained to fire first, and then ask questions afterwards. Now, will you please place your hands on top of your head, we would like to take you back to our headquarters for interrogation?'

Leila replies, 'I do not think so. I have better things to do now. Incidentally are you a married man?'

'Yes I am, why?' he replies.

Leila looks at him and says, 'Behold your family.' The captain's family are standing in front of him, he recoils in horror. His wife is standing with their two children, a tall woman blond hair, good looking, and by her side are a boy, he is about seven years old and a girl about five years old. She is in her nightdress and the two children are in their pyjamas. She looks around and says to her husband, 'what is going on here, where are we, how did we come here?'

The captain looks at his wife and says, 'I don't know' as he throws his hands in the air. He is now in a quandary and perplexed. He has never faced a situation like this in his military life.

Leila looks at him and says, 'Captain, my brother is dead and I'm going to ask you which one of your children is going to die by my hand?'

'George what is she talking about, why is she saying that one of our children is going to die?'

'Do not worry dear. He looks at Leila and enquires, 'How are you going to kill one of our children, you do not have a gun, and we have you covered. He looks at his men and says; if she moves shoot her on the spot.'

Leila answers,

'I don't need a gun as she looks at the boy. He keels over and falls on the floor. Leila says, 'George, go and take his pulse and see if he is alive!'

He walks to his son, leans over him, listens to his breathing, takes his pulse, looks up at his wife and says, 'He is dead!'

His wife starts running around the room, hands waving in the air shouting, 'How can he be dead? How did that happen?'

'I don't know,' as he looks at Leila and asks, 'how did that happen?'

'I can take the lives of the rest of your family if I wish!' She then places a shield around her family including Gia and Óisin.

'I don't think so. 'Who do you think you are?' He shouts, 'Shoot her!'

The soldiers put the rifles to their shoulders release the safety catches, press the triggers on their AK 47's and bullets fly out of their AK47's and stop about two inches from Leila's body. She walks to one side, leaves the bullets suspended in space, then proceeds to George, looks him in the eye, and says, 'Were you going to shoot everyone in this room?'

'I don't know, it was irrational behaviour. I am very fearful for my family. Please don't kill them. I'm sorry about the boy. I have to obey orders!'

Chapter 125

'Well you should be,' as she waves her hand and all the soldiers are transfixed they are unable to move. She takes all the AK47's from them without moving a muscle, dismantles them without placing a hand on them. The AK47's fall to the floor in a mangled mess, she then walks over to the suspended bullets in the air. She takes one of them, waves her hand and it travels to one inch in front of his wife as if fired by a gun. She faints!

'George, I could have let that bullet kill your wife if I so wished, I need your undivided attention now.'

He is quivering all over his body, and the perspiration is beginning to form on his forehead, he is like a frightened animal cowering on the floor. 'I want to know who sent you here to arrest me and to kill my brother.' He is in a state of panic and having difficulty breathing so she places her hand on his shoulder and says, 'you will be alright now! Mr Dankin the head of the CIA sent you to place me under arrest, am I right George?' He looks at her and nods his head and starts to cry asking, 'Am I going to die?'

'No George I am not going to kill you, I was just showing you how powerful I am. You can go now. Take your family and your little army of soldiers with you.'

'He looks at her and asks, 'What about my son?'

Leila walks back to the suspended bullets, drops them one by one on top of the dismantled guns. Now she turns around walks back to where George is standing looks him straight in the eye and says, 'You can take your son with you if you wish and the scrap metal on the floor.'

George's wife is quite hysterical; she is distraught about the whole situation. She cannot get her mind around what is happening. She walks over to Leila and asks, 'Did you kill my son?'

'Ask your husband, He had my brother killed so, an eye for an eye.'

She makes a grab for Leila but there is no substance her hands go through Leila's body. She asks, 'What are you?
Who are you?'

Leila just looks at her. She then looks at George, 'Take your wife and daughter home. I am sorry about your son, but you can take him home as well. Please leave now, take the worthless AK47's and your personal people with you and leave us.'

Gia runs over to Leila asking, 'What are you going to do about this predicament? This is not within our remit. Gia is in a panic saying, 'When we return to our planet, we will be in big trouble and we will be reprimanded for letting you have the Bio/Dna technology. We will be in very serious trouble and I am not looking forward to that. This was not supposed to happen. Everything was going so well, now it is all a gigantic problem for Óisin and me.'

Óisin throws his hands up in the air saying, 'I don't know what we are going to do, I don't think we can go back to our planet because we will certainly go to prison for a very long time!'

Leila looks at the family and then at Gia and Óisin saying, 'Do not worry, this is just a temporary hiccup, I will fix everything I promise. I should have anticipated that we would not get away without something happening to us. That is what you get for trusting people. I will be more security wise in the future.' *Leila sends a telecommunication to George telling him to place his son on the ground and watch what happens. He thinks that he is hearing things but he will try anything if it helps to bring his son back. He places him on the ground and as if by magic, the little boy sits up.* His mum runs over, bends down, gives him a very big cuddle, looks at him touches him on his head and shoulders asking, 'Are you alright?'

'Yes mum, I'm fine why?' He looks very puzzled.

George walks over, takes his son by the hand and helps him stand up. Now he knows exactly what has happened, it all falls into place. That young lady in the suite has the power over life and death and he feels very humbled. 'Come on, everyone, I think we should return to the suite and thank the young girl for giving us back our son.'

His wife looks at him and says, 'What are you talking about George?'

Trust me please. It will all be explained later, I know what to do now.'

Leila looks at the family and says, 'Incidentally the little boy is fine now I have revived him. I just placed him in a deep comatose sleep.' Leila goes to her mum takes her by the hand and says, 'Mum please believe me, I will bring Alfie back to life very shortly!'

Everyone is looking at each other and wondering how Leila is going to do that, especially Gia and Óisin. Gia walks to the side of Leila and asks, 'What are you going to do about Alfie?' Leila looks at Gia then replies, 'I will do something that will astound you and Óisin, and of course my family.'

Chapter 126

There is a knock on the door everyone look at each other, Leila walks over to the door opens it, and surprise, surprise, the little boy is standing in front of Leila, with the rest of his family are standing behind him. Now that is something to behold. Leila's family are astonished at this miraculous transformation in front of them. Leila says, 'Please, come in, my family are happy for you.' She looks at the little boy and asks, 'Are you feeling alright?'

He looks at Leila and he is wondering what she is talking about.

Ciera walks over, kneels down in front of the little boy, gives him a big hug and says, 'I'm glad you are ok.' Both families hug each other and console each other. Then Ciera looks at Leila and asks, 'What about Alfie?'

'Mum, please don't worry about Alfie.' Leila beckons George to her side and says, 'I would like you to be in the Great Hall this afternoon to tell all the leaders what happened here in this hotel this morning at four, that's if you are happy that you are a family again. Will you be my guest this afternoon?' She places this thought into George's mind so that he will remember.

'Yes of course I will. I'm more than happy to help. That is the least I can do for you. I will be in the Great Hall and give an account of everything my family has witnessed in this hotel. We are truly grateful and appreciative to you for giving us our son back,' as he gives Leila a very big hug.

'Now I must ask you to leave us. I have something very important to do,' as she guides George and his family to the door. She opens the door, gives each one a big hug as they go by, then she closes the door behind them. The anticipation of the family in the room is electric. What is Leila going to do about Alfie?

Chapter 127

Leila looks at everyone in the room gives a little smile. 'What I'm going to do now will surprise each one of you but I don't want you to worry or be frightened. Dad, could you tell me approximately the time the soldiers broke into this room, it does not have to be exactly right, do you understand dad?' 'It was about, 4.30am.' Dad replies.

'Fine, I'm going to go back in time to just before 4.30am!' Gia and Óisin look at each other then look at Leila and ask; 'What do you mean Leila?'

'Gia, I'm going astound you. I'm going to turn back the time line, just before the soldiers entered this room. Please be quiet I need to concentrate!'

Nothing is happening. Everyone is looking around, wondering what Leila is talking about, but unable to comprehend the outcome. The whole family plus Gia and Óisin, have now transported to an orbit outside the Earth. Leila has placed a very special Shield around the family including Gia and Óisin. Everything is going anticlockwise; at least everyone thinks it is. They are travelling so fast that it looks as if they are actually not moving at all. Everyone is amazed at what they see in front of them; Gia and Óisin cannot understand how Leila is able to turn time back without altering the time line but it is happening right before their eyes. The World is not moving anticlockwise. Leila the family, Gia and Óisin are moving so fast they think that the world is moving, but it isn't. Leila puts up her hand and the family, Gia and Óisin stop going around the World anticlockwise. In less than a second, Leila has taken everyone out of orbit back to the hotel room. Then something very strange happens. Before their eyes, Alfie walks out of his bedroom, there isn't a mark on him, no bullets holes in his body, no blood anywhere on his body.

He looks at everyone, and asks; 'Why is everyone here in this room?'

Ciera rushes over, she picks him up, hugs him very passionately. She is crying, 'I can't believe that he is alive.' She looks around at Leila, and she now knows that her daughter has the power over life, and death. Alfie's dad and everyone in the room rush to give Alfie a hug and a kiss, including Gia and Óisin. Alfie is flabbergasted at all this sudden interest in him, but he doesn't know why. He doesn't care; he likes what is happening to him anyway, so he keeps his mouth shut.

Gia and Óisin break away. They look at Leila and beckon to her to follow them to one side. Gia takes Leila's hand and asks; 'What is going on here Leila?'

She looks at Gia and says, I'm able to turn time back!'

'That's impossible! Even our scientists are unable to do that,' replies Óisin. 'Not any more. I can turn time back as and when I want!' Leila answers.

Gia looks at Leila in wonderment and starts to cry. She looks at Leila and says, the technology I have instilled in your mind is not supposed to turn back time, How do you account for that?'

'Gia, I've told you the technology upgrades itself. I'm light years ahead of your technology now. I have passed into a more advanced technology what you and I call BIO/DNA. It is infinite. 'There is nothing in the Universe with my power. It frightens me, but I am in total control of all aspects of this technology, please don't worry. I must go to my mum now but we will talk about your technology again!'

She turns around, walks to her mum takes her in her arms and says; 'I told you I would bring Alfie back to life, he is here now with not a mark on him, but he doesn't know anything about what happened with the soldiers. I needed to leave him here when we were in orbit. He had to stay in the hotel where he was lifeless. That way I was able to restore him back to life. It's as if it never happened. Please don't tell him anything. He doesn't need to know. It's for the best!' Leila looks around saying, 'Everyone please walk to the middle of the room!' Everyone does as Leila asks. Then she places a shield around everyone in the room.

Chapter 128

The door bursts open for the second time this morning. The soldiers run in shouting, 'Everyone stand perfectly still and place your hands in the air.'

The captain walks into the room asking; 'Who is the woman called Leila? Please step forward?'

Leila steps forward, looks the captain in the eye. She answers,' I'm Leila, 'what do you want from me?'

The captain looks at her and says; 'I'm placing you under arrest please place your hands in front of you, I have been told to take you into custody. Please don't give me any trouble I'm just doing my job!'

Leila looks around has a telepathic communication with all the relevant people in the room telling them not to interfere. *I need to go now but I'll return shortly'* She turns to the captain saying, 'I'm ready. So if you don't mind can we go now?' Leila walks to the door the soldiers walk behind her. The captain closes the door behind him. The family are a bit worried for her. Gia and Óisin know that there is no cause for concern for anyone in the room. Leila is now in control of her destiny. It hits their minds that Leila is more than likely the most powerful being in the Universe and Galaxy.

Chapter 129

The soldiers and the captain escort Leila down the corridor and into the lift. The captain presses the button for the ground floor. Then they wait until the lift stops. The lift door opens, Leila walks out the front entrance of this hotel with the soldiers around her. A car is waiting at the front of the hotel, the captain goes to the car, opens the back door. Then he indicates to Leila to sit inside the car, which she duly does. Two soldiers sit one on each side of Leila. The captain sits in the passenger seat, and then he looks back at Leila and says, I'm so sorry I have placed you under arrest. Please forgive me. I don't know why I'm telling you this but something in my mind is telling me we have met before?'

Leila knows, but she is not going to enlighten him, not yet anyway. She looks at the captain and asks; 'Captain, can I ask where I'm being taken to?' She already knows, and she knows exactly where she is being taken to.

'Sorry I'm not allowed to discuss that with you. My explicit orders are to place you under arrest then return to base, where you will be interrogated!'

'Can I ask where those orders have come from?'

'No, I have no other information to give you, so please just keep your questions to yourself!'

Half an hour later the car stops in front of a pair of big black security gates. The gates open, the car drives in and follows the road until it arrives at the back of a great building. This is an awesome looking place, a very big modern building where a lot of security lighting automatically switches itself on. Everywhere soldiers are walking about the place. Leila thinks to herself. 'I wonder who lives here,' with a smile on her face.

The captain jumps out of the front seat of the car. He walks around to Leila's door. He opens it and says, 'Please step out of the car and don't move!' He looks at the two soldiers then tells them to escort Leila inside the building.' Inside this building, she has a soldier on each side of her and the Captain behind. The four of them walk down a long corridor to a lift. The lift door opens. The two soldiers Leila and the captain walk inside the lift. He presses a button and the lift goes down. It takes about three minutes before it reaches the bottom of the shaft. This shaft is one hundred metres underground. The door opens and standing in front of Leila is Mr Dankin the head of the CIA. What a surprise. She knows exactly what he wants, so she will play along with him.

'Leila looks at him then pretends that she does not know him. She is well aware of his status but she is not about to give away any of her little secrets, at least not yet any way.

'Ah you must be Leila I have heard a lot about you, welcome to my secret underground. You will spend a lot of time here in confinement until we have gleaned all the information we need from your mind. Now please follow me!'

Chapter 130

Leila looks around the hallway, when one of the soldiers pushes her in the back saying; 'Move yourself, now follow Mr Dankin. He will take you to where you'll be staying for a very long time.'

Leila thinks, 'Well we will see about that. Maybe I can get some sleep, if I do as the soldier has asked.' She follows him. He stops in front of a metal door which is one metre thick, ten metres wide, by ten metres high, Mr Dankin takes a smart key from his pocket presses one of the buttons then the door opens very slowly. That means when the metal door is closed the timer is set, and it's not possible to open it without a smart card. She follows Mr Dankin to the other side and yet another metal door, this door opens, then they walk through to the other side. He stops in front of yet another metal door, he opens it, then indicates to Leila to go inside she looks at him. She does walk into the room in front of him. Inside there is a very large table with four chairs, no windows, no light switches. Leila has noticed that there are six video cameras placed strategically around the room. He follows her inside where he indicates her to sit on one of the chairs. He pulls up one of the chairs and sits at the table facing Leila.

He looks at her, not knowing what to say, 'Leila, normally I never interrogate people but you are different. I'm not a vicious person. I have a job to do for my President I'll find out who you are, who you are working for, and by that I mean what world government. We can do this the hard way or the easy way. That choice is yours to make. I do hope you take the easy way. You will remain in this building until I'm satisfied that the information you give me is true. I'm going to leave you now. Incidentally there is no way out of here, only the way you came in. There is no chance of anyone rescuing you. Your family, I'll take care of them, don't you worry one little bit!'

Leila looks at him and smiles, He doesn't like that, so he goes to hit her but he doesn't carry it through, his right hand fist stops about two inches in front of Leila's face. He pulls back saying; 'That would be too easy I have better ways of making you talk.' He turns, walks to the door, looks around at Leila, opens the door and walks out into the corridor. He walks twenty paces down the corridor, walks into another large room where there are rows and rows of televisions mounted on the walls, watching Leila. He walks over to one of the operators and asks; 'What is she doing?'

'Nothing sir. She is just sitting there She doesn't look worried sir!'

'She will by the time I have finished with her. You just keep an eye on her at all times. If anything happens, call me, I'm going to get a coffee, would you like one?'

'No, sir, it's not allowed in this room!'

He decides to vacate the room to go and have a coffee, and then he returns to his office. Back in his office he sits behind his desk, he picks the phone up dials a number. It's answered. He inquires, 'Is that you doctor?'

'Mr Dankin, yes it is, is that you sir?'

'Yes, doctor, it is, can you come to my office right now please? I'll be requiring your assistance very soon.'

'Yes, sir, I'll come right away!'

'Thank you, doctor. See you shortly!'

Five minutes pass and the doctor is knocking on Mr Dankin's door.

'The door is open. Come in doctor.' He pushes the door open, walks into Mr Dankin's office and sits down in front of the head of the CIA. Mr Dankin leans back in his leather chair and looks at the doctor.

'Now, doctor, I have a very special job for you and it will need a lot of discretion and tact. We have a young woman just down the corridor. I think she is a bit of an enigma, and mysterious. We don't know anything about her. I'm going to hand her over to you. I want to know what she is doing in this country and I need this information before the President goes to the United Nations Building this afternoon. I don't want any excuse, all I want is a result?'

'No worry, sir, I'll have all the information you'll need when you meet the President. This is an easy job. I could do this with my eyes closed!'

'You can go now, doctor. Don't forget I need this information as soon as possible!'

The doctor leaves Mr Dankin's office, walks back to his surgery, and goes to one of his cabinets, picks out two phials with some kind of substance inside. He places them in his case, he checks that he has two hypodermics injection syringes, places them in his case then closes the case. He picks up the phone and dials security. When the phone is answered, at the other end he says; 'This is the doctor. I need two security men at my office in two minutes?'

Then he sits down and waits. The security men arrive and they are blowing quite hard as if they ran all the way to the doctor's office. They stop at his door and knock. The doctor gets up from his chair, picks up his case, walks to the door opens it and walks out. He looks at the security men and says, 'Follow me; we have a job to do for the President!'

Chapter 131

Leila has made communication with her mum telling her that she is a prisoner somewhere in a government building, but it's not a problem. 'I need to find out what this is all about, Well I do know, so I'm going to play along with their little game. See you soon.'

Leila's door opens in walks the doctor, a tall man going bald with reading glasses perched on his nose. The two security men follow him inside. 'They are looking a bit perturbed, wondering why the doctor needs them. He looks at them and says, 'Gentlemen, secure this young woman to her chair please!'

They go round to the back of Leila, then they place her hands behind her back, they then place her hands into two leather straps making sure that they are restraining her for security reasons. The doctor places his case on the table, 'Then he opens it, facing away from Leila. He removes one of the hypodermic syringes and one phial from the case. He places the two of them on the table looks at Leila and says; 'The solution in this phial,' he points to it, 'will not hurt you. It will make you relax and feel good, so please don't struggle, all we want from you is information.' The doctor picks up the phial and the hypodermic syringe pushes the syringe into the phial pushes the plunger and withdraws the syringe with the fluid inside from the phial. Then he walks over to Leila, looks her in the eye and says, 'I'm so sorry but I need to give you an injection so that we can interrogate you!

Leila asks, 'What do you want to know about me?'

'Well, I've been told that you have very special powers and the President would like to know who you are working for!'

'I don't think I can give you any more information, but if you were to be in the Great Hall this afternoon everything will be explained!'

'But I need all the information now, that is, if you don't mind please?'

'Well I do mind, so if you would be so kind as to allow me to leave, I would be very grateful!'

The doctor lunges at Leila and tries to pierce her arm with the hypodermic needle'

However, she has anticipated his move and places a shield around her body. The doctor tries again to penetrate her arm, only to find that the needle breaks into several pieces. The doctor is flabbergasted. He looks at the needle then at Leila and steps back in astonishment saying, 'I think that was a bad needle. I'll try again!' He walks to his case there he picks up another hypodermic needle and another phial pushes the needle into the phial, again and with draws the hypodermic needle with the fluid inside, turns around and Leila is standing in front of him. He staggers back in astonishment thinking to himself, 'How did she free herself from the chair, she was secured?'

Then all the lights and the cameras stop working. The room is now in total darkness, its panic stations. The doctor and the security men are unconscious on the floor. Leila is now in Mr Dankin's office. The lights turn on. Leila is sitting in a chair in front on Mr Dankin. He jumps up, runs to the door but he is unable to open it.

Leila looks at him and asks; 'Where do you think you are going?' She levitates him back to his chair. She sits him in it. He picks up his phone and tries to phone security. Nothing happens so he places it back on its base.

'Now, Mr Dankin, you've been a naughty boy abducting me, not you personally, and then threatening my family with violence. How dare you think you could hold me in this place? Do you think for one moment that you could keep me in this building against my will? It is never going to happen. There is no building in this world able to hold me. Now, sir, there are ten security men outside your door. I'm going to let them in you keep your mouth closed.'

The door opens, the security men run in with their AK 47's rifles at the ready, safety catches off asking, 'Are you ok, Mr Dankin?'

Chapter 132

He looks at Leila, then at the security men and answers, 'Yes I'm fine I'm a bit shaken!'

Leila looks at him. She tells him to move away from his desk to the other side of the room. He duly obeys her. She stands in front of his desk then she looks at Mr Dankin and says, 'Mr Dankin, tell your men to shoot me now. Don't be afraid; tell them to obey your orders!'

He looks at the security men, throws his hands up in the air and he shouts, 'Shoot her now?' The security men put their rifles to their shoulders and pull the triggers and bullets are flying at Leila. About four hundred bullets stop two inches from Leila's body they just hang in midair. She walks to one side leaving the bullets hanging there, she looks at the security men and says; 'Get out now before I lose my temper, I could kill every one of you now, if I wish.'

One of the security men steps forward he asks, 'How could you do that? 'You don't have a gun.'

Leila looks at him, and says, there is always one idiot who wants to be a hero. Well, Mr Hero you want to prove how macho you are. Please look at all the bullets hanging in the air, point to one of them, and see what happens.' He points at one and says, 'that one.' Then he laughs out loud saying, 'what are you going to do now, shoot me. That is not possible, not without a gun in your hand, 'it's never going to happen!

One of the stationary bullets hanging in the air turns round and flies to this idiot's face and stops in midair. Leila walks over to him and asks; 'Would you like to die? I can accommodate you, what do want me to do smart boy? He faints, the bullet falls to the ground. All the rifles fly from security men's hands and fall to the ground. She has placed them in a pile in a mangled heap. Then she looks at Mr Dankin and another bullet turns round, then it flies to within two inches of Mr Dankin's face, he throws his hands up to protect his face. She leaves the bullet at the front of his face, and then she lets the other bullets fall one hundred at a time and drops them on top of the mangled rifles. She looks at the security men,' I would leave this room now and take this useless idiot with you!' She points to the soldier on the ground. She walks over to Mr Dankin, takes the bullet that is very close to his head and drops it on the ground.

'Now, Mr Dankin, I hope I have cured your curiosity because I could kill you now if I wish. Mr Dankin, all I need from you is the name of the person that told you to take me into custody. I'm waiting for the answer sir?'

He looks at her, he is finding it hard to breath then he blurts out, 'It was the Chief of staff. He wanted you away from the United Nations Building this afternoon and he needed information to help the President!'

'Well, I knew that anyway but I thought that I would give you a chance to come clean and you did. I do thank you for that. Now I have very bad news for you!' Mr Dankin has dropped down on his knees begging for mercy saying; 'I'm only doing my job!' Because he thinks that he is going to die. Leila walks over to him she puts out her hand to help him up, saying; 'I'm not going to kill you, the bad news is I'm going to raze this building to dust today, I want you to make sure that everyone has vacated the building before 12noon. Will you do that please?'

He looks at her and says, 'You are kidding me. How are you going to raze this building to the ground? That is impossible!'

'Mr Dankin, if you are in this building at 12noon you will die, but that is your choice. I'm leaving this building now and you are coming with me!' He follows her out of his office.

The doctor is running up the corridor, 'We didn't release her, sir,' as he looks into Mr Dankin's office,

What happened here?' as he looks at the carnage asking, 'How did all this happen?' Mr Dankin points at Leila and says,

That's what happened.'

'What do you mean, sir?'

'Never mind, doctor, I don't think you would understand and I don't want to talk about it!'

Leila and Mr Dankin walk down to the first metal door. She takes him by the hand. 'Mr Dankin, I'm going to show you something very special. Do you see that door sir it's made of heavy metal, 'You would normally open it with your remote?'

'Yes, I could. Why?

'I will not need to open that door.' Answers Leila. 'I want you to throw your remote as far away down the corridor as you can please. I'm going to walk through that door and you are going to come with me!'

She levitates the two of them then she moves to within one inch and while he tries to figure out what is happening the two of them are at the other side of the metal door before he understands what has happened. 'Now let us go to the big security door!' He looks at Leila and says; 'You will not be able to pass through the big security door!' 'Mr Dankin, don't you worry one little bit,' they walk up to the door.

'Now Mr Dankin do you think that this metal door will stop me from leaving this building?'

He shrugs his shoulders because he is not sure about anything now, maybe all this is a dream. She takes his hand saying, 'Are you ready to go through this metal door?'

He closes his eyes and in a second the two of them are at the other side of a bomb proof metal door!

'Now, Mr Dankin, shall we go up in the lift to the first floor, and then I can leave you in charge. At the first floor entrance she walks out of the lift she looks back then she turns round looks at him and says, 'Mr Dankin you make sure that this building is vacated before 12noon today. I hope I see you in the United Nations Building later this afternoon. Good bye.

As he blinks, she has vanished. He places both hands up to his eyes and wipes them, thinking that this is all an illusion. He is completely confused and bewildered. However, he needs to make sure that all the personal in this building, will be vacated and leave the building empty in case that the building does turn to dust by 12noon.

Chapter 133

Leila is back in the hotel in her dad's suite. Everyone is talking, trying to figure out what did happen regarding Alfie, asking each other, was this all a dream? 'Was it real?'

Gia walks over to Leila, looks her in the eye and says, 'Leila, please explain to me how you turned back time?'

Leila replies, 'It is too complicated even for you, no disrespect, Gia, but you are not up with my technology. I'm light years ahead of you or any planet in the Universe!'

Gia is astounded at what Leila has told her and says, 'Well, if what you are telling me is true I'm staggered and excited for you,' as she gives her a very big hug.

Leila's mum walks over and gives her a big hug saying, 'I'm sorry I didn't believe you when Alfie was dead. You revived him. I find it amazing that you can do all those wonderful things. Are you sure you are my daughter?'

'Yes mum, I am your daughter, 'I know that it is not easy watching me do all those wonderful things. It mesmerises me as well.'

Leila looks at Gia and Óisin and says to Gia, 'May I have a talk with you and Óisin please?'

'Yes, why not, where do you want to talk with us?'

'Shall we go and sit by the window!' replies Leila. She beckons Gia and Óisin to follow her. At the window Leila looks at Gia and says, 'What I'm going to ask you might be a little difficult for you to understand, however, I need your cooperation and help on this one?'

'Yes. Please tell me what you want, Leila, I can't stand the strain.' replies Gia.

'Would it be prudent of me to ask if I could take your spacecraft and land it on the Great Lawn in Central Park this afternoon?'

Gia looks astonished at this request made by Leila. She looks at Óisin he throws his hands in the air saying; 'It's up to you Gia, I'm happy to trust Leila. She obviously has an agenda!'

Gia looks at Leila and says; 'Ok, if Óisin is willing to trust you so am I. Yes you have our permission to take our spacecraft out of orbit and land it on the Great Lawn in Central Park. Please be careful. I don't want any damage done to it!'

'Good,' replies Leila. 'I will not let any damage happen to it. It's nearly time to go to the restaurant for breakfast.' There's a knock on the door. Dad goes and opens it, Ryan is standing in front of him with a trolley laden with their cleaned clothes, all individually in covers and beautiful laid out saying, 'Your cleaned clothes, sir' Dad looks at him, says, 'Thank you Ryan,' and hands him twenty dollars. Ryan turns around; walks back down the corridor and back to reception where he starts his daily work.

Leila says, 'Come on, everyone, it's time for breakfast. Shall we go down to the restaurant for breakfast?'

It takes about five minutes to get to the restaurant entrance. The family, Gina and Oisin walk straight in find a table to accommodate them, and then sit down. 'Mum you take Alfie to get his breakfast. I'll see to Gia and Oisin, Come on, Gia and Oisin, follow me to see what we can find for your breakfast?' The three of them walk up to the food counter. Leila points to the vegetarian meals. 'There you are, Gia, take a taste from all of them then take the one you like. Just place a portion on your plate and you do the same, Oisin?'

Gia looks at Leila and says, 'What are those white and yellow things?'

'They are eggs, they come from chickens, and you can taste a little bit. I think you might like it.'

Gia picks up a fork, picks up a little bit of the egg and places it into her mouth, samples it, nods her head then says, 'I like that, it does taste nice!'

'Fine then I'll place one egg on your plate with your vegetarian meal and you can do the same, Oisin,

He takes one egg places it on his plate and one vegetarian meal, and then he walks back with Gia to their table.

Leila says, 'I'll follow you as soon as I have picked my breakfast.' About two minutes pass and Leila is back at the table then she sits down. She looks around the table and asks, 'Shall we go into the city and maybe buy something to take back to England?'

Granddad replies, 'I think that is a very good idea!'

Leila looks around the table and says, 'As soon as I have finished my breakfast I'll go to reception and ask if there is anything special going on in New York today that we can go to see?'

Ciera replies. 'Well I think that is a good idea!

'What about Gia and Oisin? What do you think? Would you like a tour around the city?'

Gia looks a bit apprehensive and nervous. She looks at Oisin and asks, 'What do you think?'

'I'm fine with that. It could be an education for us. Yes, I think we will go and have a look at this city. That should give Gia and me a better idea of your people. Plus we can learn by mixing with them!'

Leila replies. 'Fine, I have finished my breakfast so I'll go to reception and find out what we can do this morning.' She rises up from her chair, walks out of the dining room to reception. The receptionist look up at Leila and asks, 'How may I help you?'

'My family and I have about five hours to look around your city. Is there anything of interest that we could go to see?'

'Well, there is a lot of sightseeing to do in New York. Have you any idea what you would like to see?'

Leila replies, 'Perhaps something exciting, have you anything like that?'

The receptionist has a look in her entertainment book then she looks at Leila and says, 'There is a sword fencing competition in The Grand Prospect Hall and it is open all day, now, if you and your family would like go there. It is a very palatial hall, it's very expensive but I would recommend it for its sheer elegance!'

'I'll ask the family. All being well I shall return and let you know.' Leila returns to the dining room goes and sits down with the family, then she says, 'How would you like to go and see a sword fencing competition in the Grand Prospect Hall, as we don't have anything to do for about five hours?'

Everyone looks at each other, Ciera says, 'I would like to see a sword fencing competition, what about you, Alfie?'

Alfie looks at his mum and asks, 'what is sword fencing mum?'

She looks at him and says, 'You have seen it on television, two men sword fighting with those long swords!'

'Yes, I remember there was one in the Mask of Zoro!'

'Yes, Alfie, you are quite right, would you like to go and see one?'

'Yes, please, mum, I think I would like that!'

Leila asks, 'What about you, granddad and grandma?'

'I don't think that would interest us, I think we will just go and have a look around the centre of New York.'

'What about you, JK and Delia? Would you like to come to this sword fencing competition? I'm sure that it will be very interesting.'

JK looks up and says, 'Not my kind of entertainment I'll go with dad and mum. What about you Delia would you like to see this sword fencing?'

'I'd love to come!' she answers.

Leila then looks at Gia and Oisin, 'Now I know that you have never seen this kind of sport, but it is fascinating. Can I tempt you to come?'

Gia looks at Oisin and asks, 'What do you think?'

'Well it can't do any harm, I'm up for it.'

'That's it then. I'll go to reception and hire a taxi to take us to The Grand Prospect Hall. Follow me please?'

Granddad says, 'your grandma and I will stay here for a while, and just relax you go and have a nice time. We'll see you later!'

Leila looks at JK and granddad and grandma and she says, 'I'll be in contact with you later.'

At reception Leila tells the receptionist,' We would like you to call a taxi to take us to The Grand Prospect Hall?'

'Yes, I can do that for you. Please sit down and relax over by the window. I will call you when the taxi is outside the hotel.'

Ten minutes later, the receptionist walks over to Leila and she says, 'Your taxi is waiting outside the front of the hotel!'

Leila replies, 'Thank you. Come on everybody let's go!'

Chapter 134

Up they rise from their chairs, walk out to the front of the hotel where their taxi is waiting for them.

The taxi driver sees them then he alights from his taxi, recognises Leila, goes over and says, 'You were in my taxi last night.' He opens the back door of the taxi to let his passengers go inside!

'Yes I was, and it's very nice to see you again.'

Leila sits in the front passenger seat. He closes the doors, walks around to his driving seat and sits inside, he then asks, 'Now, young ladies and young gentleman, where would you like to go to in this famous city?'

Leila looks at him and answers, 'We would like to go to The Grand Prospect Hall please!'

'No problem. Can I ask why this particular place?'

'Well, I, that is, we, would like to see some sword fencing. The receptionist at the hotel said that is the best place to go and enjoy ourselves, so will you take us there please?'

He replies, 'Yes, of course I will.'

The taxi driver looks at Leila and says, 'I watched you on television this morning and you are causing alarm because of your powers. He looks at her again, and asks, 'Are you for real?'

'Don't be afraid, I will not hurt you, and yes, I am real.'

He asks, 'who are you, where are you from?'

'I'm from England. Can't you tell by my accent?'

'Yes, but you are not like other people?'

Leila answers, 'Bill I'm as human as you. My DNA is human!'

'How do you know my name?'

She smiles looks at him, 'It's on your lapel.'

He replies, 'So it is,' as he gives a little chuckle, then he stops outside The Grand Prospect Hall.

'How much is the fare please?'

'That is ten dollars please!'

Leila takes ten dollars from her purse then hands it to the taxi driver saying, 'Thank you very much.'

He alights from his taxi, goes around to the other side of the taxi, opens the doors and everyone alights onto the pavement.

Leila looks and says, 'Thank you, Bill. Can you be at the front here to pick us up, at 2:30pm this afternoon please, and then take us to the Great Lawn? Good bye for now.'

Leila looks at this magnificent building and says, 'This is a French Renaissance Style palace, it looks awesome. Come on everyone, let's go inside and see what this wonderful building has to offer us.'

Inside the entrance is a twin staircase with marble floors, two marble columns with gilded gold ornate tops. The sides facing you are gold leaf, crafted, ornate, beautifully decorated, and stunningly eye catching!

'What do you think, Gia?'

She answers, 'It is magnificent and breathtaking. I have never seen anything so beautiful as this in my life!'

'What do you think, Alfie?'

'It's awesome.'

'Mum, what do you think?'

'Mum replies, 'I think this place looks fantastic!'

'And you, Oisin what do you think?'

Oisin answers, 'It's amazing. The opulence is spectacular, and dazzling!''

'Now let's find a receptionist.'

Off they go up the right side of the stairs where they meet a young lady.

Leila stops her and asks, 'would you be kind enough and tell me where one of your restaurants is located?'

'Yes, please follow me.'

She leads the family up another flight of stairs. 'There,' as she points to a large door you may have some refreshments in that restaurant, just walk in, find a table, and then sit down. Then a waiter will see to your needs thank you, and then she walks away.

They walk inside Ciera look around and says, 'My, my, this is very posh, I don't think we should be in here!'

'Don't demean yourself, mum, our money is as good as anybody else's. Please sit down and see what happens!'

Delia is a bit nervous, but before she can say a word, a young girl arrives at the table and asks, 'Are you ready? May I take your orders please?'

Leila looks around the table and says, 'I'll ask what is on the menu,

'She looks at the girl and asks. 'Can you do some sandwiches, and what are the ingredients please?'

She hands Leila a menu and says, 'You have a look to see what you need. I'll return in five minutes!'

'Well then, let me see what we can order from this menu. The restaurant has vegetarian, salmon, beef, chicken, duck sandwiches with a side dish of lettuce and cut tomatoes. Gia, I presume that you and Oisin will have the vegetarian, Mum, what will you have?'

'I'll have chicken please. What will you have to eat, Alfie?'

'I'll have the same as mum.'

'And you, Delia, what do you fancy?'

'I'll try the salmon please?'

'Fine I'll try the beef, and I'll order a pot of coffee and an orange for Alfie. 'Is everyone happy with that?'

Leila beckons the waiter. When she arrives at the table, Leila gives her the order. She turns round and walks to the kitchen.

Ten minutes later she walks back to Leila's table with six plates of sandwiches and a dish with diced lettuce and cut tomatoes, places them on the table then says, 'Please enjoy, I'll return with your coffee and orange!' She turns and walks away.

Two minutes and she is back with the coffee and orange, places them on the table, doesn't say a word just turns and walks away.

Leila hands out the plates with the sandwiches to the right people and says, 'Oisin and Gia help your-selves to the lettuce and tomatoes!'

At the door of the restaurant a gentleman is in an argument with the waiter and he is gesturing to Leila's table.

He pushes his way into the restaurant, then in a very brisk manner walks over to Leila's table. He then he starts to shout, 'This is my table. I have my lunch at this table every day so if you don't mind, would you please vacate it and go to another table!'

Leila looks at him and then looks around the restaurant and says, 'There are another ten tables free so why don't you have one of those?'

He looks at her, and then he makes a very big mistake. He walks over to Alfie and tries to lift him up from his chair.

Leila stands up, walks around and in a very quiet manner says, 'Please leave my brother alone!'

'No I want my table now.'

Then the manager walks over. 'Please Mr Charlton let me show you to another table?'

He's having none of this so tries to pull Alfie off his chair.

Leila winks at her mum, walks back to Mr Charlton. 'Now, sir, I see that you are all dressed up for sword fencing. Do you mind if I ask you something?'

'No I don't mind.' He looks at her in a very questionable way. 'What do you want to know?'

She looks at him, and says, 'I was wondering how good a sword fencing person you are?'

'I'm the best swords man probably in the USA. Why?'

Leila looks back at Gia and Oisin and smiles. 'Would you like to test me with a sword, 'maybe I might learn something from you?'

'I don't think so I would cut you to ribbons in about ten seconds. You're no match for me. You're just a silly little girl!'

'Why don't you try me?'

He looks her up and down, then he asks, 'Have you ever had a sword in your hand in your life?'

'No I have not, but I think I could beat you!'

He is now laughing his head off. He looks at Leila and says, you silly little girl, you are no match for me!'

'Why don't you try me? Let's make it interesting. She looks at him again. 'Why don't we have a wager? Shall we say a thousand dollars each?'

'Are you kidding me?' You wouldn't have a chance, he looks at Leila with a smirk on his face then he says, 'Look why don't you just give me your thousand dollars now, and make it easy on yourself!'

'Look, Mr Charlton, you're not afraid of me are you? You have said I'm just a little girl so what's your problem?'

By now a crowd has gathered inside the restaurant and they are goading him on. He looks around the restaurant, he then says, 'Fine. Be it on your head, what kind of sword is your pleasure?'

Leila replies. 'I'll have a Rapier, that's if you don't mind!'

'Fine,' replies Mr Charlton. 'I'll have a Rapier as well!' He can't stop laughing. 'Come on then, follow me and I'll have you kitted out!'

Leila replies, 'I don't need kitting out. I'm fine as I am thank you!'

'He looks at her again, and then he says, 'You will not be allowed unless you're kitted out.'

'Look, do you want to earn a very easy thousand dollars, or not?'

'Fine it's your body, but when I thrust and jab, it's a strike. I win, is that fair, young lady?'

Leila replies, 'Yes. I'm fine with that!' She follows him on to the sword fencing carpet. He takes two Rapiers from the sword cabinet hands her one by the handle to Leila. Then he stands back and asks, 'Are you ready? He looks around the hall then he says, 'I can't believe this young lady has challenged me to a sword fencing duel and for money. She has no chance. By now the word has got out and the hall has the biggest crowd of people ever seen in this hall for a duel of this kind.'

They are all murmuring amongst the people, 'She is going to be slaughtered.'

Leila calls the family over, then she tells them, 'Please don't worry, he will never touch me with that Rapier!'

Gia looks at her and asks, 'Are you sure? What if something goes wrong? I don't know anything about this game, is there anything I can do to help?'

'Don't worry this duel will be over in ten seconds!'

'I'm ready, Mr Charlton. You can begin when you are ready?'

Chapter 135

He lunges forward and in an instant Leila has her Rapier on his throat, 'Please don't make a move it is my strike. Thank, Mr Charlton!'

He is flabbergasted, he is trying to analyse what has happened. He looks around the audience in the hall then thinks to himself that was just a lucky strike. He looks at Leila. 'Shall we try again?'

'Are you sure? You might lose another thousand dollars!'

He replies, 'Yes but I might get even, shall we?' He points his Rapier at Leila.

He is more cautious and careful now, he thrusts and jabs on bended knee, Leila blocks and in a second she has the Rapier under his throat again.

He now is getting very nasty and he is waving his sword from left to right in a swishing movement. He is just walking around when suddenly he makes a run at Leila, waving his sword left and right, but again she has her Rapier on his throat. He backs off, walks round in a circle trying to decide what to do, this young lady is making a fool of him and he is not having that.

Leila looks at him; 'Why don't you take off those silly clothes and fight me like a man?' She is goading him now. But she is enjoying this sword fencing, she doe's find's it fascinating.

He is now raging with temper. He looks at Leila. 'I'm going to the changing rooms to remove my fencing outfit. I'll be back shortly don't leave!'

Leila replies, 'I'm not going anywhere. I'll be here when you return!'

Leila's mum runs over and asks, 'Leila, are you going to be all right?'

'Yes, mum, I'm just playing with him. I know every move he is going to make before he carries it out!'

Alfie follows his mum then he looks at his sister and says, 'You look like a movie star, I think you are awesome. I never knew that you were that good at sword fencing!'

'Thank you, Alfie, what a lovely compliment from you and I do appreciate it. Now mum and you go back and sit in your chairs I see Mr Charlton coming back, 'She also clocks a certain tall gentleman with a Rapier in his hand standing on a chair at the back of the hall.

Mr Charlton walks over to Leila looks her in the eye and says, 'I'm going to thrash you to within an inch of your life!'

'Is that so, 'She looks at him and asks, 'What do you do outside of sword fencing?'

'That is none of your business. However I'll enlighten you, I own an up market women's fashion boutique in the city. Why are you so interested?'

'Just wondered what you do for a living. Right then, en-garde.'

Mr Charlton is very weary of Leila now and he is trying to figure out what he needs to do so that he can redeem his good name.

Leila is tired of this idiot so she decides to finish this duel, she decides to put him on point, then in an astonishing move she goes beat, parry and riposte, now her Rapier is touching his throat again. She removes her Rapier, then she walks two paces, towards him, then she says, 'You are no match for me, I could cut you to ribbons but I will not do that. Will you please remain in this hall you do owe me two thousand dollars but I will trade that for some fashion clothes from your boutique!'

He puts out his hand and says, 'I think, that you're something very special, and I like you. One question, would you please tell me where did you learn sword fencing?'

'I didn't learn it anywhere that was the first time I had a Rapier in my hand!'

'That is amazing,' as he looks at her very intently saying, 'That is hard to believe, however, I have no other option,' as he throws his hands up in the air.

This audience are ecstatic, shouting, 'Bravo, bravo, 'Everyone in this hall is standing looking on in amazement.

The gentleman at the other end of the hall, jumps off the chair, runs over to where Leila is standing then he says, 'I don't believe that was the first time you had a Rapier in your hand, I think you are lying to this audience. However if you would like to try your sword fencing skills on me I would be very pleased?'

'Leila looks at him and asks, 'And you are?'

'My name is Nico-van-Karricaff and I'm the world's sword fencing champion and I'm going to teach you a lesson in sword fencing. You might have fooled Mr Charlton but you will not fool me!'

Leila looks at him, doesn't say a word. She just walks slowly around in circles, then she stops has another look then she says, 'En-garde?'

He goes for thrust and jab hoping that she will reply.

Instead she does second intention then beat, parry and riposte. He is at the mercy of Leila's Rapier which is at his throat. The audience are in shock. How did she do that, she is very good. Now there is a great hush and silence in the hall, he is the world champion?

'He shouts out, I slipped I want a return bout.'

Leila looks at him and says, 'Are you sure you want to be embarrassed again?'

'I told you that I slipped, I'll have you this time?'

Leila replies, 'Fine, I will beat you again!'

'I don't think so. I have the measure of you now? He lunges at Leila. Then he goes for a beat, parry and riposte. Unfortunately for him she is not in the place he thinks she should be. Before he realises, Leila has her Rapier at his throat saying, 'I told you that you are not good enough to beat me, now please don't ask for another chance!'

The hall is in uproar. People are throwing their coats and hats up into the air shouting, we want more, we want more.' Quite a number of people run over to Leila asking, 'Who are you? Where do you come from?'

Mr Nico-van-Karricaff walks away in a daze, not knowing what exactly happened. He knows he should have won this sword contest. But how did I loose. There is something wrong here, she is an amateur, and I'm a professional swords man, how did that happen. I'm not going to ask her for another return bout.

'Ladies and gentlemen please watch your televisions this afternoon, if you want to know about me!'

Mr Charlton walks over to Leila, puts his arm around her, then he says, 'You are the first person to beat Nico in the last four years, and you are telling me that you have never held a sword in your hand or had any sword fencing lessons?'

'Here is my mum. Please be my guest and ask her if I have ever had any sword fencing lessons before today?'

'You are this young lady's mum?'

'Yes I'm her mum. What do you want to know?'

'The question I'm asking is, has she ever had any sword fencing lessons before today?'

'Not to my knowledge and I would know, why are you asking that question?'

'I have never seen anyone as good as her in my life. It's uncanny. She doesn't seem to have a problem with sword fencing it looks like second nature to her. It's amazing. All I can say is I am really glad I had a duel with the greatest sword fencing person in the world. What name are you known by?'

'My name is Leila and I'm from England.' By now a great crowd have gathered, including Gia, Oisin, Delia, and Alfie have arrived at Leila's side, this is my family!'

He gives everyone a little cuddle especially Alfie!

'Mr Charlton may I have a word in your ear, please?'

'Of course you can. What can I do for you?'

'Let's talk about this two thousand dollars you owe me, I'm sure that you won't renege on our little bet. At least I hope not!'

'I have no reason to renege, in fact I'm very happy to pay my debt in any way you want!'

'I would like to look inside your fashion boutique shop, please. That is if you are willing to trade the money for clothes?'

'I'm sure that we can come to an arrangement. When would you like to visit my boutique?'

'In about ten minutes, first I must have a talk with my family. You just wait there where you are I'll return shortly.'

Leila walks over to the family and says, 'Who would like to come with me to Mr Charlton's fashion boutique?'

Her mum asks, 'Why would we need to visit Mr Charlton's boutique?'

'He owes me two thousand dollars on a bet, mum. Don't ask, I'll explain later.' She looks at Gia, Oisin, Delia, and not forgetting Alfie. Shall we go then?'

Mum shrugs her shoulders, the rest say, 'We're happy with that!'

Leila goes back to Mr Charlton and asks, 'Is it all right if my family come along?'

'Yes that's fine with me, I'll call a taxi!'

Leila says, 'No need to call a taxi,' as she beckons the family over to her. Before we go to your boutique I have something to show you.'

She is still holding the Rapier in her hand. She looks at Mr Charlton, then she hands him the Rapier saying, 'Please hold it up straight in front of you. He puts out his right hand, takes the sword by the handle. Now the sword is pointing at Leila. She walks up to him and smiles. She puts out her hands parallel to her shoulders. The point of the Rapier is touching the middle of Leila's body.

She pushes forward. The Rapier goes straight through her body and out the other side. He is about to cry out. O my God, I have killed her. He doesn't know what has happened. Leila is just standing there, with the Rapier protruding out the back of her body. Several people in the hall have fainted. He is aghast, and horrified at what he has done. He withdraws the Rapier from Leila's body, thinking that she is dead, but, there is no blood coming from the wound. He looks at her and asks,

'What is going on here, you should be dead, but you're still alive. How is that?' She looks at him. Mr Charlton, you can place the Rapier on the table please. Oh and I'm not dead. I don't have the time now to explain everything to you, it would take too long. 'Shall we hold hands please? That includes you Mr Charlton.' He looks perplexed and mystified. However, he places his hand in Leila's hand, and in an instant the six of them are in his fashion boutique. He looks around then he faints.

Chapter 136

Leila looks at his staff and asks, 'Can I have a glass of water please?'

One of the staff rushes into the toilet, and returns with a glass of water, Leila sits him up. He opens his eyes, he then sees Leila on one knee holding a glass of water to his lips.

She says, 'Mr Charlton please don't panic you are safe. You have a sip of water, and then you'll be fine.'

He doesn't know what is happening. He is beside himself with worry and he is very anxious about his well being. He has another look around and asks, 'How did I get here?' He then looks at Leila.

'We are in your fashion boutique. I transported you here; I don't have the time to hire taxis, as she takes him by the arm, and helps him up on his feet. The employees are looking mystified, asking each other, 'Where did all these people come from? They didn't come through the front door.'

Leila walks him to one side and says, 'I'm not like other people, I have very special powers. Please don't be frightened, you will not be hurt. Now we are in your fashion boutique will you show us around?'

He looks at Leila and asks, 'Is this real? I'm not dreaming am I?'

'No, you are not dreaming. What you see is real!'

'How did I arrive in my boutique?'

Leila answers, 'No more questions, thank you. Shall we browse around your boutique please?'

'Yes of course you can. Whatever takes your fancy, you just look around, pick anything you like with my compliments!'

'Come on, everyone. Not you, Alfie. You sit by the window be nice and quiet. Can you do that for me?'

'Yes I can do that!' as he looks at his sister.

Mum is not so keen. This is a young person's boutique so she goes and sits with Alfie.

Gia and Oisin browse but nothing takes their fancy so they go and sit with Ciera.

Delia is not overly interested, a bit too young for her but she carries on looking.

Leila picks out a Velvet Embellished Pants, a pastel green top and a black cloak with pastel green finish on the inside but it is also reversible. She picks a black pair of shoes with three inch high heels.

She walks over to Mr Charlton; 'I would like this outfit please?'

He takes the price labels off, looks at Leila and says, 'You haven't spent a lot of money on these clothes, I'll give you one thousand dollars as well. Plus, one of my special designer carrier bags as a gift. Accept this gift with my compliments, I do like you, you are a very special person and I'm very pleased I have been in your company; one question, you have never had a Rapier sword in your hand before? I find that incredible!'

Leila answers, 'I could have beaten both you and Nico together!'

He looks at her and smiles saying, 'I do believe you. When will I see you again?

'If you watch your television this afternoon, I will be addressing the world leaders in the United Nations Building!'

He looks at her; he is visibly stunned at Leila's answer. He says, 'You're not kidding me, are you?'

'No I'm not kidding you. I have no reason to lie to you. Please watch the television later this afternoon!'

She rounds up the family. They hold hands and in a flash they are gone.

He is mesmerised, looks at his staff and says, 'Did I see those people disappear into thin air?'

Not a word is said by the staff. They just look on in wonderment!

They arrive back in Leila's suite where she communicates with granddad, grandma and JK, She asks, *'Where are you now?'*

'We are in the hotel lounge having tea, please come and join us?'

She looks around. 'Anyone needing the toilet please go now, before we go down to the hotel lounge to meet the rest of the family.' No one takes her up on the offer she looks around. Shall we proceed to the lift, the door opens they go inside the lift, she presses the button for the ground floor The lift stops, the door opens, they proceed to the lounge where they meet up with granddad, grandma and JK.'

Alfie runs over to granddad, He's all excited. 'Granddad, Leila was sword fencing with the world sword fencing champion!'

'Slow down, Alfie, now what is this about Leila sword fencing with some sword fencing champion?'

'She beat him and another guy as well. It was awesome. You should have been there, granddad, she beat them twice!'

Granddad looks at Leila, 'Alright, Leila can you explain to me what happened?'

A Mr Charlton was being very abusive to Alfie, I needed to teach him a lesson, he was one of the sword fencing people, 'I couldn't resist granddad, but I need to tell you that I didn't hurt or cut any one of the two men!'

'That's good enough for me Leila. You can tell me the full story at a later date.'

'Granddad, now I have some bad news for you.'

Granddad asks, 'Bad news. Please explain?'

'I have a lot on my plate at the moment with the problem we had in the early morning. I can't take any more chances of having my family in danger, so I'm going to send everyone back home except Gia and Oisin. I know that there is going to be trouble this afternoon. I do hope that everyone will understand my predicament. It's not that I don't need you, of course I need you. I will leave immediately I have finished with this lot of idiot government officials and travel to another universe to help another race of people as you already know. I'll send each one of you to your own homes from here as we stand, Leila looks around. Any questions!'

Granddad asks, 'Does that mean you will not need us anymore!'

'No granddad, that's not what I mean, you are my family. I will need each one of you again in the future, but on this occasion it's going to be very dangerous and I need to know that everyone is safe. There will be lots of television people looking to talk to everyone of the family when you are back in England, but I'm sure that each one will be a credit to the family. I'll be in touch at all times if you need me. Is everyone ok with that?'

Granddad looks around then he says, 'I think we all agree that you're doing this to protect the family so we are happy with that!'

'Fine are you all ready?' And in a flash everyone has gone home. She communicates with them individually saying, *'I'll be in touch at all times.'*

What Leila doesn't realise is the hotel manager is standing by the lounge door and he has seen everything. He doesn't understand the implications of what he has viewed. He walks over to Leila, a little unsteady, he then asks, 'What is going on here?'

Leila looks at him then she places her hand on his shoulder and asks, 'Did you want to ask me something sir?'

He looks at her then he says, 'I don't know. I did want to ask you something but I have forgotten it. Ah I remember, now will you be vacating your rooms soon we will need them for tonight?'

'Yes, we will be leaving in about ten minutes and we did enjoy ourselves at the Ritz. Thank you for the hospitality, your staff looked after us extremely well. Oh and don't forget you must send the invoice to the White House for the attention of the President. Right, Gia and Oisin, shall we vacate our rooms? We have other issues to take care of!'

They follow her to the lift, then they go up to the suites, make sure that everything is left tidy and in place. Leila walks out of her suite locks the door, goes and knocks on Gia's door. She and Oisin walk out into the corridor to the lift. Down at reception they hand in the keys. Leila looks at Gia and Oisin let's walk into the lounge again. Inside she tells them that they are going back to the Grand Prospect Hall!'

Gia asks. 'Why?'

'Because we are being picked up by taxi then he is going to take us to The Grand Lawn in Central Park!'

Gia looks at Leila and enquires, 'Why are we going to this Grand Lawn place?'

'This is where I'm going to take your craft out of orbit and land it on The Grand Lawn. I did ask you if you would allow me to do that,' as she looks at Gia.

Gia looks at Oisin shrugs her shoulders, 'Is that all right, Oisin?'

Leila knows that they are worried about her landing the craft on the Grand Lawn. 'Look I know you are worried, 'Why don't you and Oisin go up to your craft in orbit then come down through the atmosphere then land it on The Great Lawn. Would that make your mind a little easy to take in?

Gia replies, 'Yes I think that it might be a little better, it's not that we don't trust you to land it, but it might be better on this occasion!'

'Fine, off you go then. I'll see you on The Great Lawn in thirty minutes!'

Chapter 137

In a flash the two of them are in their space craft and are making plans for the first time to land their space craft on Planet Earth.

Leila needs to go to NAB Corporation broadcasting company in New York. In a flash she is in the foyer of the building standing in front of the receptionists. They are very frightened. 'They stand up with a look of astonishment, with hands in front of their faces. One of them looks at Leila and asks, 'Who are you, where have you come from?'

Leila looks at them and says, 'Don't worry. I'm not going to hurt anyone in this building. I need to know where the overall Chief Executive's office is, I would like to have a talk with him.'

Now it's panic stations. Everyone is trying to run away from Leila. She stops them in their tracks. They look as if they are frozen to the spot. She points to one of them and says, 'You,' as she levitates her off the ground leaving the rest of the receptionists unable to move. She starts to move towards Leila as she approaches Leila, she starts to cry uncontrollably, Leila looks at her and says, 'I'm not going to hurt you. Your name is Kathy; all I need you to tell me is where is the Chief Executive's Office, please?'

Everyone is stunned by this request from a stranger who has just appeared out of thin air. Leila lets Kathy down on the carpet, places her hand on her shoulder and in an instant the two of them are in the Chief Executive's office. A very palatial and modern office beautifully laid out, with deep pile carpets with all the usual executive plush conveniences, bar, shower room and of course his own secretary in an office just outside his door

The Chief Executive jumps up from his chair and stumbles back against the large window overlooking New York shouting, 'Who are you? How did you arrive into my office, without my secretary seeing you?

'Kathy faints. Leila picks her up and places her on the couch on the left of the Chief Executive's chair. She wakes up looks at Leila and shouts, 'You stay away from me you're a witch!'

Leila looks at her and smiles, as she walks to the Chief Executive. 'Please don't panic, sir. Your name is Damien Carmichael, am I right sir?'

'Yes, but how do you know my name? I have never seen you before in my life.'

'I know the names of all the personnel in this building. That is not why I'm here, I'm here to make a very important announcement which will make world news and I have selected this media and this broadcasting corporation to announce my terms for this Planet Earth. I'm human like you. I'll be arriving above the United Nations Building this afternoon at about 3pm in my UFO, also the GIB (Grand Information Building) will be razed to the ground at noon. You will cover both of those incidents. No other building will be damaged and not one person will be harmed. You make the necessary phone calls to the fire brigade, the ambulance authority, the police, and any other authority you think will be interested. Are you clear on what I have asked you to do?'

'Yes I think so!' he answers.

Leila replies. 'Fine you can start to phone all those authorities now, please!'

She walks over to Kathy, places her hand on her shoulder and as if by magic the two of them are back in the foyer and again everyone is startled, none more so than Kathy. She doesn't know what has happened. She is totally oblivious to what is happening to her, and lost for words. Everyone is asking her, 'What happened? Where have you been?'

She just throws her hands up in the air, shouting, 'Leave me alone. I don't know what happened. One minute I'm here in the foyer, the next minute I'm in the Chief Executive's office and I don't know how I arrived there, 'It's thirty five stories high. I look around and I'm in Mr Damien Carmichael's office. I didn't go by lift. Then about ten minutes later I arrive back in this foyer and I still don't know what happened!'

Leila looks at all the receptionists, gives them a big smile and says, 'Good bye young ladies,' then in a flash she has left the building. She materialises at the front of the Grand Prospect Hall which startles everyone walking in front of the Hall. As she stands there waiting for her taxi, a car stops in front of The Grand Prospect Hall. Two young men burst out of the car waving AK 70s then they start to shout, 'we are going to kill everyone. Leila walks over to them asking, 'Why are you going to kill everyone? That is not a very nice thing to do!'

They look at her in amazement then one of them asks,

Are you crazy? Do you want to die first I can accommodate you!'

'I'm not the crazy one you are.'

Chapter 138

All the people on the pavement drop down but some run away. The two young men look at each other. Then they decide to release the safety catches of their AK 70s. But before they can pull the triggers the AK70s they fly from their hands to Leila. She looks at them in disgust saying, 'I'm fed up with idiots like you trying to kill me.' They are frozen to the pavement they can't move. 'What is your problem? I could kill you now if I wished,' then she points her finger at the two of them and she beckons them to her.

On arriving at Leila's side, she looks at them and says, 'I don't have time to worry about you today. The police are on their way so I'm going to leave you two here, which astonishes everyone including the two idiots. All the people gather around her, thanking her for saving their lives. Some of them are crying hysterically and drop down on their knees. At that moment a police car arrives. Two policemen jump out of the police car run to where Leila is standing shouting, 'Down on the floor, hands behind your back, you are under arrest.'

She does nothing she just stands there hands by her side, the two idiots drop to the floor as ordered by the police. One of the people runs over to the policemen saying, 'She saved all our lives, why are you arresting her?'

Leila's taxi has arrived. She starts to walk towards it. One of the policemen shouts, 'Stop, or I'll shoot.'

She just carries on walking to her taxi, As she arrives at the door of the taxi the policeman shouts, Do not get into the taxi or I'll shoot you.' She opens the door looks around then she says, 'Shoot me if you want I've other more important things to do!'

Chapter 139

The policeman places his legs apart; arms fully extended, then he releases the safety catch, aims at Leila, and squeezes the trigger. The bullets fly towards her then they stop two inches in front of her head. She turns, looks at the policeman then she turns the bullets around, then she sends them back to the policeman. They stop two inches from his head. He staggers back in amazement, looks to his gun then he does a very strange thing; he drops it on the ground and places his hands above his head.

She walks back and stands in front of the policemen looks them in the eye saying, 'The two idiots on the ground were going to shoot all those people,' as she points around, 'You ask those people what happened. They will give you the whole story. May I ask you a question, Tom?'

He looks at Leila very intently and in amazement. 'Before I answer your question, how do you know my name? Who are you? And yes of course you can ask me a question.'

'Why is this city of New York so violent, everyone is so unhappy, everyone wants to fight each other?'

'I agree with you. I wish someone could do something about it. But that's how things are here in New York,' says the policeman.

Leila is not worried. She can handle any situation.

The taxi driver is shaking profusely, and his eyes are unable to focus. His mind is running wild. He is thinking to himself, 'is this real or am I dreaming?' He just stands there, aghast at what he has witnessed.

Leila then takes the bullets at the front of the policemen's heads and drops them on the pavement, turns around walks to the taxi sits inside, the driver sits in the driver's seat and he is shaking badly.

Leila taps him on the shoulder and says, 'don't worry you'll be fine now. Just relax. What I'm going to do next will test your sanity, I'm not going to hurt you in any way what so ever!'

In a blink of an eye the taxi, the driver and Leila have transported to the Great Lawn in Central Park. The taxi is about fifteen metres above the ground. All the people under the taxi run for their lives from under it. Leila then lets it descend slowly to the ground. There in front of him is a UFO, Leila taps him on the shoulder then she says, 'Please don't be afraid, what you see is real, and yes, it's a UFO!'

He is mesmerised at this vision in front of him. He has never seen a UFO in his life. He looks around at Leila in a very questioning way. 'You are a very special person. I knew that there was something about you last night when I came to pick you up. I could see that something was going on but I didn't equate it with you, now I know. You are different. Are you human like me?'

'Yes, I'm human like everyone on this Planet. My DNA is human, my parents are human, in fact all my family are human but my technology is very probably twenty thousand years ahead of this planet. There is nothing that I cannot do. I must leave you now. I have a very important meeting with the World Leaders in the United Nations Building here in New York. How much is the fare?'

He looks at her and laughs, 'You owe me nothing young lady.' He pauses then he says, 'It is a pleasure meeting you, you are the most courteous, considerate and polite person I have ever met in my life.' Then he starts to cry uncontrollably.

Leila places her hand on his shoulder and says, 'Please don't cry!'

She alights from the taxi, gives the driver a little wave and walks straight to the UFO. By now a big crowd of people have gathered, and the police are trying to keep control of the situation, but it is proving difficult. The police are trying franticly keeping a cordon round the UFO. There are television crews everywhere, vying for the best positions.

Leila stands in front of this crowd, and then she says, 'Ladies and gentlemen, please move back as far as you can. We are about to take off!'

The crowd are shouting, 'Who are you? Where are you from? Are you from another world?'

Leila looks out over the crowd then she says, 'Everyone please go home and watch your televisions this afternoon. All will become clear, that's all I have to say for now. Thank you.'

In a flash she has vanished. Everyone looks on in amazement, not knowing what has happened.

Chapter 140

Inside the UFO Gia and Oisin are waiting for her.

Leila runs to Gia and says, 'What a morning. It's been manic!'

Gia enquires. 'Why?'

'I'll tell you all about it soon but not now, look at the time. Its two minutes to three. We should be at the United Nations Building now, so let's go please! 'Oisin I would like you to hover above that building I'll transport down, then, you can go into orbit and wait for me. Is that alright?'

Oisin replies, 'Yes that's fine with me!'

'Are you sure that you are comfortable on your own?' Gia enquires.

Leila replies, 'Yes I'll be fine. Now I must send a message to my mum, dad, granddad, grandma JK and Delia. *I'm fine, everyone, if there are any problems just contact me immediately. There is pandemonium here at the moment, the UFO has landed on the Great Lawn in Central Park in New York and I'm inside it. I didn't want anything to happen to the family again that is why I have sent you all home, just to be sure of your safety. I hope that everyone is happy with my decision!'*

Mum replies for everyone, *'Everything is alright at home except that we are surrounded by television people, reporters and paparazzi!'*

'Mum, don't worry, everything will turn out fine, just tell them to go home and watch their televisions there are going to be very big changes to our world this afternoon. That is all they need to know for the present. Must go now, mum, bye'

Chapter 141

It only takes seconds to materialize above the United Nations Building and the UFO hovers there. It's pandemonium under the UFO. There are thousands of people looking up at this amazing UFO, hoping, looking, for some kind of signal a message anything. The police are trying to keep order but it looks as if it's getting out of hand, plus there are numerous television people vying for the best places to get the best television to send around the world. This is a first for everyone, this is the first time a UFO looks genuine and everyone is looking up at it in anticipation, asking, 'Who are they? What do they look like?' Some people are on their knees praying, looking for something, anything that they could believe in.

Chapter 142

Hill AFB radar has picked up something big over New York and sixteen F-35 Lightning 11 are scrambled to investigate and engage with this unknown phenomenal. Air Force Colonel John Holden is in over all charge of this engagement but he does not know what he will face when he arrives at this destination. As he is watching his radar, he is amazed at what he sees. This phenomenon looks in size to be about one hundred metres in diameter, it is huge by any standard but how is it just hovering above New York and why?

He is closing fast on it, now it is visible. He can see that it is a round sphere, boy, is it big. What is it doing above New York City? 'Well I can't afford to take a chance we'll have to take it down somehow, but how?'

Then all hell breaks loose, Oisin detects that there are sixteen F-35 Lighting 11 USA fighters closing in on them at great speed. Leila we need your help!

She walks over to the console looks at Oisin and says, 'don't worry they are no match for us you just watch.'

The pilots have the UFO on their radar. They then release sixteen air to air missiles at the UFO. When they are within fifty metres of the UFO they stop, as if a barrier is in front of them. The pilots peel off right and left, wondering what is going on. Leila breaks into their intercom system asking, 'What are you trying to do? Are you trying to shoot us down on top of all those people on the ground? Colonel John Holden, I'm talking to you and you had better listen to me. Do you see that those sixteen air to air missiles you have fired at me just stopped in midair, I will send all of them back to each individual F-35 Lightning?' The Colonel shouts back, 'That's impossible. Who do you think you are?'

'My name is Leila I see that you don't believe me. Can I ask you to do something for me, Would you like to bring your sixteen F-35 Lightning's 11 into a line and just hover five hundred metres in front of me?'

The Colonel replies, 'Why would I want do that. I don't know you from Adam?

She replies, 'Because I have asked you nicely so please do as I ask, John. If you don't, I'll do it for you!

'Are you telling me that you are able to take over all my F-35 Lightning 11? That's impossible plus I do not believe you.'

'You are about to witness something well beyond your small little mind. You just watch!'

All sixteen of the F-35 lightning 11 are now under Leila's control. She forms them into a line. The pilots are trying frantically to take back control of their individual F-35 Lightning 11 and hover where they stop.

'John, now that I have your attention, at least I hope so, I am going to send the sixteen missiles back to you, and there is nothing you can do about it.'

Its panic stations aboard the F-35s, they are all shouting at the Colonel, 'Please, sir, what are we going to do?'

'What do you think we are going to do? We fire the rest of the missiles on board at our missiles and blow them up simple!

'We don't have control of our F-35s, sir!

Leila turns all the sixteen missiles around to face the F-35s. She sends them on their way back to where they came from.

The pilots are panic stricken, their hands are covering their faces but there is nothing they can do, they are helpless. When the missiles arrive, some ten metres in front of the sixteen F-35s, they stop and just hang there.

'Now, Colonel John, do you want to die with all of your colleagues? Because I can make that happen. There is nothing you or anyone on this planet can do to stop me!'

The Colonel replies, 'Fine I surrender!'

'John I'm going to transport you to my UFO now, are you ready?'

'I'm ready but what about my F-35. Will it fall out of the sky?

'Absolutely not, it's in my power to hold it there!

Two seconds and he is in the UFO.

Leila walks over to him as he is a bit dazed and disoriented and confused. For the first time in his life he is very frightened. She places her hand on him saying, 'I know you are a bit disoriented, please don't worry I'm not going to hurt you. I just need your undivided attention. You are now in our UFO. Then she points to Gia and Oisin saying, This Gia and this is Oisin, they are my god parents.'

He looks at them. 'I think that the three of you were on television yesterday afternoon, you are the people from another planet?' Replies, John.

Gia answers. 'Yes we are from another planet many light years from this planet and we greet you as friends!

'Now, Colonel John, we don't have the time to have a long discussion with you. I have a prior engagement with all the world leaders so if you don't mind I'm going to send you back to your F-35. But first, what do you want me to do with your missiles? I would like them back in our F-35s, please?'

'Fine, you have them back in the holds of your planes! John looks perplexed, 'How did you do that?

Leila answers, 'Magic, John, Magic. It's been nice meeting you,' and in a flash he is sitting back in his F-35.

Leila communicates with him again telling him the F-35s are now in his control, 'You may leave and return to your base immediately. Thank you and good bye.'

Chapter 143

Leila looks at Gia and Oisin, and then she says, 'I must leave you now, you go into orbit I'll follow you there in about two hours. Then we'll go and sort out the little problem your friends have with the Aliens trying to take over their Planet. Gia I need to tell you and Oisin something very important now,' as she looks very intently at them, the BIO/DNA technology which you gave me is now obsolete, I'm at least another ten thousand years ahead of your technology. I have left Quantum physics, nanotechnology so far behind its frightening. There is no stopping me from achieving whatever I would like to do.'

Gia looks at Leila, throws her hands up into the air saying, 'I was afraid that something like this would happen, however, as long as you remain as yourself I think that everything will be fine, but, I'm ever so pleased for you. What do you think Oisin?'

'I think that it is amazing, and he laughs out loud. We have in our midst someone that is probably, pure energy. It means that, we are very privileged to be in her presence, 'she is definitely a one off creation, and by your hand Gia. I think that you should be extremely proud of her.'

Gia replies, 'Yes of course I'm very proud and humbled to have such a wonderful being next to me, if that is what she is now. Leila looks at both of them and says, 'I'm still the same person that you gave all the technology all those years ago and nothing will ever change that. I don't feel any different. 'I have all my faculties and my wits about me.'

'I'm very happy. It means that we are in a very privileged position having Leila as our protector and I'm sure that she will do us proud not just in her world but my world and right across the Universe. She is amazing. She indeed is a one off.'

Chapter 144

Leila makes contact with Michael Hester. *'Michael you can announce me now. I'm sorry I'm a bit late but I had a little confrontation with USAF, some sixteen F-35s. They were a bit out of their depth. I sent them back to their base. Everything is fine now.'*

Michael is standing at the podium and smiles to himself. He taps the microphone, making sure it is turned on. He looks around the Great Hall, 'Ladies and gentlemen, please, our speaker from yesterday, Leila.'

Leila materializes at the podium gives Michael a light kiss on the cheeks saying, 'Good to see you again, Michael.'

He nods, points to the microphone and stands back.

Leila looks around the Great Hall. There are about one hundred SAS standing at the back of the hall poised and ready to execute all orders from their Colonel. She is not worried for herself, but she is worried about all the world leaders and their attached personnel. She decides to make all their weapons in-operable just in case they might try and use them. The Great Hall is packed to capacity. This meeting is being televised live around the world and the atmosphere is electric. You could hear a pin drop. She is dressed in the new clothes she acquired from the boutique in New York and she looks stunning and amazing. As she looks around this Great Hall silence has descended and the USA President has a big smile on his face. Leila looks at him. She then thinks to herself, 'I'll knock that smile off his face very soon. She looks out over the world leaders, sees George beckons him to the podium. He walks up and stands next to Leila.

She looks at him and says, please tell this lot of disbelievers what happened last night in my mum's suite at the hotel.' He looks a bit lost, so Leila places her hand on his shoulder saying, go on George, you can tell about your experience, and how you feel now.' He looks around the Great Hall. 'Ladies and gentlemen last night I had the shock of my life. I was given top security clearance to go to the Ritz Carlton Hotel and arrest this young lady next to me. He looks at Leila and smiles. When we burst into the suite to arrest her, a little boy ran into the room, we had no time to think but to shoot and ask questions later. The little boy was killed. Then as if by magic my family were standing in this suite next to me. I was totally in shock. I didn't know what was happening. The next thing I could see my son lying on the floor and to all intent and purposes he was dead. My wife was in total shock!'

Leila asked us to leave the suite, and take my son with me. When we arrived at the lift, Leila communicated with me, and told me to place my son on the floor. Then something very special happened, my son came back to life. I was beside myself with ecstasy and delight. That was something very special for my family, and me to behold. Now Leila is telling me that the little boy is well and alive in England, and to prove it. Leila transports Alfie to the podium! George can't believe his eyes, he runs to Alfie touches him all over his body to make sure that it's not an illusion. Then he looks at Leila and says, this is real, I'm not dreaming am I?'

'No George, you're not dreaming, that is the little boy from last night. Alfie runs to Leila asking, where am I Leila. She drops down on her knees looks at him, she then gives him a very big hug, saying, I'm sorry but I needed to bring you back here. When you're a big boy I'll explain everything to you, is that alright with you?'

'Yes, I'm fine with that.' He replies.

She looks at George and, says, 'thank you George, you can return to your family now, if you so wish!' He walks down from the podium, to where his wife is waiting for him. She gives him a big hug, and a kiss, 'then the two of them walk out of the Great hall, with a feeling of great humility.

Then she begins. 'World Leaders and people, this is my second visit to this Great Hall. I'm not going to dwell on yesterday's little talk with your President and the Prime minister of England. What I'm going to tell you now will come as a very big surprise to you World Leaders. From now on all missiles of any kind, wherever they are placed or hidden, as from now are obsolete. For those who do not understand the meaning of what I have said, they are of scrap value use only!'

There is total disbelieve at what she has told them. The German Chancellor rushes up to the podium shouting,

You can't do that. You are just playing with us. Who do think you are? You are not God.'

She elevates him six metres above the floor, looks at him and says, 'I can do anything I like, and nothing on this planet can stop me.'

The President gives a signal then the young lady from last night, Maria, walks into the Great Hall. She is surrounded by a squad of SAS soldiers. She is looking very nervous and lost as she approaches the podium. The SAS soldiers are frozen to the floor, unable to move. Leila removes all the weaponry from their person, in case it might prove dangerous.

Leila looks down at Maria. 'Please don't be afraid, Maria, come up and stand next to me.'

Maria duly obliges. She walks over to the left side of the podium up the steps, walks to the centre of the podium and stands next to Leila, She looks at her and says, 'Please don't worry I will not hurt you, neither will anyone in this hall hurt you. I'll protect you; you know that to be a fact!

'Yes, I implicitly and completely trust you, not that lot down there!'

Leila waves her hand then a vision appears in the centre of the hall.

'Ladies and gentlemen what you are about to see happened last night in the President's suite.'

A vision in 3D, it's the President's suite, at the Waldorf Hotel. The Chief of Staff goes to the door opens it escorts a young lady inside its Maria. She smiles at Leila asking, 'How do you do that, that is amazing!

Leila is smiling to herself. The whole scenario runs just like a movie. She looks at the President. She stops the movie then she says, 'Well Mr President, can you recognise anyone in that movie? Ladies and gentlemen, this is not a movie, this happened last night.'

He looks astonished his face has gone ashen white and he looks very embarrassed as does his cronies. They are cowering in their seats.

Leila runs the movie again and it proves that even the President of the USA is an out and out gangster.

He runs up to the podium shouting, 'Please, Leila, stop the movie!'

'Are you sure sir? It gets very interesting, and better as we go along!

He looks at her, 'Please have some sympathy for me I'll not give you any more trouble!

She stops it because she knows she has the President in the palm of her hand now, and she will squeeze him dry. He does not have any other options.'

'Ladies and gentlemen, I'm going to show you a vision of your future now.' In the middle of the hall and above their heads she shows the audience in 3D, a vision of Earth one hundred years ago. A very beautiful world, green and full of beautiful colours she says, 'Now ladies and gentlemen I'll show you what you have today, not so nice is it. The green is beginning to turn brown. Over population of the world is ruining the ecology of the planet. Now I'll take you one hundred years into the future. As you can see your world is burning up. Is that something you want for your grand-children? It is not very pretty is it? You can change that. I will not give you any of my technology but I can help you face up to that scenario and maybe save your world. You must place all of your resources and ingenuity to better use, technology and Quantum Computing, that is the best way to save your world.

My technology is at least twenty thousand years ahead of this world. I know that you think I'm kidding you, there is no point trying to convince you because you will never understand. My technology is infinite and I'll save this world whether you like it or not. You are so small minded in your usual phlegmatic, in different and pragmatic ways and your governments think that you will leave this world to colonize other planets. It's not going to happen, you are not wanted anywhere in the Universe because of your war mongering ways and greed. You are such a pathetic stupid people you do not realise the damage you are perpetrating on this world of yours.

I will now show you what will happen in two hundred years, Please watch the vision of your world. As you can see people are migrating from one country to another country looking for food and shelter. Food is in short supply, there are too many humans. Fighting breaks out between brothers, families, father against son, nations will start wars against other nations for survival. All this will destroy your world.'

There is total silence in the Great Hall, the representatives of all the people in the world are beginning to realise that maybe she is trying to educate them.

Leila looks around the Great Hall and disperses the vision of the future. 'Ladies and gentlemen you have a great opportunity in science to further your education especially with new materials such as graphene, this has very interesting properties it is ultra light and could be adopted and used in computers. You have coming into technology Super Conducting materials and they are intriguing to engineers because they have an amazing ability, they can generate an electrical current that flows forever as long as the material is kept cold. Now we have the advent of Plasma Projection, a very interesting subject. A very new and recent discovery and this is where all your scientists should place all their ingenuity. I'm not going to educate you how to use grapheme or super conductors or Plasma Projection materials. You need to learn how you can use these amazing materials and experiment with them. I'm sure that given time to research these wonderful new materials they will help this world to survive. Then maybe some time in the future you might be able to travel to the stars. Now I must give you new information, the first bit is that after everyone in this Great Hall has passed away, I'll still be alive. My technology is such that I will never die. I know that is very big statement to make especially now in this Great Hall, but I need you to believe me. I will never grow old. As you see me now that is the way my body will stay. I'll return from time to time to see how this world is preparing for the future.'

There is a lot of gasping and murmurings amongst the people. However, no one challenges her. 'Now for my second announcement,' she looks around smiles at Mr Michael Heston, indicates to him to come to her side. He duly obeys.

'Ladies and gentlemen, what I'm going to say now will amaze you. What this world needs now is a World President and after due deliberation and soul searching, the first World President,' She pauses for about five seconds. Each of the World Leaders is anticipating, hoping that she will choose one of them especially the President of the USA. He is about to stand up, thinking that he is going to be named the first World Leader. 'Ladies and gentlemen I give you our first World Leader,' she looks around her audience in this Great Hall, 'Mr Michael Heston.' There is total silence and disbelief, everyone looks at each other saying, 'It should be one of us!

Leila says, 'I know what you are thinking but I disagree. My instincts are always right. Mr Heston is the right person for this very important sensitive new post. You will ratify his inauguration, and he will be my President as well. He will be guided by me but, he will make his own decisions and if any nation tries to remove him, I will know and there will be a price to pay. He will have a salary befitting a World President and a house with servants. He will convene all his meetings in this Great Hall with all World Leaders once a month to discuss world problems and try and resolve them.

Mr Adams and Mr Bragin, please come up to the podium when this meeting is closed. Maria, I'll see you in the future and watch your progress. I hope that you are not too disappointed about your powers. I would like to help you, but I'm not allowed. So I bid you goodbye and I hope that you have a long life and prosper.'

Chapter 145

Leila has one other little job to finish. In a flash Commander Gruber and all the other Aliens are standing on the podium next to her. Ladies and gentlemen, this is the last time any government will incarcerate any more Aliens. I'm going to take this lot with me back to their own planets, if they so wish. Now I must leave but I will be back in the future. Then I hope to see some big improvements for everyone on this planet.' She beckons Mr Adams and Mr Bragin to the podium. The two of them obligingly walk up to the podium. Leila goes to meet them saying, 'The reason I didn't choose either of you as a world President is, I needed all the world leaders to govern their own countries for now. This World President Mr Heston will have a five year term and if he wants to run for President again it will be his decision, otherwise a new one will be elected by all World Governments I hope I'm making myself clear!'

They look at each other Mr Bragin says, 'I'm very happy with that decision,' then he looks at Mr Adams. He looks at Leila, nods his head and says, 'Well I'm not so happy about it. However you have made that decision and I'll abide by it, I promise!

Chapter 146

Mr Heston is still on the podium, Leila says good bye to Mr Bragin saying, 'thank you for being so supportive and I'll be seeing you in the future.' Then she looks at Mr Adams, 'I'll be watching you so you better behave yourself.' Then she walks across to Mr Heston takes him by the hand then she says, 'I know that this has been a very big surprise to you but, I think that you will make a very good World President and I'll will always be ready to advice you. I'll communicate with you from time to time then you can bring me up to date with everything. Now you have the power to promote whomsoever you think will be the best person as your deputy, and of course your cabinet, I'm not going to interfere in your choice of government. I must go now. I have a prior engagement in another Universe and it can't wait.' In an instant Leila and the other Aliens are aboard the UFO.

Chapter 147

Gia and Oisin greet them but they are a little surprised asking, 'Leila what are you doing with those Aliens aboard our ship? Can you explain?'

'I think that we can trust them. They know how powerful I have become, and I don't think that they will cross me.' She looks at Gruber and says, 'You will obey me, will you not, Gruber?'

'Yes, of course I will, I would not dare to cross you now. I have seen how powerful you have become and I will be pleased to stand by your side in any eventuality.'

'What about our other friends?' she asks.

He goes to them and enquires, 'What do you want to do?'

'We would like to serve with Leila, Gia and Oisin. We will lay down our lives for them, 'that's if they will allow us to serve under her.'

Gia and Oisin look bemused. They look at Leila saying, 'Leila if you are happy with this lot of Aliens, then we trust your judgement.'

'Now that we are all agreed I will transport Zaid here immediately. That is, if you are you happy with that, Oisin?'

'Yes, of course I'm happy with that!'

No sooner has the last word left his mouth then Zaid is on board. He looks surprised but he is happy to see Leila.

As he looks around, he is conscious that there are other Aliens, on board. He looks at Leila and asks, 'Who are these other Aliens. I think I know commander Gruber, 'What is he doing on this craft?'

'He is now one of my staff. He comes under my protection do you understand.' 'Yes I do.'

He looks at her and says, 'Have you come to save our planet?'

'Yes, shall we go and save Zaid's planet then? Oisin, I'm taking over the ship, that's if you don't mind!'

He looks at her and asks, 'What are you going to do?'

'Just watch!' she replies.

Zaid looks perplexed and worried. He looks at Leila then he says, 'Can I ask a question please?'

Leila replies. 'Yes of course you can. What is it you would like to know?'

'How long will it take to reach my planet? We might be too late; it may be taken over when we arrive!

She looks at him and smiles, 'Zaid, please, don't worry. I'll be above your planet before you can blink an eye. I'm monitoring it all the time and I would know if any attempt was made to take it over. Zaid I'm going to transport you back to your ship then I'll take it over, you explain to your crew. Whatever happens you are not to interfere with the controls of your ship, do you understand?

'Yes, I do understand Leila.' answers Zaid.

'It's time to go, and help a world. We are on our way to your planet, Suhriena.'

Before anyone realises what is happening Zaid shouts out, 'That is my home planet, Suhriena. Am I dreaming? That is real, am I right, Leila?'

'Yes, you are absolutely right, Zaid!'

Gia looks astonished as does Oisin. 'Is that right, Leila, we are above Zaid's planet? No question whatsoever that is astounding, I really find it amazing I'm not able to keep up with the BIO/DNA technology I have given to you. What do you think, Oisin?'

'I don't know where we are going from here,' as he begins to laugh out loud. 'I think we are in the presence of someone very special. What do you think Gruber?'

'I think we are very privileged to be in her presence, she is without doubt the most powerful being in the Universe. I'm very glad and happy to be in her presence.'

Leila looks around, then she says, 'I'm not here to have accolades given to me, I'm here to make sure that Zaid's planet is free to do what its indigenous people are lawfully allowed to pursue, so let us get down to business. Now I know that we are invisible to all those interplanetary crafts in front of us, so, Zaid, you and I will descend to your people on the planet and discuss with them what exactly what they will need to do to make these Aliens go away.'

'Gia, and Oisin, you are in charge of your craft. Commander Gruber you are in charge of the rest of the Alien contingent. Zaid, and myself are going to transport down to see what I can do to help his world.

I don't want to be disturbed while I'm in negotiations with the trouble makers surrounding the planet. However they are in for a very big surprise.

Commander, please make sure that you keep all the Aliens in line. I'm holding you responsible, if anyone of them start to give you any kind of trouble, I'll know, and I will not be too happy, I'll return to Gia's and Oisin's craft, to sort out any disagreement. Do I make myself clear?' The Commander nods his head.

The continuation of this novel will follow in a new book

Lightning Source UK Ltd.
Milton Keynes UK
UKHW011812110319
338925UK00001B/21/P